THREE
DARK
CROWNS

THREE

DARK

CROWNS

KENDARE BLAKE

HARPER TEEN
An Imprint of HarperCollinsPublishers

Library of Congress Control Number: 2016938986
ISBN 978-0-06-238543-7
ISBN 978-0-06-256412-2 (int.)

Typography by Aurora Parlagreco
16 17 18 19 20   PC/RRDH   10 9 8 7 6 5 4
❖
First Edition

THREE
DARK
CROWNS

Innisfuil Valley

Mount Horn

Sunpool

The
Black Cottage

Bernadine's Landing

Kenora

SEAWATCH MOUNTAINS

WOLF SPRING

Highgate

The Naturalist City

Sealhead
Cove

Three Dark Crowns

Map of Fennbirn

Three dark queens
are born in a glen,
sweet little triplets
will never be friends

—

Three dark sisters
all fair to be seen,
two to devour
and one to be Queen

THE QUEENS' SIXTEENTH BIRTHDAY

December 21
Four months until Beltane

GREAVESDRAKE MANOR

$\mathcal{A}$ young queen stands barefoot on a wooden block with her arms outstretched. She has only her scant under-clothes and the long, black hair that hangs down her back to fend off the drafts. Every ounce of strength in her slight frame is needed to keep her chin high and her shoulders square.

Two tall women circle the wooden block. Their fingertips drum against crossed arms, and their footsteps echo across the cold hardwood floor.

"She is thin to the ribs," Genevieve says, and smacks them lightly, as if it might scare the bones farther under the skin. "And still so small. Small queens do not inspire much confidence. The others on the council cannot stop whispering about it."

She studies the queen with distaste, her eyes dragging across every imperfection: her hollow cheeks, her pallid skin. The scabs from a rubbing of poison oak that still mar her right hand. But no scars. They are always careful about that.

"Put your arms down," Genevieve says, and turns on her heel.

Queen Katharine glances at Natalia, the taller and elder of the two Arron sisters, before she does. Natalia nods, and the blood rushes back to Katharine's fingertips.

"She will have to wear gloves tonight," Genevieve says. Her tone is unmistakably critical. But it is Natalia who determines the queen's training, and if Natalia wants to rub Katharine's hands with poison oak one week before her birthday, then she will.

Genevieve lifts a lock of Katharine's hair. Then she pulls it hard.

Katharine blinks. She has been prodded back and forth by Genevieve's hands since she stepped onto the block. Jerked so roughly at times that it seems Genevieve wants her to fall so she can scold her for the bruises.

Genevieve pulls her hair again.

"At least it is not falling out. But how can black hair be so dull? And she is still so, so small."

"She is the smallest and the youngest of the triplets," Natalia says in her deep, calm voice. "Some things, Sister, you cannot change."

When Natalia steps forward, it is difficult for Katharine to keep her eyes from following her. Natalia Arron is as close to a mother as she will ever know. It was her silk skirt that Katharine burrowed in at the age of six, all that long way from the Black

Cottage to her new home at Greavesdrake Manor, sobbing after being parted from her sisters. There was nothing queenly about Katharine that day. But Natalia indulged her. She let Katharine weep and ruin her dress. She stroked her hair. It is Katharine's earliest memory. The one and only time Natalia ever allowed her to act like a child.

In the slanting, indirect light of the parlor, Natalia's ice-blond bun appears almost silver. But she is not old. Natalia will never be old. She has far too much work and far too many responsibilities to allow it. She is the head of the Arron family of poisoners, and the strongest member of the Black Council. She is raising their new queen.

Genevieve grasps Katharine's poisoned hand. Her thumb traces the pattern of scabs until she finds a large one and picks it until it bleeds.

"Genevieve," Natalia cautions. "That is enough."

"Gloves are fine, I suppose," Genevieve says, though she still seems cross. "Gloves over the elbows will give shape to her arms."

She releases Katharine's hand, and it bounces against her hip. Katharine has been on the block for over an hour, and there is much day still ahead. All the way to nightfall, her party, and the *Gave Noir*. The poisoner's feast. Just thinking of it makes her stomach clench, and she winces slightly.

Natalia frowns.

"You have been resting?" she asks.

"Yes, Natalia," says Katharine.

"Nothing but water and thinned porridge?"

"Nothing."

Nothing to eat but that for days, and it may still not be enough. The poison she will have to consume, the sheer amounts of it, may still overcome Natalia's training. Of course, it would be nothing at all if Katharine's poisoner gift were strong.

Standing on the block, the walls of the darkened parlor feel heavy. They press in, given weight by the sheer number of Arrons inside. They have come from all across the island for this. The queens' sixteenth birthday. Greavesdrake usually feels like a great, silent cavern, empty save for Natalia and the servants; her siblings, Genevieve and Antonin; and Natalia's cousins Lucian and Allegra when they are not at their houses in town. Today it is busy and decked with finery. It is packed to purpose with poisons and poisoners. If a house could smile, Greavesdrake would be grinning.

"She has to be ready," Genevieve says. "Every corner of the island will hear about what happens tonight."

Natalia cocks her head at her sister. The gesture manages to convey at once how sympathetic Natalia is to Genevieve's worries and how tired she is of hearing about them.

Natalia turns to look out the window, down the hills to the capital city of Indrid Down. The twin black spires of the Volroy, the palace where the queen resides during her reign, and where the Black Council resides permanently, rises above the chimney smoke.

"Genevieve. You are too nervous."

"Too nervous?" Genevieve asks. "We are entering the Ascension Year with a weak queen. If we lose . . . I will not go back to Prynn!"

Her sister's voice is so shrill that Natalia chuckles. Prynn. It was once the poisoners' city but now only the weakest reside there. The entire capital of Indrid Down is theirs now. It has been for over a hundred years.

"Genevieve, you have never even been to Prynn."

"Do not laugh at me."

"Then do not be funny. I do not know what you are about sometimes."

She looks again out the window, toward the Volroy's black spires. Five Arrons sit on the Black Council. No less than five have sat on it for three generations, placed there by the ruling poisoner queen.

"I am only telling you what you may have missed, being so often away from council business, coaching and coddling our queen."

"I do not miss anything," says Natalia, and Genevieve lowers her eyes.

"Of course. I am sorry, Sister. It is only that the council grows wary, with the temple openly backing the elemental."

"The temple is for festival days and for praying over sick children." Natalia turns and taps Katharine beneath the chin. "For everything else, the people look to the council.

"Why do you not go out to the stables and ride, Genevieve?" she suggests. "It will settle your nerves. Or return to the Volroy.

Some business there is sure to require attention."

Genevieve closes her mouth. For a moment, it seems that she might disobey or reach up toward the block and slap Katharine across the face, just to relieve her tension.

"That is a good idea," Genevieve says. "I will see you tonight, then, Sister."

After Genevieve has gone, Natalia nods to Katharine. "You may get down."

The skinny girl's knees shake as she climbs off the block, careful not to stumble.

"Go to your rooms," Natalia says, and turns away to study a sheaf of papers on a table. "I will send Giselle with a bowl of porridge. Then nothing else besides a few sips of water."

Katharine bows her head and drops half a curtsy for Natalia to catch from the corner of her eye. But she lingers.

"Is it . . . ?" Katharine asks. "Is it really as bad as Genevieve says?"

Natalia regards her a moment, as though deciding whether she will bother to answer.

"Genevieve worries," she says finally. "She has been that way since we were children. No, Kat. It is not so bad as all that." She reaches out to tuck some strands of hair behind the girl's ear. Natalia often does that when she is pleased. "Poisoner queens have sat the throne since long before I was born. They will sit it long after you and I are both dead." She rests her hands on Katharine's shoulders. Tall, coldly beautiful Natalia. The words from her mouth leave no room for arguments, no space for doubt. If Katharine were more like her, the Arrons would have nothing to fear.

"Tonight is a party," says Natalia. "For you, on your birthday. Enjoy it, Queen Katharine. And let me worry about the rest."

Seated before her dressing mirror, Queen Katharine studies her reflection as Giselle brushes out her black hair in long, even strokes. Katharine is still in her robe and underclothes and is still cold. Greavesdrake is a drafty place that clings to its shadows. Sometimes, it seems that she has spent most of her life in the dark and chilled to the bone.

On the right side of her tableau is a glass-sided cage. In it, her coral snake rests, fat with crickets. Katharine has had her since she was a hatchling, and she is the only venomed creature Katharine does not fear. She knows the vibrations of Katharine's voice and the scent of her skin. She has never bitten her, even once.

Katharine will wear her to the party tonight, coiled around her wrist like a warm, muscular bracelet. Natalia will wear a black mamba. A small snake bracelet is not as fancy as one draped across one's shoulders, but Katharine prefers her little adornment. She is prettier; red and yellow and black. Toxic colors, they say. The perfect accessory for a poisoner queen.

Katharine touches the glass, and the snake lifts her rounded head. Katharine was instructed to never give her a name, told over and over that she was not a pet. But in Katharine's head, she calls the snake "Sweetheart."

"Don't drink too much champagne," Giselle says as she gathers Katharine's hair into sections. "It is sure to be envenomed, or stained with poisoned juice. I heard talk in the kitchen of pink mistletoe berries."

"I will have to drink some of it," says Katharine. "They are toasting my birthday, after all."

Her birthday and her sisters' birthdays. All across the island the people are celebrating the sixteenth birthday of the newest generation of triplet queens.

"Wet your lips, then," says Giselle. "Nothing more. It is not only the poison to be mindful of, but the drink itself. You are too slight to handle much without turning sloppy."

Giselle weaves Katharine's hair into braids, and twists them high upon the back of her head, wrapping them around and around into a bun. Her touch is gentle. She does not tug. She knows that the years of poisoning have weakened the scalp.

Katharine reaches for more makeup, but Giselle clucks her tongue. The queen is already powdered too white, an attempt to hide the bones that jut from her shoulders and to disguise the hollows in her cheeks. She has been poisoned thin. Nights of sweating and vomiting have made her skin fragile and translucent as wet paper.

"You are pretty enough already," Giselle says, and smiles into the mirror. "With those big, dark doll's eyes."

Giselle is kind. Her favorite of Greavesdrake's maids. But even the maid is more beautiful than the queen in many ways, with full hips, and color in her face, blond hair that shines even though she has to dye it to the ice blond that Natalia prefers.

"Doll's eyes," Katharine repeats.

Perhaps. But they are not lovely. They are big, black orbs in a sickly visage. Looking into the mirror, she imagines her body in pieces. Bones. Skin. Not enough blood. It would not take much to break her down to nothing, to strip away scant muscles and pull the organs out to dry in the sun. She wonders often whether her sisters would break down similarly. If underneath their skin they are all the same. Not one poisoner, one naturalist, and one elemental.

"Genevieve thinks that I will fail," Katharine says. "She says I am too small and weak."

"You are a poisoner queen," says Giselle. "What else matters but that? Besides, you are not so small. Not so weak. I have seen both weaker and smaller."

Natalia sweeps into the room in a tight black sheath. They should have heard her coming; heels clicking against the floors and ringing off the high ceilings. They were too distracted.

"Is she ready?" Natalia asks, and Katharine stands. Being dressed by the head of the Arron household is an honor, reserved for festival days. And the most important of birthdays.

Giselle fetches Katharine's gown. It is black and full-skirted. Heavy. There are no sleeves, but black satin gloves to cover the poison-oak scabs have already been laid out.

Katharine steps into the gown, and Natalia begins to fasten it. Katharine's stomach quivers. Sounds of the party assembling have begun to trickle up the stairs. Natalia and Giselle slide the gloves onto her hands. Giselle opens the snake's cage. Katharine fishes out Sweetheart, and the snake coils obediently around her wrist.

"Is it drugged?" Natalia asks. "Perhaps it should be."

"She will be fine," Katharine says, and strokes Sweetheart's scales. "She is well-mannered."

"As you say." Natalia turns Katharine to the mirror and places her hands on her shoulders.

Never before have three queens of the same gift ruled in succession. Sylvia, Nicola, and Camille were the last three. All were poisoners, raised by Arrons. One more, and perhaps it will become a dynasty; perhaps only the poisoner queen will be allowed to grow up and her sisters will be drowned at birth.

"There will be nothing too surprising in the *Gave Noir*," Natalia says. "Nothing that you have not seen before. But just the same, do not eat too much. Use your tricks. Do as we practiced."

"It would be a good omen," Katharine says softly, "if my gift were to come tonight. On my birthday. Like Queen Hadly's did."

"You have been lingering in the library histories again." Natalia sprays a bit of jasmine perfume onto Katharine's neck and then touches the braids piled onto the back of her head. Natalia's ice-blond hair is fashioned in a similar style, perhaps as a show of solidarity. "Queen Hadly was not a poisoner. She had the war gift. It is different."

Katharine nods as she is turned left and right, less a person than a mannequin, rough clay upon which Natalia can work her poison craft.

"You are a little skinny," Natalia says. "Camille was never skinny. She was almost plump. She looked forward to the *Gave Noir* as a child to a festival feast."

Katharine's ears prick at the mention of Queen Camille. Despite being raised as Camille's foster sister, Natalia almost never talks about the previous queen. Katharine's mother, though Katharine does not think of her that way. Temple doctrine decrees that queens have no mother or father. They are daughters of the Goddess only. Besides, Queen Camille departed the island with her king-consort as soon as she recovered from giving birth, as all queens do. The Goddess sent the new queens, and the old queen's reign was ended.

Still, Katharine enjoys hearing stories about those who came before. The only story about Camille that Natalia tells is the story of how Camille took her crown. How she poisoned her sisters so slyly and quietly that it took them days to die. How when it was over they looked so peaceful that had it not been for the froth on their lips, you would have thought they had died in their sleep.

Natalia saw those peaceful, poisoned faces for herself. If Katharine is successful, she will see two more.

"You are like Camille, though, in other ways," Natalia says, and sighs. "She loved those dusty books in the library too. And she always seemed so young. She *was* so young. She only ruled

11

for sixteen years after she was crowned. The Goddess sent her triplets early."

Queen Camille's triplets were sent early because she was weak. That is what the people whisper. Katharine wonders sometimes how long she will have. How many years she will guide her people, before the Goddess sees fit to replace her. She supposes that the Arrons do not care. The Black Council rules the island in the interim, and as long as she is crowned, they will still control it.

"Camille was like a little sister to me, I suppose," Natalia says.

"Does that make me your niece?"

Natalia grips her chin.

"Do not be so sentimental," she says, and lets Katharine go. "For seeming so young, Camille killed her sisters with poise. She was always a very good poisoner. Her gift showed early."

Katharine frowns. One of her own triplets had showed an early gift as well. Mirabella. The great elemental.

"I will kill my sisters just as easily, Natalia," Katharine says. "I promise. Though perhaps when I am finished, they will not look like they are sleeping."

The north ballroom is filled to the brim with poisoners. It seems that anyone with any claim to Arron blood, and many other poisoners from Prynn besides, has made the journey to Indrid Down. Katharine studies the party from the top of the main stairs. Everything is crystal and silver and gems, right down to glistening towers of purple belladonna berries wrapped in nets of spun sugar.

The guests are almost too refined; the women in black pearls and black diamond chokers, the men in their black silk ties. And they have too much flesh on their bones. Too much strength in their arms. They will judge her and find her lacking. They will laugh.

As she watches, a woman with dark red hair throws her head back. For a moment her molars—as well her throat, as if her jaw has come unhinged—are visible. In Katharine's ears polite chatter turns to wails, and the ballroom is filled with glittering monsters.

"I cannot do this, Giselle," she whispers, and the maid stops straightening the gown's voluminous skirts and grasps her shoulders from behind.

"Yes you can," she says.

"There are more stairs than there were before."

"There are not," Giselle says, and laughs. "Queen Katharine. You will be perfect."

In the ballroom below, the music stops. Natalia has put up her hand.

"You're ready," Giselle says, and checks the fall of the dress one more time.

"Thank you all," Natalia says to her guests in her deep, rolling voice, "for being with us tonight on such an important date. An important date in any year. But this year is more important than most. This year our Katharine is sixteen!" The guests applaud. "And when the spring comes, and it is the time for the Beltane Festival, it will be more than just a festival. It will be the beginning of the Year of Ascension. During Beltane, the island will see the strength of the poisoners during the Quickening Ceremony! And after Beltane is over, we will have the pleasure of watching our queen deliciously poison her sisters."

Natalia gestures toward the stairs.

"This year's festival to begin, and next year's festival for the crown." More applause. Laughter and shouts of agreement. They think it will be so easy. One year to poison two queens. A strong queen could do it in a month, but Katharine is not strong.

"For tonight, however," Natalia says, "you simply get to enjoy her company."

Natalia turns toward the steep, burgundy-carpeted stairs. A shining black runner has been added for the occasion. Or perhaps just to make Katharine slip.

"This dress is heavier than it looked in my closet," Katharine says quietly, and Giselle chuckles.

The moment she steps out from the shadow and onto the stairs, Katharine feels every pair of eyes. Poisoners are naturally severe and exacting. They can cut with a look as easily as with a knife. The people of Fennbirn Island grow in strength with the ruling queen. Naturalists become stronger under a naturalist. Elementals stronger under an elemental. After three poisoner queens, the poisoners are strong to the last, and the Arrons most of all.

Katharine does not know whether she ought to smile. She

only knows not to tremble. Or stumble. She nearly forgets to breathe. She catches sight of Genevieve, standing behind and to the right of Natalia. Genevieve's lilac eyes are like stones. She looks both furious and afraid, as if she is daring Katharine to make a mistake. As if she relishes the prospect of the feel of her hand across Katharine's face.

When Katharine's heel lands on the floor of the ballroom, glasses raise and white teeth flash. Katharine's heart eases out of her throat. It will be all right, at least for now.

A servant offers a flute of champagne; she takes it and sniffs: the champagne smells a little like oak and slightly of apples. If it has been tainted, then it was not with pink mistletoe berries, as Giselle suspected. Still, she takes only a sip, barely enough to wet her lips.

With her entrance over, the music begins again, and chatter resumes. Poisoners in their best blacks flutter up to her like crows and flutter away just as quickly. There are so many, dropping polite bows and curtsies, dropping so many names, but the only name that matters is Arron. In minutes the anxiety begins to squeeze. Her dress suddenly feels tight, and the room suddenly hot. She searches for Natalia but cannot find her.

"Are you all right, Queen Katharine?"

Katharine blinks at the woman in front of her. She cannot remember what she had been saying.

"Yes," she says. "Of course."

"Well, what do you think? Are your sisters' celebrations as glorious as this?"

"Why no!" Katharine says. "The naturalists will be roasting fish on sticks." The poisoners laugh. "And Mirabella . . . Mirabella . . ."

"Is splashing around barefoot in rain puddles."

Katharine turns. A handsome poisoner boy is smiling at her, with Natalia's blue eyes and ice-blond hair. He holds his hand out.

"What else do elementals enjoy doing, after all?" he asks. "My queen. Will you dance?"

Katharine lets him lead her to the floor and pull her close. A beautiful blue-and-green Deathstalker scorpion is pinned to his right lapel. It is still slightly alive. Its legs writhe sluggishly, a grotesquely beautiful ornament. Katharine leans a bit away. Deathstalker venom is excruciating. She has been stung and healed seven times but still shows little resistance to its effects.

"You saved me," she says. "One more moment of fumbling for words and I would have turned to run."

His smile is attentive enough to make her blush. They turn around on the floor, and she studies his angular features.

"What is your name?" she asks. "You must be an Arron. You have their look. And their hair. Unless you have dyed it for the occasion."

He laughs. "What? Like the servants do, you mean? Oh, Aunt Natalia and her appearances."

"Aunt Natalia? So you are an Arron."

"I am," he says. "My name is Pietyr Renard. My mother was Paulina Renard. My father is Natalia's brother, Christophe." He spins her out. "You dance very well."

His hand slides across her back, and she tenses when he ventures too close to her shoulder, where he might feel the roughness from a past poisoning that toughened her skin.

"It is a wonder," she says, "given how heavy this gown is. It feels as though the straps are about to draw blood."

"Well, you must not allow that. They say the strongest poisoner queens have poison blood. I would hate for any of these vultures to steal you away, looking for a taste."

Poison blood. How disappointed they would be, then, if they tasted hers.

"'Vultures'?" she says. "Are not many of the people here your family?"

"Yes, precisely."

Katharine laughs and stops only when her face drops too near the Deathstalker. Pietyr is tall, and taller than her by almost a head. She could easily dance looking the scorpion in the eyes.

"You have a very nice laugh," says Pietyr. "But this is so strange. I expected you to be nervous."

"I am nervous," she says. "The *Gave*—"

"Not about the *Gave*. About this year. The Quickening at the Beltane Festival. The start of everything."

"The start of everything," she says softly.

Many times Natalia has told her to take things as they come. To keep from becoming overwhelmed. So far it has been easy enough. But then, Natalia makes it all sound so simple.

"I will face it, as I have to," Katharine says, and Pietyr chuckles.

"So much dread in your voice. I hope you can muster a bit more enthusiasm when you meet your suitors."

"It will not matter. Whichever king-consort I choose, he will love me when I am queen."

"Would you not rather they loved you before then?" he asks. "I should think that is what anyone would wish—to be loved for themselves and not their position."

She is about to spout the appropriate rhetoric: being queen is not a position. Not just anyone can be queen. Only her, or one of her sisters, is so linked to the Goddess. Only they can receive the next generation of triplets. But she understands what Pietyr means. It would be sweet to be cared for despite her faults, and to be wanted for her person rather than the power she comes with.

"And would you not rather that they *all* loved you," he says, "instead of just one?"

"Pietyr Renard," she says. "You must have come from far away if you have not heard the whispers. Everyone on the island knows where the suitors' favors will go. They say my sister Mirabella is beautiful as starlight. No one has ever said anything half so flattering about me."

"But perhaps that is all it is," he says. "Flattery. And they also say that Mirabella is half mad. Prone to fits and rages. That she is a fanatic and a slave to the temple."

"And that she is strong enough to shake down a building."

He eyes the roof over their heads, and Katharine smiles. She had not meant Greavesdrake. Nothing in the world is strong enough to tear Greavesdrake from its foundation. Natalia would not allow it.

"And what about your sister Arsinoe, the naturalist?" Pietyr asks casually. They both laugh. No one says anything about Arsinoe.

Pietyr turns Katharine again around the dance floor. They have been dancing a long time. People have begun to notice.

The song ends. Their third, or perhaps their fourth. Pietyr stops dancing and kisses the tips of the queen's gloved fingers.

"I hope to see you again, Queen Katharine," he says.

Katharine nods. She does not notice how silent the ballroom has become until he is gone, and the chatter returns, bouncing off the south wall of mirrors and echoing until it reaches the carved tiles of the ceiling.

Natalia catches Katharine's eye from the center of a cluster of black dresses. She ought to dance with someone else. But the long, black-clothed table is already surrounded by servants like so many ants, setting the silver trays for the feast.

The *Gave Noir*. Sometimes, it is called "the black glut." It is a ritual feast of poison, performed by poisoner queens at nearly every high festival. And so, weak gift or not, Katharine must perform it as well. She must hold the poison down past the last bite, until she is shut safely in her rooms. None of the visiting poisoners can be allowed to see what comes after. The sweat and the seizures and the blood.

When the cellos begin, she almost runs to leave. It seems too soon. That she should have had more time.

Every poisoner who matters is in the ballroom tonight. Every Arron from the Black Council: Lucian and Genevieve, Allegra and Antonin. Natalia. She cannot bear to disappoint Natalia.

The guests move toward the set table. The crowd, for once, is a help, pressing close in a wave of black to push her forward.

Natalia instructs the servants to reveal the dishes from under their silver covers. Piles of glistening berries. Hens stuffed with hemlock dressing. Candied scorpions and sweet juice steeped with oleander. A savory stew winks red and black with rosary peas. The sight of it makes Katharine's mouth run dry. Both the snake on her wrist, and her bodice, seem to squeeze.

"Are you hungry, Queen Katharine?" Natalia asks.

Katharine slides a finger along Sweetheart's warm scales. She knows what she is supposed to say. It is all scripted. Practiced.

"I am ravenous."

"What would be the death of others will nourish you," Natalia continues. "The Goddess provides. Are you pleased?"

Katharine swallows hard.

"The offering is adequate."

Tradition mandates that Natalia bow. When she does, it looks unnatural, as if she is a clay pot cracking.

Katharine sets her hands on the table. The rest of the feast is up to her: its progression, its duration and speed. She may sit or stand as she likes. She does not need to eat it all, but the more she eats, the more impressive it is. Natalia advised her to ignore the flatware and use her hands. To let the juices run down her chin. If she were as strong a poisoner as Mirabella is an elemental, she would devour the entire feast.

The food smells delicious. But Katharine's stomach can no longer be fooled. It tries to twist itself shut and cramps painfully.

"The hen," she says. A servant sets it before her. The room is heavy, and so full of eyes, as it waits. They will shove her face into it if they have to.

Katharine rolls her shoulders back. Seven of the nine council members stand close at the front of the crowd. The five who are Arrons, of course, as well as Lucian Marlowe and Paola Vend. The two remaining members have been dispatched as a courtesy to her sisters' celebrations.

There are only three priestesses in attendance, but Natalia says that priestesses do not matter. High Priestess Luca has forever been in Mirabella's pocket, abandoning temple neutrality in favor of believing Mirabella to be the fist that will wrest power away from the Black Council. But the Black Council is what counts on the island now, and priestesses are nothing but relics and nursemaids.

Katharine tears white meat from the plumpest part of the breast, the meat that is farthest from the toxic stuffing. She pushes it through her lips and chews. For a moment, she is afraid she will be unable to swallow. But the bite goes down, and the crowd relaxes.

She calls for the candied scorpions next. Those are easy. Pretty, sparkling sweets in golden sugar coffins. All the venom is in the tail. Katharine eats four sets of pincers and then calls for the venison stew with rosary peas.

She should have saved the stew for last. She cannot get around its poison. The rosary peas have seeped into everything. Every sliver of meat and drop of gravy.

Katharine's heart begins to pound. Somewhere in the ballroom, Genevieve is cursing her for a fool. But there is nothing to be done. She has to take a bite, and even lick her fingers. She sips the tainted juice and then cleanses her palate with cold, clear water. Her head begins to ache, and her vision changes as her pupils dilate.

She does not have long before she sickens. Before she fails. She feels the weight of so many eyes. And the weight of their expectations. They demand that she finish. Their will is so strong that she can nearly hear it.

The pie of wild mushrooms is next, and she eats through it quickly. Her pulse is already uneven, but she is unsure whether that is from the poison or just nerves. The speed at which she eats does a good impression of enthusiasm, and the Arrons clap. They cheer her on. They make her careless, and she swallows more mushrooms than she intends. One of the last chunks tastes like a Russula, but that should not be. They are too dangerous. Her stomach seizes. The toxin is fast and violent.

"The berries."

She pops two into her mouth and cheeks them and then reaches for tainted wine. Most of it she lets leak down her neck and onto the front of her gown, but it does not matter. The *Gave Noir* is over. She slams both hands down onto the table.

The poisoners roar.

"This is but a taste," Natalia declares. "The *Gave Noir* for the Quickening will be something of legend."

"Natalia, I need to go," she says, and grasps Natalia's sleeve.

The crowd quiets. Natalia discreetly tugs loose.

"What?" she asks.

"I need to leave!" Katharine shouts, but it is too late.

Her stomach lurches. It happens so fast, there is no time even to turn away. She bends at the waist and vomits the contents of the *Gave* down onto the tablecloth.

"I will be all right," she says, fighting the nausea. "I must be ill."

Her stomach gurgles again. But even louder are the gasps of disgust. The rustling of gowns as the poisoners back away from the mess.

Katharine sees their scowls through eyes that are bloodshot and full of water. Her disgrace is reflected in every expression.

"Will someone please," Katharine says, and gasps at the pain, "take me to my rooms."

No one comes. Her knees strike hard against the marble floor. It is not an easy sickness. She is wet with sweat. The blood vessels have burst in her cheeks.

"Natalia," she says. "I'm sorry."

Natalia says nothing. All Katharine can see are Natalia's clenched fists, and the movement of her arms as she silently and furiously directs guests to leave the ballroom. Throughout the space, feet shuffle in a hurry to leave, to get as far from Katharine as they can. She sickens again and pulls on the table-cloth to cover herself.

The ballroom darkens. Servants begin to clear the tables as another twisting cramp tears through her small body.

Disgraced as she is, not even they will move to help her.

WOLF SPRING

❦

Camden is stalking a mouse through the snow. A little brown mouse has found itself in the middle of a clearing, and no matter how quickly it skitters across the surface, Camden's large paws cover more ground, even when she's sunk up to her knees.

Jules watches the macabre game with amusement. The mouse is terrified but determined. And Camden looms over it, as excited as if it were a deer or a large chunk of lamb instead of less than a mouthful. Camden is a mountain cat, and at three years old, has reached her full, massive size. She is a far cry from the milky-eyed cub who followed Jules home from the woods, young enough then to still have her spots, and with more fuzz than fur. Now, she is sleek and honey gold, and the only black left is on her points: ears, toes, and the tip of her tail.

Snow flies in twin shoots from her paws as she pounces, and the mouse scurries faster for the cover of the bare brush.

KENDARE BLAKE

Despite their familiar-bond, Jules does not know whether the mouse will be spared or eaten. Either way she hopes that it is over soon. The poor mouse still has a long way to run before it reaches cover, and the chase has begun to look like torture.

"Jules. This isn't working."

Queen Arsinoe stands in the center of the clearing, dressed all in black as the queens do, looking like an inkblot in the snow. She has been trying to bloom a rose from a rosebud, but in the palm of her hand, the bud remains green, and firmly closed.

"Pray," Jules says.

They have sung this same song a thousand times over the years. And Jules knows what comes next.

Arsinoe holds out her hand.

"Why don't you help?"

To Jules, the rosebud looks like energy and possibilities. She can smell every drop of perfume tucked away inside. She knows what shade of red it will be.

Such a task should be easy for any naturalist. It should be especially easy for a queen. Arsinoe ought to be able to bloom entire bushes and ripen whole fields. But her gift has not come. Because of that weakness, no one expects Arsinoe to survive the Ascension Year. But Jules will not give up. Not even if it is the queens' sixteenth birthday, and Beltane is in four months' time, falling like a shadow.

Arsinoe wiggles her fingers, and the bud rolls from side to side.

"Just a little push," she says. "To get me started."

Jules sighs. She is tempted to say no. She should say no. But the unbloomed bud is like an itch that needs scratching. The poor thing is dead, anyway, cut off from its parent plant in the hothouse. She cannot let it wither and wrinkle still green.

"Focus," she says. "Join me."

"Mm-hmm." Arsinoe nods.

It does not take much. Hardly a thought. A whisper. The rosebud pops like a bean skin in hot oil, and a fat, fancy-petaled red rose uncurls in Arsinoe's hand. It is bright as blood, and smells of summer.

"Done," Arsinoe declares, and sets the rose on top of the snow. "And not bad, either. I think I did most of those petals at the center."

"Let's do another," says Jules, fairly certain that she did it all. Perhaps they should try something else. She heard starlings while on the path up from the house. They could call them until they filled the bare branches around the clearing. Thousands of them, until not a single starling remained anywhere else in Wolf Spring, and the trees seethed with black, speckled bodies.

Arsinoe's snowball hits Camden in the face, but Jules feels it as well: the surprise and a flicker of irritation as the cat shakes the flakes from her fur. The second ball hits Jules on the shoulder, just high enough for the exploding snow to find its way into the warm neck of her coat. Arsinoe laughs.

"You are such a child!" Jules shouts angrily, and Camden snarls and jumps.

Arsinoe barely dodges the attack. She covers her face with her arm and ducks, and the cougar's claws sail over her back.

"Arsinoe!"

Camden backs off and slinks away, ashamed. But it is not her fault. She feels what Jules feels. Her actions are Jules's actions.

Jules rushes to the queen and inspects her quickly. There is no blood. No claw marks or tears in Arsinoe's coat.

"I'm sorry!"

"It's all right, Jules." Arsinoe rests a steadying hand on Jules's forearm, but her fingers tremble. "It was nothing. How many times did we push each other out of trees as children?"

"That is not the same. Those were games." Jules looks at her cougar regretfully. "Cam is not a cub anymore. Her claws and teeth are sharp, and fast. I have to be more careful from now on. I will be." Her eyes widen. "Is that blood on your ear?"

Arsinoe takes off her black cap and pulls back her short, shaggy black hair. "No. See? She didn't come close. I know you would never hurt me, Jules. Neither of you."

She holds her hand out, and Cam slides under it. Her big, deep purr is the cougar's apology.

"I really didn't mean to," says Jules.

"I know. We are all under strain. Don't think on it." Arsinoe slips her black cap back on. "And don't tell Grandma Cait. She has enough to worry about."

Jules nods. She does not need to tell Grandma Cait to know what she would say. Or to imagine the disappointment and worry on her face.

After leaving the clearing, Jules and Arsinoe walk down past the docks, through the square toward the winter market. As they pass the cove, Jules raises her arm to Shad Millner standing in the back of his boat, just returned from a run. He nods hello and shows off a fat brown sole. His familiar, a seagull, flaps its wings with pride, though she doubts that the bird was the one who caught the fish.

"I hope I don't get one of those," Arsinoe says, and nods at the gull. This morning, she called for her familiar. Like she has every morning since leaving the Black Cottage as a child. But nothing has come.

They continue through the square, Arsinoe kicking through slush puddles and Camden lollygagging behind, unhappy about leaving the powdery wild for the cold stone town. Winter ugliness holds Wolf Spring in a firm grip. Months of freezing and partial thaws have coated the cobblestones with grit. Fog covers the windows, and the snow is mottled brown after being walked through by so many mud-covered feet. With the clouds hanging heavy overhead, the entirety of the town looks as though it is being viewed through a dirty glass.

"Take care," Jules mutters as they pass Martinson Sisters' Grocery. She nods toward empty fruit crates. Three troublesome children are ducked down behind them. One is Polly Nichols, wearing her father's old tweed cap. The two boys she does not know. But she knows what they are up to.

They each have a rock in their hands.

Camden comes to Jules's side and growls loudly. The

children hear. They look at Jules and duck lower. The two boys cower, but Polly Nichols narrows her eyes. She has done one naughty thing for every freckle on her face, and even her mother knows it.

"Do not throw that, Polly," Arsinoe orders, but that seems to make it worse. Polly's little lips draw together so tightly that they disappear. She jumps from behind the crates and throws the rock hard. Arsinoe blocks it with her palm, but the stone manages to skip off and strike the side of her head.

"Ow!"

Arsinoe presses her hand to the spot where the stone struck. Jules clenches her fists and sends Camden snarling after the children, determined to plant Polly Nichols onto the cobblestones.

"I'm fine, call her back," Arsinoe says. She wipes the line of blood away as it runs down to her jaw. "Little scamps."

"Scamps? They are brats!" Jules hisses. "They should be whipped! Let Cam tear up Polly's ridiculous hat, at least!"

But Jules calls Camden, and the cat stops at the street corner and hisses.

"Juillenne Milone!"

Jules and Arsinoe turn. It is Luke, owner and operator of Gillespie's Bookshop, looking smart in a brown jacket, his yellow hair combed back from his handsome face.

"Small of stature but large of lion," he says, and laughs. "Come inside for tea."

As they enter the shop, Jules stretches up on her toes to quiet the brass bell above the door. She follows Luke and Arsinoe past the tall, blue-green bookshelves and up the stairs to the landing, where a table is set with sandwiches and a tray of buttery yellow cake slices.

"Sit," Luke says, and goes to the kitchen for a teapot.

"How did you know we were coming?" Arsinoe asks.

"I have a good view of the hill. Mind the feathers. Hank's molting."

Hank is Luke's familiar, a handsome black-and-green rooster. Arsinoe blows a feather off the table and reaches for a plate of small muffins. She picks one up and peers at it.

"Are those shiny black bits legs?" Jules asks her.

"And shells," Arsinoe says. Beetle muffins, to help Hank grow new feathers. "Birds," she remarks, and sets the muffin down.

"You used to want a crow, like Eva," Jules reminds her.

Eva is Jules's grandma Cait's familiar. A large, beautiful black crow. Jules's mother, Madrigal, has a crow as well. Her name is Aria. She is a more delicately boned bird than Eva, and more ill-tempered, much like Madrigal herself. For a long time, Jules thought she would have a crow too. She used to watch the nests, waiting for a fuzzy black chick to fall into her cupped hands. Secretly, though, she had wished for a dog, like her granddad Ellis's white spaniel, Jake. Or her aunt Caragh's pretty chocolate hound. Now, of course, she would not trade Camden for anything.

"I think I would like a fast jackrabbit," Arsinoe says. "Or a clever, black-masked raccoon to help me steal fried clams from Madge."

"You will have something far more grand than a rabbit or a raccoon," Luke says. "You're a queen."

He and Arsinoe glance at Camden, so tall that her head and shoulders are visible over the tabletop. Queen's familiar or not, nothing could be more grand than a mountain cat.

"Perhaps a wolf, like Queen Bernadine," Luke says. He pours tea for Jules and adds cream and four lumps of sugar. Tea for a child, the way she likes it best but is not allowed to drink at home.

"Another wolf in Wolf Spring," Arsinoe muses around a mouthful of cake. "At this rate, I'd be happy to have . . . one of the beetles in Hank's muffins."

"Don't be pessimistic. My own father did not get his until he was twenty."

"Luke," Arsinoe says, and laughs. "Giftless queens don't live until they're twenty."

She reaches across the table for a sandwich.

"Maybe that is why my familiar hasn't bothered," she says. "It knows I will be dead, anyway, in a year. Oh!"

She has dripped blood onto her plate. Polly's thrown rock left a cut, hidden in her hair. Another drop falls onto Luke's fancy tablecloth. Hank hops up and pecks at it.

"I had better go clean this up," Arsinoe says. "I'm sorry, Luke. I'll replace it."

"Do not think of it," Luke reassures her as she goes to the

bathroom. He puts his chin in his hands sadly. "She'll be the one crowned at next spring's Beltane, Jules. You just wait and see."

Jules stares into her tea, so full of cream that it is almost white.

"We have to get through *this* spring's Beltane first," she says.

Luke only smiles. He is so sure. But in the last three generations, stronger naturalist queens than Arsinoe have still been killed. The Arrons are too powerful. Their poison always gets through. And even if it does not, they have Mirabella to contend with. Every ship that sails to the northeast of the island returns telling tales of the fierce Shannon Storms besieging the city of Rolanth, where the elementals make their home.

"You only hope, you know," Jules says. "Like I do. Because you don't want Arsinoe to die. Because you love her."

"Of course I love her," says Luke. "But I also believe. I believe that Arsinoe is the chosen queen."

"How do you know?"

"I just know. Why else would the Goddess put a naturalist as strong as you here to protect her?"

Arsinoe's birthday celebration is held in the town square, beneath great black-and-white tents. Every year the tents heat up with food and too many bodies until the flaps have to be opened to allow the winter air in. Every year, most of the attendees are drunk before sundown.

As Arsinoe makes her way through, Jules and Camden follow closely. The mood is jovial, but it takes only a second for the whiskey to turn.

"It's been a long winter," Jules hears someone say. "But the madness has been mild. It's a wonder more fishers haven't been lost on their boats, taken a gaff to the side of the head."

Jules presses Arsinoe past the conversation. There are many people to see before they can sit down to their own food.

"These are very well done," Arsinoe says, and leans down to sniff a vase holding a tall spray of wildflowers. The arrangement is layered with the pinks and purples of hedge nettles and showy orchis. It is as pretty as a wedding cake, early bloomed by the naturalist gift. Each family has brought their own, and most brought extra, to decorate the tables of the giftless.

"Our Betty did them this year," says the man nearest Arsinoe. He winks across the table and beams at a blushing girl of around eight, wearing a newly knit black sweater and a braided leather necklace.

"Did you, Betty? Well, they are the finest ones here, this year." Arsinoe smiles, and Betty thanks her, and if anyone notes that a little girl can do such elegant blooms when the queen cannot open one rose, they do not let it show.

Betty's eyes brighten at the sight of Camden, and the big cat walks close to let her pet and stroke her back. The girl's father watches. He nods respectfully at Jules as they go by.

The Milones are the most prosperous naturalists in Wolf Spring. Their fields are rich and orchards bountiful. Their woods are full of game. And now they have Jules, the strongest naturalist in some sixty years, it is said. For these reasons and more, they were chosen to foster the naturalist queen and must take on all the responsibilities that go with it, including playing host to visiting members of the council. Something that does not come naturally.

Inside the main tent, Jules's grandmother and grandfather sit on either side of the honored guest, Renata Hargrove, a member of the Black Council sent all the way from the capital city of Indrid Down. Madrigal ought to be there too, but her seat is empty. She has disappeared, as usual. Poor Cait and Ellis. Trapped in their chairs. Granddad Ellis's cheeks will be sore later, from holding such a fake smile. On his lap, his little spaniel, Jake, grins a grin that looks less like friendliness and more like bared teeth.

"They only sent one representative this year," Arsinoe says under her breath. "One out of nine. And the giftless one, at that. What do you think the council is trying to say?"

She chuckles and then pops an herb-roasted, buttered crab claw into her mouth. Arsinoe hides everything behind the same easygoing smirk. She makes eye contact with Renata, and Renata inclines her head. It is not much of an acknowledgment. Barely enough, and Jules's hackles rise.

"Everyone knows her seat on the council was bought and paid for by her giftless family," she growls. "She'd lick the poison off Natalia Arron's shoes if she asked."

Jules glances at the few priestesses from Wolf Spring

Temple who have decided to attend. Sending one council member is an insult, but it is still better treatment than Arsinoe has received from the temple. High Priestess Luca has not come to her birthday even once. She went to Katharine's, occasionally, in the early years. Now it is only Mirabella, Mirabella, Mirabella.

"Those priestesses should not show their faces," Jules grumbles. "The temple should not choose sides."

"Take it easy, Jules," Arsinoe says. She pats Jules's arm and changes the subject. "The sea catch is impressive."

Jules turns to the head table, thoroughly stocked with fish and crabs. Her catch forms the centerpiece: an enormous black cod accompanied by two equally huge silver stripers. She called them from the depths early that morning, before Arsinoe had even gotten out of bed. Now they lie on piles of potatoes, onions, and pale winter cabbage. Most of their juicy fillets have already been picked clean.

"You shouldn't brush it aside," Jules warns. "It matters."

"The disrespect?" Arsinoe asks, and snorts. "No, it doesn't." She eats another crab claw. "You know, if I make it through this Ascension Year, I would like a shark as my centerpiece."

"A shark?"

"A great white. Don't be cheap when it comes to my crowning, Jules."

Jules laughs. "*When* you make it through the Ascension, you can charm your own great white," she says.

They grin. Except for her severe coloring, Arsinoe does not

look much like a queen. Her hair is rough, and they cannot keep her from cutting it. Her black trousers are the same ones she wears every day, and so is her light black jacket. The only piece of finery they could get her into for the occasion was a new scarf that Madrigal found at Pearson's, made from the wool of their fancy, flop-eared rabbits. But that is probably for the best. Wolf Spring is not a city of finery. It is of fishers and farmers and folk on the docks, and no one wears their fine blacks except on Beltane.

Arsinoe studies the tapestry hung behind the head table and frowns. Normally, it hangs in the town hall, but it is always dragged out for Arsinoe's birthday. It depicts the crowning of the island's last great naturalist queen. Bernadine, who weighed orchards heavy with fruit when she passed, and had an enormous gray wolf for a familiar. In the weaving, Bernadine stands below a tree sagging with apples, with the wolf beside her. In the wolf's jaws is the torn-out throat of one of her sisters, whose body lies at Bernadine's feet.

"I hate that thing," Arsinoe says.

"Why?"

"Because it reminds me of what I'm not."

Jules bumps the queen with her shoulder. "There is seed cake in the dessert tent," she says. "And pumpkin cake. And white cake with strawberry icing. Let's find Luke and go have some."

"All right."

On the way, Arsinoe pauses to chat with people and to pat

their familiars. Most are dogs and birds, common naturalist guardians. Thomas Mintz, the island's best fisher, gets his sea lion to offer Arsinoe an apple, balanced on its nose.

"Are you leaving?" Renata Hargrove asks.

Jules and Arsinoe turn, surprised Renata has bothered to come down from the head table.

"Only to the sweets tent," Arsinoe says. "May we . . . bring something back for you?"

She glances at Jules awkwardly. No member of the Black Council has ever shown any interest in Arsinoe, despite being annual guests at her birthday. They eat, exchange pleasantries with the Milones, and depart, grumbling about the quality of the food and the size of the rooms at the Wolverton Inn. But Renata looks almost happy to see them.

"If you go, you will miss my announcement," Renata says, and smiles.

"What announcement is that?" Jules asks.

"I am about to announce that Joseph Sandrin's banishment is over. He is already set to return to the island and should arrive in two days."

Sealhead Cove laps at the end of the long wooden dock. The weathered, gray boards creak in the brisk wind, and the rippling, moonlit sea mirrors the quiver of Jules's breath.

Joseph Sandrin is coming home.

"Jules, wait." Arsinoe's footsteps rattle across the dock as she follows Jules to the point, with Camden trotting reluctantly alongside. The cat has never cared for the water, and a thin, bent wooden board does not seem to her the most trustworthy barrier.

"Are you all right?" Jules asks, out of habit.

"What are you asking me for?" Arsinoe asks. She tucks her neck down against the wind, deep into her scarf.

"I should not have left you."

"Yes you should have," Arsinoe says. "He's coming back. After all this time."

"Do you think it's true?"

"To lie about this, at my birthday celebration, would take more nerve than even the Arrons have."

They look across the darkening water, across the cove, past the submerged sandbar that protects it from the waves and out into the deeper currents.

It has been more than five years now since they tried to escape the island. Since Joseph stole one of his father's daysailers and helped them try to run away.

Jules leans against Arsinoe's shoulder. It is the same reassuring gesture they have done since they were children. No matter what their attempted escape has cost them, Jules has never regretted trying. She would try again, if there were any hope at all.

But there is none. Beneath the dock, the sea whispers, just like it did against the sides of their boat as it held them captive in the mists that surround the island. No matter how they set the sails, or worked the oars, it was impassible. They were found, cold and scared, and bobbing in the harbor. The fishers said they should have known better. That Jules and Joseph might have made it, to be lost at sea, or perhaps to find the mainland. But Arsinoe was a queen. And the island would never let her go.

"What do you think he is like, now?" Arsinoe wonders.

Probably not still small, with dirt on his jaw and under his fingernails. He will not be a child anymore. He will have grown up.

"I am afraid to see him," says Jules.

"You are not afraid of anything."

"What if he has changed?"

"What if he hasn't?" Arsinoe reaches into her pocket and tries to skip a flat stone across the water, but there are too many waves.

"This feels right," she says. "Him coming back. For this. Our last year. It feels like it was supposed to happen."

"Like the Goddess has willed it?" Jules asks.

"I did not say that."

Arsinoe looks down and smiles. She scratches Camden between the ears.

"Let's go," says Jules. "Catching a chest cold won't improve the situation."

"Certainly not, if your eyes get red and your nose swells."

Jules shoves Arsinoe forward, back toward the marina and the long winding road up to the Milone house.

Camden trots ahead to bump against the backs of Arsinoe's knees. Neither Jules nor the cat will sleep much tonight.

Thanks to Renata Hargrove, every memory they have of Joseph is coursing through their heads.

As they pass the last dock, Camden slows, and her ears flicker back toward town. A few steps ahead, Arsinoe laments the lack of strawberry cake in her stomach. She does not hear. Jules does not either, but Camden's yellow eyes tell her that something is wrong.

"What is it?" Arsinoe asks, catching on.

"I don't know. A scuffle I think."

"Some drunks left after my birthday, no doubt."

They jog back toward the square. The closer they get, the faster the big cat moves. They pass Gillespie's Bookshop, and Jules tells Arsinoe to knock and wait inside.

"But, Jules!" Arsinoe starts, except Jules and Cam are already gone, racing down the street, past the now-empty, flapping tents and toward the alley behind the kitchen of the Heath and Stone.

Jules does not recognize the voices. But she recognizes the sound of fists when they begin to swing.

"Stop!" she shouts, and jumps into the middle of the fray. "Stop it now!"

With Camden by her side, the people reel backward. Two men and a woman. Fighting over she does not care what. It will cease to matter in the morning, after the ale wears off.

"Milone," one of the men sneers. "You're a bully with that cougar. But you are not the law."

"Aye, I'm not," Jules says. "The Black Council is the law, and if you keep on, I'll let them have you. Let them poison you out of your wits, or maybe even to death, in Indrid Down Square."

"Jules," Arsinoe says, and steps out of the shadow. "Is everything all right?"

"Fine," says Jules. "Only a brawl."

A brawl, but an escalating one. There is a small club in the drunk woman's fist.

"Why don't you look after the queen," the woman says, "and get out of here."

The woman raises the club and swings. Jules jumps back, but the end of it still catches her on the shoulder, striking painfully. Camden snarls, and Jules clenches her fists.

"Idiot!" Arsinoe shouts. She steps between Jules and the woman. "Do not push her. Do not push me."

"You?" the drunk man asks, and laughs. "When the real queen comes, we'll offer her your head on a pike."

Jules bares her teeth and lunges. She gets him square in the jaw before Arsinoe can grab her arm.

"Send him to Indrid Down!" Jules shouts. "He threatened you!"

"So let him," Arsinoe says. She turns and shoves the man, who holds his bleeding jaw. Camden is hissing, and the other two back off. "Get out of here!" Arsinoe yells. "If you want your chance at me, you'll have it! They all will, after Beltane is over."

ROLANTH

&

*T*he pilgrims gather beneath the north dome of Rolanth Temple, their lips sticky from bites of caramel cake or sweet chicken skewered with lemons, their shoulders wrapped in billowing black cloaks.

Queen Mirabella stands at the altar of the Goddess. Sweating, but not from heat. Elementals are not bothered much by temperature, and if they were, no one inside could complain of being warm. Rolanth Temple is a weather queen's temple, open to the east and west, the roof supported by beams and thick marble columns. Air moves through no matter the season, and no one shivers, except for the priestesses.

Mirabella has just filled the air with lightning. Gorgeous, bright bolts, crackling across the sky and crashing down in thick veins on all sides. Long, repeated strikes that brightened the interior like day. She feels elated. The lightning is her favorite. The lightning and the storms, the electricity coursing through her blood—it vibrates down to her bones.

But from the looks on the faces of her people, one would think she had done nothing at all. In the orange candlelight, their wide-eyed expectation is plain. They have heard the whispers, the rumors of what she can do. And they would see it all. The fire, the wind, the water. They would have her shake the earth until the pillars of the temple crack. Perhaps they even want her to shear off the entire black cliff and cast it into the sea so the temple can drift in the bay below.

Mirabella snorts. Someday perhaps. But just now it feels like a lot to ask.

She calls the wind. It blows out half the torches and sends orange sparks and embers flying from the braziers. Screams of delight fill her ears as the crowd pushes joyfully out of the way.

She does not even wait for the wind to die before raising the flames on the last of the torches, high enough to scorch the mural of Queen Elo, the fire breather, where she stands depicted on her gilded barge, burning an attacking fleet of mainland ships to the bottom of Bardon Harbor.

And still they would have more. Gathered together they have turned giddy as children. There are more in attendance than she has ever seen, packed into the temple and pressed into the courtyard outside. High Priestess Luca told her before the ceremony started that the road to the temple glowed with the candles of her supporters.

Not all who have come are elementals. Her gift has inspired other followers as well, naturalists and some who carry the rare war gift. Many who have no gift at all. They come desiring to see the rumors proved true, that Mirabella is the next queen of Fennbirn and that the long reign of the poisoners has come to an end.

Mirabella's arms tremble. She has not pushed her gift this far in a very long time. Perhaps not since she first came to Rolanth and to the Westwoods, when she was parted from her sisters at six years old and tried to batter down the Westwood House with wind and lightning. She glances at the shallow reflector pool to her right, lit prettily with floating candles.

No. Not water. Water is her worst element. The most difficult to control. She ought to have done that first. She would have, had her mind not been so clouded by her nerves.

Mirabella looks across the crowd to the back, where High Priestess Luca huddles against the curve of the south wall, layered in thick robes. Mirabella nods to her from beneath her dripping brow, and the High Priestess understands.

Luca's clear, authoritative voice cuts through the din.

"One more."

The crowd is suggestible, and in moments murmurs of "one more" weave with cheers of encouragement.

One. Just one more element. One more display.

Mirabella reaches down deep, calling silently to the Goddess, giving thanks for her gift. But that is only temple teaching. Mirabella needs no prayers. Her elemental gift coils in her chest. She takes a breath and lets it go. A shockwave passes under their feet. It rattles the temple and everyone in it.

Somewhere a vase falls over and shatters. People outside feel the reverberation and gasp.

Inside the temple, finally, the people roar.

She draws her sister's blood with a pair of silver shears. What was meant to simply trim her hair has instead shorn off an ear.

"Is this a nursery rhyme, Sister?" her sister asks. "Is this a fairy story?"

"I have heard it before," Mirabella says, and studies the crimson stain. She drops the ear into her sister's lap and runs her fingertip along the shears's sharp edge.

"Careful not to cut yourself. Our queenly skin is fragile. Besides, my birds will want you whole. Eyes in your head and ears attached. Do not drink. She has turned our wine to blood."

"Who?" Mirabella asks, though she knows very well.

"Wine and blood and back again, inside our veins and into cups."

Somewhere through the tower a little girl's voice sings; it rises up the stairs and round and round like a noose tightening.

"She is not my sister."

Her sister shrugs. Blood rolls down in a slow waterfall from the open hole on the side of her head.

"She is and I am. We are."

The shears open and close. The other ear falls into her sister's lap.

Mirabella wakes with her mouth tasting of blood. It was only a dream, but a vivid one. She almost expects to look down and see pieces of her sisters clenched in her fists.

Arsinoe's ear landed so softly in her lap. Though it was not really Arsinoe. So many years have gone by that Mirabella does not even know what Arsinoe looks like. People tell her that Arsinoe is ugly, with short, straw-like hair and a plain face. But Mirabella does not believe it. That is only what they think she wants to hear.

Mirabella kicks her sheets aside and takes a long drink of water from the glass on her bedside table. The sprawling estate of Westwood House is quiet. She imagines that all of Rolanth is quiet, even though the sunlight tells her it is nearly noon. Her birthday celebration went long into the night.

"You are awake."

Mirabella turns toward her open door and smiles weakly at the petite priestess who has stepped into her room. She is a small thing, and young. The black bracelets on her wrists are still real bracelets, not tattoos.

"Yes," Mirabella says. "Just."

The girl nods and comes inside to help her dress, along with a second initiate who had been hidden in her shadow.

"Did you sleep well?"

"Quite," Mirabella lies. The dreams have gotten worse of late. Luca says that is to be expected. That it is the way of the queens, and after her sisters are dead, the dreams will stop.

Mirabella holds very still as the priestesses brush her hair and put her into a comfortable dress after the night's revelry. Then finally, they step back into the shadows. They are always with her, the priestesses. Even in Westwood House. Ever since the High Priestess saw the strength of her gift, she has been under temple guard. Sometimes, she wishes they would disappear.

She passes Uncle Miles in the hallway that leads to the kitchen, pressing a cold compress to his forehead.

"Too much wine?" she asks.

"Too much of everything," he says, and bows clumsily before going back toward his room.

"Where is Sara?"

"In the drawing room," he answers over his shoulder. "She has not moved from there since breakfast."

Sara Westwood. Her foster-matron. A kind, devout woman, if a bit prone to worrying. She has cared for Mirabella well, and is quite gifted, specializing in the element of water. When Mirabella settles into the sitting room for tea, Sara's moans occasionally echo up the stairs from where she is likely reclined on the drawing room sofa. Overindulgence has its price.

But the night was a success. Luca said so. All the priestesses said so. People of Fennbirn will talk of it for years. They will say they were there when the new queen rose.

Mirabella puts her feet up on the green velvet chair opposite the couch and stretches out. She is spent. Her gift feels like rubber in her stomach, wobbly and uneasy. But it will come back.

"That was quite a show, my queen."

Bree leans against the door and then lazily twirls inside. She flops down beside Mirabella on the long satin couch. Her shiny, chestnut-and-gold hair is loose from its usual braid, and though she too looks exhausted, it is only the best kind.

"I hate it when you call me that," Mirabella says, and smiles. "Where have you been?"

"Fenn Wexton was showing me his mother's stables."

"Fenn Wexton." Mirabella snorts. "He is a laughing fool."

"But have you seen his arms?" Bree asks. "And he did not do so much laughing last night. Tilda and Annabeth were there for a while. We took a jug of honeyed wine and lay on his barn roof under the stars. Nearly fell through the rotted thing!"

Mirabella gazes up at the ceiling.

"Perhaps we could have smuggled you out," Bree says, and Mirabella chuckles.

"Bree, they put bells on my ankles. Large, rattling bells, like I was a cat. Like they thought I was going to sneak off."

"It is not like you have not disappeared before," Bree says, and grins.

"Never for anything so important!" Mirabella protests. "I have always been dutiful, when it matters. But they always like to know where I am. What I am doing. What I am thinking."

"They will come down on you even harder now that the Ascension Year approaches," says Bree. "Rho and those priestess guards." She rolls over onto her stomach. "Mira, will you ever be free?"

Mirabella looks at her slantways.

"Do not be so dramatic," Mirabella says. "Now, you ought to go get cleaned up. We have a dress fitting this afternoon."

The loose stair on the staircase creaks six times, and moments later, six tall priestesses file into the room. Bree makes a displeased face and stretches languorously.

"My queen," says the nearest girl. "High Priestess Luca wishes to see you."

"Very well." Mirabella stands. She thought it would be some less-pleasant errand. But it is always good to visit Luca.

"Be sure to have her back for her fitting this afternoon," Bree says, and waggles her fingers in a lazy good-bye.

Mirabella doubts she will see Bree for the rest of the day. Dress fitting or no, nothing much can keep Bree from doing exactly what she wants, and as the beloved only daughter of Sara Westwood, no one has ever much bothered to try. It would be easy to resent Bree for her freedom if Mirabella did not love her so dearly.

Outside, Mirabella keeps a brisk pace, her subtle jab at the priestesses who guard her so closely. Most of them are as hungover from her birthday as Sara, and the jarring walk turns them slightly green.

But it is not terribly cruel. Westwood House is close to the temple. When Mirabella was younger, and more able to slip her guard, she would sometimes sneak out to visit Luca alone, or to run along the temple grounds out to the dark basalt cliffs of Shannon's Blackway. She misses that space. That privacy. When she could walk with a slouch or kick stones aimed at trees. When she could be wild as an elemental queen is meant to be.

Now, she is surrounded by white robes. She has to crane her neck over the shoulder of the nearest just to catch a glimpse of the city below. Rolanth. The elementals' city, a sprawling center of stone and water running fast from the evergreen hills. Channels run between buildings like arteries to ferry people and cargo inland from the sea through a system of locks. From this height, the buildings look proud and white. The channels nearly blue. She can easily imagine the way the city once shone, when it was rich and fortified. Before the poisoners took the throne and the council and refused to let go.

"It is a lovely day," Mirabella says to break the monotony.

"It is, my queen," says one of the priestesses. "The Goddess provides."

They say no more. Mirabella knows not a one of her escorts by name. So many priestesses have come to Rolanth Temple of late that she cannot keep up with the new ones. Luca says that temples across the island are experiencing the same bounty. The strength of Mirabella's gift has renewed the island's faith. Sometimes, Mirabella wishes that Luca would attribute fewer things to the strength of her gift.

Luca meets her in the temple proper rather than upstairs in her rooms. The old woman opens her arms. She takes Mirabella from the priestesses and kisses her cheek.

"You do not look so very tired," she says. "Perhaps I should have made you work the water last night, after all."

"If you had, you would have seen nothing," Mirabella replies. "Or I may have drenched someone by accident."

"By accident," Luca says wryly. When she first met Luca, Mirabella tried to drown her by summoning a water elemental out of Starfall Lake and sending it down the High Priestess's throat. But that was a long time ago.

Luca slips her hands back beneath her layers of robes and fur. Mirabella does not know what gift Luca had before she became a priestess, but it was not the elemental gift. She is far too vulnerable to the cold.

A priestess passing by nearly stumbles, and Luca's arm shoots out fast to steady her.

"Be careful, child," Luca says, and the girl nods. "Those robes are too long. You are going to hurt yourself. Have someone hem them."

"Yes, Luca," she whispers.

The girl is only an initiate. She can still fail at serving the temple. She can still change her mind and go home.

The girl walks slower to the south wall, where three more have gathered to restore Queen Shannon's mural. The original painter captured the queen exceptionally well. Her black eyes peer out of the wall, focused and intent despite the rain and storm that obscure the lower half of her face.

"She was always my favorite," Mirabella says. "Queen Shannon and her storms."

"One of the strongest. Until you. One day your face will eclipse hers on the wall."

"We should hope not," replies Mirabella. "None of these murals depict times of peace."

Luca sighs. "Times are not so peaceful now, with decades of poisoners in the capital. And the Goddess would not have made you so strong if you were not going to need that strength." Luca takes her by the arm and leads her around the southern dome.

"One day," she says, "perhaps after you are crowned, I will take you to the War Queen's Temple in Bastian City. They have not murals there but a statue of Emmeline—bloody spear above her head, and arrows—suspended from the ceiling."

"Suspended from the ceiling?" Mirabella asks.

"A long time ago, when the war gift was strong, a war queen could move things through the air, just by the sheer force of her will."

Mirabella's eyes widen, and the High Priestess chuckles. "Or so they say."

"Why have you asked to see me, High Priestess?"

"Because a task has arisen." Luca turns from the mural and clasps her hands. She walks north, toward the Goddess's altar, and Mirabella falls in beside her.

"I wanted to wait," she continues. "I knew how tired you would be, the day after such a spectacle. But try as I may to keep you young, and to keep you here with me in this quiet place, I cannot. You have grown. You are a queen, and unless your gift has expanded to stop time, the Quickening is coming. We can no longer put off the things that need doing."

She puts her soft hand on Mirabella's cheek. "But if you are not ready, I will put them off anyway."

Mirabella places her own hand over Luca's. She would kiss the old woman's head were the priestesses not there watching. No High Priestess has ever shown favor to one queen as Luca has to her. Or caused such scandal as to leave their chambers in Indrid Down Temple and install themselves closer to their favorite.

"I am ready," Mirabella says. "I will happily do whatever you require."

"Good," Luca says, and pats her. "Good."

The priestesses walk Mirabella far out beyond the temple grounds, through the evergreen forest and toward the basalt cliffs above the sea. Mirabella has always loved the salt air, and enjoys the light breeze, and kicking her legs out fully in her skirt.

When they came to claim her from the temple, they did not tell her what they wanted. Priestess Rho leads the escort, so Mirabella thinks that it is probably to go on a hunt. Rho always leads the hunts. Every initiate in the temple is fearful of her. She has been known to strike the ones who displease her. To be a priestess is to have no past, but Mirabella is certain that Rho possesses the war gift.

Today, though, Rho is grim and sober. The priestesses carry their hunting pikes but have brought no accompanying hounds. And all the good game runs are far behind them, deeper into the woods.

They reach the cliffs and continue on to the north, farther into the rock than Mirabella has ever gone before.

"Where are we going?" Mirabella asks.

"Not much farther, my queen," says Rho. "Not much farther at all." She taps the priestess to her left. "Go on ahead," she says. "Make sure all is ready."

The priestess nods and then runs up the path to disappear around a corner.

"Rho? What are we doing? What am I to do?"

"The Goddess's bidding and the queen's duty. Is there ever anything else?" She looks over her shoulder at Mirabella and smiles meanly, and her hair peeks out from under her hood, bloodred.

The fall of their boots is loud against the stone and gravel, but it is steady. None but the girl tapped to scout ahead will go any faster, no matter how Mirabella tries to change their pace. She quickly stops trying, feeling the fool, like a bird fluttering against a cage of robes.

Ahead, the trail turns, and they round the corner and move farther into the canyon of dark rock. Mirabella catches her first glimpse of whatever it is they have brought her for. It does not look like much of anything. A gathering of priestesses in black-and-white robes. A tall brazier, burning something hot that hardly smokes. And a barrel. When the group hears them coming, they turn and stand in a row.

None of them are initiates. Only two are novices. One of the novices is dressed strangely in a simple black shift, with a blanket across her shoulders. Her brown hair hangs loose, and despite the blanket, her skin looks cold and very pale. She stares at Mirabella with wide, grateful eyes, as if Mirabella has come to save her.

"You should have told me," Mirabella says. "You should have told me, Rho!"

"Why?" Rho asks. "Would it have made any difference?" She nods for the girl to step forward, and she slips out from under the blanket and walks ahead barefoot and shivering.

"She makes this sacrifice for you," Rho whispers. "Do not disgrace her."

The young priestess kneels before Mirabella and looks up. Her eyes are clear. They have not even drugged her against the pain. She holds out her hand, and reluctantly, Mirabella takes it, and stands numb as the girl prays. When she is finished, the girl stands and walks to the cliff face.

It is all there. Water in the barrel. Fire in the brazier. The wind and the lightning, always at her fingertips. Or she could quake the rocks and bury her. Perhaps that would be painless, at least.

The girl who would become a sacrifice smiles at Mirabella and then closes her eyes, to make it easier. But it is not easier.

Impatient, Rho nods to a priestess beside the brazier, and she lights a torch.

"If you do not do it, my queen, then we will. And our way will be slower than yours."

GREAVESDRAKE MANOR

———————— ⚜ ————————

*G*iselle pours warm water over the raised blisters on Queen Katharine's skin. The shiny, fluid-filled red welts stretch in bands across her back, as well as her shoulders and upper arms. The blisters are the result of a tincture of nettles. Natalia striped Katharine with it that morning, painting it on with a soaked ball of cotton.

"She was careless," Giselle mutters. "This will scar. Don't move, Katharine." She touches Katharine gently, and a tear rolls down the young queen's cheek.

Natalia would never have made the tincture so strong. But she was not the one who made it. That was Genevieve.

"When she sees what it has done, how high they have raised, she will have that sister of hers whipped in the square."

Katharine manages to laugh a little. How she would love to see that. But she will not. Natalia will be displeased when she sees the marks. But any comeuppance Genevieve receives will be kept quiet and private.

She breathes out as Giselle gently pours more water over her shoulders. The maid has infused the bath with chamomile, to ease some of the swelling, but even so, it will be days before Katharine can dress normally without fear of the blisters popping.

"Lean forward, Kat."

She does and begins to cry again. Through the open door of her bathroom, she can see her bedroom and dressing table, and Sweetheart's empty cage. Her little snake was frightened when she fell during the *Gave Noir*. She crawled off Katharine's wrist and disappeared. She is probably dead now, lost forever somewhere in Greavesdrake's cold walls.

The nettle poisoning was not a punishment. That is what Natalia said, what she assured her in a calm, even voice as she applied stripe after stripe. But Katharine knows better. There is a price for failing an Arron, and even queens must pay it.

It could have been worse. Knowing Genevieve, she could have been injected with spider venom and forever borne scars from necrosis.

"How can she do this to you?" Giselle asks, and presses a warm cloth to the back of Katharine's neck.

"You know why," Katharine says. "She does it to make me strong. She does it to save my life."

The rooms and halls of Greavesdrake Manor are wonderfully quiet. Finally, after the many arrivals and departures of the previous days, the house is at rest, and Natalia can relax in the solitude of her study, and the comfort of her favorite leather wingback chair. Until someone knocks.

When her butler walks in empty-handed, her face falls.

"I had hoped you were bringing me a pot of mangrove tea."

"Certainly, mistress," he says. "And shall I bring a cup for your guest?"

She turns farther in her chair to see the figure waiting in the shadowy hall. She nods once, irritably, and her guest is shown in.

"After thirty years here, you would think my own butler would know that I do not want guests after I clear my house," Natalia says, and stands.

"I was wondering where everyone had gone. Even the servants have become ghosts."

"I sent everyone away this morning." She had grown tired of their faces. Their smug and accusing glares. "How are you, Pietyr?"

Her nephew comes and kisses her cheek. Until the ball, it had been years since she had last seen him, the only son of her brother Christophe. He was a child when her brother had quit the council in favor of a life in the country. But he was no child any longer, and had grown up handsome.

"I am well, Aunt Natalia," he says.

"To what do I owe this visit? I thought you would be home by now, back in the country with my brother and Marguerite."

He frowns slightly at the mention of his stepmother's name. Natalia does not blame him. Christophe's first wife had been far superior. She would have never turned him toward the temple.

"That is it precisely," says Pietyr. "I am hoping you will tell me that I never have to return there."

He steps past her without waiting for an invitation and helps himself to a snifter of her tainted brandy. When he sees her aghast expression, he says, "I am sorry. Did you want one? I thought I heard you call for tea."

Natalia crosses her arms. She remembers now that Pietyr has always been her favorite of all her nephews and even her nieces. He is the only one with her high cheekbones and ice-blue eyes. He has her same serious mouth and her same nerve.

"If you do not intend to return to the country, then what do you intend to do? Do you want me to help you find some vocation in the capital?"

"No," he says, and smiles. "I am hoping to stay here, with you. I want to help with the queen."

"You were the one she danced with for so long," Natalia says.

"I was."

"And now you think you know what help she needs."

"I know she will need something," he remarks. "I was outside this morning when you were poisoning her. I heard the screams."

"Her gift is stubbornly weak," she says. "But it is coming along."

"Oh? So you have seen improved immunities, then? But

is that due to her gift or due to your"—he lowers his voice—
"practice?"

"It does not matter. She poisons very well."

"That is good to hear."

But Natalia knows Katharine will need more than that. No
Arron queen has ever had to face a rival as gifted as Mirabella.
It has been generations since the island has seen a queen half
so strong. Even in Indrid Down they whisper that each Arron
queen is weaker than the last. They say that Nicola could be
sickened with mushrooms, and Camille could not withstand
snake venom. They say that Camille's prowess with toxins was
so lacking that Natalia had murdered her sisters for her.

But what of it? The gift matters less and less. Crowns are
no longer won, they are made, through politics and alliances.
And no family on the island can navigate those waters better
than the Arrons.

"Of course, the Westwoods are still at our backs," says
Pietyr. "They think that Mirabella is chosen. That she is
untouchable. But you and I know that if Mirabella rules, it will
not be her ruling but the temple."

"Yes," Natalia says. "Since Luca began showing the Westwoods such favor, they have become wrapped around the High
Priestess's little finger."

The fools. But just because they are fools does not mean
they are not a threat. If Mirabella wins the crown, she will
use her right as queen to replace every poisoner on the council
with an elemental. With Westwoods. And with a Westwood-led

council, the island will be weak enough to fall.

"If you have a proposal, Nephew, you ought to make it."

"Katharine has other assets," Pietyr says. "Other strengths." He holds his glass up to the light and peers through it. There is certainly no brandy as fine in Marguerite's household.

"After Beltane is over," he continues, "the delegate suitors will be in close proximity to the other queens. They could slip poison in easily, and our hands would be clean."

"The delegate suitors know the rules. None of them will chance being discovered."

"They might if they love Katharine."

"That is true," Natalia admits. Boys will do much for a girl they think they love. Unfortunately, Katharine is not well-equipped to inspire such loyalty. She is sweet but far too meek. And Genevieve is right when she says she is too skinny.

"Can you improve her in time?" she asks.

"I can," he says. "By the time I am finished, she will be such a jewel that they will forget all about politics and alliances. They will think with their hearts."

Natalia snorts. "It would be just as well if they thought with what is between their legs."

"They will do that, too."

Her butler returns with a pot of mandrake tea, but Natalia waves it away. She will have brandy instead, to seal their bargain. Even if the suitors are of no use for poisoning, it will be worth it just for the disgrace being shunned will cause to Mirabella.

"And what do you want in exchange for your aid?" she asks.

"Not so very much," Pietyr says. "Only to never return to my weakened father and his silly wife. And"—his blue eyes flash—"after Katharine is crowned, I want a seat on the Black Council."

Katharine stands quietly in a feather-light black robe as Giselle and Louise pull the sheets from her bed. After the night of the *Gave* and the morning of pain, they are ruined, stained dark with sweat and spatters of blood. Or perhaps they can still be saved. Louise has learned many tricks of laundering since becoming one of her maids. She is used to doing the cleaning after a heavy poisoning.

Katharine tugs her robe closed and winces when the fabric drags across her blisters. Beneath her hand, Sweetheart's empty cage hangs open. Her poor, lost little snake. She should have paid closer attention when she fell. She should have given her to a servant to look after before the feast began. Sick as she was, she did not even realize Sweetheart had been lost until morning. Far too late. But what truly pains her is that despite how frightened the snake must have been, Sweetheart did not bite.

Katharine startles when Louise screams, and Giselle pinches the other maid hard on the shoulder. Louise has always been flighty. But her look of surprise is warranted. There is a boy standing inside the queen's bedroom.

"Pietyr," Katharine says, and he bows.

"Has something happened to your pet?" he asks, and gestures toward her hand on the cage.

"My snake," she says. "She went missing after . . . after . . ."

"Has Natalia set servants to search the ballroom?"

"I did not want to trouble her."

"I am sure it would be no trouble," he says. He nods to Louise, who curtsies and darts off to tell Natalia. After she is gone, Pietyr dismisses Giselle as well.

Katharine tugs the robe tight around herself, despite the blisters. It is hardly what she ought to be wearing to entertain a guest.

"I am sorry for entering unannounced," says Pietyr. "I am unused to following custom and protocol. Where I am from in the country, we take all sorts of liberties. I hope you will forgive me."

"Of course," says Katharine. "But what . . . Why have you come? Everyone from the ball has already gone."

"Not me," he says, and raises his eyebrows. "I have just been talking with my aunt, and apparently, I get to stay."

He steps toward her only to divert at the last moment to inspect the perfume bottles on her dressing table. His smile speaks of mischief, and a shared secret between them, or perhaps of secrets to come.

"Stay? Here?"

"Yes," he says. "With you. I am to become your very great friend, Queen Katharine."

Katharine cocks her head. This all must be some elaborate

joke of Natalia's. Katharine has never understood her sense of humor.

"Oh," she says. "And what sort of things will we do?"

"I suppose we will do all the sorts of things that friends do." Pietyr slides his arm around her waist. "When you are well enough to do them."

"I already know how to dance."

"There is more to it than dancing."

He leans forward to kiss her, and she jerks back. It was so sudden. She stammers an apology. Though she does not know why she should be the one to apologize, when it was he who was too forward. But in any case, he does not seem angry.

"You see?" he says, and smiles. "You have been too long in the company of my aunts and your maids. They have not prepared you to court your suitors any better than they prepared you for your poison feast."

Katharine blushes scarlet. "Who do you think you are," she asks, "to say such a thing?"

"I am your servant," he answers, and touches her cheek. "I am your slave. I am here to make sure every one of the suitors does not think of either of your sisters before they think of you."

WOLF SPRING

he day of Joseph's return dawns overcast and ugly. Jules watches the whole gray affair lying in her bed in the room she shares with Arsinoe. She has hardly slept.

"They have known he was coming for weeks," she says.

"Of course they did," says Madrigal. She stands behind her as Jules sits at her dresser, pulling a brush through Jules's wild, dark brown hair.

"So why send him home now, two days after Arsinoe's birthday? He will have missed the celebration and return just in time to see the trash in the streets and the gulls and crows fighting over the leftover food."

"That's exactly why," says Madrigal. "And now they got to spring him on us, and watch us scramble like upset chickens. Poor Annie Sandrin must be out of her mind."

Yes.

Down in his family's house by the pier, Joseph's mother will be nearly overwhelmed, making things ready and barking at her husband and at Matthew and Jonah. Barking happily but barking nonetheless.

"What if he doesn't come?" Jules asks.

"Why wouldn't he come?" Madrigal tries again to pin Jules's hair up onto her head. "This is his home."

"What do you think he will be like?" she asks.

"If he is anything like his brother Matthew, then all the girls of Wolf Spring are in danger," Madrigal says, and smiles. "When Matthew was Joseph's age, he had half the town swimming after his boat."

Jules jerks under the brush.

"Matthew never cared for anyone besides Aunt Caragh."

"Yes, yes," Madrigal mutters. "He was devoted as a hound to my serious sister, just like Joseph will no doubt be to you." She throws her hands up and sends Jules's hair flying. "It's hopeless to try anything with this mess."

Jules looks sadly into the mirror. Madrigal is so effortlessly beautiful, with her honey-chestnut hair and lithe, graceful limbs. People never guess that she and Jules are mother and daughter. Sometimes, Jules suspects that Madrigal likes it that way.

"You should have slept more," Madrigal chides. "You have dark hollows beneath your eyes."

"I couldn't, not with Camden getting up and turning around every few minutes."

"And why do you think she could not sleep? Your nervousness

kept her awake. If she runs into the table and breaks anything today, it will be your fault." Madrigal steps out from behind her daughter and studies herself. She touches the ends of her soft, tan-gold waves and dabs perfume onto her long white throat.

"I have done all I can," she says. "He will have to love you as you are."

Arsinoe comes up the stairs and leans against their door. "You look great, Jules," she says.

"You ought to let him come to you," says Madrigal.

"Why? He's my friend. This is not a game." Jules twists away from the dresser and heads downstairs. She is out the door and partway down their long dirt path before she notices that Arsinoe has stayed near the house.

"Aren't you coming?"

The queen shoves her hands into her pockets. "I don't think so. This should just be you."

"He will want to see you."

"Yes. But later."

"Well, walk with me for a little way at least!"

Arsinoe laughs. "All right."

They walk together down the narrow, winding hill road that leads from the property and into town, past the docks, and into the square and the winter market. As they crest the last hill before the cove, Arsinoe stops.

"Do you ever wonder," Arsinoe asks, "what we would be doing if it had gone different?"

"Different how?" asks Jules. "If we had never tried to run

away? If we had made it? Or if they had banished us, too?"

But they only banished Joseph. Jules's sentence was to be the solitary Midwife and nurse to the queens. To live alone in the Black Cottage as a servant to the crown, her only company the queen and her king-consort during the pregnancy, and the triplets until they grew to the age of claiming. She would be in the Black Cottage now, had her aunt Caragh not volunteered to take her place.

"They should have killed me," Arsinoe whispers. "I should have offered, in exchange for letting Joseph stay. In exchange for keeping Caragh out of that cottage."

"They wanted to kill us all," says Jules. "Natalia Arron would have had us poisoned and jerking, frothing on the council floor. Right there in the Volroy."

She would have paraded their bodies through the city square in Indrid Down, if she had thought she could get away with it. They were only eleven years old at the time.

"That may still be our fate, if we step out of line," Arsinoe says. "And it will be bad. They'll craft something so we die over days. With blood running from our eyes and mouths." She spits onto the gravel. "Poisoners."

Jules sighs and looks down at the town she grew up in. Close-together wooden buildings cling around the cove like a mass of gray barnacles. Wolf Spring seems ugly today. Nowhere near grand enough for Joseph, or anyone, to come home to.

"Do you think he'll have a gift?" Arsinoe asks.

"Probably not much of one. None of the other Sandrins do.

Except Matthew, charming the fish."

"I think Matthew just told your aunt Caragh that to impress her," Arsinoe says. "His true gift is charming girls, and all the Sandrin boys have that. Even Jonah's started to chase them around."

Jules curses under her breath. That is just what Madrigal said.

"Is that what you're afraid of?" asks Arsinoe.

"I'm not afraid," Jules retorts. But she is afraid. She is very afraid that Joseph has changed and that her Joseph is gone. Disappeared in the five years they have been apart.

Camden trots ahead, paces the edge of the road, and yawns.

"I just don't know what to do with him. We can't exactly go catch frogs and snails in Welden Stream anymore."

"Not in this weather," Arsinoe agrees.

"What do you think mainland girls are like?" Jules asks suddenly.

"Mainland girls? Oh, they're terrible. Horrible."

"Of course. That's why my beautiful mother fit in so well with them."

Arsinoe snorts. "If they are anything like Madrigal," she says, "then you have nothing to worry about."

"Maybe she was right, though. Maybe I should not have come."

Arsinoe shoves her forward, hard.

"Get down there, idiot," she says. "Or you'll be late."

So Jules goes, down toward the dock, where his family

stands in their best black coats. Joseph's boat is not on the horizon yet, but his mother, Annie, is already up on a crate straining to see. Jules could wait with them. She has been welcome with the Sandrins ever since she and Joseph were children, even before her aunt Caragh and Joseph's brother Matthew were to be married. But instead she detours up through the square to watch from afar.

In the square, the tents are still up. They have been partially cleaned out but not entirely. Since the festivities ended, Wolf Spring has been nursing a collective hangover. Nothing much has gotten done. Through the open tent flaps, Jules spies platters still on the head table, covered by the shifting black wings of birds. The crows have found what is left of her cod. After they have had their fill, someone will toss the bones back into the water.

Back at the docks, more people have gathered, and not only on the pier. All around the cove, curtains and shutters have been moved aside, and here and there, folk have ventured out to pretend to sweep their porches.

There is a nudge at her waist, and she looks down into Camden's hungry yellow-green eyes. Her own stomach groans as well. On Jules's bureau in their bedroom sits an untouched tray of tea and buttered bread. She could not think of eating then. But now she has never felt so empty.

She buys a fish for Camden in the winter market, a nice, clear-eyed sea bass with a curved tail, as if it froze while still swimming. For herself she buys a few oysters from Madge's morning catch, and shucks them with her fat-bladed knife.

"Here," Madge says, and hands her a dipper of vinegar. She jerks her head toward the cove. "Shouldn't you be out there, clamoring with the rest?"

"I don't care for crowds," Jules says.

"I don't blame you." She presses another shellfish into Jules's hand. "For the cougar," she adds, and winks.

"Thanks, Madge."

Down at the docks, the crowd stirs, and the movement carries all the way up the hill and into the market. Madge's neck stretches.

"Aye, there it is," she says.

Joseph's ship has entered the harbor. It sneaked up on them; already it is close enough that Jules can make out the crewmen on the deck.

"Black sails, all," says Madge. "Someone from the mainland is trying to kiss our arses."

Jules stands as tall as she can. There is the ship. Carrying with it the moment she has been dreaming of, and dreading, for the last five years.

"You had better get down there, Jules Milone. We all know it's your face he will want to be seeing."

Jules flashes Madge a smile, and she and Camden dart out of the winter market. Her feet pound through the square, past the slack, flapping tents.

There are so many people gathered around, come to the harbor after their curiosities got the better of them. She will not be able to get through. Not even with Camden cutting a path, not unless she resorts to swatting and snarling, which Grandma Cait would never approve of and would surely hear about.

Jules paces uneasily on the slope where she watches. They unload trunks at first. Belongings and perhaps goods for trade. Gifts. Jules peers at the mainland boat. It looks out of place in Sealhead Cove, painted bright white and with plenty of gold and silver around the windows and rigging. Beneath the bleak Wolf Spring day, it practically glows.

And then Joseph steps onto the gangway.

She would know it was him even without his mother's wail. She would have known it even though he is taller, and older, and all the boyhood softness in his face has melted away.

The Sandrins throw their arms around him. Matthew picks him up in a great hug, and his father claps both of their backs. Joseph ruffles Jonah's hair. Annie has not let go of the edge of Joseph's jacket.

Jules takes half a step back. Five years is a long time. A long enough time to forget about someone. What will she do if he sees her on the hill and smiles politely? If he nods to her as he walks past with his family?

She is already backing up when he calls out her name. And then he shouts it, loud, over everyone. "Jules!"

"Joseph!"

They run toward each other, him fighting through the crowd, and her headlong down the slope. His black jacket flies open over a white shirt, and they collide.

It is no fairy-tale meeting, nothing like she imagined or day-dreamed about in all the time he was away. Her chin runs into his chest. She does not know where to put her arms. But he is there, real and solid, both changed and not changed at all.

When they pull apart, he holds her by the shoulders, and she him by the elbows. She has started to cry a bit, but not from sadness.

"You're so . . . ," she says.

"So are you," he says, and wipes her cheek with his thumb. "My God, Jules. I was afraid I wouldn't recognize you. But you've hardly changed!"

"Haven't I?" she asks, mortified suddenly that she is so small. He will think her still a child.

"I didn't mean that," he amends. "Of course you've grown. But how could I ever worry that I wouldn't recognize these eyes."

He touches her temple, beside her blue eye, and then the other, beside her green. "For the longest time I was certain I would see you, if I just looked hard enough."

But that was impossible. The council had allowed for no correspondence between them. Jules and his family had known only that he was on the mainland, fostered, and alive for the time being. His banishment was absolute.

Camden slips around Jules's leg and purrs. The movement almost seems shy, but Joseph jumps back.

"What's the matter?" asks Jules.

"Wh-what's the—?" he sputters, and then laughs. "Of

course. I suppose I have been away a long time. I had forgotten how strange Fennbirn can be."

"What do you mean 'strange'?" she asks.

"You would understand if you left." He holds his hand out to Cam for her to sniff, and she licks his fingers. "He's a familiar."

"*She* is a familiar," Jules corrects him. "This is Camden."

"But," he says, "it can't be . . . ?"

"Yes," Jules says, and nods. "She is mine."

He looks from the girl to the cougar and back again. "But she should be Arsinoe's," he says. "To have a familiar like this, it must make you the strongest naturalist in the last fifty years."

"Sixty, or so they say." Jules shrugs. "A naturalist queen rises, and the gift rises with it. Or have you forgotten that as well?"

Joseph grins and scratches Camden behind the ears. "What does Arsinoe have, then? And where is she? There are people here I want her to meet. One more than the others."

"Who?"

"My foster brother, William Chatworth Jr. And his father. They have a delegation this year."

He regards her with mischief. The temple will not like that they are here. Delegations are not allowed to arrive until the Beltane Festival, and suitors are not allowed to converse with the queens until after the Quickening is over. She wonders who these men are to have been able to bend the rules.

Joseph nods at someone over her left shoulder, and Jules turns to see Autumn, a priestess from Wolf Spring Temple, approaching with a somber expression.

"Juillenne Milone," she says gently. "Forgive the intrusion. The temple wishes to welcome Joseph Sandrin back to his home. We would take him and his family to the altar to receive a blessing."

"Of course," Jules says.

"Can it not wait?" Joseph asks, and grumbles when the priestess does not reply.

On the eastern hill of Wolf Spring, Wolf Spring Temple sits tucked, a white circle of brick surrounded by small priestess cottages. Autumn is one of only twelve priestesses who reside there. It has seemed to Jules a lonely place, whenever she has gone to pray. Except on festival days, the temple is mostly empty save for Autumn, tending the grounds, and the others in the gardens.

"And as always," Autumn says, "we extend an invitation to Queen Arsinoe, to receive a blessing."

Jules nods. Arsinoe has never set foot inside the temple. She says she will not pray to a Goddess with a turned back.

"Listen," Joseph says. "I will come to you when I'm ready. If I come at all."

Autumn's serene face falls to a scowl. She turns on her heel and leaves.

"That was not much of a welcome," Jules says. "I'm sorry."

"This is all the welcome I need." Joseph puts his arm across her shoulders. "You. Here. And my family. Come and say hello to them. I want you all with me, for as long as I can have you."

* * *

Madrigal tells Arsinoe that they are going into the hills after pheasant. She will charm them, and Arsinoe will shoot them.

"You have never gone hunting in your life," Arsinoe says, shouldering her small crossbow and bag of bolts. "What are we really going to do?"

"I don't know what you mean," Madrigal replies. She tosses her pretty, light brown hair, but the way she glances through the kitchen window, where Cait stands preparing a stew, tells Arsinoe that she is right.

Together they walk far north of the house, up the trail past the clearing and Dogwood Pond, and into the cover of the forest. Arsinoe sinks past her ankles into snow. Madrigal hums a little tune, graceful despite the drifts. Her familiar, Aria, flies far ahead above the trees. She never sits on Madrigal's shoulder, like Eva sits on Cait's. It is almost like they are not familiar-bonded at all. Or perhaps it is only that Aria never matches the outfits that Madrigal likes to wear.

"Madrigal, where are we going?"

"Not far."

It has been far already. They have walked up high, where large gray stones break through the ground. Some are only rocks, and some are the mostly buried remains of monoliths from back when the island was truly old and wore a different name.

In winter, though, they are hidden under snow, and slippery. Arsinoe has almost fallen twice.

Madrigal changes her course and walks along a rise to the

leeward side, where the snow is less deep. It is an odd little spot where the thick trunk and bare branches of a tree bend over to form a sort of canopy. At the base of the hill, Madrigal has hidden a cache of dry wood, and two small three-legged stools. She hands one of the stools to Arsinoe and begins arranging the wood for a fire, weaving in slender pieces of kindling. Then she pours oil from a silver flask onto the lot of it, and lights it with a long match.

It whooshes up hot. The logs catch quickly.

"Not so bad for a naturalist," Madrigal says. "Though it would be easier if I were an elemental. Sometimes, I think I'd rather be almost anything than a naturalist."

"Even a poisoner?" Arsinoe asks.

"If I were a poisoner, I would be living in a grand house in Indrid Down rather than my mother's drafty cottage by the sea. But no. I was thinking perhaps of the war gift. To be a warrior would be much more exciting than this. Or to have the sight and know what will come to be."

Arsinoe plunks her stool down near the fire. She does not mention that the Milone house is much more than a drafty cottage by the sea. That is all Madrigal will ever think of it as.

"Why did you come back?" Arsinoe asks. "If you are so dissatisfied? You were six years on the mainland, and you could have stayed there."

Madrigal prods the flames with a long stick. "Because of Jules, of course," she says. "I couldn't stay away and let her be raised by my dull sister." She pauses. She knows she has spoken out of turn. No one in the family will hear one word spoken against Caragh. Not since she took Jules's place in the Black Cottage. How that must annoy Madrigal, who hardly has a kind word to say.

"And you," Madrigal says, and shrugs. "A new queen. I wasn't even born when the last one was crowned, so I could not miss this. You are the only excitement this island has seen in all that time."

"Yes, excitement," says Arsinoe. "I imagine my death will be very exciting."

"Do not be so dour," Madrigal says. "I am on your side, unlike half these people. Why do you think I've brought you all the way up here?"

Arsinoe sets her crossbow and bolts beside her foot and stuffs her chilly hands into her pockets. She should have refused to come. But with Jules in Wolf Spring with Joseph, it was either this or chores.

"What do you think my Juillenne is doing down in town?" Madrigal muses, fiddling with something in her coat. She pulls out a small bag and sets it in her lap.

"Welcoming home an old friend," Arsinoe says. "Her best friend."

"*You* are her best friend," Madrigal says slyly. "Joseph Sandrin has always been . . . something else."

She pulls four things out of her bag: a curving braid of hair, a strip of gray cloth, a length of black satin ribbon, and a sharp silver knife.

"Low magic," Arsinoe observes.

"Don't call it that. That is the temple talking. This is the lifeblood of the island. The only thing that remains of the Goddess in the outside world."

Arsinoe watches Madrigal set out the items in a careful row. She cannot deny being fascinated. There is a peculiar bend to the air here, and a peculiar feeling in the ground, like a heartbeat. It is strange that she has never stumbled across this place, and this bent-over tree, before. But she has not. If she had, she would have known immediately.

"Be that as it may," Arsinoe says, "low magic is not a queen's gift. We aren't like everyone else. Our line is . . ." She stops. "Sacred," she almost said. Of the Goddess. It is true, but the words turn the inside of her mouth bitter. "I shouldn't do it," she says. "I should go down to the water and yell at a crab until it prostrates itself before me."

"How long have you tried that?" Madrigal asks. "How many times have you called for a familiar who hasn't come?"

"It will come."

"It will. If we raise your voice."

Madrigal smiles. Arsinoe never thinks of Madrigal as beautiful, though many, many people do. "Beautiful" is too gentle a word for what she is.

"Jules will help me to raise it," Arsinoe says.

"Don't be stubborn. Jules may not be able to. For her, things come too easy. The gift is there, at her fingertips. She reminds me of my sister that way."

"She does?"

"Yes. Caragh opened her eyes one day and had the gift. All of it. Just like Jules. It was not as brutally strong as Jules's is, but it was strong enough to turn my parents' heads. And she did it without work." Madrigal stokes the fire and sends up sparks. "I have wondered sometimes if Caragh isn't somehow really Jules's mother. Even though I remember giving birth to her. They were so close after I returned to the island. Jules even looks more like her."

"So, uglier, you mean." Arsinoe frowns.

"I didn't say that."

"What else can you mean? You and Caragh look similar. And Jules looks nothing like either of you. The only feature she and Caragh share is that they are both less pretty than you. Jules bonded with Caragh, but what can you expect? You were gone. Caragh raised her."

"'Raised her,'" Madrigal repeats. "She was scarcely nine years old when I returned."

She takes up the cloth in her lap and tears away errant threads until the edges are clean.

"Maybe I do feel guilt for leaving," she says, staring down at her work. "Maybe that's why I am doing this now."

Arsinoe studies the strip of gray cloth. She studies the braid of dark brown hair and wonders who it belonged to. Beneath the bent-over tree the breeze has stilled, and even the fire burns quietly. Whatever it is Madrigal is doing, they should not be doing it. Low magic is for the simple or the desperate. Even when it works, there is always a price.

"Have you noticed that no one is panicking that your gift hasn't come?" Madrigal asks. "Not Cait. Not Ellis. Not even really Jules. No one thinks you are going to survive, Arsinoe. Because naturalist queens do not survive. Not unless they're beasts, like Bernadine and her wolf." She ties a knot in the strip of cloth and uses it to anchor another knot around the braid of hair.

"Great Queen Bernadine," Arsinoe mutters. "Do you know how tired I am of hearing about her? She is the only naturalist queen anyone remembers."

"She is the only one worth remembering," Madrigal says. "And for all their savagery, the people of Wolf Spring have gotten used to that. They have accepted it. But I haven't."

"Why haven't you?" Arsinoe asks.

"I am not sure," Madrigal says, and shrugs. "Maybe because I have watched you, growing up in Jules's gifted shadow, the way I did in Caragh's. Or maybe because I want my daughter to love me, and if I save you, she might learn to."

She holds up the bit of braid and cloth. Arsinoe shakes her head. "It will go wrong. Something always does when it comes to me. Someone will get hurt."

"It will hurt when your sisters kill you," Madrigal reminds her, and presses the charm into Arsinoe's hand.

It seems like a harmless bit of junk. But it does not feel that way. It feels far heavier than any braid and strip of cloth should feel. And more alive than any rosebud in her hand.

"The Goddess is here, in this place," Madrigal says. "The priestesses pray to her like she is a being, some faraway creature, but you and I know better. We feel her inside the island. Everywhere. You felt her in the mist that night, in the boat, when she would not let you go. She is the island, and the island is her."

Arsinoe swallows. The words feel true. Perhaps once, the Goddess was everywhere, stretched out over the sky all the way to the mainland. But now she is drawn in, curled up like a beast in a hole. Just as powerful. Just as dangerous.

"Is this Jules's hair?" Arsinoe asks.

"Yes. I took it when I was brushing it this morning to put into a bun. It took forever to straighten it and braid it together."

"What about the cloth?" It looks old, wrinkled, and dirty.

"A strip of Joseph's shirt, from when he was a boy. Or so my mother says. He ruined it on a nail out by the barns, and Jules kept it after she gave him a new one. I don't know how she remembers these things." She snorts. "Of course, there are other things of Joseph's that we could use, but we don't want him charging Jules like a rutting stag."

"This is a love spell," Arsinoe says. "You are teaching me to use low magic, to do a love spell for Jules?"

"Is there any motivation in the world more pure?" Madrigal hands her the length of black ribbon. "Wrap them together and then tie them around with this."

"How do you know how to do this?" Arsinoe asks. Though in truth it feels almost as if she herself knows how to do it. Her fingers twist the braid and cloth together effortlessly, and she would have known to reach for the ribbon even if Madrigal had not instructed her to.

"Off the island there is nothing else," Madrigal whispers. "Close your eyes. Look into the flames."

"Jules would want to do this herself," Arsinoe says. "No, she would not do it at all. She does not need this."

Across the fire, Madrigal purses her lips ruefully. Every girl in Wolf Spring knows about the Sandrin boys. Their mischievous smiles, and eyes like storm clouds reflected upon the sea. All that wind in their dark hair. Joseph will be that way now. And even though Arsinoe loves Jules, and thinks of her as beautiful, she knows that Jules is not the kind of beautiful that holds a boy like that.

Arsinoe looks down at the charm, winding itself between her fingers. Moments ago, it was a scrap of nothing to be tossed into the bin or for birds to use to line their nests. But there is more to it in the knots that Madrigal tied, and the twists where Jules's hair and Joseph's shirt press tightly together.

She finishes the last wrap of the ribbon and secures the end. Madrigal takes up the silver knife and slices into the underside of Arsinoe's forearm, so fast that it takes the wound a few seconds to bleed.

"Ow," says Arsinoe.

"It didn't hurt."

"It did, and you could have warned me before you did it."

Madrigal shushes her and presses the charm into the running

blood. She squeezes Arsinoe's arm, squeezing her into the charm like milk into a bucket.

"A queen's blood," Madrigal says. "The blood of the island. Thanks to you, Jules and Joseph will never be parted again."

Arsinoe closes her eyes. Jules and Joseph. They were inseparable since birth, until she came along. Until they tried to save her, and were parted for their trouble. The Black Council imposed no punishment on Arsinoe for her part in the escape. Except for guilt. And in the years since, guilt over Jules losing Joseph has punished her plenty.

Madrigal releases her arm, and Arsinoe bends at the elbow. The bleeding has lessened, and the cut begins to throb. Madrigal did not think far ahead enough to bring along anything to cleanse the wound, or bandages. So perhaps the price of the magic will be the loss of a queen's arm.

Madrigal slides the charm into a small black bag. When she hands the pouch to Arsinoe, her fingers are sticky and red, and the charm inside feels like a small heart beating.

"After it dries," Madrigal says, "keep it somewhere safe. Under your pillow. Or braid it into your own hair, if you can keep from constantly cutting it."

Arsinoe holds the charm in her fist. Now that the magic is made, it feels wrong. A crooked thing, twisted through with good intentions. She does not know why she did it. She has no excuse, except that it was easy, and nothing has ever come easily to her before.

"I can't do this to Jules," she says. "I can't take away her will like this. No matter the reason, she wouldn't want it."

Before she can reconsider, Arsinoe throws the charm into the fire. The bag burns away like nothing, and Jules's hair and Joseph's dried scrap of shirt blacken and curl like the legs of a dying insect. The smoke that comes from it is foul. Madrigal cries out and jumps to her feet.

"Put the fire out and let's go home," Arsinoe says. She tries to sound like a queen, but she is shaky and weak, as if she has lost a pint of blood rather than a few spoonfuls.

"What have you done?" Madrigal asks sadly. "What have you just done to our poor Jules?"

ROLANTH

$\mathcal{I}$n the cloistered courtyard on the eastern side of the temple grounds, Mirabella can be alone. It is one of the few places the priestesses will let her go unescorted. One of the few places they feel is safe. Even when she prays at the altar, one or two of them are there, standing in the shadows. Only in the courtyard, and in her bedroom at Westwood House, may she be by herself. Free to think, or recline, and even to weep.

She has wept often since Rho's test in the cliffs. Most of the tears she has hidden. But not all. Word of her upset traveled quickly, and the priestesses have begun to give her suspicious glances. They cannot decide whether her weeping is a sign of weakness or of great mercy. Either way, they would prefer that she did not do it.

Mirabella tucks her legs underneath her on the cold stone bench. As she lifts her foot, a small, black-and-white tufted woodpecker lands in her footprint and hops back and forth.

"Oh," she says. It is a spritely thing, with smart black eyes. She pats the pockets of her skirt and gently shakes the folds of her cloak. "I am sorry. I have no seed for you."

She ought to have brought some. The doves cooing would have been a welcome distraction.

"It is not seed he's after."

Mirabella turns. A young initiate stands at the entrance of the courtyard, in the opening of the snow-crusted hedge. She holds her white hood tight against the chill of the wind.

Mirabella clears her throat. "What is it he is after, then?"

The girl smiles and walks into the courtyard. "He wishes to cheer you," she says.

She releases her hood, and the woodpecker flits quickly from the ground to dive into her collar.

The queen's eyes widen. "You are a naturalist," she says.

The girl nods.

"My name is Elizabeth. I grew up in Bernadine's Landing. I hope you don't mind the intrusion. It is only that you looked so sad. And Pepper always manages to make me smile."

The little bird pokes his beak out from behind her hood and disappears again just as quickly. Mirabella watches with interest. She has never seen a familiar; in the temple, a priestess gives up her gift, and familiars are forbidden.

"How is it that you have managed to keep him?" Mirabella asks.

Elizabeth rubs her tan cheek against the bird's head. "Please don't tell anyone. They would kill him on sight. I have tried to keep him away, but he will not go. I suppose I'm lucky that he is easy to hide. It is cruel to make us send them away, before we take our bracelets. What if I change my mind and leave the temple? Where will Pepper be, then? In the woods nearby? Or high in the mountains, where he may never hear my call?"

"It is cruel to make you give him up at all," says Mirabella.

Elizabeth shrugs. "My mother says that once, priestesses did not have to. But now the island is so fractured. Naturalist against poisoner against elemental. Even those few with the war gift, or those fewer with the sight gift, are hostile to one another." She looks at Pepper and sighs. "Giving them up unites us. And the sacrifice binds us to our faith. But you are right. It's still cruel."

"Could I?" Mirabella asks, and holds out her hand. Elizabeth smiles, and the little bird flies quickly to perch on the tips of Mirabella's curled fingers.

"He likes you," Elizabeth says.

Mirabella chuckles. "That is kind. But you are a naturalist. This bird will do whatever you say."

"That's not exactly how the familiar-bond works. And in any case, you would be able to tell. He would be hesitant and less bright-eyed. He might leave droppings in your palm."

"Lucky that he likes me, then," Mirabella says.

Pepper blinks once and then shoots quickly back into the safety of Elizabeth's hood.

"Seeing you here alone, so sad, I had to see if we could

help." Elizabeth settles down onto the bench beside her. "I know why you cry."

"I imagine every priestess in the temple knows."

Elizabeth nods. "But it means something special to me," she says, "as I was almost the girl sacrificed."

"You?"

"The way they make it sound," she says. "The duty and the commune with the Goddess. I almost said yes. I thought I should. Her name was Lora. The volunteer. She died believing she had done a great service. And there are worse ways to die than that."

Worse ways, like being burned alive by your sister priestesses. Mirabella tried that way of thinking. Telling herself that she had saved the girl from the flames. It did not work. It was not right, no matter how it happened.

"We are all dual-natured, Queen Mirabella. Every gift is light and dark. We naturalists can make things grow, but we also coax lobsters into pots, and our familiars tear rabbits to shreds."

"Yes," says Mirabella. "I know this."

Elementals burn down forests as easily as they water them with rain. The war gift is for protection as well as slaughter. Even those with the sight are often cursed with madness and paranoia. It is for that reason that any queens born with the sight are drowned.

"Even the poisoners," Elizabeth says, "are also healers."

"Now, *that* I have not heard," says Mirabella. Poisoners are notoriously vicious. Every one of their executions is a mess, when every executed woman or man is put to death by flamboyant poisons that bring blood to the eyes and spasms so hard they break their backs.

"It's true," Elizabeth insists. "They know the ways of healing. They have only forgotten it in the face of their hunger for council seats."

Mirabella smiles slightly. Then she shakes her head. "But it is not the same, Elizabeth. It is not the same for queens."

"Oh, I know that," the priestess replies. "And I have only been here at Rolanth for a short time. But already I can see that you are a good person, Mirabella. I don't know if you will make a good queen, but that seems to me a promising start."

A dark, black braid slides out of Elizabeth's hood, almost as dark as the queens' own. It reminds Mirabella of Bree, the way she wears it. Pepper the woodpecker ruffles his feathers. He seems to be a bird of few words.

"You are the only priestess here who has ever really spoken to me," Mirabella says. "I mean, besides Luca."

"Am I?" Elizabeth asks. "Oh dear. Yet another sign that I am not a very good priestess. Rho is always telling me so. Perhaps she is right."

Bloodthirsty Rho. The terror of the temple. Mirabella cannot remember ever seeing her be kind or hearing her utter a word softly spoken. But she will be good protection once Beltane is over and the Ascension begins. Luca is right about that.

Elizabeth cocks her head. "You are feeling a little better now?"

"I am," says Mirabella.

"Good. That rite, the rite of sacrifice—you can be sure it was Rho's idea. She wants to bring back the old ways and supplant the council once more for the temple. She thinks she can do this by force, as if she alone is the Goddess's hand. But she is not." Elizabeth smiles brightly. "You are."

"You said she did it," the High Priestess says. "And so it is done."

"I did not say that she did it well," says Rho.

Rho picks up a trinket from the corner of Luca's mahogany desk—a shiny, polished orb of opal—and makes a face. She does not like the High Priestess's rooms, up in the top floor of the temple, overlooking the cliffs of Shannon's Blackway. They are too soft, lined with pillows and blankets against the drafts. They are too cluttered, full of things, decorative things that have no use, like mosaic vases and carved, gilded eggs. Like the little opal.

Luca watches Rho wind back her arm to cast it out the window.

"Do not do that," the High Priestess cautions. "That was a gift."

"It is only a rock."

"It was still a gift. And close that window. The breeze is cold today. I cannot wait for spring. The fires of Beltane leading to hot summer nights. Will you take some soup? The kitchen tells me it is rabbit and cabbage and cream."

"Luca," says Rho. "You are not listening. The rite was a farce. Our queen was backed into a corner, and even then she would do nothing until we first let the girl feel the fire."

Luca sighs.

"The sacrifice lies buried beneath a pile of fallen stones. She performed the rite. You cannot ask her to enjoy it."

Luca herself did not enjoy it. She had listened when they cautioned her about being too soft. She believed them when they said it would be Mirabella who would be hurt by it in the end. And now an innocent is dead. Crushed under rocks that form a convenient monument to be prayed over.

"We will not ask her to do anything like this again," Luca says. "You do not know her like I do. If we press her too hard, she will buck. And if Mirabella learns to buck . . . if she remembers how . . ."

Luca looks out her west-facing window, through the trees to the roof of Westwood House. Even at that distance, the copper-cored lightning rods are still visible, standing up like stiff hairs. The Westwoods knew better, too, than to take them down.

"You were not here," Luca adds, "when they brought Mirabella from the Black Cottage. Neither was I. I was still in Indrid Down, fighting the Arron council for any scrap of power. I would not have believed Sara Westwood when she came and told me that our six-year-old queen was going to tear her house from beneath her feet had it not been for the look on her face.

"The island has not seen a gift like hers in hundreds of

years. Not since Shannon and the Queens of Old. We are its keepers but not its masters."

"That may be," says Rho. "But if she does not rise to her duty, the Black Council will keep its stranglehold for another generation."

Luca rubs her face hard. Perhaps she is too old for this. Too exhausted from a life spent trying to wrest power from the Arrons. But Rho is right. If another poisoner queen sits the throne, the Arrons of the Black Council will rule until the next set of triplets comes of age. By the time that happens, Luca will be long dead.

"Mirabella will rise," the High Priestess says. "And the temple will rein back the council. Full up with Westwoods, it will be much easier to control."

Some days later, Mirabella wakes from another dream with her mouth tasting of blood. In the dream, she, Arsinoe, and Katharine had been children. She remembers black hair fanned out in water, and dirt on Arsinoe's nose. She remembers her own hands turned to claws and tearing Arsinoe and Katharine apart.

She rises up on her forearms from being facedown in her pillows. It is midday, and her room is empty. Perhaps there are not even any priestesses lurking outside her door since Sara, Bree, and the other Westwoods are all at home.

The dreams are coming more frequently. They wake her two, sometimes three, times a night. Luca said to expect them.

That they would show her the way. She did not warn her of the dread they would make her feel.

Mirabella closes her eyes. But instead of darkness, she sees the face of the sacrificed priestess in the rocks. She sees Arsinoe's dirty nose. She hears Katharine's laugh.

Queens are not supposed to love their sisters. She has always known that, even when they were together at the Black Cottage, where she had loved them anyway.

"They are not those children, anymore," she whispers into her hands.

They are queens. They must die.

Bree knocks on her door and pokes her head in, her long brown braid swinging over her shoulder.

"Is it time?" Mirabella asks. Today they are to go into the city, where Rolanth's best artisans wait to present their finest jewels and gowns for the Beltane ceremonies.

"Nearly," Bree says. "But do not sound so glum. Look who has come from the temple."

Bree swings the door wide, and Elizabeth leans in from the opposite side. Mirabella smiles.

"Oh no," she says. "People will start saying that I will only be friends with girls who wear braids."

After Mirabella is readied and dressed, she, Bree, and Elizabeth climb into a coach waiting in front of Westwood House. Sara is already inside.

"Very good," Sara says, and taps the roof, signaling the driver to depart. "It is kind of you to join us, Priestess." She smiles at Elizabeth. "The temple will surely approve of our choices today."

"Oh, I am not here for temple approval." Elizabeth grins happily, watching the city rumble past. "I'm only escaping my chores."

Sara's lips draw into a thin line, and Bree giggles.

"We are happy to have you in any case," says Sara. "Mira, are you well? You seem pale."

"I am fine, Sara."

Sara taps the roof harder, and the driver urges the horses to go faster.

"Perhaps you are needing something to eat. There will be plenty when we arrive at the park."

Moorgate Park sits in the central district that runs alongside the channel. In spring it is pretty, full of trees and pale stones, with a gurgling ivory fountain. This time of year, the trees are bare and the grounds more open. Plenty of room for the jewelers and tailors to present their wares.

"I hope the tailor from Third Street brought that handsome son of his," Bree says.

"I thought you were seeing the Wexton boy," says Sara.

Bree snuggles back into the coach's velvet cushions.

"Not anymore. Since Mira's birthday he has forgotten how to kiss. So much tongue!" She shivers and gags and leans against Mirabella for comfort. Mirabella and Elizabeth laugh. Sara says nothing, but her eyes bulge out and her lips practically disappear.

Mirabella looks out the window. They are nearly there. In the central district, the buildings are broad, and white. What cracks there are have been carefully hidden with paint. Here, one can see how fine the city of Rolanth once was. One can see how fine it will be again, after Mirabella takes the throne.

"Here we are," says Sara as the coach jerks to a stop. She smooths the skirt of her long black dress and prepares to exit the carriage. "Bree," she mutters, "please try not to wander off."

"Yes, Mother," Bree says, and rolls her eyes.

Mirabella steps out after Sara. Through the park's open gate she can see the jewelers and dressmakers, waiting in a row. And the priestesses, of course. Always on guard.

Bree cranes her neck.

"He is here," she says, and grins.

It is easy to see who she means. A handsome boy with light brown hair stands beside the jeweler near the end of the row. He has already seen Bree as well.

"It never takes you very long," Mirabella says quietly.

"Nor should it. I have had years of practice." Bree grasps Mirabella's arm in one hand and Elizabeth's in her other. "We must find out his name."

"Enough of that," Sara says. She unlinks the girls' arms and takes her place behind the queen.

"Mother," Bree groans. "We are only picking out jewels. You do not have to treat it like the Disembarking!"

"Everything public will be formal after she is crowned," says Sara. "You had best get used to it."

As they enter the park, Sara motions to one of the novice priestesses.

"Queen Mirabella has not eaten today. Would you please prepare her something?"

The girl nods and scurries away. Mirabella is not really very hungry. The dreams of her sisters often leave her with no appetite until evening. But it will be easier to nibble than to argue with Sara.

The merchants bow when they approach the tables. The Westwoods will purchase something small from every one—a ring or bracelet, a scarf. Only a select few will be commissioned for gowns, or sets of gems.

"I can tell you without looking that we will only be buying handkerchiefs at the first table," Sara says into Mirabella's ear. "That woman has no sense of elemental movement. Everything she sews is tight and severe. Fit for a poisoner."

Approaching the woman's stall, Mirabella can see that Sara is right. It is all shimmer, and each gown is close fitted. But the tailor is so nervous. So hopeful.

"Those are very fine gloves," Mirabella says before Sara can speak. "Do you also work in leather?" She half turns to Sara. "Bree has need of a new pair for archery. And little Nico must be outgrowing his."

"Yes, Queen Mirabella," the merchant says. "I particularly enjoy working with leather."

Mirabella leaves the table so that Sara may discuss fees, and to keep from hearing her grind her teeth. From the next merchant she selects rings of twisted silver, and the next of polished gold, as Bree tugs her along in her hurry to meet her brown-haired boy.

The novice priestess returns with a tray of cheeses and bread, and a small jar of preserved tomatoes. Elizabeth takes it from her.

"Bree, slow down," she says, and laughs. "Take a moment to eat."

She does, but they are only one table away from her boy now, and the way she nibbles her cheese is highly suggestive.

"We must find something to distract her," Elizabeth whispers to Mirabella. "Perhaps these gowns. They are beautiful!"

"I do not think any gown can distract her," Mirabella says. "No matter how beautiful."

The dressmaker studies Bree. He reaches beneath his table.

"Perhaps this one," he says, and unfurls it before them.

Mirabella and Elizabeth are speechless. Bree drops her cheese.

It is not a gown for a queen. Those must be all in black. This one has a bodice embroidered with blue waves, and a gathered train of storm-blue satin cuts through the black skirt. It is splendid.

"This is the one," says Mirabella. She turns to Bree and touches her braid fondly. "You will outshine me in this. All the suitors will look at you."

"No," Elizabeth says. "That is not true, Mira!"

Perhaps it is not. A queen's raven-black hair and strange

black eyes always command attention. But Elizabeth misunderstood. Mirabella is not jealous. She could never be jealous of Bree.

Sara rejoins them and nods her approval.

"We will have three gowns," she says, "including this one to fit my daughter. Perhaps more, if we do not find anything else equal to your skill. I will call upon your shop to discuss them further."

"Finally," Bree whispers into Mirabella's ear. They have reached the jeweler and the boy.

"We will speak to his father, not to him," Mirabella says. "How will you manage this?"

Bree motions discreetly with her chin. The merchant and his son have a small, stout brazier set back from the table, to keep warm as they wait. Perhaps they are not elementals then, or perhaps their gifts are merely weak.

Bree throws her arm around Elizabeth.

"Sweet Elizabeth," she says. "You are shivering!" She turns to the boy. "May we come round and stand beside your fire?"

"Of course," he says quickly.

Mirabella's lips curl as he leads Bree and Elizabeth to the brazier. With a lazy flick of her wrist, Bree sends flames jumping up from the red embers. She looks over her shoulder at Mirabella and winks.

"Good," says Sara in a low voice. "I thought we would have to buy out the display just to give her more time to flirt."

But perhaps they will anyway. The jeweler's pieces are

exquisite. Laid out across the table, carefully cut gems sparkle in ornate settings. Mirabella's hand drifts to a necklace of three vibrant red-orange stones hanging from a short silver chain. Even on the table in the winter light they seem to burn.

"I would like this one," she says, "for the night of the Quickening."

After the purchases are made, they return to the carriage. Mirabella holds the fire necklace on her lap in a velvet case. She cannot wait to show it to Luca. She is sure the High Priestess will like it. Perhaps after the Quickening is over, Mirabella will make a gift of it to her.

"Now that that is finished," Sara says when the cart starts moving, "there has been some news. From Wolf Spring, if you can imagine."

"News?" Bree asks. "What news?"

"It seems they are housing a suitor there. His delegation has arrived early."

"But that is not allowed," says Mirabella. "Does the temple know?" She looks to Elizabeth, but the initiate only shrugs.

"They do," says Sara. "It is his family's first delegation. They are being given special treatment for a perceived disadvantage. To let them find their way here, on such unfamiliar ground. And to repay them for fostering Joseph Sandrin during his banishment."

"It has been a long time since I have heard that name," Mirabella says. She used to think of it often. Whenever she thought of Arsinoe. He was the boy who tried to run away with

101

her. Who tried to help her escape. When they were caught, she heard that he spat at Natalia Arron's feet.

Now he brings Arsinoe a suitor. It must have been hard to do, when he had so much love for her himself.

"I think you will meet him," Sara says.

"Joseph?"

"No. The suitor. Before Beltane. We will arrange for him to come here. Under the eye of the temple, of course."

"It seems a shame," says Bree. "All those suitors and you can choose only one. But still, all those suitors." She shivers with pleasure. "Sometimes I wish that I was a queen."

Mirabella frowns. "Do not ever say that."

Everyone in the coach quiets at the tone of her voice.

"It was only a joke, Mira," says Bree gently. "Of course I do not wish that. No one really wishes to be a queen."

GREAVESDRAKE MANOR

The great shadowy library of Greavesdrake is one of Katharine's favorite places. The large fireplace casts warmth everywhere except into the very darkest corners, and as she grew, the tall shelves and massive leather chairs provided many places to hide from Genevieve's slaps, or from poison practice. Today though, the fire burns low, and she and Pietyr sit out in the open. They have pulled back three sets of curtains from the eastward-facing windows and huddle in the brightest shaft of light. Warmth from the sun feels better somehow. Gentler, and less hard-won.

Pietyr hands her a bit of bread, smeared with soft, triple-cream sheep's milk cheese. He has assembled a picnic on the carpet of the finest untainted food he could find. A sweet gesture, even if it is mostly intended to fatten her up.

"You ought to try the crab soufflé," he says. "Before it gets cold."

"I will," says Katharine.

She takes a bite of the bread and cheese, but it is difficult. Even the best foods taste like mud when accompanied by nausea. She touches the small bandage on her wrist.

"What was it this time?" Pietyr asks.

"Some kind of snake venom."

It was nothing she had not been poisoned with before. But the cut used to apply it was worse than necessary, thanks to Genevieve's still-held grudge from the night of the *Gave Noir*. Pietyr has looked at the wound already, and he did not like what he saw.

"When you are crowned," he says, "there will be no more reason for that."

He serves her a small plate of scrambled egg with caviar and soured cream. She takes a bite and tries to smile.

"That is not a smile, Kat. That is a grimace."

"Perhaps we should put this off," she suggests, "until dinner."

"And let you miss two more meals?" He shakes his head. "We have to recover your poisoner appetite. Try a pastry. Or some juice, at least."

Katharine laughs. "You are the best personal attendant I have ever had. Even better than Giselle."

"Am I?" He raises an eyebrow. "I have had no practice. My house in the country is well-fortified, and well-run by Marguerite, though I am loath to admit it. I have spent my whole life being waited upon."

"Then perhaps you have learned by example," Katharine

says. "You care very much that I am crowned. But so does every Arron. Did you really come here to escape the country? What did Natalia promise you?"

"She promised me a seat on the council," he says, "after you are on the throne. But it is more than that."

He looks at her pointedly, and she blushes. He likes it when she blushes. He says that Mirabella is likely far too proud to show any pleasure at someone's interest.

"Poisoner queens are good for the island." He feeds her another piece of bread. "We have run it for a hundred years. The Westwoods are arrogant indeed if they think they can do better."

"The Westwoods," Katharine says, "and the temple."

"Yes. The temple. I do not know why they feel so slighted. Why they have to possess the entirety of the people's hearts. But they do."

Pietyr eats some bread smeared with apple jelly. He does not turn up his nose at untainted food like the rest of the Arrons do. He does not make Katharine feel small for being weak.

"It smells like dust in here, Kat," he says. "I do not know why you like it."

Katharine looks around at the tall stacks of leather-bound books. "Queen Camille liked them," she says. "She liked to read about mainland queens. Did you know that is where Arsinoe got her name?"

"I did not."

"There was a queen on the mainland who was murdered by

her sister. She was called Arsinoe too. So when Arsinoe was born weak, that is what she named her. Arsinoe the naturalist."

"Such a wicked way to name a newborn. I am almost sorry for her," says Pietyr.

"The queen knows what we are from birth. She knows our gifts. A dud is a dud, even then."

"She gave you a fine name, in any case, Katharine the poisoner. She must have known then that you would grow up to be sweet and thoughtful." He traces a finger along her cheek. "And very fair."

"Fair enough to capture the eye of every single suitor?" she asks. "Must I really?"

"You must. Imagine the look on Mirabella's face when every one of them ignores her. Perhaps she will be so dismayed that she will throw herself off the Rolanth cliffs."

That would be very convenient indeed. Though it would rob Katharine of the sight of her clawing at her throat, after it had been poisoned shut.

Katharine laughs.

"What?" Pietyr asks.

"I was thinking of Arsinoe," she says. "Of how sad and easy she will be to kill, after Mirabella is dead."

Pietyr chuckles. He draws her close. "Kiss me," he says, and she does. She is getting much better at it, and bolder. Afterward, she bites his lip gently.

He is so very handsome. She could kiss him all day and never tire of it.

"You are a fast learner," he says.

"But were you? How many girls have you practiced on, Pietyr?"

"Many," he replies. "Practically every serving girl who came through our household, and most of them in the village besides. As well as a few of my stepmother's more discerning friends."

"I should not have asked," she pouts.

He runs his hand up the side of her leg, and Katharine laughs. So many girls. So many women. But he is hers and hers alone. For now.

"You do not find me dull, after others who were more practiced?" she asks.

"No," he says, and looks into her eyes. "Never. In fact, the hardest part of all this will be something that I had not really thought of."

"What?"

"Remembering why I am here. To make you the kind of queen who wins hearts. To help you gain island support at the festival."

"What does their support matter? They will not help me kill my sisters."

"A well-loved queen has many eyes and ears. The support will matter very much, in any case, after you are crowned."

Katharine's stomach lurches, and she pushes her food away.

"It is all pressure and expectations. And I will fail. I will fail, like I did on my birthday."

"You will not fail," says Pietyr. "When you step onto your stage at the Quickening, no one will bother looking at your sisters' stages. When the suitors see you at the Disembarking, they will forget that there are other queens to see."

"But Mirabella . . ."

"Forget Mirabella. She will be stiff-backed and haughty. You will smile. Flirt. You will be the queen they want. If I can only get you to stand up straight."

"Stand up straight?"

"You are very meek when you walk, Kat. I want you to move through a room as though it is already yours. Sometimes, it even seems that you scurry."

"Scurry!"

She laughs and shoves him away. He leans back on the carpet and laughs as well.

"You are right, though. Sometimes, I do scurry. Like a rat." She grins. "But that is over. You will teach me and I will make them forget their own names. With one look."

"One look?" Pietyr asks. "That is a bold promise."

"But I will do it. And I will make you forget as well." Katharine lowers her lashes.

"Forget what?"

She looks up at him.

"That I am not for you."

When Natalia asks Katharine to accompany her to the Volroy, it can be for only one reason: to poison a prisoner. That is all she has ever gone to the palace for. She has never sat in session with the Black Council, listening to them discuss the tax on naturalist fruit or glass windows from Rolanth. Nor has she ever met with the last king-consort's representatives from the mainland, when they come to press their interests. But that is all right, Natalia says. She will one day, when she is crowned.

"He was tried in Kenora," Natalia says as they take the carriage toward Indrid Down and the black spires of the Volroy. "For murder. A stabbing, and a brutal one. It did not take the council long to determine his punishment."

The coach stops momentarily on Edgemoor Street to be allowed through the side gate and onto the palace grounds. Katharine tilts her head back in the dark shadow of the fortress, but they are already too close for her to see the top of the spires. When she is crowned, she will live there, but she has never cared for the Volroy. Despite the grandeur of the twin spires, with their flying buttresses, it is too formal and too full of hard surfaces. There are more windows and light than at Greavesdrake, yet the place is still cold. So many hallways, and drafts slide through it like notes from a flute.

Katharine leans away from the coach window as the ceiling closes over their heads.

"Are Genevieve and Lucian here today?" she asks.

"Yes. Perhaps we will meet with them afterward, for lunch. I can make Genevieve sit at a separate table."

Katharine smiles. Genevieve has still not been allowed to move back into Greavesdrake, Natalia preferring to keep the house quiet. With luck, she will not be allowed to return until after Beltane is over.

The coach stops, and they disembark and enter the building. People passing in the halls nod respectfully at the pair, buttoned up in their stark wool coats and topped with warm black hats. Katharine is careful to keep her sleeves tugged down, to hide Genevieve's bandage and the last of the scabbing blisters. They have almost healed now, much faster than she expected. Thanks to Pietyr, she is healthier and stronger. Most of the scabs have flaked off and left fresh pink skin behind. None will scar.

On the stairs that lead to the holding cells below, Katharine pauses. Deep places have always made her uncomfortable, and the holding cells have a distinct and unpleasant odor. They smell of cold and dirty ice. Whatever wind fails to escape the Volroy through its many upstairs windows falls down into the cells to rot.

"Is one murder his only crime?" Katharine asks as they tread carefully down the stone steps. The holding cells are usually reserved for prisoners of special importance. Like those who have committed crimes against the queen.

"Perhaps he could have been dealt with in Kenora after the trial," Natalia admits. "But I thought you could use the extra practice."

At the bottom, the cold-ice smell gives way to the cells' true scent: human filth and sweat and fear. It is made more pungent by the close quarters and by the heat thrown off the many torches.

Natalia sloughs her coat, and one of the guards holds her hand out to receive it before they duck through the low doorway. Another guard unlocks the last large metal door, shoving it aside so hard that the heavy steel bounces against the track.

Of the many cells in the lower level, only one is occupied. The prisoner is backed into the far corner, with his knees drawn up to his chest. He seems dirty, and tired, and not much more than a boy.

Katharine grips the bars. He has been convicted. Of a murder. But scared as he looks now, she cannot imagine him committing one.

"Who did he kill?" she asks Natalia.

"Another boy. Only a few years older than himself."

They have given him a blanket and some straw. The remains of his meager breakfast sit in the corner beside him, a small metal mug and a plate scraped clean by his fingers. The bars that separate them are solid, but she would have been safe had they been made of cloth. Whatever fight he had has drained out in the few days spent in the prison.

"What is your name?" she asks, and in the corner of her eye, sees Natalia frown. His name does not matter. But she would still like to know.

"Walter Mills."

His eyes wobble. He knows what she has come to do.

"Walter Mills," she says gently. "Why did you kill that boy?"

"He killed my sister," he says.

"Why is it not him in this cell, then? Instead of you?"

"Because they don't know. They think she ran away."

"How do you know she did not?" Natalia asks skeptically.

"I just do. She wouldn't have gone."

Natalia leans close to Katharine's ear. "We do not know if what he says is true," she says. "He has been tried. He is guilty. In any case, we can hardly bring the dead boy in for questioning." Natalia sighs. "Have you seen enough?"

Katharine nods. There is nothing to be done. The council has determined his fate. And now she knows everything she needs to know. His crime. His cause. His approximate health, age, and weight.

"Please," the boy whispers. "Mercy."

Natalia puts her arm across Katharine's shoulders and leads her out. It is not necessarily legal for Katharine to participate in executions before she is crowned. But there are no ends to the strings that Natalia can pull. Katharine has been going with her into the chamber of poisons almost since the moment of her claiming from the Black Cottage.

Inside the chamber, high up in the East Tower, Katharine unbuttons her coat and throws it over one of Natalia's beloved wingback chairs. Her gloves she leaves on. They are close-fitting, and insulated, and will provide some protection in the event of a spill.

"Are there details of the crime?" she asks.

"It was a stabbing with a short-bladed knife," Natalia answers. "Sixteen times, according to the healer's report."

Sixteen times. It is an excessive number that speaks of rage. Evidence of rage might lend credence to Walter Mills's claim of vengeance. But she cannot really know. That is what makes it so difficult.

The cabinets of poisons occupy two entire walls of the room. The collection has been amassed over the years, kept stocked and increased by countless Arron expeditions around the island and to the mainland. There are herbs and venoms and dried berries from every continent and every climate, carefully preserved and cataloged. Katharine's fingers flutter past the drawers; she mutters names of poisons as she goes. One day, she may use them to dispatch Mirabella and Arsinoe. Those will be fancy blends, indeed. But for Walter Mills, she will not be too creative.

She pauses on a drawer filled with vials of castor beans. Taken alone, the poison would provide a very slow, very bloody death, hemorrhaging from every organ.

"The boy he killed," she asks, "did he linger? Did he suffer?"

"For one long night and a whole day."

"No mercy, then."

"You do not think so?" Natalia asks. "Even though he is so very young?"

Katharine glances at Natalia. She does not often advocate for mercy. But very well. Not castor, then. Instead, Katharine opens a drawer and points at jars of dried bark of poison nut.

"A good choice."

The poison nut is housed in a glass jar. Everything is carefully contained. Even the drawers and shelves of the cabinets are lined, to keep them from leaching poison, in case of an accidental spill. Such precautions have probably saved many careless maids from perplexing, painful deaths.

Katharine sets the poison on one of the long tables, and gathers a mortar and pestle. Pitchers of water and oil stand ready to emulsify the blend. To the poison nut, she adds powdered willow to reduce his pain, and valerian to quell his fear. The dose is massive, and death cannot be escaped, but it will, indeed, be merciful.

"Natalia," she says. "Will you please call for a pitcher of good, sweet wine?"

She is always present when it is administered. Natalia has been firm about that. As queen, Katharine must be made to know what it is that she does, to see the way they struggle against their chains, or how they fight against the hands forcing the poison into their mouths. She has to see the way the crowd in the square can terrify them. In the beginning, it was difficult to watch. But it has been years now since any have made Katharine cry, and she has learned how to keep her eyes wide open.

Deep beneath the Volroy, Walter Mills sits against the wall of his cell with his hands on his knees.

"You're back so soon," he says. "Are you going to take me out of here? Into the courtyard, so the people can watch?"

"The queen has granted you mercy," Natalia says. "You will die here. In private."

He looks at the pitcher in Katharine's arms and silently begins to weep.

"Guard," Katharine says, and motions to her. "Bring a table and three chairs. Two cups."

"What are you doing, Queen Katharine?" Natalia asks quietly. But she does not stop her.

"Open the cell," Katharine says after the guard brings the table. "Set it for three."

For a moment, Walter eyes the open door, but even panicked as he is, he knows that is futile. Katharine and Natalia sit, and Katharine pours the wine into two cups. Walter stares at it as she does, as if he expects it to sizzle or smoke. It does neither, of course. Rather, it is the sweetest smelling thing in the room.

"He murdered my sister," he says.

"Then you should have brought him before us," says Natalia. "We would have dealt with him, believe me."

Katharine tries to smile at him kindly.

"You think I'm just going to drink that?" he asks.

"I think it is a great honor," Katharine says, "to take your last cups with the head of the Arrons. And I think it is a far finer thing to talk and drink until you fall asleep than to be held down and choke on it."

She holds out the cup. Walter wavers for a few moments and sheds a few more tears. But in the end, he sits.

Natalia takes the first swallow. It takes a long time, but eventually Walter finds his courage. He drinks. He even manages not to weep again, afterward.

"It's . . . ," he says, and pauses. "It's very good. Will you not have any, Queen Katharine?"

"I never partake of my own poisons."

A shadow flickers across his face. He thinks he knows now, that the rumors are true and she has no gift. But it does not matter. The poison is already in his belly.

Walter Mills drinks and drinks, and Natalia matches him cup for cup until he is rosy-cheeked and drunk. They talk of pleasant things. His family. His childhood. He breathes harder, until finally his eyes close and he slumps across the table. It will not be an hour before his heart stops beating.

Natalia looks at Katharine and smiles. Her poison gift may be weak, or may be no gift at all. But she is so very skilled at poisoning.

WOLF SPRING

❧

*J*ules knew that when Joseph returned home, certain things would have changed. She did not expect that he would fit seamlessly back into her life. She did not even know if he would find that he had a place there, after so long away. Five years may not seem like much to some, but in that time, Joseph had turned into a young man. Perhaps with a wider understanding of the world than Jules could ever hope to have from her place at the southwest corner of Fennbirn Island.

But now he is home. His family has released their held breath. And he and Jules have more than exhausted their stores of pleasantries.

"Are you cold?" he asks as they walk down the street from the Lion's Head Pub.

"No," Jules says.

"Yes, you are. Your neck has pulled down so far it's disappeared." He looks around and up the street. There is nowhere they want to go inside. Both are tired of old lovers winking at them slyly, and suspicious squints from folk who hate the mainland.

Light snow begins to fall, and Camden groans and shakes her coat. There is nothing left to do. They ought to admit it and say good night, but neither ever wants to part.

"I know a place," Joseph says, and smiles.

He takes her hand and leads her quickly down the street and toward the cove, where the mainland boat is docked.

"Only a skeleton crew will be there tonight. Mr. Chatworth and Billy are staying at the Wolverton until he departs."

"He?" Jules asks. "Don't you mean 'they'?"

"Billy's not leaving. He's staying on, straight through Beltane. To get to know Arsinoe. I thought we might introduce them soon. Take a picnic up to the pond. Have a fire."

He reaches back for her hand, and they jog down the slope to the docks. The mainland boat rocks quietly in the water. Its portholes and fastenings shine under the moonlight. Even at night, it is too bright for the likes of Wolf Spring.

"You want him to be king-consort," Jules says.

"Of course I do. My foster brother and Arsinoe on the throne, you and me on the council—it would tie everything up rather nicely."

"Me on the council?" Jules scoffs. "Leading her personal guard, more like. You certainly have everything planned out, Joseph."

"Well, I did have five years to think of it."

They cross the gangway, and Jules holds her hand back to coax Camden over.

"Is she afraid of boats?"

"No, but she doesn't like them. We go out sometimes, with Matthew. To help him fish."

"I'm glad you've stayed close," says Joseph. "Even after Caragh. Being around you, I think it lets him keep a piece of her. Something those bastards can't take away."

"Yes," Jules says. Matthew still loves her aunt Caragh, and she hopes that he always will.

Jules looks around. The decks are polished, and everything is neat and clean. Nothing smells like fish. The black sails are tied tight. But of course Chatworth would bring his finest vessel to the island. And the Chatworths must be an important family where they come from. Else how could a son become a suitor?

"Jules, this way."

Joseph leads her down to the cabins, sneaking quietly and avoiding the crew. They step through a small door into pitch darkness, until he lights a lamp. The room they have entered is also small, with a bunk and a writing desk and a few pieces of clothes still hanging in the closet. Cam stands up on her hind legs and sniffs all around the door.

The belly of the boat is warm, and Jules's neck comes out of hiding. But she wishes for some excuse to hide her face.

"I don't know what to say to you," she says. "I want things to be just like they were before."

"I know," says Joseph. "But we can't exactly play 'knights raid the castle' anymore, can we?"

"Certainly not without Arsinoe here to play the dragon."

They laugh together, remembering.

"Ah, Jules," he groans. "Why did I have to come back now? During an Ascension? Every moment with you already feels like it's stolen."

Jules swallows. It is a jolt, to hear him speak that way. They never used to say things like that when they were children. Not even during their most grand pronouncements of loyalty.

"I got something for you," he says. "It seems silly now."

He goes to the writing table and opens a drawer. Inside is a small white box, tied with green ribbon.

"It's a present, for your birthday," he says.

No one ever celebrates Jules's birthday. Jules is a Beltane Begot, a child conceived during the festival of Beltane, like the queens. It is considered very lucky, and they are all supposed to be charmed, but it is a horrible birthday to have. Forgotten and overshadowed.

"Open it."

Jules unties the ribbon. Inside the box is a delicate silver ring, set with dark green stones. Joseph takes it out and slips it onto her finger.

"On the mainland, this would mean you had to marry me," he says quietly.

One ring in exchange for a marriage. He must be joking, but he looks so earnest.

"It is a very nice ring."

"It is," he says. "But it doesn't suit you. I should have known."

"Is it too pretty for me?"

"No," he says quickly. "I meant, you don't have to pretend to like it. You don't have to wear it."

"I want to wear it."

Joseph bends his head and kisses her hands. She shivers, though his lips are warm. He looks at her in a way he has never looked at her, and she knows with both hope and dread that it is true. They have grown up.

"I want things to be just as they would have been if I had never been banished," he says. "I won't let them cost me anything, Jules. Especially not you."

"Luke. This cake is dry."

Arsinoe takes a swallow of tea to wash it down. Normally, Luke's baking is her favorite on the island. He is always trying out new recipes from the various baking books he keeps on the shelves but never manages to sell.

"I know," Luke says, and sighs. "I was short by an egg. Sometimes, I wish that Hank was a hen."

Arsinoe pushes her plate across the counter, and the black-and-green rooster pecks at her crumbs.

Jules will arrive at the shop soon with Joseph. Finally, she will have her own reunion with him. Jules says he does not blame her for his banishment. And that is probably true. But it does not change the fact that he should.

Jules and Joseph are well, though, inseparable once more, and that is enough for Arsinoe. Jules has been so happy that it is almost difficult to be around her. It seems that burning Madrigal's charm has had no ill effects at all.

Arsinoe has not told Jules, or anyone, about the trip to the bent-over tree. Nor has she told anyone about the curious and growing itch she has to go there again. It would only cause an argument. Low magic is frowned upon by those with gifts. As a queen she ought to shun it. She knows that. But she does not want to hear so out loud, from Jules.

Footsteps on the plank board outside precede the ringing of Luke's brass bell. Arsinoe takes a deep, unsteady breath. She is nearly as nervous to see Joseph as Jules was, and nearly as excited. He may have been Jules's friend first, but he became hers too. One of the few she has ever had.

She turns around with cake crumbs on her coat, scowling nervously. . . .

Jules and Joseph are not alone. They have brought a boy with them. Arsinoe grits her teeth. She hardly knows what to say to Joseph. Now she must trade stilted pleasantries with a stranger.

Jules, Joseph, and the boy come in laughing, finishing some private, hilarious conversation. When Joseph sees Arsinoe, his grin spreads across his face. She crosses her arms.

"You look just how I thought you'd look," she says.

"So do you," says Joseph. "You never did look like a queen."

Jules grins silently, but Arsinoe laughs aloud and draws him in for a hug. She is not quite as tall as he is, but almost. Certainly closer to his height than Jules is.

"Better let me in as well," Luke says, and cuts through to clap Joseph on the back and shake his hand. "Joseph Sandrin. This has been a long time coming."

"Luke Gillespie," Joseph says. "It has been a long time. Hello, Hank."

The rooster on the counter dips his head, and the shop quiets. Arsinoe searches for something to say. Another moment of silence and she will not be able to keep ignoring the stranger they brought with them. But she is not fast enough.

"I want you to meet someone," Joseph says. He turns her stiffly toward the stranger, a boy about his height, with dark blond hair and an expression that seems too pleased with itself for her liking.

"This is William Chatworth Jr. His family has a delegation this year. He's one of the suitors."

"So I've heard," says Arsinoe.

The boy holds his hand out; she takes it and shakes it once.

"You can call me Billy," he says. "Everyone does. Except for my father."

Arsinoe narrows her eyes. She would happily wring Jules's neck if Camden wouldn't have her eyes for it. She thought she would be meeting old friends. Not being ambushed by an unwanted new one.

"So, Junior," she says. "How many arses on the Black Council did you have to grease for them to let you arrive so early?"

She smiles sweetly.

"I've no idea," the boy says, and smiles back. "My father does most of the arse-greasing in the family. Shall we go?"

Jules's and Joseph's devious plan is a picnic beside Dogwood Pond. A fire and some roasted meat on sticks. Arsinoe hopes that Billy Chatworth is disappointed. Shocked by their lack of grandeur. Scandalized by her lack of decorum. But if he is, he does not show it. He seems perfectly happy to walk to the pond, sinking in snowdrifts up to his knees.

"Arsinoe," Jules whispers. "At least try to stop scowling."

"I will not. You shouldn't have done this. You should have warned me."

"If I had warned you, you wouldn't have come. Besides, it had to happen sometime. You're why he's here."

But that is only partially true. The suitors will meet all the queens, but they will only try to court the right one. The one who will be crowned. Not her. If he is excited to meet her, it is only to use her for practice before meeting Mirabella and Katharine.

"It could have happened later. I thought today would just be the three of us. Like it used to be."

Jules sighs as if there is plenty of time for that. But if there is one thing Arsinoe has never had, it is plenty of time.

As they near the pond, the boys jog ahead to start the fire. For the end of December, it is not terribly cold. If the sun would come out from behind the clouds, there might actually be a little melting. Camden bounds through the snow and kicks it up into snowy showers. Arsinoe has to admit, it is a nice day. Even with the interloper.

"Well?" Jules asks when Joseph and Billy are safely out of range. "What do you think of him?"

Arsinoe squints. Billy Chatworth wears the clothes of an islander, but he does not wear them well. He is only an inch or two shorter than Joseph, and his sandy hair is short, almost pressed flat against his head.

"He's not nearly as handsome as Joseph is," Arsinoe teases, and Jules blushes scarlet. "I knew he would grow into that Sandrin jawline. And those eyes." She prods Jules in the side until she laughs and swats her away. "Anyhow, what do *you* think of the mainlander?"

"I don't know," Jules says. "He said he had a cat that looked like me when he was younger. With one blue eye and one green. He said it was born deaf."

"Charming," says Arsinoe.

They reach the pond. Joseph takes out a packet of meat for roasting, and Camden walks up his torso to sniff. The fire is already burning hot, bright orange beside the ice and white-washed trees.

Arsinoe reaches into the nearest tree and tears down branches, one for her and one for Jules. Together, they sharpen them to points with their knives. The mainlander watches, and Arsinoe makes sure to use long, dangerous-looking strokes.

"Would you," Billy starts, and clears his throat. "Would you like me to do that for you?"

"No," says Arsinoe. "In fact, I'm making this for you."

She takes a piece of meat from the packet. It passes over her sharpened tip like butter. Then she shoves it straight into the flames and listens to it sizzle.

"Thank you," he says. "I've never met a girl so skilled with a knife. But then, I've never met a girl with a tiger before, either."

"She's a mountain cat," says Jules, and tosses Cam a chunk of raw meat. "We don't have tigers here."

"But could you?" Billy asks. "Could there ever be?"

"What do you mean?"

"Could one of you be so strong that you could call one from across the sea?"

"Maybe I am," Arsinoe muses. "Maybe that's what's taking it so long."

She smirks at Jules as she sharpens another skewer.

"I can't imagine any gift so strong," Jules replies. "I'm one of the strongest naturalists on the island, and I can't call much farther than the deep waters off the coast."

"You don't know that," Arsinoe says. "And I bet you could, if you tried. I bet you could call anything, Jules."

"I think so too," says Joseph. "She's become something fierce, since I left."

The meat comes off the skewers, and they eat in silence. It is good, marbled and tender. Arsinoe considers allowing the juices to run down her chin, but decides that is going too far.

Still, she does not speak until Jules kicks her in the foot. "How are you finding the island, Junior?"

"I am in love with it," he says. "Absolutely. Joseph has been telling me about Fennbirn since the moment he came to stay with us. It's a great pleasure to see it, and to see you, and Jules, who I have heard about even more frequently."

Arsinoe purses her lips. It is a good answer. And he delivered it so well.

"I suppose I should thank you," Arsinoe says. "For taking care of Joseph. He did tell you that I was the reason he was banished?"

"Arsinoe," Joseph says. "Don't. If I could go back, I wouldn't change it."

"But I would," she says. "I missed you."

"I missed you, too," he says, and reaches to take Jules's hand. "Both of you."

The two of them ought to be alone. As much as Arsinoe missed Joseph, it was not in the same way that Jules missed him.

Arsinoe pops the last of the meat into her mouth and then stands up.

"Where are you going?" Jules asks.

"To show Junior the views," she says. "We won't be gone long." She winks at Joseph. "Well. Not too long." Arsinoe leads the mainlander through the trees and onto the narrow, rock-edged trail that winds around the hills above Sealhead. It is an unsafe path to take in winter, unless you know the land. She almost feels guilty. But if he wants to become a king-consort, he will go through worse.

"This is a trail?" he asks, behind her.

"Yes. You can tell by the lack of trees and bushes on it."

The rocks are sharp, covered with ice more than not. A slide guarantees a cut elbow or split-open knee. A wrong step could kill. Arsinoe walks as fast as her conscience will allow, but Billy does not complain. Nor does he try to steady her. He is a fast learner.

"Is it true that on the mainland you have no gifts?" she asks.

"Gifts? Oh. You mean magic. Yes. That's true."

That is not, in fact, what she meant. And it is not true. Though he may not be aware of it, low magic is alive and well in the rest of the world. Madrigal told her so.

"They say that you did, once," she says. "And that you lost them."

"Who is this 'they,'" he asks. "They've been telling you wild tales."

"That would be a strange thing. Having no gifts. The mainland must be a strange place."

"Having them is far stranger, trust me. And you should stop calling it that. The 'mainland.' There are many lands, you know."

Arsinoe says nothing. On the island, everything that is not the island is the mainland. That is how it has always been. That is how it will always be for her, who will never have the chance to leave and see any different.

"You'll see," Billy says. "Someday."

"No, I won't. The queen might."

"Well, aren't you a queen? You look like one. Black-as-night hair, striking black eyes."

"Striking," Arsinoe mutters under her breath. She smirks. She will not be won over that easily.

They crest the last bit of hill and reach the overlook.

"There," Arsinoe says, and points. "The most complete view of Wolf Spring on the island. The Sandrins' house, and the winter market. And your boat, bobbing in the harbor."

"It's lovely," he says, and turns about. "What's that peak there?"

"That is Mount Horn. I was born at the base of it, in its shadow, in the glen at the Black Cottage. But you can't see that from here."

Billy is out of breath. That pleases her. She is only a little too warm for her scarf. When he takes her hand, it is so unexpected that she does not even try to jerk away.

"Thank you," he says. "For showing me. I'm sure you'll show me much more, before you are crowned and I am crowned beside you. Or are king-consorts crowned? That part was never exactly clear."

"You are very stubborn," she says, and tugs her hand loose. "But you're not a fool, and neither am I."

He smiles a begrudging smile that looks very much like Joseph's. Lopsided and devious. Perhaps he learned it from him.

"All right, all right," he says. "My God, this is difficult."

"It will only get worse. Perhaps you should go home."

"I can't," he says.

"Why not?"

"The crown, of course, and everything that comes with it. The trade rights to Fennbirn Island. The prestige. My father wants it all."

"And you think I can help you get it?"

Billy shrugs. He looks out over the cove thoughtfully.

"Joseph thinks you can. And I hope that's true. It would make him happy. He won't like it if you die and I marry another queen."

Arsinoe frowns. Joseph would not like it. But he would come around. They would all come around. Even Jules.

"This is all so strange," Billy says. "I boarded a boat in the bay and sailed through some mist, and there was Fennbirn, though it was never there before when I sailed in the same direction. And now here I am, taking part in all this madness."

"Looking for sympathy?" Arsinoe asks.

"No," he says. "Never. I know what you've got to do is worse. And I like what you did just now. Snatched your hand away. Made me come clean. There are not many girls who would do that, where I come from."

"There are plenty of them here," Arsinoe says. "So many you'll soon tire of us. Just don't waste your time on me, all right? I am not . . . I am not to be courted."

"All right," he says, and shows her his palm. "But we will be neighbors, for some time. So perhaps you will shake my hand and guide me carefully back down this treacherous path?"

Arsinoe smiles and shakes Billy's hand. She likes him better already, now that they understand each other.

"What do you think they're doing now?" Jules asks as she stirs the fire.

"I think everything is going according to plan," Joseph replies.

He moves closer to her on the damp, snowy log. He is warm, and the fire is warm. Jules fidgets with the green stone on her finger. On the mainland, it would have meant he wanted to marry her, he said. But on the island, it is only a ring. She has not yet found the courage to ask him which way he meant it.

"It is a bit early to say so," says Jules. "She might not even like him. And he still has to meet the other queens."

"He does. And he will. But he won't want to. After all the stories I've told him about Arsinoe, I think he is half in love with her already."

Jules does not know what stories Joseph could tell about Arsinoe to make someone fall in love, as they were only children when they were parted. But if they were lies or embellishments, Billy will discover the truth soon enough.

"It will be strange, after she's crowned," Joseph says. "Having to bow my head when she speaks."

"We will only have to do that in front of people," Jules says.

"I suppose so. But it will be hard to bow my head at all, after being so long away. I'll probably forget to bow to the High Priestess and get myself banished again."

"Joseph," Jules laughs. "They wouldn't banish you for that."

"No," he says. "But it's so different out there, Jules. Out there, men don't tremble when women speak."

"No one ought to tremble. That is why the island needs change in the Black Council."

"I know. And it will have it."

He puts his arm around her and then touches first the ring he gave her and then her hair.

"Jules," he says, and leans in to kiss her.

She jumps when their lips touch. Joseph moves back, confused.

"I'm sorry," she says. "I don't know why I did that."

"It's all right."

It feels anything but all right. But Joseph does not move away. He stays and holds her tighter.

"Jules, has there been anyone? Since I left?"

She shakes her head. She has never been ashamed of that before, but she is ashamed of it now.

"No one at all?"

"No."

No one has ever looked at her the way that Joseph looks at her. Not even Joseph, before he returned. She is not beautiful, like her mother or her aunt Caragh. She has always felt small and plain and strange. But she will not say so to him.

"I think," she says instead, "that the boys have been afraid of me."

"I would not doubt that," Joseph says. "They were afraid

of you when we were young, just because of your temper. The cougar cannot have helped."

Jules smiles at Camden.

"I should be sorry," Joseph says. "But I don't like to think about anyone else touching you. I thought of it sometimes, when I was away. And then Billy would take me out to get drunk."

Jules laughs and rests her forehead against his. There beside the pond, he feels like the boy she has known for so long. Her Joseph. He only looks different on the outside, all that dark hair and the new angles in his face. The broadness of his chest and shoulders.

"We are not the same," Jules says. "But I don't want us to have changed."

"But we have, Jules," Joseph says softly. "We've grown up. I loved you when I was a child. The way a child loves his friend. But I fell in love with you, for real, while I was away. Things can't stay the way they were before."

He leans close again, and their lips touch. He is gentle and slow. Every movement tells her that he will stop, even as his arms tighten around her waist. He will stop, if it is not what she wants.

Jules slips her arms around his neck and kisses him deeply. It is exactly what she wants. It is all she has ever wanted.

ROLANTH

"*They will come to part us soon,*" Arsinoe says. She has been in the brush, after the berries again. Bright red juice is streaked across her cheek. Or perhaps it is a cut from a thorn.

"*Willa won't let us go,*" says Katharine. "*I don't want to go. I want to stay here.*"

Mirabella would like to stay there as well. It is a warm day, newly spring. Now and again, when they grow too hot, she calls the wind to prickle their skin and to make Katharine giggle.

They are on the far side of the brook, divided from the cottage, and Willa will not cross the water to collect them anymore. It is too cold, she says. It makes her old joints ache.

"*Willa won't save you,*" Arsinoe says.

"*Yes, she will,*" says Katharine. "*Because I am her favorite. It's you she won't save.*"

"*I will save you both,*" Mirabella promises, and runs her

134

fingers through Katharine's long black hair. It is smooth as satin, and shines. Little Katharine. The youngest of the triplets. She has been Mirabella and Arsinoe's treasure since they were old enough to hold her hand.

"How?" Arsinoe asks, and drops cross-legged into the grass. She plucks a flower and rubs pollen onto Katharine's nose until it turns yellow.

"I'll call thunder to scare them away," Mirabella replies, twisting Katharine's hair into a fat braid. "And wind so strong it will blow us up onto the mountain."

Arsinoe considers this, her small brow furrowing. She shakes her head. "That will never work," she says. "We will have to think of something else."

"It was only a dream," Luca says. They are high inside the temple, in her cluttered room of pillows and trinkets.

"It was not," says Mirabella. "It was a memory."

Luca dodders about beneath a fur shawl, trying not to be irritated at being shaken from bed before dawn. When Mirabella's eye snapped open in her bed at the Westwood House, it was still dark. She waited for as long as she could stand to before coming to the temple to wake Luca, but the light peeking through the temple shutters is still the palest of grays.

"Come down to the kitchens," says Luca. "There is no one awake to call for tea at this hour. We will have to make it ourselves."

Mirabella takes a deep breath. When she lets it out, it shakes.

The memory, or the dream, if that is, indeed, what it was, still clings to her, as do the feelings it stirred.

"Be careful here," Mirabella says as she guides Luca down the steep temple stairs. She pushes the flame of their lamp up higher. Luca ought to take a room on a lower level. Perhaps a warm one, near the kitchens. But Luca will not admit that she is old. Not until she is dead.

In the kitchen, Mirabella starts a fire in the stove and heats water in a kettle while Luca searches shelves for the leaves she likes best. They do not speak again until they sit with two steaming cups of tea, sweetened with honey.

"It is only something your mind has made up. Because you are nervous. It is not surprising with the Quickening drawing near. And with you so haunted by the death of that sacrifice. Rho should never have made you do that ritual."

"It is not that," Mirabella insists. "I did not make it up."

"You were a child when you last saw your sisters," Luca says gently. "Perhaps you have heard stories. Perhaps you remember a little, about the cottage and the grounds."

"I have a very good memory."

"Queens do not remember these things," Luca says, and takes a sip of tea.

"Saying so does not make it true."

Luca looks into her cup solemnly. In the orange light of the table's lamp, every line, every furrow, in the old woman's face is visible.

"You will need it to be true," the High Priestess says. "For it is too cruel otherwise, to force a queen to kill that which she loves. Her own sisters. And for her to see that which she loves come at her door like wolves, seeking her head."

When Mirabella is silent, Luca reaches across and covers her hand with her own.

The echoes of Luca's words are so loud in Mirabella's ears that Elizabeth is almost on top of her before she hears her calling.

"You didn't hear me?" Elizabeth asks, slightly out of breath.

"I am sorry," Mirabella says. "It is so early; I was not expecting anyone to be awake."

Elizabeth gestures up the trunk of a nearby evergreen. "Pepper rises with the sun. And so I do as well."

Looking at the young priestess, Mirabella cannot help but smile. Elizabeth has a way of making it impossible to be sad. Her hood is down, and her dark hair has not yet been braided. Her tufted woodpecker darts onto her shoulder, and she feeds him a palm of seed.

"It is nice also," she says, "to be up so early that we don't have to worry about being seen."

Mirabella grasps Elizabeth gently by the wrist. The bracelets the priestess wears are only that: bracelets made from black ribbon and beads. She is only an initiate and can still change her mind.

"Why do you stay?" Mirabella asks. "When I met you, you said that they would take Pepper and kill him if they knew. But your bond is so strong. Why do you not go?"

Elizabeth shrugs. "And go where? I was a temple child, Mirabella. Did I tell you that?"

"No."

"My mother was a priestess of Kenora Temple. My father was a healer who she often worked with closely. My mother didn't give me up to foster. I grew up there. The temple is all I know. And I am hoping . . ."

"Hoping what?"

"That you will take me with you to Indrid Down Temple, after you are crowned."

Mirabella nods. "Yes. Many people in Rolanth hope for similar things."

"I'm sorry," says Elizabeth. "I do not mean to add to your burden!"

"No." Mirabella hugs her friend. "You have not. Of course I will take you with me. But think on these"—she holds Elizabeth's bracelets—"I do not necessarily have to bring you to the temple. You have choices. You have all the choices in the world."

Rho does not like being called to Luca's chambers. She stands near the window, shoulders squared and back stiff. She never tries to make herself at home. She never looks at home anywhere, except perhaps when she is supervising the younger priestesses at their tasks.

Luca can see why Mirabella does not like her. Rho is severe, and uncompromising, and when she smiles, it does not reach her eyes. But she is one of the best priestesses Luca has ever known. The queen may not care for Rho, nor Rho for the queen, but Rho will certainly be of use.

"She said that," Rho says, after Luca tells her of Mirabella's early visit. "She remembers her sisters."

"I do not know if it is true. It might only be the dreams playing tricks. It might only be her nerves."

Rho looks down. It is clear that she does not think so.

"And so?" Rho asks. "What do you wish to do?"

Luca leans back in her chair. Nothing. Perhaps nothing need be done. Or perhaps she was wrong all this time and Mirabella is not the chosen queen. She wipes at her mouth with the back of her hand.

"You will look a fool," Rho says, "after supporting her. It is too late to change course."

"I will not change course," Luca says angrily. "Queen Mirabella is chosen. She has to be."

She looks over Rho's shoulder, at the large mosaic hanging on the wall. A depiction of the capital city of Indrid Down, the six-sided dome of its temple and the great black spires of the Volroy.

"How long will it be before we can look at that and think of it only as the capital?" Luca asks. "Instead of as the poisoners' city?"

Rho follows her gaze and then shrugs.

"It was, once," says Luca. "It was once ours. Ours and the queen's. Now, it is theirs. And the council is theirs. They have grown too strong to listen, and we belong nowhere."

Rho does not respond. If Luca had hoped for pity, she ought to have summoned a different priestess.

"Rho, you have seen her. You watch her like a hawk above a mouse. What do you think?"

"Do I think she can kill them?" Rho asks, and crosses her arms. "Of course she can. A gift like hers could sink a fleet. She could be great. Like the Queens of Old."

"But?"

"But," Rho says darkly, "it is wasted on her. She can kill her sisters, High Priestess. But she will not do it."

Luca sighs. Hearing it finally spoken does not shock her. In truth, she has suspected it for some time, feared it since meeting Mirabella on the banks of Starfall Lake and nearly being drowned. The child was so angry. She had grieved the loss of Arsinoe and Katharine for nearly a year. Had she been as strong then as she is now, Luca, and every Westwood besides, would be dead.

"If only there were a way to channel that rage," she mutters.

"Perhaps you will think of one," Rho says. "But I have thought of something else."

"What?" Luca asks.

"The way of the White-Handed Queen."

Luca cocks her head. White-Handed Queens are queens who ascend the throne without ever spilling a drop of their sisters' blood. Without staining their hands.

"What are you talking about? Mirabella was born one of the common three."

"I am not talking about the Blue Queen," Rho says, referring to the rare fourth-born twin, who is deemed so blessed that her sisters are drowned by the Midwife as babies.

"Then what?" Luca asks.

"In the old legends, there were other White-Handed Queens," says Rho.

"Queen Andira, whose sisters were both oracles, with the sight gift," Luca says. Queens with the sight gift are prone to madness, and put to death. But neither Arsinoe nor Katharine are oracles.

"Another," says Rho. "Still another. I speak of the White-Handed Queen of the Sacrificial Year."

Luca narrows her eyes. Rho has been thinking on this for a long time. A Sacrificial Year refers to a generation in which two of the queens are nearly giftless. So weak that they are viewed less as kills than as sacrifices.

Rho has dug deep. Only temple scholars are likely to have heard even the vaguest allusion or parable of the Sacrificial Year.

"This may be such a year," says Luca. "But I fail to see how it will help, if Mirabella will not claim the sacrifices."

"In some Sacrificial Years, the people take the sacrifices for her," Rho says. "The night of the Quickening, in the most sacred of places, the people rise up and feed the other queens into the fires."

Luca watches Rho carefully. She has never read that. "That is not true," she says.

Rho shrugs. "Enough whispering will make it true. And it would be quick, and clean, and it would spare the queen's soft heart."

"You want us to—" Luca starts, but then glances at the door and lowers her voice, "sacrifice Arsinoe and Katharine at Beltane?"

"Yes. On the third day. After the Quickening Ceremony."

Bloodthirsty Rho, always seeking final solutions. But Luca never imagined she would hatch anything like this.

"The council would have us killed."

"Mirabella would still have the throne. And besides, they would not, if the island was with us. Not if the rumor was spread. We will need Sara Westwood."

Luca shakes her head. "Sara would not agree."

"Sara has become a pious woman. She will do as the temple instructs. And so will its priestesses. Besides, it will do the island good, to be reminded of its old legends."

Old legends. Legends that they spin out of thin air.

"I do not want to give up on Mira so quickly," she says, and Rho frowns. "But it is something to consider."

GREAVESDRAKE MANOR

--- ⚜ ---

K atharine and Pietyr sit with Natalia around a table picked clean of food. Lunch was a loin of pork from a poisoned hog, the sauce made from butter and milk from a cow that had been grazed on henbane. Stout oat bread to sop it up. There was also a soufflé of jack-o'-lantern mushrooms. Natalia does not care to eat untainted food, but everything she served contained poisons to which Katharine has acquired a near immunity.

Natalia calls for more wine. Her dining room is pleasantly warm. Fire crackles in the fireplace and thick red curtains hold in the heat.

"How was Half Moon's gait today?" Natalia asks. "One of the grooms worried he was swelling on his right rear pastern."

"His gait was fine," Katharine replies. "And there was no heat in the leg."

Half Moon is her favorite black gelding, named for the white crescent on his forehead. Had he showed any signs of lameness, Katharine would never have taken him out. Beneath the table, she moves her knee against Pietyr's.

"Did you notice anything, Pietyr?" she asks.

"Not at all. He seemed perfectly sound."

He clears his throat and moves his knee away from hers, as if he fears that Natalia can sense their contact. When they are in her presence, he is always careful to maintain distance, even though Natalia knows what they do. Even though he is there at Natalia's insistence.

"I have some exciting news," Natalia says. "A delegation has arrived early from the mainland. And the suitor wishes to meet with Katharine."

Katharine sits up straighter and glances at Pietyr.

"He is not the only one to meet, mind you," Natalia continues. "But he is a promising start. We have had dealings with his family for a number of years. They fostered Joseph Sandrin during his banishment."

"I will look upon him kindly, then," Katharine says.

"No more kindly than you would look upon any other," says Natalia, even though she means exactly the opposite. "His name is William Chatworth Jr. I do not know when we will be able to arrange a meeting. He is in Wolf Spring at present, having audiences with Arsinoe, the poor boy. But when we do, will you be ready?"

"I will be."

"I believe you," says Natalia. "You have looked much better these past weeks. Stronger."

It is true. Since Pietyr has come, Katharine has changed. Genevieve would still say that she is thin and too petite. After so many years of poisoning, it is unlikely that she will ever fully recover, or regain, the growth she has lost. But her hair and her complexion and the way she moves have all improved.

"I have a present for you," Natalia says. Her butler, Edmund, enters holding a glass enclosure. Inside, a small red-and-yellow-and-black coral snake stretches toward the top.

"Look who I found sunning herself in a window," Natalia says.

"Sweetheart?" Katharine exclaims. She pushes her chair back nearly hard enough to knock it over and runs to Edmund to reach inside. The snake recoils slightly and then wraps herself around her wrist.

"I thought I killed her," she whispers.

"Not quite," Natalia says. "But I am sure she would like to return to her familiar cage and the warmth of her lamp. And I need to speak to Pietyr alone."

"Yes, Natalia." Katharine smiles once at each of them and then leaves, nearly skipping.

"One small gift turns her back into a child," Natalia says.

"Katharine loves that snake," says Pietyr. "I would have thought it dead."

"It is dead. It was found limp and cold in the corner of the kitchen three days after the *Gave Noir*."

"Then what is that?" Pietyr asks.

Natalia shrugs. "She will not know the difference. This one is trained the same as the first one."

She motions again for Edmund, who brings a silver tray and two glasses of her favorite tainted brandy.

"You are making progress," Natalia says.

"Some. She still only thinks to dress in a way that covers a rash or a jutting rib. And when she is frightened, she still scurries like a rat."

"Come, Pietyr. We have not treated her so poorly."

"Perhaps not you. But Genevieve is a monster."

"My sister is only as severe as I allow. And Katharine's poison training is not your concern."

"Not even if it makes my task harder?"

He blows blond hair out of his eyes and slumps in his chair. Natalia smiles behind her brandy. He does remind her so much of herself. One day, he might even rise to become the head of the family, if no suitable daughter comes of age.

"Tell me," she says. "Is she ready to meet this delegate?"

"I suppose. He should not be hard to impress, in any case, coming from Wolf Spring. Everyone knows that Arsinoe has a face like oatmeal."

"She may have," Natalia says. "But Mirabella does not. To hear the Westwoods tell it, she is more beautiful than the night sky."

"And just as withdrawn and cold," says Pietyr. "Katharine,

at least, has a sense of fun. And she is sweet. You have not beaten that out of her."

There is something in Pietyr's tone that Natalia does not like. He sounds too protective. Almost possessive, and that will not do.

"How far have you gone?" she asks.

"What do you mean?"

"You know what I mean. Teach her all the tricks you like, but you cannot go too far, Pietyr. Mainlanders are strange. They will want her to go into her marriage a maid."

Natalia watches him carefully, to see if he will wriggle. He seems disappointed—frustrated, perhaps—but not afraid. He has still not dared to take that step.

"Are you sure they would not value her skill in the bedroom instead?" he asks. Then he shrugs. "I suppose if they do, I can teach her that after they are wed."

He finishes the last of his brandy in one large swallow and sets the snifter on the table. He would like to be allowed to go, to follow after Katharine and dress and undress her like a doll.

"It is probably for the best, Nephew," says Natalia. "If you were to bed her, I fear she would fall in love with you. She seems nearly in love with you already, and that is not what we intend."

Pietyr pushes his empty glass back and forth between his fingers.

"Is it," she says, more sternly.

"Do not worry, Aunt Natalia," he says. "Only a king-consort is fool enough to fall in love with a queen."

Katharine has still not put the snake away when Pietyr comes into her rooms. She has missed her so, she cannot bear to part with her, and sits at her vanity mirror with Sweetheart coiled around her hand, her nose practically pressed to the snake's poisonous head.

"Katharine," he says. "Put her away. Let her rest."

Katharine does as she is told, standing up to lower the snake gently into the warm cage. She leaves the top of it open to reach inside to stroke the snake's scales.

"I cannot believe she survived," Katharine says. "Natalia must have had all the servants searching."

"She must have," says Pietyr.

"So." She removes her hands from the cage and folds them onto her lap. "I am really to meet my first suitor?"

"Yes."

She and Pietyr stand close together without touching and without looking each other in the eyes. Pietyr runs his fingers along the back of her brocade-covered chair and worries at a loosening thread.

"Are you sure I cannot poison my sisters first?"

Pietyr smiles. "I am sure. This must be done, Kat."

He looks through the scant space between her curtains, out at the overcast sky and all the shadows in the courtyard. The small lake they rode beside that morning lies like a slate-gray puddle to the southeast. Soon, it will be bright blue, and the courtyard will be green and sprouting daffodils. Already the weather has turned warmer. The dawn brings more fog than frost.

"Mirabella will be hard to overcome," Pietyr says. "She is tall and strong and beautiful. In Rolanth, there are already songs about her hair."

"Songs about her hair?" Katharine asks, and snorts aloud. She ought to care about this. But in truth, she would not mind if all the suitors preferred Mirabella. None of them will kiss the way Pietyr kisses. He holds her with such desperate wanting that she cannot even catch her breath.

"Do you think the suitors will kiss like you do, Pietyr?" she asks, just to see his lower lip stick out.

"Of course not. They are mainland boys. All fumbling and drool. It will be difficult for you to pretend to enjoy it."

"They cannot all be bad," she says. "I am sure to find one who I like."

Pietyr arches his brow. His fingers dig into the back of the chair but relax when he sees her expression.

"Are you teasing me, Kat?"

"Yes." She laughs. "I am teasing you. Is that not what you have taught me to do? To counteract my sister's regal formality with smiles and a beating heart?"

She touches his chest, and he grasps her hand.

"You are too good at it," he whispers, and pulls her up against his chest.

"You will have to laugh at their jokes," he says, "even when they are not funny."

"Yes, Pietyr."

"And get them to talk about themselves. Make them remember you. You must be the jewel, Kat. The one who stands out from the others." He releases her hand a little reluctantly. "No matter what you do, they will still want to try all three. Even plain-faced Arsinoe. And Mirabella . . ." He breathes deeply through his nose. "Whatever gown she wears to the Quickening, you can be sure they will be dying to tear it off her."

Katharine frowns. "I suppose she will be presented as the prize."

"And what a prize," Pietyr sighs, and Katharine thumps him in the chest. He laughs.

"Now, I am teasing." He pulls her closer. "I would not touch that elemental if she got down on her knees and begged. She pretends to be crowned already. But she is not. You are our queen, Kat. Do not forget it."

"I will never," she says. "We will do good for the island, Pietyr, when I am crowned and you are the head of the Black Council."

"The head?" he asks, eyes sparkling. "I think Natalia would have something to say about that."

"Of course, Natalia will remain in her position as long as she wishes," Katharine amends. "But not even she can stay there forever."

Behind them, the coral snake climbs the side of the cage. Its scaled head slips above the opened hatch and pauses there, tasting the air with its tongue. Unaware, Katharine lets her arm drop back to rest on the top of the table. The snake does not like the movement. It curves back to strike.

"Katharine!"

Pietyr's arm darts forward. The snake's fangs catch him in the wrist. He holds the reptile gently until it releases, even though he ought to break its neck. Katharine will not be safe around it, and no harm can be allowed to come to her so close to the Quickening.

"Oh," Katharine says. "I am so sorry, Pietyr! She must still be out of sorts."

"Yes." He puts the snake back into the cage, making sure to close the lid tightly this time. "But you should use caution with her from now on. Retrain her. Even a few weeks on her own may have been enough to turn her wild."

Twin drops of blood dot Pietyr's arm. The wound is not bad. As strong an Arron as he is, the venom will only cause a little redness.

"I have salve that will help," Katharine says, and goes into the other room to fetch it.

Pietyr eyes the snake ruefully as he holds his wrist. Reacting was the right thing to do. Katharine would have been sick with the venom for days, even after receiving treatment. But he did so without thinking. And he had been afraid that Katharine would be hurt. Truly afraid.

"Only a king-consort is fool enough to love a queen," he says quietly.

WOLF SPRING

---

*A*rsinoe and Billy walk side by side through the winter market. Since their introduction and their afternoon at Dogwood Pond, it has proved difficult for Arsinoe to get away from him, but in the market, Arsinoe does not mind. Jules is often with Joseph, and without her there, Arsinoe feels exposed in crowded places. In bustling parts of town, like the market, wicked glances sting like bees. Any in the crowd could grow brave enough to reach around and slit her throat.

"Arsinoe?" Billy asks. "What's the matter?"

She studies the surly winter faces of fishmongers she has known since she came to Wolf Spring. A good number of them consider her weakness a disgrace and would see her dead.

"Nothing," she says.

Billy sighs. "I am not in the mood for the market today," he says. "Let's buy something to eat and walk up into the orchards.

It's not too cold for that."

On the way, they stop at Madge's shellfish stand so that Billy can pay for two fried stuffed clams. He barely fumbles with the coins this time. He is learning.

They eat quickly as they walk, to keep them from getting cold. Madge stuffs her clams with chunks of crab and buttered bread crumbs. When she feels particularly generous, she dices in some nice, fat bacon.

As they walk past the docks, toward the road that heads up over the hill and into the apple orchards, Billy stares down at his clamshell, turning it over in his hands.

"Staring at it won't make it grow a new one," Arsinoe says. "You should have bought three."

He grins and draws his arm back to throw the shell into the cove as far as he can. Arsinoe throws hers as well.

"Mine went farther," she says.

"It did not."

Arsinoe smiles. Actually, she could not tell.

"What happened to your hand?" Billy asks.

Arsinoe tugs her jacket sleeve down to cover the scabbing from the new rune she cut into her palm.

"I cut it on the chicken coop," she says.

"Oh."

He does not believe her. She should have made up something else. No chicken coop could leave behind such an intricate design. And she has still not told Jules what she and Madrigal are doing.

"Junior," she says, looking closer at the docks. "Where is your boat?"

The slip where it has bobbed since Joseph's return is empty, and the entire cove looks darker because of it.

"My father's returned home," he says. "It is easy enough to come and go. A short sail to the mist and through it. My God, I feel mad just saying that aloud. Madder, knowing that it's true."

"Easy to come and go," Arsinoe mutters. Easy for anyone but her, anyway.

"But listen, when he returns . . ."

"What?"

"He intends for me to meet your sisters. We're to travel to Indrid Down and the Arrons. And Queen Katharine."

Of course. He wants his son to wear the crown. He has no particular loyalty to the naturalists, no matter how fond he became of Joseph during his banishment.

"You never call me 'Queen Arsinoe' anymore," she notes.

"Do you want me to?"

She shakes her head. To be called a queen feels like a nickname. Like something that only Luke calls her. They walk up the road and then wave to Maddie Pace when she rumbles past in her oxcart. Arsinoe does not need to look to know that Maddie has twisted around in her seat to stare at them. The whole of the town is interested in their courting.

"I don't know if I want to meet the rest of you," Billy says. "It feels a little like befriending a cow on its way to slaughter."

Arsinoe chuckles. "Be sure to tell my sisters that, when you meet them," she says. "But if you don't want to meet them, then don't."

"My father isn't the sort of man you say no to. He gets what he wants. He won't have raised a failure."

"And what did your mother raise?" she asks, and he looks at her, surprised.

"It doesn't matter," he says. "She never wanted this. You know mothers. They'd keep us attached to their apron strings forever if they could."

"I do not know that," Arsinoe says. "I do know that you sound a little like you are sulking. Don't forget the difference between what a lost crown means for you and what it means for me."

"Yes. You're right. I'm sorry."

She looks at him from the side of her eye. It cannot be easy, to be a stranger here and to give up everything familiar for a crown and an unfamiliar life. He has tried to be fair, and she should try also. And she should keep her distance. It will not be easy for him to see her dead, should they become close. But she has so few friends. She cannot turn one away.

Arsinoe pauses. Without thinking, she has turned them onto the trail that leads to the woods, and the old stones, and the bent-over tree.

"No," she says, and changes their direction. "Let's take another path."

"What do you think your sisters are like?" Billy asks.

"I do not know and I do not care," Arsinoe says. "They are

both probably in training for the Quickening Ceremony. Less than three months now."

"Beltane," Billy says. "It's held every year, isn't it?"

"Yes. But this year is different. This Beltane is the start of the Ascension Year."

"I know that," he says. "But how is it different? Does it still last for three days?"

Arsinoe cocks her head. She can only say what she has heard. Neither she nor Jules has ever attended one. To go, you must be at least sixteen.

"It is still three days," she says, "and there is always the Hunt. The ritual hunt to provide meat for the feasts. Then normally there are daily blessings, and rites that the temple performs. But this year there won't be much of that. Everyone will be preparing for the Disembarking the night after the Hunt, and the Quickening on the night after that."

"The Disembarking," he says. "Where you are presented to the suitors."

"Where the suitors are presented to us," she says, and punches him in the arm.

"All right. Ow. And the Quickening. That's when you demonstrate your gift. How are you going to manage that?" he asks, and braces for another hit.

Arsinoe chuckles instead. "I thought I would learn to juggle three herring," she says. "Katharine will eat poison, and Mirabella . . . Mirabella can fart cyclones for all it will matter. The island will love her best."

"Fart cyclones," Billy says, smirking.

"Yes, you would like that, would you?"

He shakes his head. "And after Beltane is over, that's when you are courted, officially," he says. "And when . . ."

"And when we can kill one another," Arsinoe says. "We have a whole year to do it. Until the next year's Beltane. Though if Mirabella comes charging like an angry bull I could be dead within the week."

They tramp through snow, ice-crusted from melt, into the resting earth of the orchard. They walk deeper down into the valley until the birds stop singing and the wind breaks.

"Do you ever wonder what happened to your mother?" Billy asks. "After she had you and left the island with her king?"

"King-consort," she corrects him. "And no, I don't."

There are stories, of course. Tales of great queens who left the island to become great queens again on the mainland. Others tell of queens who live out the rest of their lives peacefully and quietly, with their consorts. But Arsinoe has never believed a word. In her mind, every last queen lies at the bottom of the sea, drowned by the Goddess the moment she was done with them.

Jules runs her hand through the dark hair at Joseph's temple. It is soft, and long enough to twist around her fingers. They are alone in the Sandrin house today. Joseph's father is out on the *Whistler* with Matthew, and his mother and Jonah have taken a carriage to Highgate to secure hardware for the boats. It is a good thing, too, since Billy's father sailed home to the mainland and robbed them of the use of Joseph's cabin.

"This is just as uncomfortable as on the boat," Joseph says. He lies half on top of her, with Camden stretched across their lower legs.

"I didn't notice," Jules says. She pulls him down and opens her mouth beneath his. From the way his arms tighten around her, she can tell that he does not really notice either.

"Someday soon, though, we will have to find a bed big enough for the two of us, and your cougar."

"Someday soon," she agrees. But for now, she is glad of the cramped quarters, and the lack of privacy. As much as she loves Joseph, she is not ready to go further. With Camden hindering their movements, she can kiss Joseph for as long as she likes without feeling they ought to do more.

Joseph lowers his head and kisses Jules's collarbone, where it peeks through her disheveled shirt. He rests his chin against her and sighs.

"What is it?" she asks. "Your mind is on something else today."

"My mind is only on you," he says. "But there is something."

"What?"

"Do you remember that boat in our western slip?" he asks. "The shiny little daysailer with the new deck and fresh stripe of blue paint?"

"Not really."

The Sandrins' shipyard has been full of jobs like that for

months. Vanity repairs, from all along the coast. Mainlanders will arrive on the island soon, and the island wishes to show a fresh face. They have even had jobs from the fishers of Wolf Spring, who say the word "mainlander" through curled, disdainful lips. They may speak of mainlanders and spit, but they will use that spit to shine their own shoes.

"What about it?" she asks.

"I'm to sail it up to Trignor to return it to its owner. I leave as soon as my mother and Jonah return from Highgate."

"Oh," Jules says. "Why does that trouble you?"

Joseph smiles. "It will sound foolish to say so out loud, but I don't want to be parted from you, even for a short time."

"Joseph." Jules laughs. "We have been together almost every moment since you've returned."

"I know," he says. "And I will not be gone long. If the winds are good, I can reach Trignor by nightfall. It should not take more than a few days at most, to catch the coaches back to Wolf Spring. Still"—he pulls himself farther on top of her— "perhaps you could come with me?"

Traveling on a small craft with Camden and long days of rumbling coaches does not sound pleasant, but being with Joseph would make it so. She slips her arms around his neck and hears Arsinoe's voice: *Jules and Joseph, inseparable since birth.*

"I can't," says Jules. "I have neglected Arsinoe enough already. She's had to work on her gift with my mother, and I can't ask her to take on any more of my chores. She's a queen."

"The best queens don't mind extra chores."

"Still," Jules says. "I shouldn't leave her here. And you should not ask me to. You love her too, remember. As much as you love me."

"Nearly as much, Jules," he says. "Only nearly."

He drops his head to rest against her shoulder.

"We will not be parted for long, Joseph. Don't worry."

ROLANTH

The dream is a bad one. Mirabella wakes to the sound of her own cry. It is a sudden waking; the edges of the dream blur into the familiar air of her bedroom, her body trapped half inside each consciousness and her legs tangled in damp sheets. She sits up and touches her face. In the dream, she had been crying. Crying and laughing.

Her door clicks open softly, and Elizabeth pokes her head in. She has taken over much of Mirabella's personal escort, and Mirabella exhales, relieved that it is her outside her door tonight.

"Are you all right?" Elizabeth asks. "I heard you shouting."

Pepper the woodpecker flies from her shoulder and flits around the queen from hip to head, making sure she is safe.

"I heard it too," Bree says. She pushes the door wider, and both girls go inside and close it tight behind them. Mirabella tugs her knees up to her chest, and Bree and Elizabeth climb onto the bed. Bree flicks her wrist and lights the candles on the dresser.

"I am sorry," says Mirabella. "Do you think I woke anyone else?"

Bree shakes her head. "Uncle Miles could sleep through the battle of Bardon Harbor."

Sara's and young Nico's rooms are too far away. So is the servants' quarter on the first floor. It is only the three of them, one wakeful spot in a darkened house.

"Mira," Bree says, "you are trembling."

"I'll get some water," says Elizabeth, and Pepper lands beside the pitcher and chirps to guide the way.

"No," Mirabella says. "No water."

She stands up to pace. The dreams of her sisters cling to her, sometimes for days. They do not fade like other dreams do.

"What was it?" Bree asks.

Mirabella closes her eyes. This one was not a memory but a series of images.

"It would be impossible to describe," she says.

"Was it about," Elizabeth asks hesitantly, "the other queens?"

The other queens, yes. Her sweet sisters, dead and stuffed upright in chairs with greening skin and stitched-shut mouths. Then a flash of Katharine, lying on her back with her chest cracked open, nothing inside but a dry, red hole. Finally Arsinoe, screaming at her without sound because her throat is too clogged with thick, dark blood.

Mirabella, they said. *Mirabella, Mirabella.*

"I held them underwater," Mirabella whispers. "In the stream beside the cottage. The water was so cold. Ink came out of their mouths. They were only children."

"Oh, Mira," Bree says. "That is awful, but it is only a dream. They are not children."

"They will always be children, to me," Mirabella says.

She thinks of what it felt like when Arsinoe and Katharine went limp, and rubs her hands together as though filthy.

"I cannot do this anymore."

Luca will be disappointed. She has put faith in her and raised her to rule. So have the Westwoods, and the city, and the Goddess herself. She was created to rule. To become the queen the island needs. If she goes to see Luca in the temple, she will tell Mirabella that exact thing. That these dreams, and these feelings, have been put in her path for a reason. As a test.

"I have to leave," Mirabella says. "I have to get away from here."

"Mirabella," says Elizabeth. "Be calm. Take some water."

She accepts the glass, and drinks, if only to please her friend. But it is hard to swallow. The water tastes like something has died in it.

"No. I have to go. I have to leave." She goes to her closet and pushes open the doors. She rifles through cloaks and dresses, all black, black, black.

Bree and Elizabeth stand up. They hold their hands out to try to stop her, to try to soothe her.

"You can't go," says Elizabeth. "It's the middle of the night!"

"Mira, you will not be safe," Bree adds.

Mirabella selects a dress of lined wool. She puts it on over her nightclothes and opens a drawer for long stockings.

"I will go south. I will not be seen."

"You will be!" Elizabeth says. "They will send a party after you."

Mirabella pauses, still trembling. They are right. Of course they are right. But she has to try.

"I have to go," she says. "Please. I cannot stay here anymore and dream of my sisters talking to me from dead bodies. I cannot kill them. I know that you need me to; I know that is what I am meant to do . . ."

"Mira," says Bree. "You can."

"I won't," she says fiercely.

Elizabeth and Bree have moved to block the door. They are sad, and worried, and moments from waking Sara and alerting the temple. Mirabella will spend the rest of her time until Beltane locked in Luca's rooms and under constant guard.

Mirabella steps into her boots and laces them. Whoever they send after her will certainly catch her, but they will have to work for it.

She steps forward, ready to force her way through her friends.

"Wait," Elizabeth says. She holds up one hand and goes out the door. If she calls down the hall, there may not be time for Mirabella to run. But Elizabeth does not call out. She comes back into the bedroom carrying her white priestess's cloak.

"Take this," she says. "Keep the hood up and your hair covered." She smiles her sweet, gentle smile. "No one looks twice at a priestess. They only bow and get out of the way."

Mirabella hugs her gratefully. The cloak is a little short. But it is large, cut to cover Elizabeth's ample curves, and covers Mirabella's dress completely.

"Elizabeth," Bree says but then stops. She takes Mirabella by the arm. "Let us come with you, at least."

"No, Bree," Mirabella says gently. "I would not have you know anything of this. When they find me gone, they will seek someone to blame. Someone to punish. Do not let it be you or Elizabeth."

"I promise," Bree says. "We will look after each other."

Mirabella smiles sadly and touches Bree's face.

"I have never seen you look so frightened," she says, and hugs her tightly. "Please understand, Bree. I love them. Just like I love you. And I cannot stay here and let the temple force me to kill them."

She releases Bree and holds her arm out for Elizabeth. She has been lucky to have them.

By the time Mirabella makes her way south, through and out of the Westwoods' grounds, dawn has started to pink in the east. It must have been later than she thought, when the dream woke her. Already, fires and lamps burn in the city as early tradespeople and smiths prepare for the day. She tugs the white cloak down to conceal her face.

She takes the main road into Rolanth. It might be wiser to keep to the secondary passages, but that is the way she knows by coach, and a slightly greater risk of being seen is better than becoming lost.

When the road turns toward the locks and the city center, Mirabella holds her breath at the sound of people. Ahead on the sidewalk, a woman beats dust from a rug and calls a morning greeting to a neighbor emptying a bucket into the gutter. Mirabella keeps her head low, but Elizabeth was right. The woman does no more than nod before stepping out of her way. If anyone wonders what a priestess is doing in the city at such an hour, none of them stop her to ask.

As she leaves Rolanth, she looks back once, across the rooftops and the softly smoking chimneys, her city in the growing light. Beyond that, settled back in the tall evergreens, Sara and the rest of Westwood House will be waking. In the temple, Luca is probably already having tea.

It is difficult to leave them, but getting out was easier than she thought it would be, all things considered.

WOLF SPRING

❧

*B*eside the fire, beneath the bent-over tree, Arsinoe's
head spins. Madrigal has cut deep into her arm this
time, to let enough blood to soak three lengths of cord. The
cord will keep the blood until they have need of it. And for
low magic strong enough to kill another queen, they will need
all that Arsinoe can spare.

They have not discussed yet what that magic will be. A
curse, perhaps. Or an unlucky charm. It does not matter. All
Arsinoe knows is that she grows stronger every day.

"That's enough," Madrigal says. She lowers the cords carefully into a glass jar. "These will not keep forever. We should
put them to use right after Beltane."

Madrigal slides the jar into a sack of black cloth and slings
the strap across her body. "Here," she says, and presses a cup of
something to Arsinoe's lips. "Cider. Take some."

"Did you bring any nuts?" Arsinoe asks. "Bread? Anything
to eat?"

She holds the cup shakily and sips. The sides of the cup are sticky and smeared with Madrigal's fingerprints in Arsinoe's blood.

"Jules is right," Madrigal mutters. "You are mostly stomach."

She hands the queen a small packet: cheese and a dozen naturalist-ripened blackberries.

"Thank you," says Arsinoe. Her arm throbs and stings as Madrigal cleans and binds it, but it is a good sting. In fact, Arsinoe has not felt this hopeful in her entire life.

"I never would have guessed," Arsinoe says, "that you would be the one to help me. With anything."

Madrigal scrunches up her nose. On her, even that is pretty.

"Yes," Madrigal says. "I know."

She sits back, and wraps herself in a warm fur, sulking for never being appreciated. But no one can blame Cait and Ellis. Since she was a girl, Madrigal has preferred comfort to work. Caragh used to tell of a time when Madrigal made flowers grow in a swirling pattern, only to pluck them to put in her hair. And this all while cucumbers were dying in the garden.

"Where is my Juillenne today?" Madrigal asks.

"Saying farewell to Joseph. He sails northwest up the coast for Trignor."

Madrigal stares into the fire. "Lucky Jules," she says, "to have a boy like that. I didn't think she had it in her, what with those funny eyes of hers. And looking like her father the way she does."

"Her father?" Arsinoe asks. "I didn't think you remembered Jules's father."

"I don't. Not really. I remember the fires of Beltane. And thinking how wonderful it would be if I conceived a baby on that sacred night. How strong she would be. How much she would love me." She snorts. "I don't remember who her father was. But she does not look a thing like me, so she must look like him."

"Do you think he knows?" Arsinoe asks.

"Knows what?"

"That he has a daughter and that she is the strongest naturalist on the island."

Madrigal shrugs. It is not likely. And if he did, it would not matter. Beltane Begots are sacred in the eyes of the temple. And much like the queens, in the eyes of the temple, they have no recognized fathers.

Arsinoe leans back. With the cheese and fruit in her belly, she is warm again and no longer shaky. She stretches her legs out and pushes the soles of her shoes near the coals.

"Joseph is so handsome," Madrigal says wistfully.

"He is," Arsinoe agrees.

"Seeing him and Jules together makes me realize how long I have been on my own. Perhaps I ought to work a spell. To bring a lover like that to me."

"Hmph," Arsinoe snorts, eyes half closed. "You don't need low magic for that, Madrigal."

"Perhaps not. But if I used just an inch off one of these

cords," she says, and pats the black bag in her lap, "I could have the best-looking man on the island."

Arsinoe eyes her sideways, to make sure she is joking before beginning to chuckle. Before long the chuckle becomes a laugh, and then they are both laughing. But even had they not been, they would still not have heard Camden and Jules's silent approach.

The mountain cat arrives at the fire before Jules does, but it is not enough warning to try to feign innocence.

Jules looks from her mother to Arsinoe.

"What is this?" she asks.

Arsinoe grimaces. They sit below the sacred stones, surrounded by rags soiled by queen's blood. Arsinoe's sleeve is drawn up above her elbow and shows the bandage clearly.

"This is what you do?" Jules half shouts at her mother. "The moment I turn my back? You bring her here and cut her open? You teach her low magic?"

"Jules," Arsinoe says, and stands. She stretches an arm out, as if to shield Madrigal, which only makes Jules angrier. Camden begins to growl.

"I am helping her," Madrigal says.

"Helping her?" Jules reaches for Arsinoe and tugs her so hard Arsinoe nearly trips over the log she was seated on. "You cannot do this. It is dangerous."

Madrigal shakes her head. "You don't understand it. You don't know anything about it."

"I know that there's always a price," Jules says. "I know it is for the simple, and the desperate, and the weak."

"Then it is for me." Arsinoe rolls her sleeve down to cover the bandage and the cuts of the runes on her palm.

"Arsinoe, that is not true."

"It is true. And I will use it. It's all I have."

"But you don't know what it will cost."

"It will be fine, Jules. Madrigal used it when she was on the mainland, and she is safe."

"Those who speak against it are only coughing up temple superstition," Madrigal agrees as she douses the fire.

She and Arsinoe walk around the hill silently, eager to get Jules out of their sacred place. Jules follows behind, angry.

For as long as Arsinoe can remember, she and Jules have not quarreled over anything more important than the size of a slice of cake. Her shoulders slump.

"It will take time," Madrigal says softly. "But she will come around."

THE WESTERN COAST

It is better when there are no carriages or carts and she can travel by the roadside. At least the air is open there and she can see a patch of unobscured sky. Mirabella looks up at the fading light. It has been two whole days of walking since she fled Rolanth, separated by a few uncomfortable hours of dozing against this broad trunk or that. The country to the south is not meadows and sheer cliff sides. It is made up of denser forest and softly rolling hills. So many trees. Even in winter, without their leaves, they box her in. She does not understand why naturalists love the woods so.

She picks up her skirt to step over a mostly thawed puddle in the ditch, trying to preserve it even though the priestess's cloak that Elizabeth loaned her is edged with dark watermarks and mud. The journey has not been easy. Her legs ache, and her stomach is empty. Yesterday, she used a bit of lightning to stun a trout, but she is not skilled at hunting without the priestesses and their hounds.

She misses Bree and Elizabeth. Luca and Sara. Even Uncle Miles and excitable little Nico. But she will bear it. She cannot stop for too long in any one place, and she cannot go often into cities. Soon though, she will have to trade for new clothes and a meal with a vegetable in it so her teeth do not fall out.

Mirabella steps quickly up the ditch as something approaches on the road. Whatever it is sounds large. Several carriages perhaps. A search party from Rolanth?

She will have to get far into the trees to keep them from seeing her and her from seeing them. The sight of poor Luca pressed against the window would break her heart.

When she is deep in the woods, she stops and listens. Only one carriage passes. Probably a rickety wagon headed for Indrid Down, perhaps carrying a load of wool, or sheep's milk and cheese. Not long ago she smelled sheep fields and guessed that she was passing through Waring and its many farms.

But she is not certain where she is. She has studied maps since she was a child, but the island looks much smaller on paper, and she has not seen a sign since passing one for North Cumberland early this morning. By now, with the sun setting, she must be at least as far as Trignor. Perhaps even Linwood. Another few days and she will have to skirt the boundary of Indrid Down.

Where they will catch you, you silly girl, Luca says in her head.

Mirabella brushes black hair out of her eyes. Somewhere

to the east, thunder rumbles. Tired as she is, she does not even know if she is the one who called it, but she craves it all the same and turns farther from the road to follow the scent of the storm.

She walks faster as the cliffs and open sky call. Above the trees, rich black clouds roll in until she can no longer tell what time of day it is or whether it has crossed into night.

She breaks through the tree line. For a moment, she fears that she has somehow walked in a wide circle. The cliffs she stands on are so like the Blackway of home. But it is not the Blackway. A flash of lightning shows the cliff face in white and pale gold, softer stuff than her beloved black basalt.

"A little more," she says to the wind, and it races around her and squeezes. It blows the ruined cloak back off her shoulders.

Mirabella steps to the cliff edge above the sea. Lightning illuminates the water in greens and blues. There must be a path down. She wants to wade out and be soaked to the waist.

The only way she finds is steep and lined with wet rocks. It is treacherous, but she takes her time, delighting in the wind and rain. Tomorrow, the people who live here will speak of this as a Shannon Storm, named for the queen whose mural decorates the largest portion of Rolanth Temple. They will talk about it over breakfast tables. It will damage roofs and leave downed trees to clear. People will sing the song of Shannon and tell of how she could summon hurricanes and send them out like pigeons on errand.

They are only tall tales, perhaps. One day, they will call

great fires a Mirabella Flame and say that she could scorch the sun. Or they would have, had she not run away to disappear.

Mirabella looks out to the sea and takes down the hood of her cloak, so the rain can slick her hair. Then the lightning flashes, and she sees a boat topple down.

"No."

The craft is small and the waves rough. Perhaps the storm tore it out from its slip. No one could be unlucky enough to be caught in the middle of such a monster, in a boat as tiny as that.

The boat rolls itself and rights again. The sail has come loose and blows, wet and flapping. It has not been abandoned or dragged unmanned out to sea. One lone sailor clings hopelessly to the mast.

Mirabella looks in all directions, but there is no one down the beach, no town, no glow of friendly fires. She screams for help back toward the road, but it is too far.

The boat will roll again, and fail to come upright. It will sink down deep and be tossed in the restless currents until there is nothing left.

Mirabella holds up her palm. She cannot stand there and do nothing as the sailor drowns. Even though she is weary and water has always been her most difficult element.

"Use the wind," she says to herself, but she has never used the wind to move anything but her own body or a few small belongings. Luca's scarf or Sara's hat.

Mirabella studies the water. She can try to push the boat

back out, far enough into the sea perhaps, that it might escape the storm.

Or she can try to bring it in.

Either choice is risky. She could shatter the boat against the cliffs. She could lose control of the water and swamp it. Or the hull could be impaled on an unseen, rocky outcropping lurking beneath the surface.

She clenches her fists. There is no more time. She focuses her gift on the water around the boat, working it and shifting its currents to slide the small craft toward the shore. She calls too much wind, and the boat jumps forward like a spooked horse.

"Goddess," Mirabella says, teeth clenched, "guide my hand."

The boat pitches sloppily back and forth. The boom wags like a dog's tail, and the sailor makes a grab for it. He misses, and the boom catches him clean across the back. He falls over the side and into the sea.

"No!" Mirabella shouts.

She uses her gift to sift through the water, separating it down deep. She has never done anything like this before. The ocean's layers, its currents, and cold and churning sand move as she commands. It is not easy, but the water obeys.

The boy breaks the surface, cradled in the current she has created. He is smaller than the boat and easier to manage.

When he strikes the beach, his body rolls hard onto the wet sand. She did not know how to be gentle. She has probably broken all his bones.

Mirabella scrambles down the steep path. She slips and crabs her way, cutting her palms bloody against the sharp rocks. She runs across the sand to the boy and presses her torn hands to his chest.

Water drains from his mouth. He is so pale, lying on the edge of the surf. He could be any other sea creature, spit out of the waves belly up.

"Breathe!" she shouts, but she cannot put wind into his lungs. She is no healer. She does not know what to do.

He coughs. He begins to shiver, violently, but that is better than being dead.

"Where am I?" he asks.

"I do not know," she says. "Somewhere near Trignor, I think."

She takes off her cloak and drapes it over him. It will not be enough. She will have to get him warm, but as far as she can see there is no cover.

"This was," she says, and shakes him by the shoulder when he seems to again lose consciousness. "This was not the best place to come ashore!"

To her surprise, the boy laughs. He is about her age, with thick, dark hair. His eyes, when they meet hers, are like the storm. Perhaps he is not a boy at all, but some elemental thing, made by the crashing water and the endless thunder.

"Can you walk?" she asks, but he slips away again, shivering so hard his teeth clack. She cannot carry him. Not up the trail and not down the long stretch of beach that might lie between them and the next town.

Where the cliffs cut in toward the road, they slant so that the opening is narrower at the top than the bottom. It is not a cave. It is barely an overhang, but it will have to do.

Mirabella slips her arm beneath him and pulls him across her shoulders, dragging him, waterlogged and limp. The sand sucks at her boots. Her already-weary legs burn in protest, but they manage to reach the cover of the cliffs.

"I have to find wood to keep a fire," she says. He lies on his side, shaking. Even if she gets him warm, he may not survive the night. He may have swallowed too much of the sea.

Pieces of dark, wet driftwood and blown-down sticks from the trees above litter the beach. Mirabella gathers them and arranges them under the cover of the cliffs into a great heaping mess, threaded through with seaweed and errant shells and pebbles.

She is shaking too. Her gift is close to exhausted.

When she calls fire to the wood, none comes.

Mirabella kneels and rubs her hands together. Next to the lightning, fire is her favorite. To have it ignore her is like watching a most loved pet turn tail and run away.

The boy's lips have turned blue.

"Please," she says, and pushes her gift as hard as she can.

At first, there is nothing. Then slowly, a tendril of smoke rises from the pile. Soon, flames warm their cheeks and begin to dry their clothes. The fire sizzles and spits when the rain from the Shannon Storm hits it, but there is nothing to be done about that. She is too tired to order the clouds away. The storm will pass when it passes.

Beside her, the boy's shivering has eased. She wrestles him out of his jacket and shirt and spreads them out on the sand, as close to the fire as she can without risk of them catching. She lays Elizabeth's cloak out as well. It will keep him plenty warm, if she can get it dry.

The boy moans. If only Luca were there. She would know what to do.

"Cold," the boy mumbles.

Mirabella did not drag him up from the depths and across the sand only to watch him die now. She knows only one thing to do.

She unfastens her dress and slips out of it. She lies behind the boy and wraps her arms around him, sharing her heat. When her cloak is dry, she will use it to cover them both.

Mirabella jerks awake. After covering them with Elizabeth's dry cloak, she had begun to doze, staring into the fire, and dreamed of Arsinoe and Katharine until the pieces of driftwood became their finger bones and the knots of wet, steaming seaweed became their hair. They burned and fell apart into charcoal as they tried to crawl out of the sand like crabs.

The boy lies in her arms. Beads of sweat dot his forehead, and he struggles, but she holds him tight. He must stay warm. In the morning, he will need fresh water. She can probably find some if she goes up the cliff trail back into the trees. Even after the rain, there will still be ice in the woods, frozen on branches or into logs.

Mirabella adjusts her position and the boy's arm slides around her waist. His eyes open slightly.

"The boat," he says.

"It is at the bottom of the sea." Cracked and broken, most likely, given the force of those Shannon waves.

"My family," he whispers. "They'll have to replace it."

"Do not worry about that now," Mirabella says. "How do you feel? Do you hurt anywhere?"

"No." He closes his eyes. "I'm cold. I'm so cold."

His hand wanders tentatively across her back, beneath the cloak, and Mirabella's pulse quickens. Even half-drowned, he is one of the most handsome boys she has ever seen.

"Am I dead?" he asks. "Did I die?"

His leg moves between hers.

"You did not die," she says, her voice breathless. "But I must get you warm."

"Make me warm, then."

He draws her mouth to his. He tastes of salt. His hands move slowly over her skin.

"You are not real," he says against her lips.

Whoever taught this boy to kiss has taught him well. He pulls her on top of him to kiss her neck. He tells her again that she is not real.

But perhaps he is the one who is not real. This boy with eyes like the storm.

Mirabella wraps her legs around him. When he moans this time, it is not from the cold.

"I saved you," she says. "I will not let you die."

She kisses him hungrily, her touch waking him up, pulling him out of the dark. He feels like he belongs in her arms. She will not let him die. She will make them both warm.

She will set them both on fire.

WOLF SPRING

*J*oseph's mother had a dream. A dream of her son, pulled under by waves. It was more than a nightmare, she said, and Jules believes her. Joseph had a touch of the sight when he was a boy. Such a gift had to have come from somewhere. But others were skeptical until the birds returned from Trignor with word he had never arrived.

Luke pushes a cup of tea into Jules's hand. He has brought a pot down to the pier with a stack of teacups tucked in his elbow.

"Sorry," he says when hot tea splashes over the edge and burns her knuckles. "And I'm doubly sorry that I didn't have enough hands to carry the cream. But here." He reaches into his jacket pocket and drops in a handful of sugar cubes.

"Thank you, Luke," Jules says, and Hank the rooster clucks on his shoulder as Luke moves through the gathering of worriers and rubberneckers, offering cups.

Jules is too anxious to drink. The birds brought with them

word of a storm off the coast, a monstrous storm that swung into the island from the wide-open sea and devastated land from Linwood to the port at Miner's Bay.

Billy steps up beside her and places firm fingers on her shoulder.

"Joseph is a strong sailor, Jules," says Billy. "It's most likely that he pulled in at a cove somewhere to ride it out and went on like nothing happened. We'll hear something of him soon. I'm sure of it."

Jules nods, and Arsinoe leans against her on the other side. Camden leans against her legs. Despite words of reassurance, many boats have already left the Sealhead to go out searching, including Matthew on the *Whistler*, and Ms. Baxter said she would take her *Edna* out into deeper waters.

Jules looks out at the cove. From where she stands on the pier, the sea looks vast and mean. For the first time in Jules's life, it looks ugly. Indifferent and unblinking, nothing but grasping waves and a seafloor sated by bones.

She has hated the sea only one time before: the night they tried to escape and it refused to release its hold on Arsinoe. Bobbing against that mist, thick as a net, she had hated it so much she had spit in it.

But she had only been a child. Surely the Goddess would not hold on to that one bitter spell and wait all these cruel years to send it back on her.

"I don't know why we're doing so much," someone whispers, "for an upstart boy who smells of the mainland."

Jules rounds on the small crowd. "What did you say?" she asks. Her teacup shatters in her fist.

"Easy, Jules," Arsinoe says, and drags down her arm. "We'll find him."

"I won't hear any word spoken against Joseph," Jules growls. "Not until he's returned. Not until you can be brave enough to say it to his face."

"Come away, Jules," Arsinoe says as the crowd backs down from Jules's fists. "We'll find him."

"How?" Jules asks. But she lets Arsinoe lead her off the pier. "Arsinoe, I've never been so scared."

"Don't be," the queen says. "I have a plan."

"Why does that frighten me?" Billy mutters, and follows them off the docks.

Arsinoe, Jules, and Billy leave Wolf Spring within the hour on three of Reed Anderson's saddle horses. Arsinoe's and Billy's are long-legged and finely boned. Jules's mount is thicker, stronger, so that it can occasionally support the extra weight of a mountain cat.

A change of Joseph's clothes is tucked into a bag behind Arsinoe's saddle, along with a sharp silver knife.

THE WESTERN COAST

When Mirabella wakes, she is alone beneath Elizabeth's cloak. The storm has passed, and the fire has burned down, but she is still warm enough from the memory of the boy's embraces. He was her first. How excited Bree will be to find out . . . if Mirabella can ever return to Rolanth to tell her.

She pokes her head out. It is still early. The water does not yet sparkle, but day has begun to coat the beach with gray, hazy light. The boy sits with his back to her, dressed again in his trousers and shirt, his head in his hands.

Mirabella pushes up onto one elbow. Her dress is somewhere underneath her. She considers trying to discreetly slip back into it.

"Are you well?" she asks quietly.

He turns slightly.

"I am," he says. He closes his eyes. "Thank you."

Mirabella blushes. He is just as handsome in the day as he was beside the fire. She wishes he would come back and lie with her. He seems so far away.

"What," he says, still half turned. "What happened?"

"You do not remember?"

"I remember the storm, and you and me," he says, and stops. "I just don't understand how it . . . How I could have done this."

Mirabella sits up and tugs the cloak around her. "You did not want to," she says, alarmed. "You did not like it."

"I did like it," he says. "It was wonderful. None of this . . . None of it is your fault."

She sighs, relieved, and moves close to wrap them both in the cloak. She kisses his shoulder and then his neck. "Come back to me, then," she whispers. "It is not day yet."

He closes his eyes when her lips touch his temple. For a moment she thinks he might resist her altogether, but then he turns and takes her in his arms. He kisses her fiercely and presses her into the sand beside the spent coals.

"I don't know what I'm doing," he whispers.

"You seem to know very well what you are doing," Mirabella says, and smiles. "And you may do it again."

"I want to. God damn it all but I want to."

He pulls back to look into her eyes.

She watches his expression change from disbelief to despair.

"No," he says. "Oh no."

"What is it?" she asks. "What is the matter?"

"You're a queen," he croaks. "You're Mirabella." He backs away.

He had not recognized her then, last night. A part of her had wondered, feared that he would return her to Rolanth. But a larger part had not cared.

"No," he says again, and she laughs.

"It is all right. It is not wrong, to lie with a queen. You will not be punished. You will not die."

"What are you doing here?" he asks. "Why aren't you in Rolanth? Why do you have a white cloak?"

She studies him warily. It is not the fact that she is a queen that he regrets.

"What is your name?" she asks.

He is not an Arron; he does not have the coloring. And his clothes have the look of a craftsman, well-worn and many times mended. He must have sailed from a great distance. His accent is different from any she has ever heard.

"My name is Joseph Sandrin."

Mirabella's blood runs cold. She knows that name. He is the boy who loves Arsinoe. The one who was banished for trying to help her escape.

She takes up her dress from the sand and slips into it quickly while underneath Elizabeth's cloak. She has slept with the boy her sister loves. Her stomach lurches.

"Did you think that I was her?" she asks, finishing the fastenings of her dress. "Did you think that I was Arsinoe?"

Given his confusion from the storm and the cold, that might absolve him at least.

"What?" he asks. "No!"

And then he laughs in surprise.

"If I had touched Arsinoe the way I touched you"—he stops and turns solemn once again—"she'd have hit me."

Hit him. Yes. Arsinoe always hit first when they were children. Especially if she really cared for you.

Joseph stares out at the waves. The water is quiet now. Shimmering and calm, playing innocent after last night's rages and mischief.

"Why did this have to happen?" he asks. "After I waited so long for her."

"For who?"

"For the girl I've loved my whole life." He does not give Mirabella her name. Fine, then. Let him keep it.

"She does not ever need to know," Mirabella says. "You are unhurt. You are alive. You can go home."

Joseph shakes his head. "I will know." He looks at her and touches her cheek. "The damage has already been done."

"Do not say that. Damage, like what happened was something terrible. We did not know!"

Joseph does not look at her. He stares sadly at the sea. "Mirabella. It might have been better if you had let me drown."

They cannot stay on the beach forever. They dig in the low tide's sand for cockles and clams and then dry their rewetted clothes beside a fresh fire, but they are lingering. Their time is up.

"Where will you go?" Mirabella asks.

"Inland, to the road. I was to ride the coaches back to Wolf Spring. I suppose I still will."

Joseph looks at the queen by his side. She is nothing at all like Arsinoe. And nothing at all like he expected. He has heard that Mirabella lives as though she is already crowned, that you must drop to your knees if she passes in the street. He has heard she is locked away in the Westwood estate or kept carefully hidden in the temple. In his mind, she became a holiday ornament, only taken out during celebrations and never to be played with.

This Mirabella is not like that. She is wild and brave. Her black hair is not braided or pinned to her head. He wonders if this is the queen who everyone in Rolanth sees. If all the rumors have been untrue. Or perhaps this Mirabella only appears on beaches, after a storm. If that is so, then she is his and his alone.

They kick sand over the remains of the dead fire, and Mirabella leads Joseph up the path to the top of the cliffs.

"It is easier going up than down," she says, and shows him the cuts on her palms.

When they reach the top, they walk together through the trees, toward the road.

"You will probably have to walk to the next town to find a coach," Mirabella says. "I had been following this road for at least a day and I did not hear many pass me by."

Joseph stops. "What are you doing out here? Why aren't you in Rolanth, surrounded by your future court?"

It sounds like mocking, the way he says that. But that is not the way he means it. He takes her hand. "It is not safe to be out here alone."

"You sound like my friend Bree," she says. "I will be fine."

"It has occurred to me that you are headed south because Katharine and Arsinoe are in the south. But that can't be. Movements against the other queens are not allowed until after Beltane, unless the rules have changed. Have they? I have been gone a long time."

"They have not changed," she says. "I slip away on occasion. To be by myself. It is lucky for you that I did!"

"That's true," Joseph says, and smiles. "I suppose I owe you."

"I suppose you do."

They have nearly reached the road, but they are not eager to part. Their steps slow, almost to dragging. When Joseph suggests that he accompany her farther south, Mirabella kisses him on the cheek.

One kiss leads to more. They will have so little of each other, they must take what they can. By the time the sun begins to sink, they have not traveled far, but at least beneath the trees, it is easier to find wood for a fire.

THE ROAD FROM WOLF SPRING

*J*ules uses her gift to urge the horses faster. They have never been so game in their lives. Even so, they and their riders must all rest for the night in Highgate, and upon reaching the outskirts of Indrid Down, Arsinoe uses Billy's father's money to wheedle them new mounts, as well as a cart-lead back to Wolf Spring for the horses loaned to them.

Jules pats each of their old mounts and kisses their cheeks. They were good, and they will be sore from the speed of the journey.

"All right," Arsinoe says. "Let's go."

"Wait a minute, at least," Billy says, stretching his back. He is a pampered city son, unused to haste and dozing in the saddle. "I haven't even adjusted my stirrups."

"You can ride without them."

"Not as well as if I use them."

He reaches for the leathers and the girls give in, taking a

moment to adjust their own stirrups. They check and double-check their girths, and Jules feeds Camden a strip of dried, smoked fish.

Arsinoe would like to be on the road. Whenever they stop, Jules looks miserable. But they are nearly there. The point where Joseph would have sailed around Cape Horn, and where the storm might have come upon him.

"We take to the woods now," Arsinoe says.

"Why's that?" Billy asks.

"You'll see."

She swings into the saddle and turns around to face the spires of the Volroy. Indrid Down is her sister's city, for now, and as such, Arsinoe is forbidden to enter without an invitation. But after Beltane, that will change, and if she ascends, those spires will be hers, even though it makes her dizzy just to look at them.

They ride fast through the maze of cobblestone streets, out to where the roads change to gravel, and then to dirt, until they jump the last ditch and disappear into the trees. The going is slower in the forest, and the Indrid Down horses do not like it—fancy, jet-black things that they are—but Jules manages to keep them moving. Camden is tired, and rides draped across the front of Jules's saddle, massive and purring and clinging to the horse's neck. It is a testament to the strength of Jules's gift that her horse does not drop dead from fright.

"We should have kept to the roads," Billy says. No one answers, and he says no more. Since they left Wolf Spring, no one has said what they all know to be true: if Joseph went into the frigid water, he is gone. Dead within minutes, and no amount of searching will bring him back. They will know soon. If Arsinoe's spell leads them to the water's edge, they will know for sure.

When they step into a clearing large enough to hold them all, and a fire besides, Arsinoe halts her mount.

"All right," she says. "Let's gather wood."

"Gather wood? We've only just started on these horses," says Billy.

Arsinoe pulls together fallen branches. The fire does not need to last long. Jules strips birch bark with her knife and drops a mound of white- and peach-colored curls over the top of the pile.

She kneels beside the fire as Arsinoe lights the match. "Are you going to need my hair?" Jules asks.

Arsinoe looks at her, surprised. But of course she knows. Jules has always been able to read her better than anyone else.

Arsinoe reaches into her leather bag and pulls out the small silver blade. She takes it from its sheath. It is slightly curved, sharp and mean-looking, and longer than their common knives by half. She takes out the clothes of Joseph's that she brought and sets the knife on top of them.

"What's going on?" Billy asks. "What are you doing?"

Arsinoe feeds the fire up higher with dry weeds and small twigs. There is no one around for a long way in all directions. They passed no fences coming in, and heard no barking dogs.

It is windless and a little warm and eerily silent except for the pop and crackle of burning wood.

Jules rolls up her sleeve.

"I thought you made flowers bloom and forced cougars to balance books on their heads," Billy whispers.

"Jules doesn't force that cat to do anything." Arsinoe grabs the knife and searches through the pile of clothes with the tip. "And she can make flowers bloom. Not me, though. All I've got is this."

"Low magic," Jules explains.

"Magic for the giftless." Arsinoe grabs Joseph's shirt and tears a strip from the bottom with her teeth.

"Why do I not like the sound of that?" Billy asks. "Why does it seem like you've kept it a secret?"

"Because I have," Arsinoe says.

"Because it lies," says Jules. "Because it kicks back."

"Then why are you using it now?" asks Billy.

Arsinoe tilts the knife back and forth. "Do you want to find Joseph? Or not?"

Jules watches it fearfully as it wags in Arsinoe's hand. She has never fooled about with low magic, not even as a child, when many of the island grew curious. Low magic is not something to be played at. It is not owned, like a gift is. It is something let off its leash. The priestesses of the temple sometimes call it a sideways prayer: perhaps answered and perhaps not, but always with a price.

"All right," Jules says, and holds her hand out.

"Wait!" Billy says before Arsinoe can make a single cut. "Joseph wouldn't want you to do this. He wouldn't approve of it!"

"I know. But he would do it for me, if I were the one who was missing."

"Close your eyes," Arsinoe says. "Think of Joseph. Think of nothing else but Joseph."

Jules nods. Arsinoe takes a steady breath and cuts into the meat of Jules's hand, into the soft mound of flesh just above her thumb. Thin red blood runs in stripes, circling around to drip to the ground. Arsinoe slices carefully, carving out the elaborate web of symbols that Madrigal showed her.

She holds Jules's hand above Joseph's shirt. "Squeeze."

Jules closes her fingers. Blood drizzles onto the fabric. When there is enough, Arsinoe drops the bloody mess onto the fire and quickly binds Jules's cuts with the strip of cloth she tore.

"Breathe the smoke."

"Did you take too much blood?" Jules asks. "I don't feel right. My eyes . . ."

"Don't be afraid. Think of Joseph."

The smoke smells acrid from the burning blood. Arsinoe and Billy watch with morbid fascination as Jules breathes it in and the spell inside it hollows her out. It makes of Jules a vacant vessel for whatever the smoke desires. If Arsinoe has done everything right, what it will desire is Joseph.

"Is she all right?" Billy asks.

"She will be," Arsinoe says, though truly, she does not know. It does not matter now. It is too late to turn back.

Arsinoe and Billy lead the horses in Jules's wake as she lumbers jerkily through the trees. It is not easy; the horses are skittish and nervous without Jules's gift to calm them, and they are afraid of the thing that Jules has become: magic encased in skin, with no person left inside.

"What are you doing to her?" Billy whispers.

"I am not doing anything to her," Arsinoe replies. "She's looking for Joseph."

It is looking for Joseph. It is not Jules. But when he is found, it will let Jules go, or so she hopes.

Camden bumps against Arsinoe's leg and grunts nervously. The spell seems to have made the cougar slightly ill. She does not want to be near the shell that is and is not Jules, and stays close to Arsinoe and the horses.

Billy looks from the cat to Arsinoe.

"How long have you been doing . . . that?" he asks, and jerks his head over his shoulder.

"Why?"

"Because I don't think you know quite how to do it," he says.

The corners of his mouth turn in a disappointed frown. Arsinoe punches him in the arm.

"It's working, isn't it? And besides, I don't think that you are exactly the best person to judge."

Jules told her that Joseph thought Billy was already half in love with her. But he is not. Arsinoe sees through him, all the way down to his father's darker designs. He will marry the queen. *The* queen, for *the* crown. But it has been pleasant, becoming his friend. And it is not as if she does not understand his reasons.

Ahead, Jules moans. Then she half shouts, and breaks toward the coast. Toward the water. Arsinoe looks at Billy nervously, and he squeezes her shoulder.

A moment later, Jules changes direction and darts straight ahead.

Arsinoe shoves her horse's reins into Billy's hands.

"Take them," she sputters. "Cam, with me!"

The cougar needs no more encouragement. She seems to sense that Jules is returning to herself. Her ears prick forward and she purrs as they run together after Jules.

Joseph and Mirabella walk hand in hand. Even after spending a long morning beside a fire, they have to be nearing the capital. No matter how slow they walk, they must soon part. Neither can put it off any longer.

Joseph will return to Wolf Spring. To his girl, and to where he belongs, and this strange interlude will be over.

But not forgotten.

"It is foolish to be sad," Mirabella said the night before, as they lay together. "Things are the way they are. Even if you were free, I could never keep you."

Mirabella freezes at movement in the trees, and Joseph steps protectively in front of her. Perhaps it is a search party from Rolanth. She almost hopes so. Then they will drag her off, and she will not have to walk away from him of her own accord.

A girl's cry sounds through the woods. Joseph's fingers slip from hers.

"Jules?" he calls out. "Jules!"

He looks back at Mirabella, perhaps with regret. Then he runs through the trees.

Mirabella follows at a safe distance. Just close enough to see the girl who crashes through the leaves, running through low brush like an animal.

"Joseph!"

The girl throws herself against his chest with no grace, and he wraps his arms around her. She sobs, very loud sobs for a body so small.

"Your mother had a dream," she says. "I was so afraid!"

"I am fine, Jules." He kisses her head. She jumps up and presses her lips to his.

Mirabella's heart feels as if it is hanging on the outside of her chest. She shrinks back into the trees as Joseph kisses this girl he has loved his whole life.

Something else shakes the brush, and a large golden cat jumps up on them both.

Mirabella watches as they pet and stroke the cougar. They are naturalists, then. And such a strong familiar is befitting a queen. Arsinoe must be near. Arsinoe, her sister.

And then she sees her. Running up with a grin that Mirabella recognizes, her short hair flying over her shoulders.

Mirabella wants to shout. She wants to hold her arms wide open. But she is too afraid to move. It has been so long since she has seen Arsinoe, but she is just the same. There are even shadows of dirt on her impish face.

Through the trees, another boy approaches, leading three horses. Perhaps an attendant.

"We thought you were dead," Arsinoe says.

"I see that. You didn't even bother to bring a fourth horse."

Everyone laughs except the girl, Jules.

"That is not funny . . . yet," she says.

They do not see Mirabella. She watches them embrace, and listens to their laughter. But no matter how many times she opens her mouth, she cannot find the courage to speak. Instead she ducks behind a tree and suffers quietly. It will not be long before they walk away.

Arsinoe breathes a sigh of relief watching Jules and Joseph embrace. Jules is herself again. The moment she saw Joseph, the spell released her.

"Are you hurt?" Billy calls from farther back. The horses are still nervous, and he has his hands full trying to hold them steady.

"No," says Joseph. "But the boat's gone. I got caught in the squall and it went under. I barely made it to the shore."

"I thought I taught you to sail better than that," Billy says, and laughs.

"You didn't teach him to sail at all," Arsinoe says over her shoulder. "He's been on the boats since he was old enough to walk."

"Jules." Joseph looks down at her hand, wrapped in blood-soaked cloth. "What happened?"

"Later," Arsinoe interjects. "Isn't it enough that you are not drowned? And we ought to get you out of these woods and over a hot plate of food."

"You're right," says Joseph. He puts an arm around Jules. As he does, he glances back, into the trees. Arsinoe's eyes follow, and she sees a flash of black skirt. As they leave the meadow, she discreetly drops her knife. It is easy enough to pretend to notice it missing a moment later, and go back for it alone.

Mirabella does not hear anything before Arsinoe steps around the tree trunk. Not so much as a snapping twig.

"Arsinoe!"

"You're not very good at hiding," Arsinoe says. "Those lovely black skirts of yours are sticking out all over."

Mirabella stiffens at the tone of Arsinoe's voice. Her eyes flicker to Arsinoe's hand, curled around the handle of a knife. Everyone told her that her sisters were weak. That killing them would be easy. But it does not feel easy. So far, Arsinoe is much better at this game.

"What are you doing here?" Arsinoe asks.

"I do not know," says Mirabella. She sounds like a fool. When she left Rolanth, she never imagined she would meet one of her sisters and hear her voice. But here they are. Together, as if they were led.

"You have grown tall," Mirabella says.

Arsinoe snorts. "Tall."

"Do you remember me?"

"I know who you are."

"That is not what I asked," says Mirabella. It is hard to believe how much she wants to reach out to Arsinoe. She had not realized until this moment how much she has missed her.

She takes a half step forward. Arsinoe steps back and tightens her grip on the knife

"That is not why I am here," Mirabella says.

"I don't care why you're here."

"You do not remember, then," says Mirabella. "That is all right. I remember enough for us both. And I will tell you, if you will listen."

"Listen to what?" Arsinoe's eyes dart suspiciously to the shadows of the trees. The naturalists have taught her to be afraid. They have taught her to hate, just as the temple has tried to teach Mirabella. But it has all been lies.

Mirabella holds out her hand. She does not know what she will do if Arsinoe takes it, but she has to try.

Hoofbeats rumble. Arsinoe steps back as riders burst through the trees. They are not alone anymore. Armed priestesses close in on them, circling and circling.

"What is this?" Arsinoe growls. "An ambush?" She glances at the knife in her hand as if considering taking Mirabella hostage. "Jules!" she shouts instead. "Jules!"

It is only moments before the girl and the cougar bound into the clearing, with Joseph close behind. But they are cut off. The priestesses use their mounts to push them into a tight group.

"No, Arsinoe," Mirabella starts.

"Queen Mirabella!"

Mirabella scowls. It is Rho, seated astride a tall white horse. She holds the reins in one hand. In the other, she carries one of the long, serrated knives of the temple.

"Are you injured?"

"No. I am fine! I am safe! Stop this!"

Rho charges the horse in between the sisters, so violently that Arsinoe falls back onto the leaves.

"Rho, stop!"

"No," Rho says. She drags Mirabella up into the saddle in front of her as though she weighs nothing. "It is too soon for this," she says loudly. "Not even you can break the rules. Save your killing for after the Quickening!"

On the ground, Arsinoe glares up at her. Mirabella shakes her head, but it is no good. Rho signals to the priestesses, and they gallop off together, veering north and leaving Arsinoe and Joseph far behind.

"The High Priestess is not pleased with you, my queen," Rho says into Mirabella's ear. "You should not have run away."

STARFALL LAKE

✺

———————————   ◊   ———————————

*L*uca meets Sara Westwood on the bank of Starfall
Lake. It is far inland from Rolanth, a large, deep
lake with more width than length. It is where the Blue Heron
River originates and where they brought Mirabella to meet
Luca for the first time. It is a long way to come for a pot of tea
and a cooling lunch, but at least there are fewer ears pressed
against doors to hear what they are saying.

Sara greets the High Priestess and bows. More gray has
come into her hair this year, and there are faint lines in the corners of her eyes. By the end of the Ascension, Sara may become
an old woman.

"Has there been no word?" she asks.

"Nothing yet," says Luca. "But Rho will find her."

Sara stares out across the steely blue lake. "Our Mira,"
she says sadly. "I did not know she was unhappy. After she
first came to us, I never expected she would begin to hide her

emotions. What if she is hurt?"

"She is not hurt. The Goddess will protect her."

"But what will we do?" Sara asks. "I do not know how much longer we can keep this secret. The servants begin to suspect."

"They will have no proof, once Mirabella is returned. Do not worry. No one will ever know that she was gone."

"What if it is not Rho who locates her? What if—"

Luca grasps her arm. If the High Priestess's touch has been good for anything, it has always been good at stemming panic. And Luca has no time for panic today. She did not ask Sara to come all this way just to calm her fears.

She leads Sara up the bank, to a copse of evergreens and a large stone, dark and weathered and flat as a table. Her priestesses have set it with tea and bread and soup reheated over a small cooking fire.

Luca readies her old bones and climbs onto the rock. She is pleased to discover it is not a difficult climb, and they have set out a pillow for her, along with a soft folded blanket.

"Will you sit with me?" she asks. "And eat?"

"I will eat," Sara says, looking gravely at the stone table. "But I will not sit, High Priestess, if it is all the same to you."

"Why not?"

"That stone is sacred," Sara explains. "Elemental priestesses once sacrificed hares on it and threw their hearts into the lake."

Luca runs her hand across the rock. It seems more than just a rock now, knowing all the blood it has drunk. And it is not only rabbits' blood it has tasted, she is sure. So many things on the island are more than what they seem. So many places where the Goddess's eye is always open. It is fitting that Luca has come to this one, to discuss the sacrifice of queens.

Luca tears the bread in half and hands a piece to Sara. It is a good, soft bread, with an oat crust, but Sara does not take a bite. She worries it between her fingers until it turns to crumb.

"I never thought she would do something like this," Sara says. "She has always been so dutiful."

"Not always," Luca notes, and chews. There was a time when Mirabella listened to no one, and nothing. But that was long ago, and far away from the dignified young queen she has become.

"What are we to do?"

Luca swallows her tea and fights the urge to slap Sara across the face. Sara is a good woman, and her friend these many years. But there is no firmness in her jaw. It will take a backbone of steel to hold together a Black Council led by her. Sometimes, Luca pities the High Priestess who comes after, for she will be the one who has to do it.

"What are we to do," Luca says. "Indeed. Tell me, Sara, what do you know about the White-Handed Queens?"

"They are blessed," she says hesitantly. "Fourth-borns."

"Yes, but not only that. A queen is said to be White-Handed any time her sisters are killed by means other than her own doing. Be that by being drowned by the Midwife before they come of age, or put to death for some unfortunate curse, or,"

Luca says slowly, "being sacrificed by the island, for the one true queen."

"I had not heard of that," says Sara.

"It is an old legend. Or at least, I thought it was only a legend. Something of a whisper, about the Sacrificial Years. It is so old, it is no wonder we have overlooked the signs."

"What signs?"

"The weakness of Arsinoe and Katharine. The boundless strength of our Mira. And of course, Mirabella's own reluctance to kill." Luca presses her hand to her forehead. "I am ashamed to say that all this time, I thought that her only flaw."

"I do not understand," Sara says. "You believe that Mirabella is reluctant to kill because she is meant to be White-Handed? And Arsinoe and Katharine . . . will be sacrificed?"

"They are made as sacred offerings on the night of the Quickening."

Luca drums her fingers on the stone. It vibrates down deep, like a heartbeat.

"These are old tales," she says. "Tales that tell of a queen, born much stronger than her sisters. The only true queen born to that cycle. On the night of the Quickening, the people recognize this, and feed the other queens into the fires."

Luca waits tensely. Sara does not speak for a long time. She stands still, her hands clasped piously over her stomach.

"That would be much easier," she says finally, and Luca relaxes. Sara's eyes are downcast, but whether she truly believes the tale does not matter. Rho is right. Sara will do as the temple bids.

"Do not burden yourself," Luca says. "What comes to pass will come to pass. It is only that I would see the island prepared. You have always been a strong voice for the temple, Sara. It would be best if the people began to hear of this before they must watch it happen."

Sara nods. She will be as good at spreading their tale as she has been at expanding Mirabella's fame. By the night of the Quickening, the people will be waiting and wondering. Perhaps they will pick up the knives themselves.

One of the novice priestesses approaches to warm their cups with fresh tea. Through the folds of her robes, Luca glimpses the silver of the temple's long, serrated blades. Come Beltane, every faithful priestess will carry one.

It is not a lie, Rho told her. It is part truth. And it is for the good of the island. Someone must take things in hand, if their chosen queen will not.

After the Quickening Ceremony, when the crowd at Beltane is drunk, and in ecstasy from Mirabella's performance, the priestesses will step forward to take Arsinoe's and Katharine's heads. They will cut them at the necks and sever the arms at the shoulders. And when it is over, they will have a new queen.

GREAVESDRAKE MANOR

———————— ⚜ ————————

*T*he Arrons welcome the Chatworth delegation the only way they know how: with a party, though not a great, glittering party in the north ballroom. While there is plenty that glitters, the party they throw for the Chatworth boy is meant to be an introduction between the queen and her potential king-consort. They will hold this meeting in the small dining room on the second floor, where it can be more intimate. And where Katharine can be placed at the heart, like a centerpiece.

It is exciting to have the house prepared for a party again, and filling up with people. Cousin Lucian has returned with servants from his household, and he bows whenever he sees Katharine in the halls. There is a curious smile on his face when he does it, and she cannot decide whether the joke is with her or on her.

Unfortunately, the return of people to Greavesdrake also

meant the return of Genevieve, who has taken her exile very personally. As the younger sister, she hates when Natalia excludes her, and since her return has insisted on being involved in every aspect of the planning.

"My scalp is still sore from so many styles braided into it," Katharine says, leaning back against Pietyr. They have hidden themselves away in the stacks of the library, one of the few places she can be alone with Pietyr since Genevieve returned.

"Poor Giselle's fingers must ache as well," she continues. "Genevieve is never pleased with my hair."

"Your hair is beautiful," says Pietyr. "It is perfect."

Genevieve had ordered braid after braid and bun after bun. She ordered beads of jet and pearl to be woven in, only to tear them out again. And all that just to declare that Katharine's neck is still too thin, and she should wear her hair down to hide it.

"Sometimes, I think that she wants me to fail," Katharine whispers.

"Do not listen to her," Pietyr says, and kisses a sore red scab near her temple. "After the suitor has gone, Natalia will order her back to her house in the city. You will not have to see her again until Beltane."

She twists in his arms to kiss him.

"You must kiss the Chatworth boy just like that," he says. "It will be difficult to find the right moment during this small, ill-conceived dinner party. But there will be a time when you can steal away."

"What if I do not like him?"

"You may grow to. But if you do not, it does not matter. You are the queen and must have your choice of consorts."

He touches her cheek and then lifts her chin. He would not see any of the delegates ensnared by Mirabella. And neither would she.

William Chatworth Jr. is a handsome enough boy. His looks are not striking, like Pietyr's, but he has strong shoulders, a solid jawline, and very short hair the color of wet sand. His eyes are an unremarkable shade of brown, but they are steady, even seated as he is in the midst of a poisoners' dinner party.

He came alone, without his mother or even his father, and with only two attendants as an escort. From the tense look on his face, it was not his idea. He has been thrown into the wolves' den. But there are worse houses for a mainlander to stumble into. Many of the Arrons have had close contact with the last king-consort. Of all the families on the island, they have the most knowledge of the mainland and its customs.

Aside from a stiff bow and an introduction, he and Katharine have not spoken. He has spent most of the evening talking with Cousin Lucian, but now and again, Katharine raises her head and finds him studying her.

The meal is served: seared pink medallions of meat with a sliver of golden baked potato tart. Untainted, of course. The Arrons do their best to look impressed, though only those who are terribly hungry will do more than pick at it.

Genevieve takes Katharine by the arm and digs her fingers in deep. "Do not make a pig of yourself," she says, "just because there is no poison in it."

To further make the point, she twists the skin inside Katharine's elbow. It hurts so badly that Katharine nearly cries out. Tomorrow there will be a dark black bruise to be covered by sleeves and gloves.

Across the table, Pietyr watches with a tightened jaw. He looks ready to leap across their dinner plates and wrap his hands around Genevieve's neck. Katharine catches his eye, and he seems to relax. He was right, after all. It is only until the Chatworth boy leaves. Then Genevieve will be banished again.

After the dinner is over, with the food pushed back and forth to appear as though eaten, Natalia moves the party into the drawing room. Edmund serves the digestif, which must be poisoned, for the Arrons flock to it like birds to a crust of bread. A maid carries a silver tray with a green bottle and two glasses: something special for the queen and her suitor.

"Let me," Katharine says. She takes the bottle by the neck and the glasses by the stems. Across the room, Cousin Lucian sees her coming and bows away from the Chatworth boy's side.

"Will you take a drink, William Junior?" she asks.

"Of course, Queen Katharine."

She pours for them both, and the champagne sparkles and fizzes.

"You may call me Katharine, if you'd like," she says. "Or even only Kat. I know that the full title can be a mouthful."

"I'm not used to saying it," he says. "I should have practiced."

"There will be plenty of time for that."

"And please, call me Billy. Or William. Some folk here have taken to calling me Junior, but I would rather it didn't spread."

"It is a strange custom, naming the child the same as the parent. Almost as if the parent hopes to one day inherit the body."

They chuckle together.

"According to my father, a fine enough name can be used again," he says.

Katharine laughs. She looks around the room. "Everyone is watching us and pretending that they are not. I would not have chosen to meet you this way."

"Oh?" he says. "What way would you have preferred?"

"On a trail somewhere, on a fine spring day. On horses so that you would have to prove your mettle by catching me."

"You don't think that my coming here on my own proves my mettle?"

"That is true," she says. "It most certainly does."

He is nervous, and drinking fast. Katharine refills his glass.

"The Arrons have lived here a long time," he says, and Katharine nods.

The Arrons are entrenched at Greavesdrake. And it is more than their poisons and their morbid artwork on the walls—still lifes of butchered meat and flowers, and black snakes curled around nudes. They have seeped into the manor itself. Now every inch of wood and shadow is also a part of them.

"Of course, the Arrons' ancestral estate lies in Prynn," Katharine says. "Greavesdrake Manor is the rightful home of the stewards of the queen, and it goes as the queen goes."

"You mean that if Arsinoe becomes queen, the Milones would live here?" Billy closes his mouth quickly over the question, as if he has been instructed not to mention her sisters' names.

"Yes," Katharine replies. "Do you think they would like it? Do you think it would suit them?"

"No," he answers, and raises his eyes to the high ceilings, the tall windows obscured with velvet drape. "I think they'd be more likely to live in tents in the yard."

Katharine blurts laughter. Real laughter, and her eyes find Pietyr's, out of guilt. He has drawn away into the far corner, pretending to listen to the council concerns of Renata Hargrove and Margaret Beaulin, but the whole time watching Katharine jealously. She does not want to think so, but it would be easier if Pietyr were not there at all.

"Billy," she says, "would you care to see more of the manor?"

"It would be a pleasure."

No one objects when they move into the hall together, though there is a momentary hush in the already hushed conversation. The second they are free of the drawing room, Katharine takes a great, heaving sigh. When the mainlander looks at her strangely, she blushes.

"Sometimes I think I have had so much ceremony I could scream," she says.

He smiles. "I know what you mean."

She does not think that he does. But he will soon enough. The entire Beltane Festival is one ritual after another: the Hunt, the Disembarking, and the Quickening. His poor mainland mind will addle trying to remember all the rules and decorum.

"There will be no break from it, I suppose," he says. "Not even from meetings of this kind. How many suitors will there be, Queen Katharine?"

"I do not know," she says. "Once, there were many. But now Natalia thinks it will only be six or seven."

But even that number seems a burden when she thinks of Pietyr. How can she ask him to stand aside and watch? It is what he says he wants, but she knows that he is lying.

"You don't sound excited," Chatworth says. "None of you queens seems to want to be courted. The girls I know back home would go mad to receive so many suitors."

Katharine tries to smile. She is letting it slip, leaving him open to be snatched up by Mirabella and the Westwoods. She forces herself to step in close and to tilt her face up to his.

When she kisses him, his lips are warm. He moves them against hers, and she almost pulls away. She will never be lost in him the way she is in Pietyr. There is no point even in hoping. She will have many more moments like this when she is queen. Passionless moments spent silently screaming until she can return to Pietyr.

"That was lovely," Chatworth says.

"Yes. It was."

They smile awkwardly. He did not sound like he meant it any more than she did. But they lean forward anyway, to do it again.

WOLF SPRING

❧

"You hate her, don't you?" Joseph asks, sitting with Arsinoe at the Milones' kitchen table as Madrigal washes fresh rune-cuts on Arsinoe's hand. They are all the way up her wrist now, with bloodletting wounds on the inside of each arm.

"Mirabella, you mean?" Arsinoe asks. "Of course I hate her."

"But why? When you don't even know her?"

For a moment in the forest, when Mirabella held out her hand, she almost made Arsinoe believe something different. And then the priestesses came, looking more like soldiers than temple servants, and whatever flicker was there vanished. Her sister is cunning and strong. She came very close. It must take all those soldiers to keep her in check. To keep her from stealing away and killing her sisters too soon.

"I don't think it is strange at all," Arsinoe says. "Don't you see? It has to be one of us. It has to be her. My whole life I have heard that it has to be her. That I have to die, so that she can lead. That I do not matter, because she's here."

Across the kitchen, Grandma Cait throws a towel over her shoulder, shooing off her crow, who flies into another room and returns with a jar of salve. She lands on the table and knocks it against the wood.

"I'm not touching that," says Madrigal. "It's oily and it smells."

"I'll do it then," Cait says gruffly, and uses the same towel to shoo her daughter out of her chair.

Cait's hands on Arsinoe's wounds are rough as she works the salve into the cuts. Rough because they are worried, but she says nothing. No one has said anything about Arsinoe's use of low magic. Since it brought Joseph home, even Jules has kept her mouth shut.

It is not in Cait's nature to hold her tongue. But chastising Arsinoe would do no good. She has been indulged for too long and has become used to doing as she pleases.

"You ought to let this air awhile. Before you wrap it up again."

Cait holds Arsinoe's hand a moment and then pats it firmly and sets it on the table. Arsinoe frowns. The Milones have loved her well, but they have loved her as one loves a doomed thing. Only Jules ever thought differently. And now Madrigal.

"I don't suppose it matters that none of those things are Mirabella's fault," Joseph says, and Cait smacks him with her towel.

"Stop defending that queen, Joseph Sandrin," she snaps.

"But she saved my life."

"Is that all it takes to buy your loyalty?" Cait asks, and Joseph and Arsinoe smile.

Joseph stands when Jules comes through the front door. He leans down and kisses Arsinoe on the forehead.

"You saved me too," he says. "You found me." He rests his hand on Arsinoe's shoulder. "But I don't want to see any more cuts on Jules, do you understand?"

"Not even if you go missing again?"

"Not even then."

She harrumphs. "You sound like a temple acolyte."

"Maybe so," he says. "But there are worse things to sound like."

Arsinoe does not see Jules again until much later, when Jules slips into their shared bedroom, with Camden behind her. Were it not for the sad dragging of the mountain cat's tail, Arsinoe might never have known that something was wrong.

"Jules? Are you just coming back?"

"Yes. Did I wake you?"

Arsinoe sits up and searches her bedside table until she finds her matches. She lights the candle to see Jules's troubled face.

"I wasn't sleeping that well, anyhow." Arsinoe holds her hand out to Camden, but the big cat only groans. "What's the matter? Has something happened?"

"No. I don't know." Jules climbs into her bed without

changing clothes. "I think that something might have happened with Joseph."

"What do you mean?"

"He's different since the accident."

Jules sits back quietly against her pillows, and Camden jumps up to lie beside her, and rests her large paws on her shoulder.

"Do you think," Jules starts. "Do you think something could have happened with your sister?"

"My sister?" Arsinoe repeats. Jules almost never refers to the other queens that way. It sounds near accusatory, though Arsinoe cannot believe that is how she means it. "No. Never. You are imagining things."

"He keeps finding ways to mention her," Jules says.

"Only because she saved him."

"They were together for two nights."

An uncomfortable ball forms in Arsinoe's gut. She wishes that Jules would stop talking about this. She does not want to know it.

"That doesn't mean anything. She was . . . she was likely using him to find me. Perhaps she even sent the storm."

"Maybe," says Jules.

"Have you asked him?" Arsinoe asks, and Jules shakes her head. "Then ask. I'm sure he will tell you there was nothing. Joseph has been waiting for you for years. He would never . . ."

Arsinoe pauses, and glances down the hall toward Madrigal's room. When Joseph came home, they had worked a spell.

Soaked in her blood and then knotted together. But she had destroyed it before it could be finished. Or at least she thought she had.

"Sleep, Jules," Arsinoe says, and puts out the light. "It will be better in the morning."

That night, neither girl sleeps well. Jules and Camden compete for space in the bed, grunting and pushing at each other with paws and knees. Arsinoe listens to the rustle of blankets for a long time. When she finally closes her eyes, her dreams are of Joseph, drowning in a bloodred sea.

In the morning, Cait sends Jules and Arsinoe down into town, on orders to procure proper festival clothes. Gowns, she said, and grimaced when she said it. Cait, like Arsinoe, has no use for gowns. The brown and green wool dresses she wears to tend her household are all she needs. But even she will need one. This Beltane will be the elder Milones' first since Jules was born. As Arsinoe's stewards, every Milone must attend. Beltane, Cait says, is for the young and the obligated.

"Will we see Joseph first?" Arsinoe asks.

Jules wrinkles her nose.

"To make him come shopping?"

"There is no reason we ought to suffer alone. He and I can try on jackets and get kicked out of Murrow's for eating crab claws. It'll be grand."

"All right," Jules says. "He will not be on the boats, anyway."

Joseph will not be on the boats for a very long while. It did not sit well with anyone to nearly lose him so soon after he was regained. Least of all with his mother. She has grounded him and Jonah both and set them instead to working in the shipyard. Even Matthew has been restricted from going out too far on the *Whistler*, though that means sacrificing his best runs.

Arsinoe inhales warming morning air. Wolf Spring has begun its thaw. Soon enough, the trees will bud and everyone will be in much finer spirits.

"Wait, Jules! Arsinoe!"

A petite black crow soars overhead and wheels around to flap twice in Jules's face.

"Aria!" Jules sputters. Camden rears up to halfheartedly swat the bird, but the crow is too fast and makes it back to land at Madrigal's feet.

"I'm coming with you," Madrigal says. She looks very pretty in a light blue dress and tall brown boots. Her hair is curled and bounces around her shoulders. Over her arm is a basket draped in white cloth. Arsinoe smells baked bread.

"What for?" Jules asks.

"I know more about gowns than either of you," she says. "And it is too fine a day to spend indoors."

Jules and Arsinoe look at each other and sigh. After the poor night of sleep, neither has the energy to argue.

They find Joseph with Matthew, talking on the deck of the *Whistler*.

"Here they come," Matthew says with a broad smile. "Three of our favorite girls."

"Matthew Sandrin," Jules says, casting a glance at her mother. "You are too polite." But she grins when Joseph jumps onto the dock and pulls her close.

"They are very sweet," says Madrigal.

"They are, indeed, though I could stand to see less of it," Matthew says, and tosses a coil of rope at Joseph's head.

"We've come to take him away from you," says Arsinoe.

"And what will you give me in return? Your pretty company while I bring in the crab pots?"

Arsinoe blushes. Matthew Sandrin is the only boy who has ever been able to make her blush. How she used to envy Aunt Caragh, even as a child.

"Perhaps this will do for a trade." Madrigal holds out her basket. "Fresh oat bread and some cured ham. Two ripened hothouse tomatoes. The best we had. I ripened them myself."

Matthew leans over to take the basket.

"Thank you," he says. "This is unexpected."

"I will come back for the basket later," says Madrigal. "Will your run be long?"

"Not with my mother watching."

"Come on." Jules waves her hand. "If we get this over with soon enough, we can still make it to Luke's for tea."

Their destination is Murrow's Outfitters, the only likely place to find festival clothes suitable for a queen.

"Maybe one of those lace ones?" Joseph suggests once they are inside, and Arsinoe grasps one by the sleeve.

"Lace," she mutters, singsongy. "Lace, lace, I will strike you in the face."

"Not lace, then," he says. But there is not much to choose

from. What dresses they have are plain cotton things in blues and greens.

"Will you need something?" Arsinoe asks, and holds a jacket up to his chest. "Perhaps for the Hunt?"

"For the feast, you mean," Madrigal says. "Naturalist boys will be shirtless for the Hunt. Bare-chested, except for the symbols we paint on them. As this is your first Beltane, Jules, you had best think of some pretty markings for Joseph." She smiles and holds a dress up to Jules, who swats it away much like her cougar would. "Will Matthew join the Hunt this year?"

"I don't know," says Joseph. "He may. He may not. He says it is for the young."

"But Matthew is not old! He cannot be more than thirty!"

Joseph squeezes Jules's hand. Matthew is only twenty-seven. The same age as Luke. But Luke seems much younger. He has not known the sadness that Matthew has. The loss. All of Matthew's years must have felt long, after they took away Caragh.

"I'm going to go talk to the clerk," Joseph announces. "Perhaps they can still have things brought in from Indrid Down, if the fear of poisoned dresses has not taken hold yet."

"He doesn't seem different to me," Arsinoe whispers to Jules after he has gone.

"Perhaps you were right," Jules says.

"Why don't you take him and get out of here for a little while? We are not having any luck."

"Are you sure?" Jules glances at her mother. "I can stay."

"Go," Arsinoe says, and grimaces at a dress of lace and

black ribbons. "That way you can witness my shame for the first time at the Disembarking, like everyone else."

Jules nudges her shoulder, and Arsinoe watches as she goes to whisper into Joseph's ear, some foolish lovers' talk that she cannot ever imagine saying herself.

Of course Jules is wrong. Joseph may have done his share of looking, but he has only ever had one girl in his heart. Except as they leave the shop, Arsinoe catches Joseph's guilty reflection in the glass of the window.

"Arsinoe?" Madrigal asks. "What's the matter?"

"Nothing," she says, but she grasps Madrigal by the wrist. "That first spell beneath the tree, when Joseph came home . . . That did not come to pass. That was destroyed. Wasn't it?"

"I do not know," Madrigal answers. "I warned you not to burn it."

She had not warned her not to burn it, Arsinoe remembers as she and Madrigal walk through the streets toward the square and Gillespie's Bookshop. She had only suggested she should not have, after the charm had already been burned.

Low magic will come back to bite. How many times has she heard that and in how many voices? From Jules and from Cait. Long ago, from Caragh.

"What if we did some kind of harm?" she asks. "Some kind of wrong, to Joseph and Jules."

"If you did, there is nothing to be done about it now," Madrigal says. "It will work its will, out in the world. Whatever you did has to be borne." She shoves Arsinoe playfully. "My Jules is in love and happy. You are worrying for nothing."

But all through Luke's excellent tea service of poppy seed cake and diced chicken sandwiches, it is all she can think about. When Madrigal excuses herself to go to the docks to check on Matthew's afternoon catch, Arsinoe barely hears her.

"You know," Luke says, and the way he twists Hank's tail feathers tells her he has been working up to this for the last several minutes, "all this searching through Murrow's is a waste. When I could make you something twice as good as anything from his tailors."

Arsinoe looks at Luke and grins.

"Luke, that's brilliant," she says. "I do need you to make the most beautiful dress that anyone has ever seen. I just need you to make it to fit Jules."

Jules and Joseph sit beside Dogwood Pond on a wide, dead log while Camden paws at melting ice chunks to lick the water off her pads. Now that it is thawing, the pond is not as pretty as it was in hard winter. It is muddy and soggy and smells of decomposing plants. But it is still their place, the same place they have been sneaking away to since they were children.

"I don't think Arsinoe will ever find a dress," Joseph says. He throws a waterlogged stick into the open water near the pond's center. "Or if she does, I don't think Cait will be able to get her to wear it."

"I don't think it will matter," says Jules, "if she has no gift to show at the Quickening. The other day, I asked her what she was going to perform, and she said she was planning on gutting a fish. Making fillets."

Joseph chuckles. "That's our Arsinoe," he says.

"She is insufferable, sometimes."

Joseph holds Jules's hand and kisses it. It does not need to be bandaged anymore. The cuts from Arsinoe's spell have nearly healed. But she keeps it covered, anyway, as Arsinoe keeps her own arm and hand hidden when she is in town.

"Madrigal should be strung up for getting her involved in this," Joseph says.

"Yes, she should," Jules agrees. "Though I mind it less, since it brought you home. And less, too, since it has given Arsinoe hope. Let it keep her safe until her real gift comes."

"Isn't that what you and the cat are supposed to be for?"

So everyone says. Jules and Camden have been guardians to the queen for a long time. And they will continue to be until it is over, one way or another.

"Still, she does not have much time. She had best think of something, and it had best be grand. Beltane is only a few weeks away."

Joseph looks down.

She and Joseph have planned to be together, the first night of the festival. They have come very close already, in his bedroom or pressed into the mattress in the belly of the mainland boat, but Jules wanted to wait. She is a Beltane Begot, and somehow, she has always thought that her first time with Joseph would be at Beltane.

"I know you don't like to think about it," Joseph says. "But do you ever wonder what will happen if Arsinoe loses? What your life will be like?"

Jules plucks dead reeds beside the log and twists them. He did not say "killed." But that is what it means. And part of Jules has secretly thought that if Arsinoe died, she would find a way to die right along with her. That she would be there, fighting.

"I have not thought about it often," she says. "But I have. It doesn't seem like we should go on after that. But we will. I suppose I'll take over the house. The fields and the orchard. Goddess knows Madrigal isn't going to do it."

"She might. You don't know. And that would leave you free to think about other things."

"What other things?"

"There's a whole other world out there, Jules."

"You mean the mainland," she says.

"It's not so bad. There are parts of it that are astounding."

"Do you . . . want to go back there?"

"No," Joseph says, and takes her hand. "I would never. Unless you wanted to. I'm just saying that . . . if our world ends here, we could start over again, out there." He lowers his head. "I don't know why I'm talking about this. Why I'm thinking about it."

"Joseph," she says, and kisses his ear, "what is the matter?"

"I don't want to lie to you, Jules. But I don't want to hurt you, either."

He stands abruptly and walks to the edge of the pond.

"Something did happen the night that Mirabella saved me."
He stuffs his hands into his pockets and stares out at the water.
"I was almost drowned. Freezing cold. Delirious." He stops and
then curses under his breath. "Ah, Jules! I don't want to sound
as though I'm making excuses!"

"Excuses for what?" Jules asks quietly.

He turns to face her. "I was delirious at first," he says.
"Maybe even when it started. But then I wasn't. And she was
there, and I was there, and we . . ."

"You what?"

"I didn't mean for it to happen, Jules."

Perhaps not. But it had.

"Jules? God, Jules, please say something."

"What would you have me say?" she asks. It is difficult to
think. Her body is numb, made of the same wood she sits on.
A warm weight presses into her lap. Camden's heavy head. A
growl that is aimed at Joseph rumbles in her throat.

"Call me some horrible name," Joseph says. "Tell me what
a fool I am. Tell me . . . tell me you hate me."

"I could never hate you," she says. "But if you do not leave
now, my cat will tear your throat out."

ROLANTH

"Come away from that window, Mira," Luca says. "And try this on."

Mirabella gazes a few more seconds down at the cliffs of the Blackway, where she and Bree often held footraces as girls. Bree grew out of it, but Mirabella never had. Her love of the wind and the open spaces brought her to the edge of those cliffs often. Or at least it did, before every door was locked.

"What for?" Mirabella asks. "It is not much, and it can be tightened. It will fit."

Luca sets the garments down. They are the clothes Mirabella will wear the night of the Quickening Ceremony. Two gathered black bands of fabric that will be soaked and resoaked in a boil of herbs and extracts to keep them from burning off her body.

For the Quickening Ceremony, she will perform a fire dance.

"What will the music be?" Mirabella asks. "Strings? Flutes?"

"Drums," Luca replies. "A long line of great skin drums. To roll out a rhythm for you like a heartbeat."

Mirabella nods.

"It will be beautiful," Luca goes on. She lights a lamp with a long tapered candle, and leaves the top open. "The nighttime ceremony and the fire glowing orange. Every eye on the island will be on you."

"Yes," Mirabella says.

"Mira," Luca says, and sighs. "What is wrong with you?"

The High Priestess's tone is sympathetic. But it is also frustrated, as if she cannot understand why Mirabella should be unhappy. As if Mirabella should be glad to be home and captured, grateful that she was not whipped in the square.

But though Luca knows what happened on the road, how she met her sister and held out her hand, she does not know everything. She does not know that Mirabella also met a boy and that the meeting broke her heart. And she does not know that for just one moment, there was a flicker of trust in Arsinoe's eyes.

"Where is Elizabeth?" Mirabella asks. "You promised you would not send her away."

"And I have not," says Luca. "Not forever. She will be back from her punishment soon."

"I want to see her as soon as she returns."

"Of course, Mira. And she will want to see you. She was most worried."

Mirabella purses her lips. Yes, Bree and Elizabeth were most worried. And they were loyal. They did not give her up, even after a dozen welts were put upon their backs. She should have known that would happen. Just as she should have known that the temple would condemn Elizabeth as a conspirator the moment Mirabella was found wearing her white cloak. Mirabella said she had stolen it when Elizabeth was not looking. No one believed her.

She should have found a way to keep them safe. It will be hard to face Elizabeth when she returns. As it will be hard to face Arsinoe at Beltane, unable to explain how it had all been a mistake. Mirabella grimaces. Thinking of what lies ahead makes her chest tighten. Her only comfort is to relive her nights with Joseph, and even those are sullied by his love for another girl.

"He ran to her," she whispers, hardly realizing she is speaking aloud. "Like he had not seen her in a hundred years."

"What?" Luca asks. "Mirabella, what did you say?"

"Nothing." She holds her hand out toward the warmth of the lamp's flame. One flicker of her finger and the fire jumps from the wick and onto the back of her hand. Luca observes, pleased as it inches up Mirabella's wrist and around her arm like a curious worm. This is how it will start. Slow and warm. The drums will fill her ears. The fire will reach for her, and she will embrace it, let it have the run of her body as she spins with her arms flung out. She will wrap herself in it like chains and let it burn. Perhaps it will burn her love for her sisters right out of her heart.

* * *

Days later, Mirabella is walking through the woods near Westwood House when she hears a woodpecker rapping on a tree. She looks up. It is a small black-and-white tufted. Perhaps it is Pepper. She thinks it is him, though to her, one woodpecker tends to look much like the next.

"Keep to the path, Queen Mirabella."

One of her priestess escort nudges her back to the center. As if she would try to run, surrounded as she is. There are six of them now, and all young and fit. When the wind moves their cloaks, it reveals the silver glint of their mean, serrated knives. Had the priestesses always carried those? Mirabella does not think so. Certainly not so many and not so often. Now, it seems that every initiated priestess wears them.

"How things have changed," she says.

"They have, indeed," the priestess says. "And whose fault would that be?"

Ahead, the gabled roof of Westwood House rises through the trees, dotted with lightning rods like so many hairs. She cannot wait to get inside. There, she will be free at least to walk the halls. Perhaps she will take tea in to Sara, as a peace offering. Sara worried so severely when she ran away. There is so much white now, in her twisted bun. And when Mirabella was returned, she held her so tightly.

"Mira!"

Bree dashes up to them on the path, brown braids swinging. Her eyes are red as though she has been crying.

"Bree? What is the matter?"

Bree shoulders past the priestesses and takes hold of Mirabella's hands.

"Nothing," she says. But she cannot mask it. Her expression crumples.

"Bree, what is it?"

"It is Elizabeth," she says, and rounds on the priestesses with her teeth bared. "I ought to set your robes on fire!" she shouts. "I ought to murder you in your sleep!"

"Bree!"

Mirabella tugs her friend tight to her side.

"We told you she did not have anything to do with it!" Bree sobs. "We told you that the cloak was stolen!"

"What did you do?" Mirabella asks the priestesses. But they seem to be as alarmed as she is.

Mirabella and Bree start to run, pushing through the escort.

"Do not run, Queen Mirabella!"

Several try to grab her arms, but the effort is halfhearted, and she wrenches loose. They know where she is going. She and Bree race the rest of the way up the path, out of the trees, and around the side of the house.

Elizabeth is there in the drive. She stands with her back to them beside the stagnant stone fountain. The priestesses who accompanied her lower their eyes when Mirabella approaches.

Mirabella breathes a sigh of relief. Elizabeth is home. She seems stiff, but she is alive.

"Elizabeth?" Mirabella steps closer.

The young priestess half turns.

"I am all right," she says. "It is not so bad."

"What is not so bad?" Mirabella asks, and Elizabeth allows the sleeves of her robes to fall away.

They have cut off her left hand.

The stump is wrapped in rough white bandages, and blood has soaked through and dried brown.

Mirabella stumbles to her friend and drops to her knees, clutching Elizabeth's skirt. "No," she moans.

"They held me down," Elizabeth says. "But that was for the best. They used their knives to saw through, you see, and it took more time than with an ax. So it was better that they held me. It felt good to be able to fight and struggle."

"No!" Mirabella shouts, and feels Bree's hand on her back. Elizabeth touches the top of her head.

"Do not cry, Mira," she says. "It was not your fault."

But it was. Of course it was.

WOLF SPRING

" *S* he will forgive him soon," Madrigal says, speaking of Jules and Joseph. "As angry, and as hurt, as she is, she misses him more. And I believe him when he says he loves her. I don't think he has smiled once since she sent him away."

"How do you know?" Arsinoe asks, and Madrigal shrugs.

"Because I have been down to the docks," she says. "I have seen him working. All frowns. Not even your Billy can make him laugh."

Arsinoe's lips curl despite herself when Madrigal calls Billy that. Hers. It is a lie, but it is a funny one. And it is true what Madrigal says. Jules will forgive Joseph soon. And so will Arsinoe. It has not been easy for her either, to think of him with Mirabella. In some way, it has felt as though he betrayed her too.

"It does not suit him." Madrigal sighs. "Sandrins are not meant to be so serious. So sad. They were made to laugh and have not a care in the world."

"He deserves his misery," Arsinoe says. "Every cruel word she gives, and some from me besides. Who will take care of Jules if I fail and do not survive? I was counting on him to look after her."

"I will look after her," Madrigal says, but she does not meet Arsinoe's eyes when she says it. Madrigal has never been good at looking after people. And Jules would never allow her to.

"I suppose our Jules is perfectly equipped to take care of herself," Arsinoe says, her anger cooling. "And perhaps she will never have to try. I still may become queen."

"You may, indeed," Madrigal says. She takes up her small silver knife and passes it through the fire. "But the time for waiting is over. Now we will make something happen."

Madrigal picks up a jar filled with dark liquid. It is mostly Arsinoe's blood, both fresh and from the soaked cords she collected before. The cords have been rewetted with water from the cove. She walks to the trunk of the bent-over tree.

"What are you doing?" Arsinoe asks.

Madrigal does not reply. She splashes the jar onto the side of the hill, across the exposed slabs of sacred stone, across the trunk of the twisted tree and the roots that web through the rocks and bind it there. When she whispers something to the bark, the tree seems to breathe. To Arsinoe's astonishment, coffee-colored buds pop out along the tree's branches like gooseflesh.

"I didn't know it bloomed," she says.

"It does not, or at least not often. But tonight it must. Give me your hand."

Arsinoe walks to the tree and holds out her hand, expecting pain. What she does not expect is for Madrigal to yank her palm against the trunk and drive her knife all the way through it.

"Ah! Madrigal!" Arsinoe screams. The pain streaks up her arm and into her chest. She cannot move. She is trapped, pinioned, as Madrigal begins to chant.

Arsinoe does not know the words, or perhaps it is only that they are spoken too quickly. It is hard to hear anything over the pain of the knife in her hand. Madrigal walks back to the fire, and Arsinoe drops to one knee, trying to fight the urge to tear her hand free. The blade is buried deep into the wood. She pulls on the handle gently, and then harder, but it will not come out.

"Madrigal," she says through her teeth. "Madrigal!"

Madrigal lights a torch.

"No!" Arsinoe shouts. "Leave me alone!"

Madrigal's face is determined in a way that Arsinoe has never seen before. She does not know if Madrigal means to fuse her hand to the tree, but she does not want to find out. She takes a breath, preparing to pull loose, even though it will mean cutting between the bones of her middle fingers.

Quick as lightning, Madrigal reaches forward and yanks the knife out of the trunk. Arsinoe scrambles back, hugging her hand to her chest as Madrigal sets the tree alight. It ignites in bright yellow flames, and reeks of burning blood.

Arsinoe falls over, and the world goes dark.

That night, in a bed she has no recollection of returning to, Arsinoe dreams of a bear. A great brown bear, with long, curved claws and pink-and-purple gums. She dreams of it roaring before a scalded, bent-over tree.

It is barely dawn when Arsinoe shakes Jules gently awake, evoking growls from both the girl and the cougar who shares her pillow.

"Arsinoe?" Jules asks. "What is it? Are you all right?"

"I'm better than all right."

Jules squints at her in the pale blue light. "Then why are you waking me so early?"

"For something grand," Arsinoe says, and grins. "Now, get up and get dressed. I want to fetch Joseph and Billy, too."

It does not take long for Jules to get dressed and washed, and to gather her unruly waves with a thick piece of ribbon at the nape of her neck. They are out of the house and on the road into town long before anyone else begins to stir. Even Grandma Cait.

Jules did not object when Arsinoe wanted to bring Joseph. But when they reach his house, she will not go up to knock.

Arsinoe finds that she does not want to either. Eager as she is to reach the bent-over tree, she feels guilty, and oddly shy, disturbing the Sandrins so early. But just as she is about to gather pebbles to shoot at Joseph's window, Matthew comes through the door.

He startles when he sees them. Then he smiles. "What are you two about, at this hour?"

"Nothing," Arsinoe says. "We're looking for Joseph. Is he awake?"

"Only just," says Matthew. "I'll get him moving for you."

"And the mainlander too," Arsinoe calls after him as he goes back inside.

"When they come out," Jules says, leaning against her mountain cat, "will you tell me what we are doing here?"

"Perhaps it is a surprise," Arsinoe says. She paces around Jules. Arsinoe's blood is up, and not even the loosely wrapped hole in her hand causes her any pain. But she is still hesitant to say what she has seen. She is afraid Jules will tell her it was only a dream. And she is afraid that Jules would be right.

It seems like forever passes before the boys come out, looking confused and bedraggled. Joseph brightens when he sees Jules. Billy smoothes his hair when he sees Arsinoe, and Arsinoe coughs to cover her smile. Billy has not seen her since he returned from meeting Katharine, and even though she would not admit it, she was worried that he would return devoted to the poisoners.

"This is a welcome sight," Billy says. "Did you miss me so much that you had to see me the moment I arrived back in Wolf Spring?"

"I thought you had been back for days," Arsinoe lies. "And I am not here for you, but for Joseph."

"I heard you call for me. 'The mainlander too.' I'm not deaf."

Arsinoe says nothing. She is too busy watching Joseph stare at Jules, and Jules stare at her cougar.

"Arsinoe, are you listening to me? I said, where are we going?"

"North," she says distractedly. "Into the woods."

"Then we'll pass by the Lion's Head. I'll buy us some food."

"I don't really want to stop."

"But stop you will," says Billy, "if you want my company. You are dragging us out before breakfast."

They drag the Lion's Head's kitchen boy out before his breakfast as well, and it takes longer than usual for fried eggs and rashers of bacon doused in beans. Arsinoe is antsy all through the meal, though she does manage to eat her entire plate and part of Jules's besides.

Afterward, she leads them on a curving path through the alleys and streets of Wolf Spring, taking the most direct route to the tree. She bends her arm to elevate her wounded hand. It has begun to throb.

Perhaps that is a good omen. Or perhaps she should have brought Madrigal. It may have been only a dream, after all, and she is leading them through the melting snow for nothing.

When they are a good distance into the trees, Jules recognizes the direction they are heading in and stops.

"Tell me, Arsinoe," she says. "Tell me now."

"What?" Joseph asks her. "What's wrong? Where is she taking us?"

"It's more low magic," Jules replies. She looks at Arsinoe's freshly wounded hand. "Isn't it?"

"I still don't understand what's so different about low magic," Billy says, and looks at Jules. "And what you do with that cougar."

"It is different," Joseph says. "Jules's gift belongs to her. Low magic is for anyone. You, me . . . even back home we could do it. But it's dangerous. And it's not for queens."

"Wait," Billy says. "You're saying that back home, you could have . . ." He makes a twirling motion with his wrist that Arsinoe does not like. Joseph nods, and after a moment, Billy shrugs. "That's not possible," he says. "And I can't imagine you doing spells. You're like my own brother."

"What does that matter?" Arsinoe asks.

"It doesn't," Billy says quickly. "I don't know. . . I—I know I have met Luke, and Ellis, and so many other men, but . . . spells? I suppose I thought that spells were still only for girls."

"Why would they be only for girls?" Arsinoe asks, but she cannot really blame him for not knowing.

"Never mind that, now," Jules says. "Arsinoe. Answer the question. Why are you bringing us to that place?"

"Because I saw my familiar," Arsinoe says.

Jules and Joseph straighten. Even Camden pricks her black-tipped ears. Arsinoe holds up her hand and unrolls the bandages to reveal the angry, red-crusted wound that runs all the way through the center of her palm.

"We used my blood. I was bound to the tree, and we woke

my gift. Madrigal . . . Somehow, she must have known that in that sacred space, we would be heard, if only my blood would soak into the roots."

It sounds like madness. But she was there. She felt something pass through her and into the trunk. Into the stones and into the island. There, beneath the bent-over tree, as in so many other places, the island is more than just a place. There, it breathes and it listens.

"What did you see?" Jules asks. "And where?"

"In my dream last night. A bear. A great brown bear."

Jules makes a soft, astonished sound. To have a great brown as a familiar would make Arsinoe the strongest naturalist queen the island has ever seen. Stronger than Bernadine and her wolf. Perhaps stronger even than Mirabella and her lightning. Jules does not want to believe in Arsinoe's use of low magic, but even she cannot help hoping.

"Are you certain?" Jules presses.

"I am not certain about anything," Arsinoe says. "But that is what I saw. What I dreamed."

"Can it be true?" Joseph asks.

Arsinoe clenches her injured fist, and the tenuous scabs give way to leak more blood, as though that might make it so.

"The temple might rethink their backing of Mirabella," Joseph says.

"Would that bother you?" Jules asks. She turns to Arsinoe. "Perhaps he should not be here. Perhaps he should not come."

"I only meant that nobody cares whether the new queen is

an elemental or a naturalist," Joseph says softly. "As long as she is not a poisoner."

Jules frowns. She does not move, even though Arsinoe paces loops in the direction of the tree.

"It can't hurt, can it?" Billy asks. He takes a few steps after Arsinoe. "To go look?"

Arsinoe claps him on the shoulder. "Right you are, Junior! Let's go!"

She moves quickly through the trees, picking her way across lingering snow and patches of melting ice. She does not look back. Even though she cannot hear Jules's and Camden's silent feet, she knows they are there. Whether she approves or not, Jules would never let her go alone.

As they near the tree, the image of the bear hangs behind Arsinoe's eyelids. Even in the dream it was enormous. It blotted out everything else. In her mind, it is only shining brown fur and a roar. White fangs and curved black claws long enough to disembowel a running deer.

"It will be a tame bear, won't it?" Billy asks.

"As tame as Camden is tame," Joseph says.

"Not tame at all, then," Jules says. "But not a danger to friends."

"That cat is tamer than half of my mother's spaniels," says Billy. "But I can't imagine a bear behaving the same."

They round the curve of the hill to the sunken patch of land before the bent-over tree and the ancient surfaces of the sacred stones.

The tree is intact. The night before, it had seemed to explode in yellow fire, but the only mark it bears is a charred patch stretching from the trunk to the lowest branches. Its limbs are free of the buds that Arsinoe remembers Madrigal blooming, and every drop and spatter of blood is gone, as if it never was. Or as if it had been drunk.

"What happened here?" Jules asks through a grimace. She steps gingerly around the dormant coals and floats her hand over the blackened part of the trunk. Then she wipes her fingers against her jacket, even though she never touched it.

"I think . . . ," says Billy. "I think that even I feel something. A vibration, almost."

"This place feels tired," says Joseph. "As if it has been used up."

"No," says Jules. "It feels like what it is. Outside. It is not what the rest of these trees are. Not what the rest of this ground is."

"Yes," Arsinoe adds breathlessly. "That's exactly right."

Prickles rise on the back of Arsinoe's neck. It has never felt quite like this. As if Jules's apprehension and Billy's nerves are leaching into the air.

"Was it supposed to be here?" Joseph asks. "Is this where you saw it?"

"Yes."

It was there, before the tree. Roaring as the branches burned behind it.

But the branches are not burned. And she has led them all this way for nothing.

"How long do we wait?" Billy asks. "Should we . . . whistle for it?"

"It is not a dog," Arsinoe snaps. "It is not a pet. Just . . . a little longer. Please."

She turns and searches the trees. There is no sound. No wind and no birds. It is as still and silent as it always is.

"Arsinoe," Jules says gently. "We should not be here. This was a mistake."

"No, it's not," Arsinoe insists.

Jules was not there. She was not the one joined to that tree, bleeding into it. She did not feel the change in the air. Madrigal said that a queen's blood would really be worth something, and she was right. Arsinoe's low magic is strong.

"The bear will come," she murmurs. "It will come."

She begins to walk north.

"Arsinoe?" Jules asks, and takes a step, but Billy puts out his arm.

"Give her a moment," he says. But he follows her himself, keeping his distance as she searches.

When it arrives, it is not difficult to spot. The great brown bear is massive and trundling drowsily down the hillside. Its shoulders swing in dismal arcs as it tries to find its way down to her through the close-growing trees.

Arsinoe nearly shouts. But something holds her back. The bear does not look the way it did in her dream. With its claws dragging through the mud and its head lolling, it looks as if someone has pulled it up out of a ditch already dead and forced it back onto its rotting feet.

"It will recognize me," Arsinoe whispers, and forces her legs to take a step. Then another.

She smells something decaying. The bear's fur moves the way dead fur moves when it is disturbed by colonies of maggots and ants.

"Jules," she whispers, and dares to look back. But Jules is too far away. She cannot see.

"Arsinoe, come away from it," Billy says. "This is madness!"

But she cannot. She has called it, and it is hers. She holds out her hand.

At first, it does not seem to know that she is there. It keeps on lumbering, and to add to its list of wrongs, there is something the matter with its gait: its left shoulder slams down harder than its right. She sees streaks of red in its paw print. An overgrown claw has dug into its foot, as is common in very old or sick bears.

"Is it?" Billy asks. "Is it your familiar?"

"No," she says, and the bear's angry, bleary eyes finally meet hers.

"Run!" she shouts, and turns as the bear roars. The ground shakes beneath its weight when it comes after her.

They race down the hill, and time slows. Several years ago, when she and Jules were children, a farmer brought his dead hounds into the square to warn people of a rogue bear. A hunting party found and killed it a few days later. It had only been a common black, but those hounds had barely looked like hounds anymore, split from nose to tail by the common black's claws. All these years later, Arsinoe remembers the way one dog's jaw dangled by the tiniest piece of skin.

Mud from the bear kicks up around her shoulders. She is not going to make it.

Jules screams and runs toward her, but Joseph grasps her around the waist.

Good boy. He cannot let her risk herself. He has to look after her, the way Arsinoe always knew that he would.

Arsinoe's foot slides in the mud, and she falls forward onto her face. She closes her eyes. Any moment, and the claws will tear through the backs of her legs. What's left of her blood will stain the ground.

"Hey!" Billy shouts. "Hey! Hey!"

The fool has come closer, right into the bear's sight line. He waves his arms, and pelts the bear with ice and mud balls he scoops into his hands. They do not do anything besides bounce off, but it gives Arsinoe time to climb to her feet.

"Run!" he screams. "Run, Arsinoe!"

But Billy has exchanged her life for his. The bear will be on him in moments. Perhaps he thinks that a worthy trade, but she does not.

Arsinoe throws herself between Billy and the bear. It strikes out hard with its paw. The brunt of the force easily pops her shoulder out of the joint. The rest she takes across her face.

Red paints the snow in drizzles.

Camden snarls and races up the hill to collide with the great brown in a blur of golden fur.

Billy wraps his arm around Arsinoe's ribs and heaves her up.

"It's hot and cold," she mumbles, but cannot get her mouth to work properly.

"Come on," Billy says, and Jules cries out. Camden wails pitifully. She stops abruptly when she is thrown hard against a tree.

"No!" Arsinoe screeches. But the sound is barely heard over Jules, screaming, louder and louder until it hardly sounds like her voice. The great brown begins to shake its head and then to paw at itself. It scratches at its chest like it is trying to claw out its own heart.

For an instant, in the midst of Jules's shouts, it seems that the bear hovers in midair.

Then it falls over, dead.

Sweat rolls off Jules as though it is the middle of Wolf Spring summer, and she collapses onto one knee. The bear is dead, its great paws flung out on all sides. It lies still and looks almost peaceful now, no longer too old and too sick, but out of its misery.

"Jules," Joseph says, and crouches beside her. He puts his arm across her shoulders and turns her face to his. "Are you all right?"

"Y-yes," she says. She takes a breath. She is fine. And whatever she used to kill the bear, to explode its heart inside its chest, has gone. Perhaps back into the heart of the gnarled, bent-over tree.

"Cam," she says. "Arsinoe."

"I know," says Joseph. He runs through the trees, up the hill to where Arsinoe and Camden lie. Billy has torn the sleeves from his shirt and tied tight strips around Arsinoe's upper arm. He presses the rest of the cloth hard to her face.

"She didn't have enough blood to begin with," he growls. "We have to get her to a doctor. Now."

"There aren't any," Joseph says quietly. "There are healers."

"Well, whatever they have here," Billy snaps. "She needs them."

"They'll be at the temple," says Jules, coming close to kneel beside them. "Or at their houses in town. Oh Goddess. The blood . . ."

"The houses are closer, aren't they? You can't panic now, Jules. You have to listen. This cheek here is going to bleed like crazy, and the snow will make it look like more. Can you help, or will you faint?" Billy asks.

"I will not faint."

"Can we risk moving her?" Joseph asks.

"We don't have a choice," says Billy. "The bleeding is too severe. I can't stop it."

He and Joseph look at each other gravely over Arsinoe's body. Jules can hardly see, her tears rise so quickly. Billy said she should not panic, but she cannot help it. Arsinoe looks so pale.

"All right," Billy says. "Get under her hips and legs. I've got her shoulders and I have to keep pressure on her face."

Jules does as she is told. Warm blood coats her hands almost instantly.

"Joseph," she says. "Camden. Please don't leave Camden."

"I won't," he says, and kisses her quickly. "I promise."

Jules and Billy carry Arsinoe through the trees, back down the path. Joseph follows behind with Camden across his shoulders. The big cat groans softly. When Jules glances over her shoulder, Cam is licking his ear.

By the time they reach Wolf Spring, all are exhausted. The first healer's house is not more than four streets away, but they are not going to make it.

"The Wolverton," Billy says, and gestures with his chin. He kicks at the door until it opens, and he shouts at Mrs. Casteel until there are running feet everywhere.

"Isn't there anyone of any use in this town!" Billy bellows.

They set Arsinoe on the sofa near the entrance and wait. When the healer finally arrives with two priestesses in tow, to burn the wounds closed and pull them tight with string, they shove Jules and Billy out of the way.

"What is this?" one of the priestesses asks. "How did she get these wounds? It was not another attack from Rolanth? Did Mirabella come again, through the woods?"

"No," Jules says. "It was a bear."

"A bear?"

"We—" Jules says, and stops. Everything happened so

quickly. But she should have known. She should have protected her.

"We were walking," Joseph says from behind her. "We went off the path. The bear came upon us suddenly."

"Where?" the priestess asks, and touches the serrated knife hanging from her hip. "I will send a hunting party."

"That isn't necessary," Jules says. "I killed it."

"You?"

"Yes, her," Joseph says with a tone of finality. "Well, her and a mountain cat."

He slips his arm around Jules's waist and turns her away from any more questions. They walk slowly to stand near Billy, who kneels, stroking Camden's head. The cat still cannot walk, but she is purring.

"Joseph?" Jules asks. "They will live, won't they?"

"You made Camden strong," he says, and squeezes her tightly. "And you and I both know that Arsinoe is meaner than any bear."

GREAVESDRAKE MANOR

❧

*T*here is no shortage of poison in Greavesdrake Manor. Open any cabinet or drawer, and one is likely to find some powder, or tincture, or jar of toxic root. It is whispered in the streets of Indrid Down that when the Arrons are ousted, the Westwoods will have the place gutted. That they fear that every wall has been tainted. The fools. As if the Arrons have been so careless with their craft. As if they would ever be so careless about anything.

Natalia stands before the fireplace in the poison room, taking late-morning tea with Genevieve. Katharine is beyond them, laboring at the tables. Mixing and blending in her protective black gloves.

"It has finally happened," Genevieve says. "The weather has turned, and the fire is too hot. You shall have to start opening windows."

"Not here," Natalia says. Never here. In this room, the right breeze passing over the wrong powder could instantly mean a dead queen.

Genevieve scowls and half turns in her chair. "What is she doing back there?"

"Working," Natalia replies. Katharine has always worked very well at her poisons. Ever since she was a child, she bent over the tables and vials with such enthusiasm that Genevieve would drag her away and slap her, to try to force more seriousness. But Natalia put a stop to that. That Katharine takes joy in crafting poisons is the thing about her that Natalia most loves.

Genevieve sighs. "You have heard the news?" she asks.

"Yes. I assume that is why you have come home? To make sure that I heard the news."

"But it is interesting, is it not," Genevieve says. She sets down her teacup and brushes biscuit crumbs from her fingers and onto her plate. "First the attempt in the Masthead Woods and now Arsinoe is near death in her bed?"

Behind them, the clattering and clinking goes quiet as Katharine stops to listen.

"They say it was a bear attack," Natalia says.

"A bear attack on a naturalist queen?" Genevieve narrows her eyes. "Or is Mirabella simply more clever than we assumed? An 'accidental' death like this would not look like a strike against her."

"She was not concerned with strikes against her when she left Rolanth to murder Arsinoe in the forest," Natalia says. She glances at Katharine. That attack rattled them all. Masthead is only a half day's ride from Indrid Down. The upstart elemental had come far too close.

Natalia leaves the fireplace and crosses the room to put a hand on Katharine's small shoulder. The table is a mess. It seems that she has pulled poisons from every shelf and every drawer.

"What do you have here, Kat?" she asks.

"Nothing yet," the young queen replies. "It must still be boiled down and concentrated. And then it must be tested."

Natalia looks down at the glass jar, filled with two inches of amber liquid. There is no end to the combinations that can be created here. In many respects, the poison room at Greaves-drake is superior even to the chamber at the Volroy. It is more organized, for one. And it houses many stores of Natalia's own special blends.

Natalia runs her hand fondly across the wood. How many lives has she dispatched from this table? How many unwanted husbands or inconvenient mistresses? So many mainland problems, handled here, to honor the alliance and the interests of the king-consort.

She reaches for the jar, and Katharine tenses, as if Natalia needs to worry.

"Do not spill it on the wood," Katharine explains, blushing. "It is caustic."

"Caustic?" Natalia asks. "Who would require such a poison?"

"Not Arsinoe, certainly," says Katharine. "She may yet have mercy."

"Mercy," Genevieve mumbles, listening from her fireside chair.

"Mirabella, then?" Natalia asks.

"They are always saying that she is so beautiful," Katharine says. "But that is only skin deep."

She looks up at Natalia so shyly that Natalia laughs and kisses the top of her head.

"Natalia."

It is her butler, Edmund, standing straight-backed beside the door.

"There is someone here to see you."

"Now?" she asks.

"Yes."

Katharine looks from her poison to Genevieve. She has not finished, but does not like to stay when Genevieve is there and Natalia is not.

"That is enough for today," Natalia says. She pours the poison deftly into a glass vial and plugs it. Then she tosses it into the air and catches it. When she opens her palms to Katharine, the poison is gone, disappeared up her sleeve. An easy trick, and always good for a poisoner to learn. She wishes that Katharine were better at it.

"I will keep it for you to finish later."

Natalia's visitor waits for her in her study. It is not an unfamiliar face, but it is unexpected. It is William Chatworth, the father of the first suitor, already seated in one of her wingback chairs. Her favorite one.

"May I offer you a drink?" she asks.

"I brought my own," he says. He reaches into his jacket and shows her a silver flask. His eyes pass over her bar with contempt. They linger on her brandy, infused with hemlock and with a handsome black scorpion suspended near the bottom.

"That was not necessary," she says. "We always keep stores of untainted goods for guests."

"And how many have you accidentally poisoned?"

"None of any consequence," she says, and smiles. "We have partnered with mainlanders for three generations and never poisoned one who did not already have it coming. Do not be so paranoid."

In the chair, Chatworth has a familiar, drapey air, as if he owns it. He is just as handsome and arrogant as he was when they first met all those years ago. She leans down and slides her hand over his shoulder and onto his chest.

"Don't," he says. "Not today."

"All business, then. I suppose I am disappointed." She sinks into the chair opposite. William is a very good lover. But every time she beds him, he seems to think less of her. As if she gives something during the bedding that she does not take back afterward.

"I do love the way you talk," he says.

She sips her drink. He may love the way she talks. He also loves the way she looks. His eyes never stop moving over her body, even now, as he discusses business. For mainland men, all roads with women lead somehow right back between their legs.

"How did you find my son?" he asks.

"He is a fine young man," Natalia says. "Charming, like his father. He seemed very fond of Wolf Spring."

"Don't worry," Chatworth says. "He will do as he's told. Our agreement is still in place."

Their agreement. Struck so long ago, when Natalia required somewhere for Joseph Sandrin to be banished to. Her friend and lover had been an easy choice. She was not able to kill the Sandrin boy as she would have liked, but she would not be denied everything. There is always something to be gained if one looks hard enough.

"Good," she says, "It will be well worth it for him to obey. The trade agreements alone will elevate your family beyond reckoning."

"Yes," he says. "And the rest?"

Natalia finishes her brandy and rises to pour another.

"You are so squeamish," she says, and chuckles. "Say the words. 'Assassinations.' 'Murders.' 'Poisonings.'"

"Don't be vulgar."

It is not vulgar. But she sighs.

"Yes," she says. "And the rest." She will kill whoever needs killing, discreetly and from great untraceable distance, as long as their alliance holds. Just as she has, and the Arrons have, for every king-consort's family.

"But why have you come?" she asks. "So urgent and unexpectedly? It cannot have been just to rehash old bargains."

"No," he says. "I'm here because I've learned a secret that I don't like. One that could end all of our well-laid plans."

"And what is that?"

"I've just come from Rolanth, brokering a meeting between my son and Queen Mirabella. And Sara Westwood told me a secret that I don't think you know."

Natalia snorts. That is unlikely. The island is good at remaining hidden but terrible at hiding anything from her.

"If it is from Sara Westwood, you have wasted your horse's legs," Natalia says. "She is nothing but a sweet woman. Sweet and devout. And two more useless words I have never heard."

"Most of Fennbirn is devout," Chatworth says. "If you had one ear to your temple, you wouldn't need me to tell you what I'm telling you now."

Natalia's eyes flash. If she dips her letter opener into her brandy, she can stab him in the neck. It will be a race to see whether he dies of the poison or the blood loss.

"They're planning to assassinate the queens," he says.

For a moment, the words sound so ridiculous that Natalia cannot process his meaning.

"What?" she asks. "Of course they are. We all are."

"No," says Chatworth. "I mean the temple. The priestesses. After your ceremony at the festival. They're going to ambush us. They're going to kill our queen and the one from Wolf Spring. She called it 'a Sacrificial Year.'"

"'A Sacrificial Year,'" Natalia repeats. A generation of two weak queens and one strong. No one doubts the truth of that.

But she has never heard of the weak queens being slaughtered by priestesses at the Quickening Ceremony.

"Luca," she whispers. "How clever you are."

"Well?" Chatworth says, and leans forward in his chair. "What are we going to do?"

Natalia shakes her head and then affixes a bright smile to her face.

"We are not going to do anything. You have already done your part. Let the Arrons handle the temple."

"Are you sure?" he asks. "What makes you think that you can?"

"Only that we have, for the last hundred years."

WOLF SPRING

When Arsinoe wakes, she knows there is something wrong with her face. At first she thinks that she has slept wrong, perhaps pressed too hard into the pillow. Except that she is lying on her back.

The room is quiet, and bright as midday; she does not know how long she has been asleep. The blue-and-white curtains are drawn closed. Plates of untouched food crowd the writing desk.

"The bear," she whispers.

Jules appears beside her, tired, her brown hair a wavy mess of tangles.

"Don't move," she says, but Arsinoe pushes herself onto her elbows. When she does, her right shoulder screams.

"Let me help at least." Jules pulls her up and stacks pillows behind her back.

"Why aren't I dead?" Arsinoe asks. "Where is Camden?"

"She is all right," Jules says. "She is there."

She nods toward where the cougar lies on Jules's bed. The big cat appears to be lounging in relative ease. She has a few cuts, and one of her forelegs is wrapped and held in a sling, but it could have been worse.

"Her shoulder is broken," Jules says quietly. "By the time anyone thought to tend to her . . . It will never heal right."

"This is my fault," Arsinoe says, and Jules looks down.

"You could have been killed," Jules says. "Madrigal should never have taught you."

"She was only trying to help me. It is not her fault that something went wrong. We all know that they do, sometimes, with low magic. We all know of the risk."

"You say that like you are going to do it again, anyway."

Arsinoe frowns. Or she tries to. Her mouth will not work properly. And her cheek is odd and heavy. There is a part of her face that she can no longer feel, as if a stone has grown into the skin.

"Will you open a window, Jules?"

"Of course."

She walks to the other side of the room, to push back the curtains. The fresh air is a relief. The room smells stagnant, like blood and too much sleep.

"Luke was here," Jules says. "He brought cookies."

Arsinoe reaches up to her face and strips the bandages.

"Arsinoe, don't!"

"Get me a mirror."

"You have to stay in bed," Jules says.

"Don't be thick. Bring me one of Madrigal's."

For a moment, it seems that Jules will refuse. That is when the first real fear sets in. But eventually she goes to ransack Madrigal's dresser until she finds a mirror with a pretty pearlescent handle.

Arsinoe runs her good hand over her black cap of hair, smoothing it where it sticks up from having rested on her pillow. Then she raises the mirror and looks.

She does not blink. Not even when Jules begins to cry behind her hand. She has to make herself see it. Every inch of stitched-together red. Every angry black knot that holds together what is left of her face.

Most of her right cheek is gone, hollow where it should be plump. Lines of dark stitches cross from the corner of her mouth to below the outside edge of her eye. Another, larger line of stitches covers the hollow of her cheekbone, all the way down to her chin.

"Well," she says. "A hairsbreadth higher and I would have needed to wear an eye patch." She starts to laugh.

"Arsinoe, stop."

She watches the stitches pull in the mirror until blood spurts down her chin. Jules tries to calm her, and calls for Cait, and Ellis, but Arsinoe only laughs harder.

The cuts stretch open. The salt from her tears burns. It is a lucky thing that she never cared about what she looked like.

Jules finds Joseph in his family's shipyard, sifting through a tangled mess of rope and rigging. It is a warm day, and he has taken his jacket off and rolled up the sleeves of his shirt. She watches him dismally as he wipes sweat from his brow. He is the kind of handsome that draws every eye.

"Jules," he says when he sees her, and sets down his pile of rigging. "How is she?"

"She is Arsinoe," she says. "She tore her stitches out. They are putting them back in now. I couldn't stay. I couldn't take any more."

He rubs his fingers clean on a handkerchief. He would take her hand if he thought she would let him.

"I was going to bring her flowers," he says, and chuckles. "Can you imagine? I want to see her, but I don't know if she will want to see me. If she will want to be seen."

"She will want to see you," says Jules. "Arsinoe will never hide from anything."

Jules turns to face the water, obscured by boats in dry dock, barely visible past the edge of the pier.

"I feel strange," she says. "Without Camden. Without Arsinoe. As if I've lost my shadows."

"They will be back," Joseph says.

"Not like they were."

Joseph wraps tentative fingers around her shoulder until she leans back into him. For a moment, it seems that he could hold her up, take all her weight in just one hand.

"I love her too, Jules," he says. "Almost as much as I love you."

Together, they look out at the cove. It is quiet, nothing there

but low waves and wind, and it seems like you could sail forever.

"Joseph . . . I wish we had gotten her off the island five years
ago."

Billy does not smile when he comes into the room, and that is
good. Or better, at least, than the guilty, shaky, forced grins that
the healers and the Milones have been trying to wear. He holds
his hand up. He brought her flowers. Vibrant, yellow-orange
blooms that do not come from any hothouse in Wolf Spring.

"My father sent for these," he says. "All the way from my
mother's favorite florist. He sent for them the moment we heard.
Before we knew whether you would live or die. He said we
could use them either way, for courting or condolences. Shall I
stomp on them?"

"In a naturalist house?"

She takes them. They have small velvet petals, and smell a
little like the oranges they import in the summer.

"They are lovely," she says. "Jules will be able to keep them
blooming for a long time."

"But not you," he says.

"No. Not me."

She sets the flowers on her bedside table, near the windowsill and the dry, curled shell of her dead winter fern. Billy sets
his jacket on a chair, but instead of sitting in it, takes a seat at
the foot of her bed.

"How have you come to be here?" he asks. "If you are truly

"Do you want to see it?" She touches her face.

"Are we little boys now?" he asks. "Comparing scabs?"

"If we were, I would win."

She turns her head and pulls off her bandages. The stitches pull at her cheek but do not bleed.

Billy takes his time. He sees it all.

"Should I lie and tell you that I have seen worse?" he asks, and she shakes her head. "There's a rhyme about you, you know," he says. "Back home. Little girls sing it when they skip rope.

> *"Three Black Witches are born in a glen,*
> *Sweet little triplets*
> *Will never be friends.*

> *"Three Black Witches, all fair to be seen.*
> *Two to devour,*
> *And one to be queen.*

"That's what they call you, on the mainland. Witches. That's what my father says that you are. Monsters. Beasts. But you are not a monster."

"No," she says quietly. "And neither are the rest of us. But that doesn't change what we have to do." She takes his hand and squeezes it softly. "Go back to the Sandrins', Junior. Go back and read your letter."

INDRID DOWN

*P*ietyr Renard has never been invited inside the Volroy, but he has always dreamed of it. Ever since he was a child and his father told him stories. There is nothing in the halls to catch sound, he said. The Volroy defies adornment, as if there are too many other important things inside for it to be bothered with tapestries. Only the chamber where the council meets has anything but smooth black surfaces, and that is a relief sculpture depicting naturalist blooms and elemental fires, poisoner venoms and the warrior's carnage. He used to sketch the poisoner portion for Pietyr, charcoal on white paper, a knotted nest of vipers on a bed of oleander petals.

He promised to take Pietyr there as soon as he came of age. But that was before the house in the country, and his new wife.

"This way," says an attendant, who leads Pietyr up the stairs of the East Tower, where Natalia waits.

He does not really need a guide. He has walked the Volroy a thousand times in his imagination.

As they pass a window, he looks out at the West Tower. Huge and hulking, it blots out everything else. Up close, it does not give the grand impression that it does at a distance, slicing into the sky like an engraved knife. From here, it only looks black and mean, and locked up tight until the new queen comes.

The attendant stops outside a small door and bows. Pietyr knocks and then enters.

The room is a small, circular study that looks almost like a priestess's hovel, an odd little space hollowed out of a rock. Beside its solitary window, Natalia seems nearly too big for it.

"Come," she says.

"I was surprised that you summoned me here," he says.

"I knew it was what you were waiting for," she says. "A glimpse of your prize. Is it everything you imagined?"

Pietyr looks out the window and whistles.

"I must admit that I always thought there should be three towers instead of two. Three, for the queens. But now I see. The construction is astounding! Even two is a supreme achievement."

Natalia walks across the room and bends before a small cupboard, her footsteps loud as a horse's hooves on a cobblestone drive. There are very few floor coverings. It must make the servants' legs ache terribly.

Natalia pours two glasses of straw-colored liquid. May wine. He can smell it from the window. It is a strange choice.

A drink for a poisoner child. He takes it and sniffs, but he does not detect any added toxins.

"What is the occasion?" he asks. "I have not had May wine in years. My stepmother used to make it for me and the cousins in the summer. Sweetened with honey and strawberry juice."

"Just as I used to make it for Katharine," Natalia says. "She was always so fond of it. Though at first it made her sick as a dog, the poor thing."

Pietyr takes a sip. It is very good, even unsweetened.

"It is from a Wolf Spring vineyard," Natalia says. "Naturalists may be a filthy lot, but they know how to grow a grape. A small sun in every fruit, they say." She snorts.

"Aunt Natalia. What is the matter?"

She shakes her head. "Are you a pious boy, Pietyr? Do you know much of the temple?"

"Not overmuch," he says. "Marguerite tried with me, after she and Father married. But it was too late."

"It is never too late. She persuaded your father to leave the council, did she not? To give up the capital and his family." She sighs. "I wish Paulina had not died. It was a great insult to her when Christophe married Marguerite."

"Yes," he says. "But this is not why you brought me here."

Natalia chuckles.

"You are so like me. So direct. And you are right. I summoned you here because the temple is moving against us. Have you heard whispers of something called 'the Sacrificial Year'?"

"No," Pietyr says.

"I am not surprised. You are quite sequestered, with Katharine. The Sacrificial Year refers to a generation of queens where one is strong and two are weak."

"A generation like this one."

"Yes," she says. "And that much of the story is true. Even I remember that—a story told to me by my grandmother, told to her by hers. But the temple has decided to deviate."

"How?"

"They are saying that in Sacrificial Years, the two weaker queens are taken apart by a mob following the Quickening Ceremony."

"What?" Pietyr asks. He sets down his wine unsteadily, and it sloshes onto the window ledge.

"They are saying that a great mob rose up and tore the arms and heads from their bodies and tossed them into the fires. And they intend to do it to Katharine and Arsinoe. They are trying to make Mirabella a White-Handed Queen."

Pietyr holds his breath. White-Handed Queens are well-loved by the people. They are second only to a Blue Queen. But there has not been one in two hundred years.

"That part of the Sacrificial Year story is not true," Natalia says. "At least not as I have ever heard it."

"Is old Luca so desperate, then?" he asks. "There must be something wrong with their elemental."

"Perhaps. Or perhaps the temple is only seizing upon opportunity. It does not matter. What matters is that we know."

"How do we know?" Pietyr asks.

"I was informed by a foolish bird from the mainland. He whispered it into my ear."

Pietyr runs his hands over his face. Katharine. Sweet Katharine. They intend to take her arms and her head. They intend to burn her.

"Why am I the only one here, Natalia? Where are Genevieve and Lucian and Allegra?"

"I have not told them. There is nothing that they can do." She looks out the window, across the city and into the countryside. "Nothing on this island happens without my knowing. Or so I thought. But I do know that every ceremonial blade that the temple possesses is on its way to Innisfuil. Every priestess will be armed."

"So we will arm ourselves in kind!"

"We are not soldiers, Nephew. And even if we were, there is no time. We would need every poisoner in the city. At Innisfuil, the elementals and the temple priestesses will outnumber us three to one."

Pietyr grasps his aunt by the arms and squeezes hard. He may not have seen her often growing up, but he knows enough from his father's stories to recognize when she is not herself. The matriarch of the Arrons does not just accept that she has been outplayed.

"We will not stand by and let them behead our queen," Pietyr says. He softens his hands and his voice. "Not our Katharine. Not our Kat."

"What would you do to save her, Pietyr?" Natalia asks.

"At Beltane, we are nearly powerless. The priestesses oversee everything, from the Hunt to the Quickening. It will be close to impossible to maneuver within them."

"Close to impossible," he corrects. "But not impossible. And I will do whatever I have to do. I will do anything."

She curls her lip.

"You love her."

"Yes," he says. "And so do you."

WOLF SPRING

❧

*E*llis carves Arsinoe a mask to cover her healing cuts. It is so thin and closely fitted that it can rest on her face by virtue of her nose alone, but he chisels holes in the sides and then strings fine black ribbon to be tied behind her head. The mask is lacquered black, and stretches over her good cheek and the bridge of her nose to taper to her chin on the right side. He paints bright red slashes across it, down the cheek and from the eye, at her request.

"It will make quite the impression on the suitors," he says. "When they step off of their ships. They'll wonder who you are. And what is behind the mask."

"They'll be horrified to find out," she says, and touches Ellis on the arm when he frowns. "The mask is wonderful. Thank you."

"Let me help you put it on," says Jules.

"No," says Arsinoe. "Better to save it. For the Disembarking, like Ellis says."

Cait nods sternly. "A good idea. It is far too pretty a thing to be worn around for no reason."

She claps her hands together, and flour flies. She has been rolling out a piecrust for the last of the fall's jarred apples. Jules has already cut long strips for the lattice. Madrigal was to help as well, but that morning she was nowhere to be found.

Outside, something rustles against the corner of the house, near the chicken coops. Jules looks out the window.

"It's Billy," she says. "He's caught in the barberry bush. He must have come up through the orchard."

"I'll go," Arsinoe says, and pushes away from the table. It is a relief to be out of bed and on her feet again. Perhaps she will take him up the hill path. Or perhaps not. The hill path winds too close to the bent-over tree, where none of the Milones want her to go. But oh, how she itches to.

Outside, Billy is kicking at thorns. "What the hell is this devil plant?"

"Barberry," Arsinoe says. "Cait plants them around the coops to discourage the foxes. What are you doing here?"

He stops struggling. "That's not a very warm welcome. I've come to see you. Unless you are in a black mood."

"'Black mood'?"

"A grim mood," he says. "Depressed. Dark. Mean." He chuckles. "God, you are so strange sometimes, you people."

He holds out his hand, and she pulls him out of the bush.

"I thought you might want to get away from here," he says. "Away from your sickbed."

"Now, that is a good idea," she says.

He takes her down to the cove, to one of the Sandrins' slips. In it is a pretty daysailer with light blue sails and a painted yellow hull. Arsinoe is not really supposed to sail. Not since she tried to escape. But it has not been expressly forbidden.

It is a good day to be on the water; the cove is as calm as she has ever seen it, and a few of the namesake seals' heads bob out near the point of the rocks.

"Come on," he says. "I asked Mrs. Sandrin if she would prepare us a lunch." He holds up a basket covered with a cloth. "Fried chicken and fingerling potatoes. Soured cream. She said it was one of your favorite meals."

Arsinoe considers the basket, as well as the poorly hidden glances from Mr. Bukovy as he haggles prices with two market merchants. What are they whispering about her these days? The scarred queen. Attacked by her sister in the woods and nearly done in by a bear. Even those who are loyal will have their doubts now. Even Luke.

"Fried chicken?" she asks, and steps into the boat.

Billy casts off. It is not long before they are past the seals, sailing north along the west side of the island.

"If we go farther, we might see frothbacks," Arsinoe says. "Whales. We should have brought Jules. She could make them pull the boat, and we could tie down the sails."

Billy laughs. "You sound almost bitter, you know," he says.

Not almost. She does. So many times she has wished for just a fraction of Jules's gift. She reaches up and touches the bandaged gashes on her cheek. They will not even be healed to scars at Beltane. They will be red and scabbed and ugly.

"When do you leave for the Disembarking?" Arsinoe asks.

"Soon," Billy says. "Longmorrow Bay is not far. My father says we won't stop at night, and if the wind holds, we will even be early. Besides, we only have to make it as far as Sand Harbor. Then it's a slow processional into the bay. I remember that much from Joseph."

"I suppose he has told you everything," Arsinoe says.

"I should have paid better attention," Billy says. "But none of it was real to me until I passed through the mist and watched Fennbirn grow larger."

Arsinoe looks back at the island. It looks different from the sea. Safer. As if it does not breathe and demand blood.

"I'm disappointed that the suitors miss the Hunt," he says. "That's the only part of the festival that sounds like real fun."

"Don't be too sad. When you are king-consort, you will lead the Hunt every year. And even if you don't become king-consort, the suitors participate in the Hunt of the Stags next year, before the wedding."

"Have you ever been to where we're going? To Innisfuil?"

"No," says Arsinoe. "Though it's very near to the Black Cottage, where I was born."

"And where Jules's aunt Caragh is now," Billy recalls. "That will be hard. For her to be so close. Will Jules and Madrigal try to see her, do you think?"

"Jules may have a temper, but she will not break the council's decree. No matter how unfair. And as for Madrigal, she and Caragh never really cared for each other."

"Do no sisters care for each other on this island?" he asks, and Arsinoe snorts.

"Speaking of sisters, shouldn't you be courting mine? Why are you not in Rolanth, with Mirabella?"

"I didn't want to go, after you were hurt. I will see her at the festival, like everyone else."

His words give Arsinoe a warm feeling in her belly. He is good, this mainlander. And though he was not lying when he said she would make for a poor wife, he will make a very good king-consort to one of her sisters. She does not dare to think he would make a good king-consort for her. Such hopes are dangerous.

Billy eases the sails as he turns the daysailer away from the island, bearing off into open water.

"We shouldn't go out too far," Arsinoe says. "Or it will be dark by the time we return."

"We aren't going back to Wolf Spring."

"What?" she asks. "Then where are we going?"

"I'm doing what any civilized person ought to do. I'm taking you off this island. Straight through the Sound, and home. You can disappear if you want. Or you can stay with me. I'll give you anything you need. But you cannot stay here."

"Stay with you?"

"Not with me, exactly. I will have to come back for the festival. If I don't, my father will have my scalp. But if I am not made king, I will return and find you. And my mother and sisters will all help in the meantime."

Arsinoe sits quietly. She did not expect this. He is trying to save her, to take her away from the danger by force. It is such a mainlander thing to do. And a brave thing to do for a friend.

"I can't let you. You'll be punished if I go," she says.

"I'll make it seem that you pushed me overboard and left me to swim," he says. "You have tried it before; no one will doubt me."

"Junior," she says. She looks out at the sea, half expecting to see the mist net rising. "It will not let me go. Didn't Joseph tell you?"

"It will be different this time," he says. "This boat isn't from Fennbirn. It's mine, and it comes and goes as it pleases." He touches the mast as if stroking the neck of a horse. "I sent for it. The last time my father went home, I had him tow it back for me. A gift for Joseph, I said. For he and I to sail."

Hope rises in Arsinoe's throat. He makes it sound possible.

"Billy. You have been a good friend to me. As good as I have ever had. But I can't go. Besides, you ought to have faith. Even with this ruined face, I may still win."

"No you won't," he snaps. "Arsinoe. They're going to kill you. And not before next year's festival. Not someday—some months away. Now. My father told me what they're planning. That is why he sent his letter. The priestesses of this bloody, godforsaken island. They're going to tear you and Katharine apart. They're going to throw you into the fires in pieces and crown Mirabella before the dawn of the next day."

"That is not true," she says, and then listens as he tells her what he has learned about the plot and the Sacrificial Year.

"Arsinoe, do you believe me? I wouldn't lie. I could never come up with it."

Arsinoe sits quietly. To her right lies the island—permanent and unbothered by the waves. Anchored down deep. If only there were a way to snap off the lot of it and set it to drift. If only it were just an island rather than a pretty, sleeping dog with sand on its paws and cliffs on its shoulders, waiting to wake and rip her open.

"Your father could be wrong," she says.

But he is not. Billy is telling the truth.

Arsinoe thinks of Luke and the Milones. She thinks of Joseph. She thinks of Jules.

"We were going to fight," she says. "Even though it was a losing battle. But I thought I had more time. I don't want to die, Junior."

"Don't worry, Arsinoe. I won't let you. Now, grab that rope. Help me go faster."

THE BELTANE FESTIVAL

Innisfuil Valley

THE WESTWOOD ENCAMPMENT

"They have not found anything. No trace of her. She was not hiding in a Wolf Spring attic, and the boats have dragged nothing up in their nets but fish. Arsinoe is gone."

"She cannot be gone," Mirabella says, and Bree purses her lips.

"May not be, might not be," Bree says. "But she is."

"That is good," says Elizabeth. "If she has fled, no one can force you to harm her. And she will be unable to harm you."

Harm. It is a mild word for what they must do. But she would not expect anything harsher from Elizabeth.

Mirabella stands before the tall mirror as Bree laces her into a long black dress. It is a comfortable one, loose and not too heavy. Good for lounging about in on a day when she does not have to be seen.

Elizabeth kneels on the floor, searching through their many

trunks for a soft hairbrush. As she does, she forgets her injury and knocks the stump of her wrist against the corner of one of the lids. She hugs her arm tightly and bites her lip. Pepper the woodpecker flies fast to her shoulder.

"Elizabeth," Mirabella says. "You do not have to do that."

"Yes, I do. I must learn ways to use it."

Shadows pass by outside. Priestesses, always close at hand. Always watching. In Mirabella's lavish black-and-white tent, laid out with thick rugs and a bed, soft pillows and tables and chairs, it is easy to forget that it is not a room with dense walls but canvas and silk, where they are easily overheard.

Bree finishes lacing the dress and stands beside Mirabella in front of the mirror.

"Have you seen some of the boys here?" she asks loudly. "Putting up tents in the sun with their shirts off their backs? Do you think that naturalist boys are really as wild as they say?"

Mirabella holds her breath. Naturalist boys. Like Joseph. She has not told Bree and Elizabeth about what happened between them. Though she longs to, she is afraid to say it out loud. Joseph will be at the festival. She could see him again. But he will be with Juillenne Milone. And no matter what happened between Mirabella and Joseph on the beach, and in the forest, no matter that they were so tangled in each other that they could not hear the storm, Mirabella knows that she is the interloper in their story.

"Probably not," Mirabella says equally loudly. "But I am sure that you will find out and tell me."

The shadows move along, and Bree squeezes Mirabella's shoulder. It will be a long day inside, after two long days of travel. The jolting carriage from Rolanth made all their stomachs uneasy, particularly the stretch around the mouth of Sand Harbor, which smelled of salt and fish tossed onto a warming beach.

Mirabella peeks out through the tent flap. There are so many people, laughing and working in the sun. She has not seen much of the valley. They kept her hidden in the carriage until her tent was ready and immediately brought her inside. What view she did have was of predawn cliffs and thick, dark trees surrounding the broad clearing.

The priestesses say she ought to feel more like herself here. More like a queen, when she is at the island's heart and so near to the Goddess's pulse in the deep, dark chasm of the Breccia Domain. But she does not. Mirabella feels the island hum beneath her feet, and she does not like it at all.

"Where is Luca?" she asks. "I have hardly seen her."

"She is busy with the search," Elizabeth says. "I have never seen her so agitated or so angry. She can't believe your sister could be so defiant."

But that is Arsinoe. She was always that way, and it seems that growing up in Wolf Spring has only made it worse. Mirabella could see it in her eyes, that day in the forest. She could see it in Joseph's eyes as well. Wolf Spring raises its children defiant.

"Luca is also busy overseeing whatever they are moving in

those crates," Bree says. "Crates and crates and crates. And no one can say what is in them. Do you know, Elizabeth?"

The priestess shakes her head. That is not surprising. The temple does not trust her anymore, and with only one hand, she would not be of much use loading and unloading.

"Do you think," Elizabeth asks, "that they will still find her? Could she really have gotten away and survived?"

"No one thinks so," Bree says gently. "But it is better that she should die this way than any other."

THE ARRON ENCAMPMENT

*T*he poisoners arrive in the night, their whole clan descending upon the festival grounds like ants. They set their tents by moonlight and only the smallest of lamps, working so quietly that when day breaks upon a dug-in encampment, many of the heavier-sleeping priestesses stare at it with open mouths.

Inside her tent, Katharine paces. Pietyr was to bring her breakfast, but he has been gone for too long. It is not fair that he should be free to wander the meadow while she must stay inside until the Disembarking. Perhaps if she can find Natalia, they might take a walk together.

She steps out of the tent, directly into Bertrand Roman.

"Best to stay inside, my queen," he says, and places his huge mitts on her shoulders to move her back through the flap.

"Take your hands off her." Pietyr steps between them and shoves Bertrand away, though the great brute is not shoved far.

"It is for her own safety."

"I do not care. You are never to touch her that way again."

He slips his arm about Katharine's waist and draws her inside.

"I do not like him," he says.

"I do not like him either. I have not seen him since I was a child and he showed me how to poison with oleander milk," Katharine says. "I did not think he needed to demonstrate on an entire batch of kittens!"

"Yet who better to lead an armored escort," Pietyr mutters. "We must not be lax about your safety."

But there were others who could be just as effective. Choosing brutal Bertrand Roman was Genevieve's idea. Of that, Katharine has no doubt.

Pietyr climbs onto her makeshift bed and lays out what food he has found. Most of the food is still unpacked or is being carefully hoarded for the feasts. But he has managed some bread and butter, and some hard-cooked eggs.

"Pietyr," Katharine says. "There is a flower in your hair."

He reaches up and plucks it from his ear. It is only a daisy, common in the field.

"Where did you get it?"

"Some priestess or another," he says, and Katharine crosses her arms. "Kat." He rises and wraps his arms around her. He kisses her face until she giggles. He kisses her lips and her neck until she slips her hands under his shirt.

"It is unfair of me to be jealous," she says.

"It does not matter," he says. "It is our lot. To drive each other mad with jealousy. You will kiss a suitor, and I will kiss a priestess, and it will make your fire for me burn even higher."

"Do not tease," she says, and he smiles.

Outside the tent, poisoners converse as they move and unpack chests. Preparation for the night's Hunt has begun. Every poisoner at Innisfuil will soon be stringing bows and readying crossbows, dipping their arrowheads and bolts in dilutions of poisonous winter rose.

"I wish I could take part in the Hunt," Katharine says. She walks to the bed and kneels to smear butter across a bit of crust. "It would be nice to take a horse into the hills and flush quail and pheasant. Will you go on horseback? Or on foot?"

"I will not go at all," he says. "I will stay with you."

"Pietyr. You do not need to. I will only be a bore, worrying about the *Gave Noir* and the Disembarking."

"No," he says. "Do not worry about any of that."

"It will be hard to think of anything else."

"Then I will help you."

Pietyr pulls her to his chest and kisses her again until they are both breathless.

"Do not think of it, Kat. Do not worry." He lays her back on the bed. "Do not be afraid."

He moves on top of her, his warm breath in her ear. Something has changed in Pietyr; his touch is desperate and slightly sad. She imagines it is because he knows they will soon be parted by one suitor or another, but she does not say a word for fear he will stop. His kisses make her dizzy, even if she does not understand it when he traces his finger across her skin, first where her arm and shoulder meet, and then in an invisible line across her throat.

THE MILONE ENCAMPMENT

*J*ules raises the mallet high above the tent stake. She means to tap. But when she swings, the impact splits the wooden stake in two. A waste of a perfectly good stake, but at least it frightens the onlookers. Since Arsinoe disappeared, Jules has had no peace. Everyone thinks she must know where Arsinoe went.

Even Billy's father. The day after the boat went missing, William Chatworth finally paid the Milones a visit, but only to pound on their door demanding answers. Demanding punishment. But there is no one to punish. The queen is gone, and Billy has gone with her.

Ellis bends down with his white spaniel, Jake.

"I didn't mean to split it," Jules says.

"I know," he says. "Don't worry. Jake can pull this out, and there are more on the cart."

Jules wipes her brow as the dog sets to digging up the stake.

Their main tent lies on the grass like a dead bat's wing, and smells just as sour. It is nothing like the fine tents housing Mirabella and Katharine. Not that it matters. They do not really need to put it up. Without Arsinoe, they did not need to come to Innisfuil at all.

Jules toes the edge of the tent, and a hole in it that needs mending.

"This is shameful," she says. "We should have taken more care. We should have treated her like a real queen."

"We did," Ellis says. "We treated her like a naturalist queen. Nose in the dirt. Running with us and fishing. Naturalist queens are queens of the people; it's why they make such good ones, when they are strong enough to manage it."

"Scat!"

Jules and Ellis turn and see Cait chase Camden from her tent. Eva caws and flaps around the cougar's head.

"What's the matter?" Jules asks.

"Nothing much," Cait says. "She is only after the bacon." She gestures with her chin. "Here's Joseph."

He waves a greeting, walking slightly hunched. The eyes of the island have been on him too since Billy and Arsinoe disappeared.

"Hallo, Joseph," Ellis says. "Have you and your family settled in? Where are you camped?"

"Just over that way," he says, and points to the east. "Though my parents decided to stay behind with Jonah, so it's just me and Matthew."

"Have you scouted ground for the Hunt?" Cait calls.

"No. Not yet."

"Then you'd best get after it. You and Juillenne both. If you go slowly enough, you can take this beast with you."

At her mention, Camden looks at Jules hopefully. Her left foreleg and shoulder are healing poorly, but her eyes are bright and yellow green. *I am not useless*, they seem to say. *I am still alive and eager.*

"Let's go," Jules whispers, and the cat canters ahead on three legs.

"Do a good job of it," Cait says. "There will be more deaths this year, just on account of so many jostling feet." She looks out across the enormous meadow. "It won't be long before these tents start to spill over onto the beaches."

And more will come, on top of that. Folk without any tents at all, to sleep out under the stars.

"Jules," Joseph says when they are inside the trees.

"The undergrowth is not thick," Jules says. That will make for easier going, but hunting in the darkness of the trees is always perilous. People trip and are trampled underfoot. They break their bones on uneven ground. Or they are caught by a careless blade or arrow.

"Jules."

He touches her shoulder.

"How are you? I mean, after all this."

"Shouldn't we be happy?" she asks, and shrugs him off. "Haven't we always wanted her to find a way off the island?"

"Yes," he says. "But I didn't think it would be so suddenly. And without word. I didn't think she would go without us."

Jules's eyes sting. "That does cut. But I don't blame her. She saw her chance."

Camden scouts ahead and grunts at the edge of a slippery washout along the widening banks of a creek. During the Hunt, Cam will be kept in the camp with the other familiars. Though she would love to join, it is no place for the snap-able bones of dogs and birds, and any could be mistaken for prey.

"Mirabella is here," Jules says. In the corner of her eye, Joseph tenses. "Did you see the carriages that brought her? Gilded and spotless. The horses had not a hair of white between them. If not for all the silver on their harnesses, they would have looked like shadows."

"I didn't see them," he says. "I haven't seen her, Jules."

"I'm saying that it's good that Arsinoe is gone," Jules continues. "She was never going to win. Maybe she could have, if she'd had the Westwoods or the Arrons behind her instead of us. If we had been able to give her . . . anything . . ."

"Arsinoe was happy," Joseph says. "She was our friend, and she got away. You made her strong enough to get away."

Camden's ears flicker backward as a branch pops beneath a foot. Other hunters scouting the woods. Joseph raises an arm in greeting. It is no one they know. They are probably naturalists but could have any gift. At Beltane, the people mix and mingle, though the tents do not reflect it. The naturalists are camped near other naturalists, and all the Indrid Down and Prynn tents are together. Even during the Hunt, only those with the war gift will venture outside their parties, and them only because they are so few and because they know the naturalist gift will provide a better opportunity for a kill.

"It's nearing time," Joseph says. His eyes are bright. Sad as he is for Arsinoe, he is still a young wolf, and this is his first time running with the pack.

"I don't imagine you had any hunts so grand when you were on the mainland," says Jules.

"No. We hunted, but it was nothing like this. It was daylight so we could see, for a start."

In the distance, toward camp, someone beats a drum. The day has turned late without them noticing. Soon, the fires will burn high and people will jump through them. Naturalists will trade their clothes for deerskin and streaks of black-and-white paint on their bodies.

By the time they return to the meadow, the sun has dipped behind the trees and turned the light to dusky yellow. And Cait was right. In their absence, Innisfuil has filled to near bursting. Tents edge together with barely a step of space between them, and the paths and fire pits are crowded with excited, smiling faces.

They reach Joseph's tent, and he skins out of his shirt.

"Are you going to keep those?" Jules asks, gesturing to his tan, mainlander trousers.

"I don't see why not," he says. "Everyone thinks I'm from the mainland, anyway."

He helps her out of her own shirt, down to her soft leather tunic and leggings. She is not much in the mood for hunting, but the naturalist blood in her veins will not let her stay behind. Already it tugs her toward the trees.

"Will you paint me?" Joseph asks. He holds out a jar of black.

At first, she does not know what to paint. And then she does.

She dips four fingers and drags lines down his shoulder. She dips them again and drags lines down his right cheek, before doing the same to herself.

"For Arsinoe," she says.

"That is perfect," he says. "But just one more."

"One more?"

He takes her by the wrist.

"I would wear your handprint, over my heart."

Jules's hand hovers over his chest. Then she covers her palm with paint and holds it against his heartbeat. As she does, she presses her lips to his.

She missed his touch. The heat of it, and the strength of his arms around her. Since Mirabella, sometimes it has felt like Joseph had never come back to the island at all. But he is there, even if Arsinoe is not, and even if their promises to each other about Beltane, and being together for the first time, have been spoiled.

Joseph holds on to Jules tightly. He kisses her as if he is afraid to stop.

She raises her hands to his chest and pushes him away.

"Joseph. I was wrong to do that."

"No," he says breathlessly. "You weren't. We can stay here all night, Jules, we don't have to hunt."

"No."

He touches her face, but she will not look in his eyes. What she would see there might change her mind.

"Will you never forgive me?" he asks.

"Not now," she says. "I do not want to feel like everything between us has been ruined. I want it to be right again and to go back to the way it was."

"What if it never does?" he asks.

"Then we will know that it was never meant to be."

THE BRECCIA DOMAIN

❖

"*I*t is so black," Katharine says.

"Yes," says Pietyr. "But you ought to know what black is, being a queen."

His voice comes from a distance behind her. He refused to go so close to the edge. But the moment Katharine saw the Breccia Domain, she dropped onto her belly and slithered up to it like a snake.

The Breccia Domain is the deep chasm in the ground that they call "the heart of the island." It is a sacred place. They say it has no bottom, and seeing it, Katharine cannot describe its darkness. It is so black that it is almost blue.

Pietyr sneaked her out as soon as Natalia and Genevieve were distracted by the Hunt. They slipped quietly into the deep southern Innisfuil woods, where hunting is forbidden, until the trees opened up on the stark gray rocks and the dark fissure in the island, like the wound from a jagged blade.

"Come out here with me," she says.

"No thank you."

She laughs and hangs her head over the edge. Pietyr cannot feel what she feels as a queen. This place is for her kind.

She takes another deep, deep breath.

The Breccia Domain feels. The Breccia Domain *is*, in that way that so many other sacred places on Fennbirn are, but the Domain is where all those other places connect. It is the source. Had Katharine been raised in the temples like Mirabella, she might have better words for the hum in the air and how it makes the back of her neck prickle.

The cold, dense air of it rushes into her blood and makes her so giddy that she laughs.

"Kat, come away from it now," Pietyr says.

"Must we go so soon? I like it here."

"I do not understand why. It is a morbid place in the middle of nowhere."

She rests her head on her hand and continues to look down into the fissure. Pietyr is right. She should not like it so well. In generations past, the Domain is where they would throw the bodies of the queens who did not survive their Ascension Years. Genevieve says that at the bottom of the hole, they lie in piles. Shattered.

But now Katharine does not think so. The Breccia Domain is so vast and deep. Those queens cannot be broken at the bottom. They must all still be falling.

"Katharine, we cannot stay here all night. We must return before the Hunt is over."

She takes one last, long look into the blackness and sighs.

Then she stands and brushes dust off her gown. They had better go back. She will need rest before tomorrow.

Tomorrow, they will prepare for the Disembarking at sunset, when she and Mirabella will see their suitors for the first time, as well as each other. She wonders whether the pretty elemental will be surprised to see her weak poisoner sister looking so healthy.

"What a waste," Katharine says. "Kissing that mainland boy, Billy Chatworth. Only to have him run off with Arsinoe."

"What do you mean kissing him?" Pietyr asks. "You kissed him?"

"Of course I did," she says. "Why do you think I left the drawing room? So that you would not have to watch."

"That is kind, but soon I will not be able to avoid it," he says. "You will have to pretend that I am not there, Kat. You will have to pretend that I do not exist."

"Yes, but I will only be pretending. And none of them will touch me here at Beltane. I will not be alone with them until after the Quickening."

Pietyr looks away, and Katharine walks to him and kisses him quickly. She will steal many more kisses from him tonight, and tomorrow night, hidden away from Genevieve's disapproving eye.

"We will not be parted," she whispers against his lips. "Even though we will always have to hide."

"I know, Kat," he says, and wraps his arms around her. She rests her head against his chest.

It will be hard but not impossible. They have gotten very good at hiding.

THE HUNT

❧

When the Hunt began, Jules was so close to Joseph that they were almost touching, standing near the front of the naturalist horde as the drums counted down. The High Priestess sounded the horn, and they ran with the rest, the only sounds in their ears the cries of other hunters, and the crushing of grass beneath their feet.

They stayed together for a while, running, as the naturalists' gifts drew game willingly into the trees. Then she looked to her right, and he was not there.

She searched for him every place she could think of. She even took up one of the torches to search the ground, in case he had fallen. But she did not find him, and now the woods are quiet.

"Joseph?" she calls. The other naturalists and those few with the war gift have left her far behind. For a time, she heard their victory cries, but now there is not even that. The poisoners with

301

their tainted blades and arrows have taken the high hunting ground in the hills below the cliffs, and the fast, light-footed elementals will have flooded the northern woods behind their precious queen's tent.

"Joseph!" she calls again, and waits.

He will be all right. He is fit and an able hunter. It is easy to lose track of a companion in such a trampling crowd; perhaps they were foolish to try to stay together in the first place.

Jules holds her torch out and peers into the dark. The night air chills her skin now that she is no longer running. After a moment, she sets off in the opposite direction of the pack. She has come this far already. There is no reason she should not find some game.

Mirabella sits before a cold plate of fruit and cheese. She stands quickly when something thumps outside her tent. Moments later, Bree and Elizabeth drag her unconscious guards inside.

"What is this?" she asks.

Bree looks very pretty in a black belted tunic with silver edging and high, soft boots. She and Elizabeth both wear cloaks of dark gray wool. Hunting cloaks.

Mirabella studies the unconscious priestesses. At least, she thinks that they are unconscious. They are both so still.

"What have you done?" Mirabella asks.

"We have not killed them," Bree says in a tone that suggests she would not care if they had. "They are only drugged.

A poisoner's trick, I know, but what good is being in a meadow full of poisoners if you cannot get even a simple sleeping water?"

Elizabeth holds out a folded gray cloak for Mirabella.

"We will be discovered," Mirabella says. She looks down at Elizabeth's side, where her hand should be. "We cannot risk it."

"Do not use me as an excuse," the priestess says. "I may be of the temple, but they will not control me." Beneath her hood, her olive cheeks are flushed with excitement.

"You will make a very bad priestess someday," Bree says, and laughs wickedly. "Why do you even stay? You could come and live with us. You do not belong with their lot."

Elizabeth thrusts the cloak into Mirabella's arms.

"It is not so bad, being a pariah," she says. "And just because the priestesses have turned on me does not mean that the Goddess has. Now come. We do not need to be gone long. Only long enough to see the naturalists. The real hunters, with feathers braided into their hair and bones around their necks."

"And their bare chests," says Bree.

"We can put these two back at their posts when we return," Elizabeth says. "Perhaps they will wake and be too ashamed to admit they fell asleep."

There is a dagger and slingshot tucked into Bree's belt, and a crossbow slung over Elizabeth's shoulder. Not for game but for protection. Mirabella's eyes dart to her friend's missing hand. She will need help, to reload.

"All right," she says, and slides into the cloak. "But quickly."

* * *

Jules hears the bear before she sees the den dug into the side of the hill. She moves her torch so the light falls across the entrance, and he looks back at her with bright, firelit eyes.

He is a great brown. She was not seeking him. She was on the path of a stag and would have caught up with her quarry over the next rise.

The bear does not want trouble. He has most likely retreated back into his winter den in order to avoid the hunters.

Jules draws her knife. It is long and sharp and can go through a bear's hide. But the bear will still kill her if he decides to fight.

The bear looks at the knife and sniffs. Part of her wants him to come. She is surprised by that, by the heat of her anger and the weight of her despair.

"If you are looking for the queen," she says, "you came too late."

It is not necessary to see the elementals or the poisoners to know that the naturalists will have the largest cache of meat. So many hunters flood the trees, and there are so many shouts of victory. Most who Mirabella sees have game tied to their belts: rabbits or nice fat pheasants. No one who attends the naturalist feast will be eating field-raised goat; that is certain.

She and Elizabeth and Bree have run far with the hunters. Perhaps farther than they meant to. But the parties move so fast. It is nearly impossible to keep from being caught up in their current.

"The naturalist gift grows strong," Mirabella says, thinking of Juillenne Milone and her mountain cat.

"I have heard whispers," says Elizabeth, "of a girl with a cougar for a familiar."

"They are not only whispers," says Mirabella. "I have seen her. In the forest that day, with my sister."

"With your sister?" Bree asks. She sounds alarmed. But in the dim light of the moon, she is only a shadowed shape.

"What?" Mirabella asks. "What is the matter?"

"Did you not wonder if the naturalists had grown clever as well as strong? That perhaps they had hidden Arsinoe's strength all this time and that cougar is truly hers?"

"I do not think so," Mirabella says.

"And besides," adds Elizabeth. "Mountain cat or no, Arsinoe is gone."

Mirabella nods. They ought to be heading back to the encampment. The poisoned priestesses will soon wake. But before she can say so, another hunting party comes upon them and sweeps them up into their run.

"Jules!"

It is only a harsh whisper, scarcely able to be heard above the cries of the hunters and Bree's and Elizabeth's laughter.

"Jules!"

Mirabella slows and then stops. Bree and Elizabeth run on without her.

"Joseph?"

He is alone, holding a low-burning torch. There are black

marks on his face and on his shoulder. But it is him.

When he sees her, he freezes.

"Queen Mirabella," he says. "What are you doing here?"

"I do not know," she says. "I probably should not be."

He hesitates a moment and then takes her by the hand and pulls her behind a broad tree trunk where they will not be seen.

Neither knows what to say. They grip each other's hands tightly. Joseph's jawline is smeared with blood, just visible in the light of the dying torch.

"You are injured," Mirabella says.

"It's just a scratch," he says. "I tripped over a log when the Hunt began. Lost my party."

Lost Juillenne, is what he means. Mirabella smiles slightly. "It seems you are injured often. Perhaps you should not be allowed out alone."

Joseph chuckles. "I suppose I shouldn't. Since I've been back here, I have become a bit . . . prone to accidents."

She touches the trace of blood on his chin. It is nothing serious. It only adds to his wildness, when coupled with the black stripes on his face and down his bare shoulder. She wonders who painted them, and imagines Jules's fingers sliding over Joseph's skin.

"I knew you would be here," she says. "Even after Arsinoe's escape. I knew. I hoped."

"I didn't think I would see you," he says. "You are supposed to be hidden away."

Hidden away. Kept prisoner, under heavy guard. But she

and Bree have been thwarting the temple's attempts to lock her up since they were children. It is a wonder the priestesses have not given up by now, or gotten better.

Mirabella slips her hand up Joseph's chest to curl around the base of his shoulder. He is warm from running and his pulse jumps at her touch. She presses closer until their lips are almost touching.

"You do not know me like you know Jules," Mirabella says. "But do you want me just the same? Did it matter, what happened that night, in the storm?"

Joseph breathes hard. He looks at her from beneath a lowered brow. He does not have much resistance left. He did not have much to begin with.

She slides her other arm around his neck, and he kisses her hard, pressing her into the tree.

"It mattered," he says against her. "But God, I wish it hadn't."

THE ARRON ENCAMPMENT

⚜

*T*he poisoner kill is mostly birds, and a few rabbits. It will be nothing compared to the naturalist kill, but that is to be expected. The Hunt is truly the naturalists' portion of Beltane.

Katharine joins Natalia in the long, white kitchen tent and finds Natalia wrist deep in feathers, plucking a pheasant.

"Should I," Katharine starts, "have brought the servants?"

"No," Natalia says. "The few we have brought are tasked with other things. But there are still birds to be plucked. Beltane makes servants of us all."

Katharine rolls up the sleeves of her gown and grabs for the nearest bird.

Natalia nods approvingly. "Pietyr has been a good influence on you," she says.

"He did not teach me to pull feathers," says Katharine. "I may make a mess of it."

"But you are self-assured. You are charming. You have grown up since he has come."

Katharine smiles back and puffs feathers away from her nose. Most of the birds are destined for the feasts, but a few of the best will be reserved for the Quickening Ceremony and her *Gave Noir*.

"Is that not why you brought him to Greavesdrake?"

"It is," Natalia says. "It was his task to make you a fanciable woman, and he has." There is a bit of blood on her fingers. She has been pulling too hard and has torn the skin. "It was my task to develop your gift and to keep you safe. My task to make you the queen."

"Natalia, what is the matter?" asks Katharine. "You sound as though you think you have failed."

"Perhaps I have," she says, and lowers her voice to a barely audible whisper, though there is no one else in the tent, and no nearby shadows on the canvas.

"I hoped that Arsinoe's escape would change their plans," Natalia goes on. "That they would be too busy searching for the hideous brat. Or that they would deem it unnecessary. But I have seen the crate's moving, and I know what is inside. All those serrated knives."

Across the table, Katharine keeps working. The faraway, vacant look in Natalia's ice-blue eyes, and the dread in her voice, chills Katharine to the bone.

"Arsinoe was a clever thing," Natalia says. "A coward but clever. Using that mainland boy to sneak her away . . . Who would have thought it possible?"

"I do not think that they made it," Katharine says. "I think they are both at the bottom of the sea. With fish biting away their cheeks."

Natalia laughs. "Perhaps. But if she is at the bottom of the sea, she is still not here. And they will have only one target."

"'They'? Natalia, what are you talking about? Is something wrong? Do you think I will fail the *Gave Noir*?"

"No. You will not. It will be a spectacular success."

Katharine flushes shamefully. The *Gave* is the thing she dreads. Since long before the humiliation of her birthday. Failing before Natalia and Genevieve is bad enough. To fail before the island will be so much worse.

"'Spectacular'? That is not likely," she says.

Natalia pushes the dead birds to the side. Her eyes travel over Katharine like she is seeing her for the first time.

"Do you trust me, Kat?"

"Of course I do."

"Then eat from the *Gave* until your belly is swollen." Her hand darts out to grab the young queen's as fast as the strike of a snake. "Eat it without fear. *And trust that there will be no poison.*"

"What? How?"

"The priestesses may think that they are smart," Natalia says. "But no one is better at sleight of hand than I am. And I will do anything to make you appear strong. So that no one will be able to say that this is a Sacrificial Year."

THE MILONE ENCAMPMENT

❧

"We used to share our meat," Ellis says, "instead of dividing into separate feasts. Poisoners, naturalists. Warriors. Elementals. Even the giftless. We were all one on festival days when I was young."

"When was that, Granddad," Jules asks. "One or two hundred years ago?"

Ellis grins and sends Jake over the top of the table to nip her fingers.

The morning after the Hunt is quiet. Everyone in the meadow is either working or resting. Or tending their wounded. As predicted, many within the great horde were injured. But there has been no word of any deaths. Some have begun to whisper that this Beltane is blessed.

But it cannot be blessed with Arsinoe gone.

Camden climbs clumsily onto Jules's lap and sniffs at the bandaged cut on Jules's shoulder. It is not from the bear. The great brown she left where she found him, snug in his den. Instead, she went on to her stag and brought him down fast, one cut with her knife across his throat. But a thrashing hoof caught her as she held him down.

Jules reaches over the table and slices Cam a thick piece of the stag's heart.

"That stag is the finest take of the Hunt," Cait says. "By rights that heart should go into a stew for the queens."

"Send the rest of it, then," Jules says. "All the queens are not here. And Arsinoe would want Cam to have her portion."

Behind the table, Madrigal's tent rustles. Jules frowns and squeezes her cougar. That tent has been rustling since she woke. Rustling and giggling. Madrigal is not alone.

"Get up and out of there," Cait says, and kicks the flap. "There's work."

The tent flap rises. Matthew holds it up so that Madrigal can duck beneath his arm.

Cait and Ellis freeze. Matthew has been with Madrigal, but that does not make any sense. He loves Aunt Caragh. Or he did. Madrigal's fingers slide down the open collar of his shirt, and he smiles. Grins, even, like a guileless hound that has been chasing thrown sticks.

Jules jumps up from the table so quickly that she unseats Camden.

"What have you done?" she shouts. Her hand slams down. Everything on the tabletop shakes. "Get away from him!"

"Jules, no!" Ellis grasps Camden around the neck just as

she is set to spring. Matthew steps in front of Madrigal to shield her, and Jules growls.

"I," Madrigal says. "I . . ."

"I don't care if you are my mother! You shut your mouth!"

"Juillenne Milone."

Jules quiets. She clenches her fists, and her teeth, and tears her eyes from Matthew and Madrigal to look at her grandmother.

"You get out of here now," Cait says calmly. "Go."

Jules takes several deep breaths. But she calms, and Ellis releases Camden. She turns on her heel.

"Jules, wait," says Madrigal.

"Madrigal," Cait says. "Keep quiet."

Jules stalks away into the Beltane crowd. She is lost in it in seconds.

For a while she walks without purpose, an angry girl and a mountain cat cutting a wide path. Matthew and Madrigal seemed so at ease. Not at all like new lovers. With Madrigal's frequent disappearances, it is impossible to determine when it started.

"I hate her," Jules says to Camden quietly. Selfish Madrigal, constantly acting without thought. She had created chaos for Jules's whole life and never did anything to fix it beyond pouting. Now she has Matthew. She always did like to take things from Caragh. Even this last thing. The only thing Caragh had left.

"Jules!"

She turns. It is Luke, shouldering his way through people.

She had not been sure he would come. Loyal Luke. He had believed in Arsinoe since the beginning. He was the only one who never doubted.

When he reaches Jules he wraps her in a warm embrace. Hank the rooster flutters down from Luke's back to peck a hello to Camden.

"I am glad you're here," Jules says. "You are one of the only welcome sights I have had at this festival."

He holds out a package wrapped in brown paper.

"What's this?" she asks.

"The dress I made for Arsinoe," he says.

Jules squeezes the fabric inside the bag.

"Why did you bring it?" she asks. "When she is not here to wear it?"

"It was never for her. She asked me to make it for you. She told me to make it well and to make it shine. For you and the eyes of your young man."

Jules holds the package to her chest. Sweet, foolish Arsinoe, to think of her instead of herself. Or perhaps not. Perhaps she had only done it because she knew even then that she intended to run away.

"Did she really leave us, Jules?" Luke asks. "Or was it the mainlander? Was she taken?"

Jules cannot imagine Arsinoe doing anything she did not want to do. But it is possible. And the thought will comfort Luke.

"I do not know," she says. "She may have been."

Luke sighs. Around them the faces are jovial. Untroubled festival faces. Most are probably glad that Arsinoe is gone. It is one less obstacle in Mirabella's path. Now there is only Katharine. A poisoner, rumored to be weak and sickly.

"I suppose we ought to support Mirabella now," Luke says. "I suppose we will have to grow to love her. It will be easier to do, since she didn't have to slay our Arsinoe."

Jules nods grimly. She will never love Mirabella, but for her own, small reasons. It does not mean she will make a poor queen.

"I saw the suitors' ships when I passed Sand Harbor," Luke says. "Five of them, though Billy's doesn't really count."

Jules nods grimly as Luke tells her which flags the ships bear. Two from the land of Bernadine's consort. One from Camille's. One from someplace he cannot identify. But Jules is no longer listening. Billy's father's ship is at Innisfuil. With Billy aboard it? Somehow she does not think so. She doubts that Chatworth has any more knowledge of Billy and Arsinoe's fate than anyone else.

"Strange, isn't it?" Luke ponders. "The way we take mainlanders in to our bosoms, just so we can keep them out?"

In the harbor to the southeast, the delegation ships will wait until sunset, when they begin the procession toward Longmorrow Bay. There, they will lay anchor for the Disembarking. Had Arsinoe been with her, Jules might have taken Camden across the cliffs to spy. Now it hardly matters. Let Mirabella choose whoever she likes. He will have little power on the island. King-consorts are figureheads. Symbols of peace with the mainland.

"What is that?" Luke asks, and points.

Priestesses run down the path from the cliffs in a black-and-white line. Jules and Luke press forward to get a better view. So do many others. Small as she is, Jules has to jump to see over their heads and shoulders.

There is a disturbance near the Westwood tents. Or perhaps it is in the High Priestess's tent. They are so close together that it is hard to tell. Luke prods a tall fellow in the back.

"Oi, do you know what's going on over there?"

"Can't be sure," the man replies. "But it sounds like they caught the traitor queen."

"That can't be," Luke says.

"I think it is. There are priestesses coming now."

"Let us through!" Jules shouts. But the crowd is too dense. She growls, and Camden snarls and jumps against the man's back, slicing his shirt. The edges of the fabric soak red, and he cries out.

The crowd parts. They also scream at her—horrible naturalist slurs about her and her beast. But she does not care. Behind her, Luke has gone for Cait and Ellis. If it really is Arsinoe, as Jules both prays and fears that it is, then she will need them all.

THE HIGH PRIESTESS'S
ENCAMPMENT

*I*t does not take long for the Black Council to assemble in the tent that Luca designated. The tent is small and mostly empty, with only a few rugs, and stacks of crates inside. It is flimsy and impermanent, but the weight of the people standing beneath it makes it seem as substantial as solid rock.

The poisoners Paola Vend and Lucian Marlowe, and war-gifted Margaret Beaulin, stand to one side with Renata Hargrove. Natalia Arron stands at the head. The head of the snake, Luca sometimes calls her. Behind her are the other Arrons of the council: Allegra, Antonin, Lucian, and Genevieve. Genevieve stands close at Natalia's shoulder. She is Natalia's ears on the council, they say. Her knife in the dark. Mirabella dislikes her on sight.

It is only by chance that Mirabella is there. She was with Luca when the priestesses came with the news of Arsinoe's capture, and Luca did not have time to argue with her about leaving.

Across the tent, Mirabella and Jules briefly lock eyes. It is a charged moment in the midst of charged moments, and it does not last long. But afterward, Mirabella will remember the fierceness in Jules's expression and how much she looked like the cougar beside her.

"Queen Mirabella should not be here," Natalia says in her cold, steady voice. She is the only one in the tent whose heart does not appear to be pounding. "She has no voice on the council."

"There are many here who do not have a voice on the council," Cait points out.

"Cait," Natalia says. "Of course you may stay. As fosters, all you Milones may stay."

"Aye, and we thank you," Cait replies sarcastically. "But is it true? Has she been found?"

"We will know soon enough," says Luca. "I have sent priestesses to the coast to collect these travelers, whoever they may be."

The Black Council sneers at the word "travelers," and Natalia shushes them like children. "If one of these travelers is indeed Arsinoe, then Queen Mirabella should go. You know better than anyone that they are not to meet until the Disembarking."

"They have already met once," Luca says. "Another time will do no harm. The queen will stay. She will stay and be silent. As will you, young Milone."

The cougar pins its ears. The elder Milones each place a hand on Jules's shoulders.

The priestesses return from the beach with tromping footsteps and jostling bodies. Mirabella listens tensely as the crowd mutters and gasps. And then the tent flap opens, and the priestesses throw Arsinoe inside.

Mirabella bites the inside of her cheek to keep from crying out. It is hard to tell that it is Arsinoe at first. She is soaked to the bone, and shaking, crumpled into a ball on the thin temple rug. And her face is ruined by deep, stitched gashes.

The priestesses stand guard with their hands on the hilts of their knives. They are ridiculous. The girl can barely stand let alone run.

"What happened to her face?" Renata Hargrove asks, disgusted.

"So there really was a bear," Genevieve mutters over Natalia's shoulder.

The stitched-together cuts are bright red. Irritated by the salt water.

More noise rumbles outside the tent flap, and two more priestesses enter with a boy struggling between them. Through his soaked, sand-streaked clothes, Mirabella recognizes him as the boy who was in the woods when Arsinoe and Jules found Joseph. He had been holding the horses. She had thought he was an attendant. But he must be the suitor, William Chatworth Jr.

The boy wrenches loose of the priestesses and kneels near Arsinoe, shivering.

"Arsinoe," he says. "It's going to be all right."

"Arsinoe, I'm here!" Jules shouts, but Cait and Ellis hold her back.

Lucian Marlowe reaches down and pulls Chatworth up by the collar. "The boy should be killed," he says.

"Perhaps," says Natalia. "But he is a delegate." She steps toward him and holds his chin in her hand. "Did you knowingly take Queen Arsinoe, mainlander? Did you attempt to help her flee? Or did she take control of your vessel and do it herself?"

Her voice is carefully neutral. Anyone listening would believe that she does not care one way or another how he answers.

"We were caught in a squall," he says. "We barely made it here. We did not mean to leave."

Margaret Beaulin laughs aloud. Genevieve Arron shakes her head.

"He didn't know," Arsinoe whispers from the carpet. "I made him. It was me."

"Very good," says Natalia. She flicks her wrist, and two priestesses take Billy by the arms.

"No," he says. "She's lying!"

"Why should we believe the word of a mainlander over one of our own queens?" Natalia asks.

"Take him to the harbor," she says. "Send word to his father. Tell him that we are most relieved that he has been returned unharmed. And hurry. He does not have long to recover before the Disembarking."

"This whole place is mad," Billy growls. "Don't you touch her! Don't you dare touch her!"

He struggles, but it is not difficult to remove him, exhausted as he is.

With him gone, every eye falls on Arsinoe.

"This is unfortunate," Renata says.

"And unpleasant," says Paola. "It would have been better had she stayed lost. If she had drowned. Now there will be a mess."

Genevieve slips out from behind Natalia and leans down close to Arsinoe's ear.

"She has been very stupid," she says. "Another boat and another boy. She has not even come up with a different plan."

"Get away from her." Jules Milone's voice is a growl. Genevieve looks for a moment at the cougar, as if unsure it was not the one who actually spoke.

"Quiet," the High Priestess says. "And you, Genevieve. Get back."

Genevieve clenches her jaw. She looks to Natalia, but Natalia does not disagree. At Beltane, the temple rules. The Goddess rules, whether the Black Council likes it or not.

Luca kneels before Arsinoe. She takes the queen's hands between her own and rubs them.

"You feel like ice," she says. "And you look like a belly-up fish." She motions to one of the priestesses. "Bring her water."

"I do not want water."

Luca sighs. But she smiles at Arsinoe kindly, trying to be patient. "What do you want, then? Do you know where you are?"

"I tried to get away from you," Arsinoe says. "I tried to run, but the mist wouldn't let go. We fought. We paddled. But it held us like a net."

"Arsinoe," Cait says. "Do not say any more."

"It doesn't matter, Cait. Because I couldn't get away. She held us in that fog until she spit us out, right into this cursed harbor."

Arsinoe's arms tremble, but her eyes do not waver. They are red, and weary, full of hatred and despair, but they remain fixed on the High Priestess's face.

"Does she know?" Arsinoe asks. "Does your precious queen know what you are planning?"

Luca inhales sharply. She tries to pull away, but Arsinoe does not let go. Priestesses advance to help, and grasp Arsinoe by the shoulders.

"Does she know that you are planning to kill me?"

The priestesses force Arsinoe facedown onto the rug. Jules shouts, and Ellis holds Camden tight by the neck to keep her from leaping.

"Does she know?" Arsinoe shrieks.

"Kill her," Luca says calmly. "The escape cannot be pardoned a second time." She motions to the priestesses, and they draw their knives. "Take her head and her arms. Cut the heart separate from the body. And throw it all into the Breccia Domain."

Arsinoe struggles as the priestesses move upon her. They pin her down. They raise their knives. The council looks on in shock. Not even the poisoners were ready for this. The only one not slightly green is war-gifted Margaret Beaulin.

"No!" Jules shouts again.

"Get her out of here," Natalia says. "For the girl's own good, Cait. She does not need to see this."

Cait and Ellis struggle with Jules and drag her out of the tent. Mirabella steps forward and takes Luca by the arm.

"You cannot do this," she says. "Not here. Not now. She is a queen!"

"And she will have the death rites of a queen, though she dies in disgrace."

"Luca, stop. Stop it now!"

The High Priestess pushes Mirabella back gently.

"You do not have to stay either," she says. "Perhaps it would be better if we escorted you out."

On the thin rug, Arsinoe is screaming as the priestesses tear at her, pressing her down, pulling her limbs to lay flat. It seems that she is crying red tears, but it is only that the stitches in her face have begun to stretch.

"Arsinoe," Mirabella whispers. Arsinoe used to chase Katharine like a monster through the muddy bank. She was always dirty. Always angry. Always laughing.

One of the priestesses places a foot on Arsinoe's back and

yanks her arm hard to pull it out of joint. Arsinoe yelps. She does not have much fight left. It will not be difficult to saw through her arms and head.

"No!" Mirabella shouts. "You will not do this!"

She calls down the storm almost without knowing it. Wind bows the sides of the tent and tears at the flaps. The priestesses upon Arsinoe are so focused that they do not notice until the first bolt of lightning shakes the ground beneath them.

The Black Council scatters like rats. Before she can send the flames from the candles after them, or lightning comes straight for their heads. Luca and the priestesses try to reason with her, but Mirabella brings the storm down harder. Half the tent collapses beneath the force of the wind.

In the end, they all run.

Mirabella gathers Arsinoe into her lap and brushes salty, filthy hair from her sister's cheeks. The storm calms.

"It is all right now," Mirabella says softly. "You will be all right."

Arsinoe blinks her tired black eyes. "You're going to pay for this," she says.

"I do not care," says Mirabella. "Let them execute us both."

"Hmph," Arsinoe snorts. "I'd like to see them try."

Mirabella kisses her sister's forehead. She is weak and feverish. The knotted wounds that line her face are swollen and slightly torn. Every bit of her must sing with pain. Yet Arsinoe does not wince.

"You are made of stone," Mirabella says, and touches

Arsinoe's stitched-together cheek. "It is a wonder that anything was able to cut you at all."

Arsinoe struggles out of Mirabella's arms. That too is like the sister she remembers. Always a wild thing, not made for cuddling.

"Is there water?" Arsinoe asks. "Or did you turn it into an arrow and stab Natalia Arron through the heart?"

Mirabella retrieves the pitcher from where the storm cast it onto the floor. Most of it spilled, but there is still a cupful, sloshing against the sides. "There is not much," she says. "I was not focused. I only wanted to keep them away. It was like that day at the Black Cottage."

"I don't remember that day," Arsinoe says. She upends the pitcher and swallows greedily. She may throw it up as soon as she stands.

"Try, then. Try to remember."

"I don't want to." Arsinoe sets down the pitcher. It takes a moment, but eventually, she is able to rise.

"Your shoulder," Mirabella says. "Be careful."

"I'll get Jules to put it back in. I should go."

"But," Mirabella says, "the council and Luca . . . They will be waiting."

"Oh," Arsinoe says. She takes a step and holds her breath and then takes another. "I don't think they will. I think you made your point."

"But if you let me . . ."

"Let you what? Listen, I know you think you did something

really grand just now. But I'm here. I'm caught. We all are."

"You hate me, then?" Mirabella asks. "You want to kill me?"

"Yes, I hate you," Arsinoe says. "I always have. I didn't try to escape so that I could spare you. It was not about you."

Mirabella watches her sister limp toward the tent flap.

"I suppose I have been very stupid," Mirabella says. "I suppose . . ."

"Stop sounding so sad. And stop looking at me that way. This is what we are. It doesn't matter that we didn't ask for it."

Arsinoe grabs on to the flap of the tent. She hesitates as though she might say more. As though she might be sorry.

"I hate you a little less now," she says quietly, and then she is gone.

THE MILONE ENCAMPMENT

❧

$\mathcal{J}$ules is waiting for Arsinoe just beyond the half-collapsed tent. Arsinoe will not take a shoulder to lean on, but she accepts Jules's arm, and tugs the collar of her shirt over her face. It at least provides a small shield from the spit and fruit peelings as they navigate the crowds.

"Everyone stay back!" Jules shouts. "No one say a word!"

They do stay back, thanks to Camden. But they say and throw plenty.

"Just like being at home, eh?" Arsinoe says grimly.

Inside her tent at the Milone encampment, safe from prying eyes, Cait and Ellis tend to her. Luke and Joseph are there as well. Even Madrigal. When Ellis sets Arsinoe's shoulder, Luke weeps.

"Queen Mirabella is one for the rules," Ellis says. "She will not even let priestesses harm a queen before her time."

"Is that why she stopped them?" Jules asks. "Or does she just want to do it herself?"

"Whatever the reason, I think that the temple will find her harder to control than they thought," says Ellis.

"Is Billy all right?" Arsinoe asks. "Has anyone heard?"

"He was safe when they escorted him toward Sand Harbor," Joseph says. "I'm sure he's there now, preparing for the Disembarking."

"The Disembarking," Madrigal says. "We do not have long until sundown."

"Be silent, Madrigal," Jules says. "She does not have to worry about that."

"No," Arsinoe says. "I do. I'm here, and I won't have you getting into any more trouble on my account."

"But—" Jules says.

"I would rather walk up those cliffs than be dragged by priestesses."

Cait and Ellis look at each other solemnly.

"We had best finish preparing for the feast, then," Cait says. "And dig our blacks out of mothballs."

"I can help," Luke says. He looks very handsome, and very smart, in his festival clothes. But Luke is always better dressed than the rest of Wolf Spring. "If I'm staying and eating, I ought to pull my weight." He takes Arsinoe's hand and squeezes. "I am glad to see you back," he says, and follows Cait and Ellis out of the tent.

Arsinoe sits down on the makeshift bed of pillows and blankets. She could sleep for days, even in a tent that smells like mold, with no furniture besides a wooden trunk and a table with water in a cream-colored pitcher.

"I should wring your neck," says Jules.

"Be nice to me. My neck was almost severed, not one hour ago."

Jules pours Arsinoe a cup of water before sitting on the trunk.

"I need to tell you something," Arsinoe says. "I need to tell you all."

They gather close. Jules and Joseph. Madrigal. They listen as she tells them what Billy told her. About the Sacrificial Year, and the priestess's plot to assassinate her and Katharine.

"This can't be true," Jules says when Arsinoe is finished.

"But it is. I saw it in old Luca's eyes." Arsinoe sighs. "Luke should go. Someone should get him out. He would stand between me and a thousand priestesses' knives, and I don't want him to be hurt."

"Wait," Joseph says. "We can't give up now, after all this. There has to be some way . . . some way to stop them."

"To outmaneuver the High Priestess at the Beltane Festival?" Arsinoe asks. "It isn't likely. You should . . . ," she says, and pauses. "You should take Jules away, too, Joseph. For the same reason as Luke."

"I'm not going anywhere," Jules says. Her eyes flash at Joseph like he intended to grab her right that instant.

"I don't want you to see it, Jules. I don't want any of you to see it."

"Then we'll stop it," says Madrigal.

They turn to look at her. She sounds very sure.

"You said that the temple is using the guise of the Sacrificial Year," Madrigal says. "One strong queen and two weak ones."

"Yes," says Arsinoe.

"So we will make you strong. They cannot strike after the Quickening if the island does not see weakness. Their lie will not hold."

Arsinoe looks at Jules and Joseph.

"That might work," Arsinoe says wearily. "But there is no way to make me strong."

"Wait," Jules says. Her eyes are unfocused and faraway. Whatever it is that she is thinking, she is so distracted that she does not even respond when Camden tugs on her pant leg with very sharp claws.

"What if there was a way to make you *look* strong?" Her eyes snap back to Arsinoe's. "What if on stage tomorrow night, you call your familiar, and it arrives in the form of a great brown bear?"

Arsinoe inadvertently touches the cuts on her face. "What are you talking about?"

"I saw a great brown in the western woods," Jules says. "What if I could get him to go to you? I could hold him on that stage."

"That is too much, even for you. A great brown bear, in the midst of the crowds and clamor . . . You couldn't hold him. He'd tear me apart in front of everyone." Arsinoe cocks her head. "Though I suppose I would prefer that he do it, rather than the priestesses."

THREE DARK CROWNS

"Jules can do it," Madrigal says. "But just to hold the bear on stage will not be enough. It must be made to obey you, or no one will believe. We will need to tie it to you, through your blood."

Jules grabs her mother by the wrist. "No. No more."

Madrigal jerks away and shakes the touch off dismissively. "Juillenne. There is no choice. And it will still be dangerous. It will not be a familiar-bond. You won't be able to communicate with it. It will be more like a pet."

Arsinoe looks at Camden. She is no pet. She is an extension of Jules. But better a pet than a torn-out throat or losing her head and arms.

"What do we need?" Arsinoe asks.

"Its blood and yours."

Jules inhales shakily. Joseph takes her by the elbow.

"This is too much," he says. "Holding a bear is one thing, but taking his blood? There must be some other way."

"There isn't."

"It's too dangerous, Jules."

"You've been gone a long time," says Madrigal. "You don't know what she can do."

Jules puts her hand over Joseph's.

"Trust me," she says. "You always have before."

Joseph clenches his jaw. It seems that every muscle in his body might burst from tension, but he manages to nod.

"What can I do to help?" he asks.

"Stay away," says Jules.

"What?"

"I'm sorry but I mean it. This is the hardest thing I have ever asked of my gift. I can't be distracted. And I don't have much time. It will take a while, to move him from the woods. I will have to take him around the valley, where he won't be seen. Even if I sneak out tonight, after everyone is asleep, I may not make it in time. And if the Hunt drove him farther away . . ."

"It is the only chance we have," Arsinoe says. "Jules, if you're willing, I would try."

Jules glances at Madrigal. Then nods.

"I'll leave tonight."

THE DISEMBARKING

*A*rsinoe is the last queen to take her place atop the cliffs for the Disembarking. By the time she makes her way through the meadow and up the path, the valley has emptied. Everyone has assembled on the beach, to stand beside tall, lit torches and await the ships.

Arsinoe adjusts the mask on her face. Even the lightest touch on her inflamed cuts hurts. But she must wear the mask. She wants to, after Ellis went to so much trouble. Besides, the painted red streaks will look fierce against the firelight. Though perhaps not as fierce as her actual wounds.

She steps up to the makeshift pavilion atop the cliffs, and looks down toward the people. They will see what they will see. Dressed in black pants, and a black shirt and vest, Arsinoe does not hide.

On the farthest pavilion from Arsinoe, Katharine stands, still as a statue, surrounded by Arrons. A strapless black gown hugs the young queen tight, and black gems circle her throat. A live snake slithers around her wrist.

On the center platform, Mirabella's gown billows around her legs. She wears her hair loose, and it blows off her shoulders. She does not look at Arsinoe. She stares straight ahead. Mirabella stands as though she is *the* queen and there is no reason to look anywhere else.

The Arrons and Westwoods step away from their pavilions. Arsinoe panics and grabs for Jules.

"Wait," she says. "What am I supposed to do?"

"The same thing you always do," Jules says, and winks.

Arsinoe squeezes her hands. It ought to be Jules standing up there between the torches, beautiful, in the dress that Luke made. Back in the tent, Madrigal touched Jules's lips with copper and red, and braided her hair with ribbons of copper and dark green, to match the ribbon edging of the gown. If it were Jules on the platform, the island would see a beautiful naturalist with her mountain cat, and they would have no doubts.

Arsinoe glances down at the beach and her head spins.

"I'm afraid," she whispers.

"You are not afraid of anything," Jules says, before stepping back down the cliff path to wait with her family.

The drums start, and Arsinoe's stomach flutters. She is still weak from the boat, with a belly full of salt water.

She pushes her legs out and squares her shoulders. She will not fall or sicken. Or tumble down the cliffside to the delight of her sisters.

She looks again at Mirabella, beautiful and royal without effort, and at Katharine, who is lovely and wicked-looking as black glass. Compared to them, she is nothing. A traitor and a coward. Giftless, unnatural, and scarred. Compared to them, she is no queen at all.

In the bay, five mainland ships wait, anchored. As Arsinoe watches, each ship sends its launch; each launch carries a boy who hopes to become an island king. All are decorated and lit with torches. She wonders which one belongs to Billy. She hopes that his father was kind when he returned.

The drums quicken, and the crowd turns away from the queens to watch the launches approach. The crowd, all in black, must make an imposing sight to come ashore to, but only one suitor seems afraid: a tan, dark-haired boy with a red flower in his jacket. The others lean forward, smiling and eager.

Billy's launch lags behind as the others come ashore. The suitors are too far below for words or introductions. That will come later. The Disembarking is all ceremony. First looks and first blushes.

Arsinoe raises her chin as the first boy bows to Katharine. Katharine smiles and drops half a curtsy. When he bows to Mirabella, she nods. When he finally bows to Arsinoe, it is with surprise, as if he had not noticed that she was there. He stares at her mask for too long. He offers only a partial bow.

Arsinoe does not move. She stares them down to the last and lets the mask do its job. Until Billy comes ashore.

Her heart warms. He does not seem weak or injured.

Billy stands below the cliffs and looks up at her. He bows, deep and slow, and the crowd murmurs. Arsinoe holds her breath.

He bows only to her.

THE ARRON ENCAMPMENT

*P*oisoners are allowed no poison in their Beltane feasts. Those are the rules, as decreed by the temple, so that any Beltane reveler may partake of the offerings. It seems very unfair to Natalia, when the elementals are free to blow wind through the valley, and the naturalists let their filthy familiars run wild.

On Natalia's plate, a headless, roasted bird shines up at her, completely devoid of toxin. She will not stoop to eating it. Yesterday, it was singing joyfully in the scrub bushes. What a waste.

She stands with a huff of disgust and then goes inside the tent. The flap moves behind her, and she turns to see Pietyr.

"They should let us do as we wish with our own feast," he says, reading her mind. "It is not as if anyone is brave enough to try our food, anyway."

She looks out into the night, the bonfires and milling people. He is right, of course. Not even those who have had too much to drink will dare touch what the poisoners prepare. There is too much fear. Too little trust.

"The delegates may venture close enough to eat," Natalia says. "And we do not want to be poisoning them. It would create a spectacle if they had convulsions on the rug."

And they cannot afford to lose a one. There are fewer and fewer suitors every generation. On the mainland, the number of families who share the secret of the island has dwindled. One day, Fennbirn may be nothing more than a rumor, a legend to delight the mainland children.

Natalia sighs. She has seen a few of the suitors standing before Katharine's feast already. The first was the handsome boy with broad shoulders and golden-blond hair. He seemed to like the look of her very much, though they will still not be allowed to speak.

"I hope you have taught her to flirt from a distance," Natalia says.

"She knows how to use her eyes," Pietyr says. "And her movements. Do not worry."

But he is worried. She can see it in the drag of his shoulders.

"It is unfortunate that the Chatworth boy proved loyal to Arsinoe," Pietyr says.

"Is it? I am not so sure. I have been assured that he will fall into line."

"It did not seem that way on the beach. Right now he is probably lingering outside of Arsinoe's feast, like a dog hoping for scraps."

Natalia closes her eyes.

"Are you all right, Aunt? You seem tired."

"I am fine."

But she is tired. Katharine's Ascension Year is the second of her lifetime. It will probably be her last. It was all so much easier with Camille, when Natalia was still a girl and her mother was still alive to act as the head of the family.

Pietyr stares through the tent flap.

"The country fools dare one another to come close to our feast," he says. "Such is our influence. It is hard to believe that it will all be over tomorrow. It is hard to believe that the priestesses have won."

"Who says that they have?" Natalia asks, and Pietyr looks at her in surprise. "You say that I am tired, but why do you think that is? You asked me to find a way to save our Kat. All day long, I have been preparing food for a *Gave Noir* with no poison in it."

"How?" Pietyr asks. "With priestesses overseeing everything?"

Natalia inclines her head. No poisoner is better at sleight of hand than she is.

"Natalia, they will test it."

Natalia does not reply. He acts as though she has not been slipping poison into things unnoticed for most of her life.

THE HIGH PRIESTESS'S ENCAMPMENT

"*J* do not believe the brat returned," says Rho, standing with Luca outside the High Priestess's tent, watching the last of the temple crates be moved.

"It is a curious thing," Luca says. "Queen Arsinoe washing up on our beach was certainly not something I expected. But it was not her choice."

"Her part in the story is not over yet, it seems," says Rho. "Or perhaps the Goddess is as mindful of tradition as our Mirabella, and no queen leaves unless she is dispatched by her sister's hand."

"What have you heard, Rho?" Luca asks, her eyes on the crates. "About today's debacle? What are the whispers?"

"The only whispers I have heard are about Arsinoe's return. When they mention Mirabella's storm they only talk about her rage. Nobody suspects why the storm was actually called."

Rho steps away to bark at one of the priestesses for failing to notice that the crate she is carrying has been damaged. She jerks it from her and cuffs her on the back of the head. The initiate, barely thirteen years old, runs away, crying.

"You did not need to do that," says Luca. "It was in no danger of cracking."

"It was for her own good. Had it broken open, she might have lost most of her hand."

Rho grasps the crate and twists. The sides splinter apart. Packed inside are three dozen of the temple's serrated knives.

Luca takes one of the knives out of the crate. The long, slightly curved blade glows ominously in the light from the festival bonfires. She does not know how old it is, but the handle is well-worn and comfortable. It might have come from any number of temples before finding its way to Innisfuil. Perhaps it came from a naturalist place and was used primarily for cutting wheat. But no matter where its origin, there is little doubt it has tasted blood.

She turns the knife back and forth. As High Priestess, it has been years since she has carried one.

"You will have to lead them tomorrow," Luca says. "In the silence after Mirabella's fire dance ends. Before I am to speak. Go over the top of the Arrons and get to Katharine. Do not take long. I want you to be at the fore when we take Arsinoe."

"Yes. I will be there. The Milone girl with the mountain cat is the only one likely to give me any trouble. I will take the cat first, if it tries to stop us."

Luca thumbs the blade of the knife and does not realize it

has cut through the pad of her finger until blood wells over the edges of her skin.

"They must all be this sharp," she says. "So it is fast and they do not even feel it."

THE MILONE ENCAMPMENT

The Milone feast is the most popular feast of the festival, and not only because of the roasted meat of Jules's fine stag. Almost despite herself, Arsinoe made an impression at the Disembarking. People crowd the grounds around the table and tents to get a closer look at her and her black painted mask. She was nothing like the other queens, standing on those cliffs. Now, they wonder if there is more to her than meets the eye. If there is something that they missed.

"There's the last one," Joseph says through a mouthful of stew. He gestures with his head into the milling bodies, and Arsinoe sees a suitor, the one with golden-blond hair, staring at her from across the tables. She allows herself a grin, and a glance toward Billy, who watches protectively from nearby.

"That makes all of them," says Luke.

Arsinoe had not expected to see any. So much attention is strange.

"If I knew how these mainlanders enjoyed indifference, I wouldn't have worried so much," she says, and looks at Billy again. "I wish Junior didn't have to stay away. Someone go and fetch him. Let the temple wag their tongues."

Jules laughs. "Look who is drunk on triumph," she says. "No, Arsinoe. You have broken more than enough rules already." She touches Joseph. "Joseph and I will go and keep him company."

"Before he starts a fight with one of the other suitors in your name," Joseph says, and grins.

Before they go, Jules nudges Arsinoe's shoulder. The night grows late. It will not be long before the fires burn lower and she will leave for the woods after the great brown bear.

Arsinoe looks Jules a long time in the eyes. Brave girl. Her gift is so strong, but a great brown bear may be stronger.

"I wish I didn't need you," Arsinoe says. "Or I wish I could go with you."

"I will be careful," says Jules. "Don't worry."

Billy is sullen when Jules and Joseph join him on the edge of the feast. He stands with arms crossed, watching the other suitor with open hostility.

"We brought you some of Ellis's stew," Joseph says, and shoves a bowl into his hands. "Since you haven't ventured close enough to get any for yourself."

"I didn't know how close I was allowed to get," Billy says. "And after the way we were found, I thought it best to keep some distance."

THREE DARK CROWNS

"But you didn't think it was a bad idea to bow only to her? Your father is going to have your head."

"Believe me, I know. I don't know what I was thinking." He sips the stew.

"It was a help to her," says Jules. "Look at all these people. What you did had a hand in this. And what you did before. Trying to take her away."

Billy lowers his head. "I'm sorry about that. Not telling you. I had to do it, knowing what these priestesses have planned. And here she is, back here, anyway. Damn it all."

"It'll be all right. We have our own plan."

"What is it?" Billy asks, and Jules whispers it into his ear. His face brightens at once. "Joseph always said you were a glorious thing. And that dress. You are ravishing in that dress."

"Ravishing? That's a very fine word."

"Perhaps, but it is the right one."

Jules blushes and slides closer to Joseph to hide beneath his arm.

"Well," Billy says, and sighs. "You don't need to keep me company. I intend to stay here all night until those priestesses escort me back to my launch."

"Are you sure?" Joseph asks, but Jules tugs his arm. They wave good-bye and walk off through the crowds.

"What are we doing?" Joseph asks as she slips her hand into his.

"I thought it a good idea if we were seen," she says. "So that

345

when I am not here tomorrow, anyone wondering will think that I am only off in a tent somewhere with you."

The night is filled with bonfires and laughter. Slender girls pull boys into a dance with rosy, warm cheeks, and in Luke's gown, Jules feels as beautiful as any of them.

"I have never seen you like this," Joseph says, and the way his eyes move over her body fills her with pleasure. "Luke will have to close down the bookshop and become a tailor."

Jules laughs. The weight that she felt when Beltane began has lifted. Arsinoe has returned. And they will not stand by and let her be killed. They will take action, and the idea buoys her so completely that Camden leaps in a joyful circle, as if she were a kitten.

In the corner of her eye, a girl slides her fingers down a boy's bare chest. Many couples tonight will disappear into tents or to the soft ground beneath the trees.

"How did we get here?" Joseph asks.

Jules has navigated the fires in a slow circle, so that they are standing directly beside her tent.

She pulls Joseph inside. "I feel like I should apologize, for the time I've wasted," she says.

"No," Joseph says. "Don't ever apologize."

She lights a lamp and closes the tent flap. Her tent is not very large, and her bed is nothing more than a thin roll of blankets. But it will have to do.

She steps close and slides her fingers under the collar of his shirt. His pulse races before she raises her lips to kiss his throat. He smells of the spices used to prepare the feast. His arms wrap around her.

"I have missed you," she says.

"Before the Hunt, you didn't want me," he starts, but she shakes her head. Everything hurt before. Now, everything is different.

Jules draws his mouth down to hers and presses her body fiercely against him. She is bold tonight. Perhaps it is the gown or the energy of the fires.

They kiss hungrily, and Joseph's hands clutch Jules's back.

"I am so sorry," he says.

She unbuttons his shirt. She moves his hands around to the fastenings of her dress.

"Jules, wait."

"We have waited long enough."

She backs up toward her makeshift bed, and they lower to their knees.

"I have to tell you," he says, but Jules stops him with her lips and her tongue. She does not want to hear anything—about Mirabella. It is over. Done. Mirabella does not matter.

They lie down together, and Jules hands glide under Joseph's shirt. She would touch all of him tonight. Every inch of bare skin.

Joseph holds himself on top of her carefully. He kisses her shoulders and her neck. "I love you," he says. "I love you, I love you."

And then he squeezes his eyes closed, and his face crumples.

He slides off her and rolls onto his back.

"Joseph? What's the matter?"

"I'm sorry," he says, and covers his eyes with his hand.

"Did I do something wrong?" Jules asks, and Joseph squeezes her tightly.

"Just let me hold you," he says. "I just want to hold you."

THE ARRON ENCAMPMENT

❖

After the feast ends, and the fires burn low, Katharine and Pietyr lie in her tent, side by side, Pietyr on his back and Katharine on her belly, listening to the last of the night's revel. The air smells of sparks and smoke, of different woods burning, and different meats cooking. Below those warm scents, there is evergreen needles, and salt air from over the cliffs.

"Do you believe Natalia?" Pietyr asks. "When she says that she will be able to alter the *Gave Noir*?"

Katharine drums her fingers atop his chest. "She has never given me any reason to doubt her."

Pietyr does not reply. He was quiet during the feast. Katharine climbs on top of him to try to cheer him with kisses.

"What is wrong?" she asks. "You are not yourself. You are so tender." She lifts his hand and drops it on her hip. "Where is your usual demanding touch?"

"Have I been such a brute?" Pietyr asks, and smiles. Then he closes his eyes. "Katharine," he says. "Sweet, foolish, Katharine. I do not know what I am doing."

He rolls onto his side and then grasps her chin. "Do you remember the way to the Breccia Domain?" he asks.

"Yes, I think so."

"It is there," he says, and points through the tent in the direction of the southern woods. "Through the trees behind the five-sided tent with white rope. Straight back from there until you reach the stones and the fissure. You have to cross the stream. Do you remember?"

"I remember, Pietyr. You lifted me over the water."

"But I will not, tomorrow night. I will not be able to."

"What do you mean?" Katharine asks.

"Listen to me, Kat," Pietyr says. "Natalia thinks that she has this all in hand. But if she does not . . ."

"What?"

"I will not be there tomorrow night at the Quickening," he says. "If it goes wrong, I could not bear to watch it."

"You have no faith in me," she says, hurt.

"It is not that. Katharine, you must promise me something. If anything goes wrong tomorrow night, I want you to run. Straight to me, at the Breccia Domain. Do you understand?"

"Yes," she says softly. "But Pietyr, why—"

"Anything, Kat. If anything goes wrong. Do not listen to anyone. Just go there. Do you promise?"

"I do, Pietyr. I promise."

The Quickening

THE WESTWOOD ENCAMPMENT

*lizabeth drapes the black cloak over Mirabella's back, and Bree ties it before her chest. It hangs carefully over the wet, herb-soaked black cloth wrapped around her hips and breasts. It is all she will wear for the Quickening Ceremony, except for the fire.

"Your young man will not be able to take his eyes off you," Bree says.

"Bree," Mirabella says, and shushes her. "There is no young man."

Bree and Elizabeth exchange conspiratorial smiles. They do not believe her, since they found her at the edge of the meadow after the Hunt, flushed and breathless. But Mirabella cannot bring herself to tell them about Joseph. He is a naturalist, and loyal to her sister. That may be too much for even Bree to understand.

Outside, the light turns orange, on its way toward pink and

blue. The ceremony begins on the beach at sundown.

"Have you seen Luca yet?" Mirabella asks.

"I saw her heading to the beach late this afternoon. She will have much to do. I don't know whether she will make it back to see you before it is time." Elizabeth smiles reassuringly. Yes, the High Priestess must be busy. It is not that she is furious with Mirabella for interfering with Arsinoe's execution.

"You ought to be angry with her, anyway," Bree says.

"I am," says Mirabella. She is, and she is not. Luca has been dear to her all these years. The strife between them these past months has not been easy.

"What are these priestesses about, Elizabeth?" Bree asks, peering out from between the tent flaps. "They are all acting strangely. Huddled together. Muttering."

"I don't know. I am one of yours now, and they know it. They tell me nothing."

Mirabella cranes her neck to look. Bree is right. The priestesses have not behaved normally all day. They are even more hard and aloof than usual. And some seem afraid.

"There is something in the air," Bree says, "that I do not like."

THE MILONE ENCAMPMENT

Arsinoe buttons another vest over another black shirt and straightens the ribbon on her mask. Behind her, Madrigal fidgets in a soft black dress.

"Did Jules tell you?" Madrigal asks. "That she saw me with Matthew?"

Arsinoe stops. She turns to Madrigal, surprised and disappointed.

"Matthew?" she asks. "You mean Caragh's Matthew."

"Don't call him that."

"To you and to all of us, that's who he is. I imagine that Jules was not too happy."

Madrigal kicks at a pillow and tosses her pretty chestnut hair.

"No one was happy. I knew that you wouldn't be. I knew just what you would say."

Arsinoe turns away from her again. "If you knew what we

would say, then our words must not matter much. You did it anyway."

"Do not fight with me today! You need me."

"Is that why you told me now?" Arsinoe asks. "So I couldn't give you the tongue-lashing you deserve?"

But she does need Madrigal. On a small circular table sits the beginnings of the spell—a small stone bowl of water that has been boiled and cooled, scented with herbs and red rose petals. Madrigal pouts as she lights a candle and warms the edge of her knife in the flame.

"I haven't seen Jules yet," Arsinoe says, changing the subject. "If she doesn't make it in time . . ."

Madrigal takes up the bowl and walks toward her with the knife. Arsinoe rolls up her sleeve.

"Do not think that way." She slices deep into Arsinoe's arm. "She will be here."

Arsinoe's blood drizzles into the bowl like honey from a comb. It blooms bright red in the water and stirs up the herbs and ground petal bits. Between her blood and the bear's, it will be half water and half blood. She cannot imagine having to drink it.

"Will the magic still work if I throw this up onto the stage?"

"Hush," says Madrigal. "Now, you can't carve the rune into your hand. There are too many old rune wounds there, and this one can't afford to be muddied. You'll have to draw it. Then press it to the bear's head, coated in the potion. Save enough to pool into your palm after drinking the rest."

"Are you sure I have to drink it all? Can't the bear and I share it?"

Madrigal presses a cloth to the cut and squeezes Arsinoe's arm hard. "Stop joking! This is no small spell. It will not make the bear your familiar. Perhaps not even your friend. If Jules is not strong enough to hold it after guiding it through the valley, then it may still tear you apart in front of everyone."

Arsinoe closes her mouth. They should not have asked Jules to do this. Joseph was right—it is too much. Holding the bear in the quiet woods would be difficult. Holding it steady in front of a roaring crowd and blazing torches seems nearly impossible.

"If only we could dye Jules's hair black and let her be queen . . . ," Arsinoe says sarcastically.

"Yes," says Madrigal. "If only."

Outside the tent flap, Jake barks.

"Arsinoe," Ellis says. "It's time."

Madrigal holds the young queen by the shoulders and gives her one steadying shake. "When Jules arrives, she'll get the blood to me, and I will send the potion to the stage with her. It's all right. There is still time."

Arsinoe steps out of the tent, and a lump lodges in her throat. Standing outside her tent are not only the Sandrins and Luke and the Milones, but half of the naturalists in the valley.

"What are they doing here?" Arsinoe whispers to Joseph.

"This?" Joseph asks, and smiles. "Seems that someone heard rumor of your performance. Queen Arsinoe and her great brown bear."

"And how did that happen?"

"Once Luke caught wind of it, the entire valley knew within an hour."

Arsinoe looks at the people. Some smile at her in the torchlight. Her whole life they have thought her a failure, yet at the first hint of hope, they move to follow her, as if it is what they wanted all along.

Perhaps it was.

QUEEN KATHARINE'S STAGE

$\mathcal{T}$he temple decreed the order of the Quickening performances. Katharine is to be first. The priestesses have set the long mahogany table with the poisoner's feast. The torches are lit. She needs only to climb up onto her stage and begin.

Katharine cranes her neck to view the crowd. The sea of faces and black-clad bodies stretches in front of all three stages and along the coast. Katharine's stage is in the middle. Directly before hers is a raised dais, where the suitors sit, with High Priestess Luca.

"So many priestesses," Natalia mutters from beside her.

"Yes," Katharine says. Her stomach tenses. Natalia is a strong source of comfort, but she wishes that Pietyr had changed his mind about not attending.

"All right, Kat," Natalia says. "Let us go."

They walk up together. Katharine smiles as luminously as

she knows how, remembering not to look rigid and formal like her elemental sister. But still the crowd's eyes on her are somber. When Mirabella takes her stage, no doubt they will grin like fools.

Genevieve and Cousin Lucian stand in the front row. She nods to them, and for once, Genevieve does not scowl.

Katharine and Natalia take their places at the head of the table.

"Trust me," Natalia says. "Say the words loud."

Katharine's gown rustles against her legs. It is a very fine garment to be ruined by *Gave Noir* stains. She can only hope that none of those stains will be caused by her sickening.

Before them, priestesses remove the lids from each poison dish and announce the contents. Inky cap mushrooms stuffed with goat cheese and wolfsbane. Codfish stewed in yew berries. Tartlets of belladonna. Deathstalker scorpions, sugared and buttered, beside a dish of clotted oleander cream. And cantarella wine. The centerpiece of the feast is a great, golden pie baked into the shape of a swan.

The air fills with delicious scents. The first three rows of poisoners lift their noses to scent the air like alley cats at a kitchen window.

"Are you hungry, Queen Katharine?" Natalia asks, and Katharine takes a breath.

"I am ravenous."

Natalia stands to one side as Katharine eats. Her bites at first are tentative and small, as if she does not believe. But as the feast progresses, and the poisoners clap, she grows more confident. Pink-tinged sauce drips down her chin.

The mainland boys on the dais wet their lips. What wonder they must feel, watching this girl who cannot die. It does not even matter that it is not real.

Katharine pushes away the plate of candied scorpions. She ate three, clever enough to leave the tails crumbled in the yellow sugar. All that remains is the swan pie.

Natalia guides Katharine around the side of the table, and the queen tears through the crust to scoop out the meat. That is all. Katharine washes it down with a full goblet of wine and empties it to the last drop.

She slams her hands down on the table. The crowd cheers. Louder, it seems, out of sheer surprise.

Natalia raises her eyes to the dais and finds Luca's cold, stony gaze.

Natalia smiles.

QUEEN ARSINOE'S STAGE

*F*rom her place behind the stage to Katharine's right, the *Gave Noir* looks as grotesque as Arsinoe expected a ritual feasting of poison to look. She is unfamiliar with many of the poisons listed in the dishes, but even she must admit to being impressed as pale, petite Katharine swallows them down. By the time it is over, Katharine is coated in berry glaze and meat gravy to the elbows, and the crowd is screaming.

Arsinoe clenches her fists and then remembers the rune drawn in her palm and quickly releases them. It cannot be smudged or muddied. This is not the best day to ask her palms not to sweat.

"Arsinoe."

"Jules! Thank the Goddess!"

Jules presses the small black bowl of potion into Arsinoe's hand. Arsinoe makes a face.

"Pretend that it's wine," Jules says.

Arsinoe stares down into it. Drinking seems impossible. Though it is no more than four mouthfuls, it is four mouthfuls of salty, metallic, and tepid liquid. Blood from her own veins and the veins from a bear.

"I think I see a piece of fur," Arsinoe says.

"Arsinoe! Drink it!"

She tips the bowl back until it knocks against the wood of her mask.

The potion tastes just as bad as she feared. It is surprisingly thick, and the herbs and roses do not help, providing only unwanted texture and chewiness. Arsinoe's throat tries to close, but she manages to force it down, remembering to save enough to pool in the palm of her rune hand.

"I'll be just beside the stage," says Jules, and disappears.

The priestesses announce Arsinoe, and she steps up. The eyes of the crowd are as heavy as they were atop the cliffs, but she cannot think about them now. Somewhere, not far away, a bear is waiting.

She walks to the center of the stage, the hastily assembled boards creaking beneath her feet. The blood-taste coats her tongue and rolls in her belly. She keeps her rune hand carefully cupped to her chest. It will work. It will look like she is praying. Like she is calling for her familiar.

"Here, bear, bear, bear," Arsinoe mutters, and closes her eyes.

For a few moments, all is silent. And then he roars.

People scream and part a wide path as he lopes toward the stage from the cover of the cliffs. He climbs up beside her without hesitation. The sight of his long, curved claws makes the cuts on her face itch. Somewhere to her right, Arsinoe hears Camden snarl and hiss.

Arsinoe may not have long. Jules may not have much control. She has to get the blood and the rune pressed to his forehead.

He comes closer. His fur touches her hip, and she freezes. His jaws are large enough to take half her rib cage in one bite.

"Come," she says, surprised that her voice does not crack. The bear turns his snout to look at her. His bottom lip hangs down, as bears' bottom lips do. His gums are mottled pink. There is a black spot on the tip of his tongue.

Arsinoe reaches out, and presses the bloody rune into the fur between the bear's eyes.

She holds her breath. She stares into the bear's brown and gold-flecked eyes.

The bear sniffs her face and slobbers on her mask, and Arsinoe laughs.

The crowd cheers. Even those naturalists who doubted her throw their arms into the air. She ruffles the bear's brown fur and decides to push her luck a little further.

"Come on, Jules," she says, and raises her arms in a wide V. "Up!"

The bear slides backward. Then he stands on his hind legs, and bellows.

The beach fills with cheers and shouts, the barking and cawing of happy familiars. Then the bear drops back onto all fours, and Arsinoe throws her arms around his neck and hugs him tight.

THE DAIS

⁂

he High Priestess watches the girl embrace the bear, and claps with the others. She has no choice. Amid the cheers and celebration, her eyes seek Rho, who faces her with eyes full of blood. Luca shakes her head. It is over. They have lost.

Rho shakes her head. She bares her teeth and reaches for the handle of the knife at her side.

QUEEN MIRABELLA'S STAGE

"No one expected such a showing from Katharine and Arsinoe," Sara Westwood says as she adjusts the fall of Mirabella's cloak. "But it does not matter. It is still you they have come to see."

Mirabella cranes her neck toward where Katharine sits on her stage, in the middle of a poisoned table, and farther right, where Arsinoe stands, calmly stroking an enormous brown bear. She is not so sure that Sara is correct. But she can only do what she can do.

The drums start before the priestesses call her to the stage. They extinguish all the torches, so her stage is dark, except for the warm, red glow of one brazier.

Mirabella climbs the steps in three fast strides. She throws aside her cloak, and the crowd hushes. The quiet is absolute.

The drums beat faster in time with her pulse. She reaches for the fire, and it leaps onto her hands. A murmur passes through the crowd as the flames stretch up her arms and roll across her belly.

Working the fire is slow and sensuous. More controlled than when she calls the wind and the storms. The flames are bright. They do not burn her, but her blood still feels like it is boiling.

She spins. The crowd gasps, and fire crackles in her ears.

In the midst of the people straining toward her is Joseph. Seeing him nearly makes her take a misstep. His face is the face he wore on the night they met, lit by flames on a darkened beach. How she longs to pull him up onto the stage. She would clothe them both in fire. Burn them up together rather than far apart.

She throws her head back as he calls her name.

"Mirabella."

QUEEN KATHARINE'S STAGE

⚜

*N*atalia watches the girl spin, on fire. The crowd is a sea of blank, enthralled faces. Mirabella has them in the palm of her hand.

Something is shifting in the many rows of priestesses that line the stages. Their fingers slip inside their cloaks, to rest on the hilts of their knives. One priestess with hair as red as blood stares at Natalia with a gaze so intense that she has to look away.

The strength of Mirabella's performance is difficult to believe. Even Natalia feels the pull, the draw to move toward her on the stage.

She blinks and turns toward Luca and the old woman's dark, burning eyes. The ruses that Natalia and the naturalists carried off do not matter. The temple will not waver. They will make the Sacrificial Year come true.

QUEEN ARSINOE'S STAGE

J ules can hardly hold the bear and watch Mirabella dance at the same time. The noise and movement of the crowd make him nervous, and beside Arsinoe, he begins to bob his head and scratch at the boards.

Jules refocuses.

"It is all right," she whispers, with beads of sweat upon her brow, and in her mind, the bear tugs. He tugs hard.

The crowd surges toward Mirabella, and Jules grits her teeth. When will the girl be done? The dance feels like it has gone on forever, though the people do not seem to mind. Jules takes a deep breath, and searches for Joseph. He will be somewhere watching, proud of her for what she has done with the bear.

Only he is not looking at Jules at all. He is at the very front of Mirabella's stage. Pressing toward her with the crowd.

Jules can hardly believe the look in his eyes. If she were to shout his name at the top of her lungs, he would not hear her. He would not hear her if she were standing right beside his ear. The lust on his face sickens Jules's stomach. He has never looked at her the way he looks at Mirabella.

In the midst of her dance, Mirabella reaches toward Joseph through the flames. Everyone can see. They must all know that they are together. That Jules is a fool.

In her chest, Jules's heart turns sharp as a shard of glass, and something snaps. As it does, so does her hold on the bear.

Arsinoe knows that something is wrong when the bear starts shaking his head. His eyes change from serene to frightened and then to angry.

She steps back.

"Jules," she says, but when she tries to get Jules's attention, she cannot. Jules is staring intently toward Mirabella's stage like everyone else.

The bear paws the wooden boards.

"Easy," Arsinoe says, but she can do nothing. The low magic that binds them is not the same as a familiar-bond. The bear is afraid, and Jules has lost control.

There is no time to warn anyone as he roars and leaps from the stage and into the people, swiping sharp claws and throwing his head back and forth. No one can scatter. They are crowded together too tightly as they strain for Mirabella's stage. Not even his claws cutting them down parts enough of a path, and the bear turns back for the stages.

"Jules!" Arsinoe shouts. But her shout is lost within the rest as the crowd begins to realize what is happening.

The bear climbs onto the middle stage, and Katharine screams. He barrels through the table of the *Gave Noir*, dashing it to pieces and sending it tumbling down to the sand. But he does not make it to Katharine. She is quick, and dives off the side to safety.

Priestesses draw their knives and advance with terrified faces. The bear slashes at the nearest one, and her white robes do nothing to hide all the red and loops of entrails that its claws rake out of her. At the sight of so much blood, the courage of the others fails, and they turn to flee with the crowd.

High Priestess Luca stands and shouts. The suitors watch in horror.

On the far stage, Mirabella has stopped dancing, but fire still burns across her chest and hips. It does not take the bear long to focus on her. He charges, tearing down torches and anyone who happens to be in his way. Mirabella cannot move. She cannot even scream.

Joseph leaps onto the stage, right in the bear's path. He covers Mirabella with his body.

"No," Arsinoe says. "No!"

Jules must know that it is Joseph. She must see. But it may be too late to call the bear back.

QUEEN MIRABELLA'S STAGE

*P*riestesses shout to protect the queen. But all Mirabella hears is the bellowing of the bear. All she feels are Joseph's arms around her.

The bear did not strike them. It reared up on its hind legs. It roared. But in the end, it pawed at its face as though in pain and then dived off the stage to run down the beach.

Mirabella lifts her head and looks down at the scattered, panicked crowd. Most have found their way to safety through the cliffs and back into the valley. But several bodies lie motionless before the stages. The young priestess who attended Katharine's stage lies now at the foot of it, her arms bent, her robes and her abdomen laid open for all to see. And so many more have been wounded.

"Are you all right?" Joseph whispers into her ear.

"Yes," she says, and clings to him.

He kisses her hair and her shoulder. White-robed priestesses surround them with knives drawn.

"Calm yourselves!" Luca shouts, standing on the dais beside two shaky suitors. "It has gone!"

Mirabella peers over Joseph's arm at the ruined stages. Arsinoe stands alone, her arms fluttering at her sides. Perhaps she did not realize the extent of the carnage she would cause.

"She sent that bear for me," Mirabella says. "After everything I did to save her. She would have let it tear me apart if not for you."

"It doesn't matter," Joseph says. "You're safe. You're all right." He holds her face in her hands. He kisses her.

"Where is Queen Katharine?" Natalia Arron shouts. "Luca! Where is she?"

"Do not panic," says the High Priestess. "We will find her. She is not amongst the fallen."

Natalia looks around wildly, perhaps to form her own search party. But all her poisoners have fled. Moans erupt from the foot of her stage, and she grimaces.

The bear knocked the *Gave Noir* off the edge, at the foot of the crowd. The poisoned food lies dashed across the sand. Several dog familiars lap eagerly at it.

"They have eaten some," a woman weeps. "Stop them! Call them back!"

Natalia steps quickly to the front. "Isolate the food," she orders, her composure regained and her voice even and deep. "The dogs must be brought to my tent for treatment. Quickly. Gather them up and keep the rest of them clear."

Across the stages, Arsinoe retreats in the company of the Milones. The mask she wears makes any expression unreadable.

"How could she?" Mirabella asks, heartbroken. But even to her ears, it seems a foolish question for a queen to ask.

Joseph shushes her as he kisses her hair.

"Away from her now, naturalist." Rho reaches out and drags Joseph back without effort. He does not struggle much when he sees the serrated knife in her hand.

"Leave him alone, Rho," Mirabella says. "He saved me."

"From his own queen's attempt," Rho says. She jerks her head, and three more priestesses come forward to lead Joseph away. Rho grabs Mirabella by the arm. Her fingers dig in deep, until Mirabella yelps.

"Back to your tent now, my queen. The Quickening is over. The Ascension Year has begun."

THE BRECCIA DOMAIN

❧

*B*ranches scrape at Katharine's face as she runs through the trees in the southern woods. Her heart pounds, and her knee throbs from when she fell against the stage. She falls again when her skirt twists in a bramble. With no torch, she has only the light of the moon as a guide, and there is not much of that deep in the trees.

"Pietyr!" she calls, weak and breathless. She did as she was told and ran straight from the Quickening to the five-sided tent and into the woods beyond.

"Pietyr!"

"Katharine!"

He steps out from behind a tree, holding a small lamp aloft. She stumbles to him, and he catches her against his chest.

"I do not know what happened," she says. "It was so awful."

The bear would have killed her. Split her open just like it had that poor priestess. It will be a long time before she can forget the crazed look in its eyes, and the sharp, wild arc of its claws.

"I hoped it would not come true," Pietyr says. "I hoped that Natalia was right. That she had it under control. I am so sorry, Kat."

She rests her head on his shoulder. He was kind to meet her here, away from everyone, for a few moments of solace. His arms take the chill from her skin, and the strange, deep-earth smell of the Breccia Domain calms her as she breathes it in.

Pietyr rocks her back and forth. He steps with her slowly until it is almost like dancing, and their feet slide across the smooth surface of the rock at the sides of the crevasse.

"Perhaps I should have stayed with Natalia," Katharine says. "She could be hurt."

"Natalia can take care of herself," says Pietyr. "She is not the one in danger. You did the right thing."

"They will be coming for me soon. Looking. We do not have long."

Pietyr kisses the top of her head. "I know," he says regretfully. "The bloodthirsty temple."

"What?"

"I was not supposed to love you, Kat." He takes her face in his hands.

"But you do?"

"Yes," he says, and kisses her. "I do."

"I love you, too, Pietyr," says Katharine.

Pietyr steps back. He holds her gently by the shoulders.

"Pietyr?" she asks.

"I am sorry," he says, and then he throws her. Down, down, down into the bottomless pit of the Breccia Domain.

THE ASCENSION YEAR BEGINS

THE ARRON ENCAMPMENT

A day and a half after the disaster of the Quickening, Innisfuil Valley is nearly empty. The naturalists and the elementals have gone. So have the giftless and those few with the war gift. Even most of the poisoners have returned to their homes, except for the Arrons and those families most loyal to them.

Many priestesses still remain, including High Priestess Luca, as they organize search parties and scour the cliffs for Katharine. But they have searched the entire valley. The shore and the forest on all sides. Poor Pietyr has searched nonstop since Katharine disappeared.

But they have found no body and no answers.

Natalia sits in her tent, alone. She has not searched since yesterday, and the longer the search goes on, the less she wants to find her. Today, the body would still be Katharine. But soon, it would bloat and then decay. Natalia does not know if she can bear to find Katharine's little bones, held together by sinew and a rotted black dress.

She drops her head into her hands, too tired to stand. Certainly too tired to take down tents and return to Indrid Down. To face the council and pretend that there is anything left for her to do.

The tent flap opens, and High Priestess Luca walks inside in her white robe and black collar. Natalia straightens, but it cannot be news of Katharine. If it were, Luca would have sent someone to fetch her instead of coming by herself, with no escort.

"High Priestess," says Natalia. "Please. Come in."

Luca half turns and makes sure that the tent flap is closed. Then she raises her nose and sniffs.

"This tent, Natalia. It smells like dying dogs."

Natalia purses her lips. The familiar hounds brought to her after the Quickening died messily. There was no time to assemble a tidy poison. She used what she had on hand, and they convulsed and vomited on the rugs and pillows.

Luca takes down the hood of her robes and unfastens her collar, showing off a wrinkled neck and fine, bright white hair.

"I must depart soon," she says. "For Rolanth and Mirabella."

"'Must,'" Natalia says with bitterness.

"A small contingent of priestesses will remain here. They will search until the little queen is found."

For a moment, the two women regard each other. Then Natalia gestures to the chair opposite her at the small table.

Luca snaps her fingers and has a pot of tea brought in. When they are settled, and alone again, she sighs and leans back wearily.

"One of the delegations has fled," Luca says. "The dark one, with the red flower in his jacket. His family was superstitious. They said this generation was cursed."

"This was not a terribly successful Beltane," says Natalia, and Luca laughs, once.

"If only we had taken that brat's head and arms when we had the chance."

"If only your Mirabella had let us."

Luca adds cream and two lumps of sugar to her tea and sets a thin baked biscuit on her plate.

"There is no poison in it," Luca says wryly of the tea. "Perhaps you can squeeze that snake of yours into your cup."

Natalia smirks and then sips. "What can be done about Arsinoe?" Natalia asks.

"What about her?"

"She attacked the queens before the end of the Quickening. Before the Ascension Year had begun. It is a crime, is it not?"

"A violation by a day. It was a show of strength, whether we like it or not. The people will push back if we punish her publicly."

"What good is the temple if it cannot enforce its own laws," Natalia grumbles.

"Indeed," says Luca. She takes a sip of tea, and eyes Natalia over the rim of her cup. "That lovely *Gave Noir* that you set," she says. "All that poison, fallen into the sand. I snuck a bit of it into one of my priestess's dinner. And oh!" Luca's face lights up briefly. "She lived! She did not even sicken. Unlike those poor dogs you dispatched. What did you give them, Natalia? Arsenic?"

Natalia drums her fingers against the table. The High Priestess raises an eyebrow.

"Do not whine about our weakness now," says Luca. "When we are only what you have made of us. When it is you who have turned the people away."

"If the people turn away from your preaching, then it is not our fault. We have never sought to impose council will on the temple."

"No," says Luca. "Only to silence our voice." She studies Natalia quietly. They have been adversaries for many years but have spent little time alone together, and never when they were not battling over something.

"It is strange," Luca says, "that you have turned away from the Goddess. When she is the one who creates the queens. Whose power on this island preserves our way of life. I know," she says when Natalia rolls her eyes. "You think it is you. The strength of your gift that keeps us safe. But who do you think gave that to you? She is the source of this thing you revere, yet you do not revere her. In your pride, you forget that she has given and that she is the one who may take it away."

ROLANTH

---

*L*ooking out the window of the bouncing coach, the streets of Rolanth are strangely quiet. The city expected Mirabella to return in triumph. Now that she has not, there is an air of loss. Shops in the central district have pulled down most of the Beltane decorations, though a few modest ribbons and wreaths remain. She was not exactly beaten, after all. Her Quickening performance was nearly a success.

Nearly. But thanks to Arsinoe, she had not even gotten to finish.

It will not be long until they are safely back at Westwood House. Though it will not be the same as it once was. Now that Katharine is missing and presumed dead, the temple will take a defensive position until it is determined what happened. Rho will have a small army near Mirabella night and day. Already armed priestesses surround the coach, as well as Sara and Uncle Miles's coach ahead of them.

Mirabella doubts that Arsinoe will launch another attack so soon. But the temple will be ready for anything.

"I froze when that bear charged," Mirabella whispers, and Bree and Elizabeth raise their heads from where they rest against the windows. "At first I thought it was a mistake. But it came right for me."

Her friends look down sadly. They will not tell her that Arsinoe did not mean it. And she does not want them to. She has had days to relive that terror, and for the hurt in her heart to turn to anger. Perhaps Arsinoe also murdered Katharine. Perhaps she had some other creature waiting for her when she ran away into the woods.

Sweet little Katharine. Who she and Arsinoe used to swear to protect.

"Elizabeth," Mirabella says. "You are a naturalist. Could you have done what Arsinoe did with that bear?"

Elizabeth shakes her head. "Never. Not with fifty of me. She is . . . stronger than any naturalist I have ever seen."

"Or even heard of," Bree says with wide eyes. "Mira, what will we do? If it were not for that boy, Joseph, you would be dead."

Mirabella told them, afterward, who Joseph was and what happened between them. It came out in a rush, in her tent, when she was heartbroken in so many ways. Betrayed by Arsinoe and dragged away from Joseph, possibly forever.

"Dear Joseph," Elizabeth says. "His love for you may save you again. If he is truly Arsinoe's good friend, perhaps he will stop her. Perhaps he will help us."

"I will not ask him to take sides," Mirabella says.

"But someone will. Arsinoe. Or Luca. I don't think that someone as strong as Arsinoe will hesitate to use her advantages."

"That is good," Mirabella says. "I do not want her to hesitate. I want her to push me and push me until I hate her."

She looks back out the window, to escape the knowing sadness in Bree's and Elizabeth's eyes. They knew it would come to this. Everyone knew, except for Mirabella. But she is through being sentimental. Seeing that bear, and Arsinoe's cold face behind that mask, showed her the truth.

The sisters she loved at the Black Cottage are gone. Arsinoe saw her chance, and she took it. So next time, Mirabella will take hers as well.

GREAVESDRAKE MANOR

———————— ⚜ ————————

After a week of searching, Pietyr traveled back to Greavesdrake with Natalia. But once they arrived, he would not stay. Without Katharine, there was nothing for him there.

Natalia did not try to convince him otherwise. The boy was miserable. Even his dull country house was preferable to Greavesdrake, haunted by Katharine's ghost.

Before he left, they had one last drink together in her study.

"You had me so convinced about the Sacrificial Year and the temple," he said. "I thought they were going to take her head. I did not even think of Arsinoe."

Now he is gone, packed into a carriage, and Natalia is again alone. Genevieve and Antonin went directly to their houses in town, fearful of her mood. They would not dare return without an invitation.

The servants too refuse to look her in the eye. It would be

nice if any of them were decent enough to pretend that everything was all right.

Natalia walks down the main hall and listens to the spring wind rattle branches against the windows. The manor feels drafty this year. She will need workmen from the capital to inspect the windows and doors. It may not be hers for much longer, but she will not let the grand old house fall into disrepair.

In the long, red hallway that attaches to the staircase to her bedroom, she notes dust on the sconces and a small stack of clothing folded and set just inside the door to the hall bath. She stoops over to pick it up and stops.

She is not alone. There is a girl, standing in the foyer.

Her dress is a ruin, and her hair knotted and twisted through with filth. She does not move. She could have been standing there for a very long time.

"Kat?" Natalia asks.

The figure does not respond. As Natalia walks closer, she begins to fear that it is a figment of her imagination. That her mind has fractured, and at any moment, the girl will vanish or dissolve into a pile of lice.

Natalia reaches out, and Katharine looks up into her eyes.

"Katharine," Natalia says, and crushes the girl to her chest.

It is Katharine, dirty and cold but alive. Cuts mar every inch of her skin. Her mangled hands hang limp by her sides, tipped in dark red with most of the fingernails torn off.

"I did not fall," Katharine croaks. Her voice is rough, as

though her throat is filled with grave dirt.

"We must get you warm," Natalia says. "Edmund! Bring blankets and run a bath!"

"I do not want that," says Katharine.

"What do you mean, sweetheart? What do you want?"

"I want revenge," she whispers, and her fingers trail bloody streaks down Natalia's arms.

"And then I want my crown."

WOLF SPRING

hough the townspeople would like to see her, Arsinoe spends her time in the Milone house or down in the orchard. She is not hiding, exactly. But it is easier there, where no one stares with newfound respect and where she does not have to explain where her bear is.

Telling the people that the bear was not actually her familiar will be difficult. They may be impressed by her ruse, but they will still be disappointed that she will not be riding it into town.

"Are you accepting visitors?" Billy asks, walking up from the orchard.

"Junior," she says, and he smiles. He has recovered from their time in the mist, at sea, and looks very well in a light brown jacket. With the young leaves stuck to his shoulder, he hardly looks like a mainlander at all.

"I have never heard you sound so glad to see me," he says.

"I wasn't sure you were still here. I thought your father

might have packed you up and sailed you home."

"No, no," Billy says. "I am to begin formally courting soon, just like the other suitors. He's a dogged man, my father. He does not give up. You'll come to know that about him."

He holds out his hand. In it is a box wrapped in blue paper and tied with green-and-black ribbon.

"He sent this, you see? As a peace offering." He shrugs. "It isn't much. Sweets from our favorite shop back home. Chocolates. Dipped nuts. A few taffies. I thought you would like it, though. Since you are mostly stomach."

"A gift? Really?" Arsinoe says, and takes the box. "I guess the bear changed his mind about me."

"It changed everyone's minds about you." He sighs and then nods to the house. "How are things, here?"

Arsinoe frowns. Since the Quickening, Jules has been miserable. She has barely spoken to anyone.

Joseph walks up behind Billy with his hands in his pockets. The look upon his face is grim and determined.

"What are you doing here?" Arsinoe asks.

"I'm here to see Jules. I need to talk to her about what happened."

"You need to grovel is more like. To both of us."

"To both of you?" he asks, confused.

"She must really be something," Arsinoe says. "That elemental sister of mine. To make you forget every promise that you ever made. To Jules. And to me."

"Arsinoe."

"Do you want me to die now, instead of her? Would that make you happy?"

She shoves past him hard on the way to the house. There is plenty more she would like to say to Joseph, but it is only right that Jules should have her turn first.

"Let me put these away," she says, and shakes the candy box. "And then I'll go find her for you."

It does not take long to find Jules walking in one of the southern fields with Ellis, discussing the spring plant. When Jules sees her, her face falls, as if she knows.

"You have to talk to him sometime," Arsinoe says.

"Do I?" says Jules.

Ellis puts a gentle hand on his granddaughter's shoulder and walks back down the rows, holding Jake in his arm. The little white spaniel has scarcely walked a step since Beltane. Ellis is just so grateful that he was not taken by the poison, like those unlucky familiars who ate from the fallen *Gave Noir*.

Jules lets Arsinoe walk her around to the front of the house, where Joseph and Billy wait.

Arsinoe takes Billy by the elbow, and leads him away so Jules and Joseph can have some privacy.

"All right," says Jules. "Let's talk."

Jules lets Joseph inside the bedroom she shares with Arsinoe and closes the door softly in Camden's face. She does not know what will be said or how angry she will get. But if Camden were to injure him, she may regret it later.

Outside, Joseph had seemed tense but collected, as if he had rehearsed many times whatever dressing down he intended to give her. Inside, he shrinks. He looks at her bed, where they spent so many moments together.

"How could you do it?" he asks softly. "How could you send that bear?"

"I stopped it, didn't I?" Jules snaps. "And that's what you have come here to say? To accuse me? Not to tell me you're sorry for falling in love with someone else?"

"Jules. People died."

She turns away. She knows that. Does he think she is stupid? It all happened so fast. One moment she had the bear, and the next . . . It was the most difficult thing she had ever done, bringing him back under control. But she could not let him hurt Joseph.

She leans against the writing desk and pushes a wrapped blue box.

"What is this?" she asks.

"Billy brought it for Arsinoe," he says. "It's a box of sweets."

Jules tugs off the lid. She does not have much of a taste for sweets. Certainly not like Arsinoe does.

"He chose well," she says.

"Jules. Answer the question. Why did you do it?"

"I didn't!" she cries. "I didn't mean to let him go. I had him. Until I watched her dance. Until I saw you, and the way you looked at her. Like you have never looked at me."

Joseph's shoulders slump. "That is not true," he says. "I have looked at you. I see you, Jules. I always have."

"Not like that," Jules says. In her mind, she sees the bear charging. She does not know whether she would have stopped it from killing Mirabella. She only remembers the rage, and the hurt, and how her world turned red.

Jules reaches into the box of candy and puts a piece into her mouth. It tastes like nothing, but at least he cannot ask any more questions while she chews.

"The night of the Disembarking," she whispers. "In my tent. When you wouldn't touch me. It was because of her, wasn't it?"

"Yes."

He says it so simply. One word. As if it requires no further explanation. No justifications. As if it does not make Jules's head begin to spin.

"Do you not love me anymore, then? Did you ever?" She pushes away from the writing desk and stumbles, her stomach weak and pained. "I've been quite an idiot, haven't I?"

"No," Joseph says.

Jules blinks. Her vision goes black, and bright, and then black again. Her legs go numb below her knee.

"Jules . . . I . . ."

"Joseph," she says, and her voice makes him look up. He reaches out and grabs her to his chest as she falls. "Joseph," she says. "Poison."

His eyes grow wide. They flash to the box of sweets as Jules begins to fade, and he screams for Cait and Ellis.

* * *

"It's my fault," Joseph says.

"Shut your mouth," Arsinoe says. "How can it be your fault?"

They sit beside Jules's bed, as they have since the healers left. They could do nothing, they said, but watch and wait for the poison to paralyze her lungs or her heart. Cait threw them out after that. She threw them out and wept for hours, bent over the kitchen table.

"Dammit, where is Madrigal." Joseph grasps Camden's fur, where she lies atop Jules's legs.

"She can't handle it," Arsinoe says. But she knows where Madrigal is. Gone to the bent-over tree, to pray and make bargains of blood magic. Gone to beg for her daughter.

Ellis knocks softly and pokes his head in.

"Arsinoe. The mainlander is outside, asking for you."

Arsinoe stands and wipes at her eyes. "Don't leave her, Joseph."

"I won't," he says. "I'll never. Never again."

In the yard, Billy waits with his back to the house. He turns when he hears her, and for a moment, she thinks he will try to hug her, but he does not.

"I didn't know, Arsinoe. You have to believe me. I didn't."

"I know that," Arsinoe says.

His face floods with relief. "I'm so sorry," he says. "Will she be all right?"

"I don't know. They don't think so."

Billy slips his arms around Arsinoe, slowly and tentatively, as though she might bite. She probably would bite if he did not feel so solid and good to lean on.

"They'll all pay for this," she says against his shoulder. "They will bleed and scream and get what they're owed."

Two days after Jules was poisoned, she opens her eyes. Arsinoe is so exhausted that she is not sure whether she is hallucinating until Camden climbs onto Jules's chest and licks her face.

Madrigal wails with joy. Ellis kneels beside the bed and prays. Cait sends her crow, Eva, out after the healers again.

Joseph can only weep and press Jules's hand to his cheek.

Arsinoe carries another pot of flowers from Joseph into their bedroom and sets them on the windowsill. There is almost not enough room. So many offerings crowd the space that it is beginning to look like a hothouse. As she arranges the blossoms, a few of the buds open with pert little clicks. She turns to Jules, sitting up against her pillows.

"Feeling better, are we?" Arsinoe asks.

"I just wanted to see if I still could," Jules says.

"Of course you can. You will always be able to."

She walks to the bed and sits, scratching Camden's haunches. Jules looks much better today. Finally strong enough, perhaps, to hear what Arsinoe has been dying to tell her.

"What?" Jules asks. "What is it? You look like Camden after she has gotten into the eggs."

Arsinoe peers down the hallway. The house is empty. Cait

and Ellis are in the orchard, and Madrigal is in town, with Matthew.

"I have to tell you something," Arsinoe says. "About the candy."

"What? Is it about Billy? Did he do it?"

"No. I don't know. I don't think so." She swallows and looks at Jules with bright eyes.

"I ate it too."

Jules stares at her, confused.

"When I put the box on the desk," Arsinoe says. "Before I came to get you in the field. I ate three of them. Two chocolates and a taffy."

"Arsinoe."

"When have you known me to turn away candy?"

"I don't understand," says Jules.

"Neither did I," Arsinoe says. "Not at first. You were so sick, and Joseph said you only ate one. And I was so worried about you that for a while I didn't think about it at all. But then you woke up. And I knew."

Arsinoe leans forward on her elbows.

"I haven't been a giftless queen all this time, Jules. Unable to sprout a beanstalk or turn a tomato red or get some stupid bird to sit on my shoulder." Her voice grows louder and faster until she catches herself and quiets. "All this time I thought I was nothing. But I'm not nothing, Jules."

Arsinoe looks up and smiles.

"I'm a poisoner."

ACKNOWLEDGMENTS

Hi there. This one was quite the odyssey. Years in the making. Lots of folks to thank. But where to begin?

With the idea, I guess. Writers are often asked where we get our ideas, and I never have a good answer. So it's quite a thrill that this time I do. Thanks very much to my friend Angela Hanson and her beekeeping pal, Jamie Miller, for having the conversation about swarming bees that started all this. The blueberry ale was also pretty good. Bees and beer, you guys know how to have a good time.

Next up, the shove from idea to writing. I have to thank my agent, Adriann Ranta, for that (and for many, many other things). When I told Adriann about this, her eyes lit up. Then she politely listened while I told her about another book I wanted to write first. She even read that one after I wrote it. But I knew she wanted this. So, thank you, Adriann, for championing 3DC back when it was a vague bit of nothing, and for shepherding it through.

Thank you to my wonderful editor, Alexandra Cooper. You brought so much into the world of the queens. And I love your persnicketiness. That's not a word. Or is it? Whatever, you know what I mean. You are also a fantastic champion for a book to have. These queens be lucky.

Thank you to the entire book-creating team at HarperTeen: Aurora Parlagreco, designer extraordinare, and Erin Fitzsimmons, art director of legend! Olivia Russo, publicity wizard, and Kim VandeWater and Lauren Kostenberger, marketing powerhouses. Jon Howard, for more editorial excellence. The fabulous copy editor, Jeannie Ng. I am in awe of how much passion you all put into your projects. And how much you get done!

Virginia Allyn, rad map. John Dismukes, kickin' crowns. Both of these folks are such talented artists.

Thanks to Allison Devereux and Kirsten Wolf at Wolf Literary.

Thank you to Amy Stewart, who I have never met but whose excellent book *Wicked Plants: The Weed That Killed Lincoln's Mother & Other Botanical Atrocities* helped a lot, poison-wise. Of course, I took many liberties, so don't blame her for any stretched facts.

Thank you to the novelist April Genevieve Tucholke for reading an early draft and telling me she liked it.

Thanks to the readers, the librarians, the bloggers, the booksellers, the booktubers, the book lickers (I've seen a few of you—no shame; lick proudly).

Thanks to my parents (ready for another book-release barbecue?); my brother, Ryan; and my friend Susan Murray. Thanks to Missy Goldsmith.

And thanks to Dylan Zoerb, for luck.